Secret Paths presents
The Storyteller's Quest ~ Book Three

I0667217

The Starless Square

Alan McCluskey

First published in March 2016
Secret Paths Editions, Mureta 2, 2072 Saint-Blaise, Switzerland.

Copyright © Alan McCluskey
Cover illustration by Alan McCluskey

ISBN 978-2-940553-06-8

Other books by the author

The Reaches - The Storyteller's Quest Book One
The Keeper's Daughter - The Storyteller's Quest Book Two

Boy & Girl
In Search of Lost Girls

Table of Contents

Prologue

The rising sun eclipsed the last remaining stars and cast a promising glow over the emerging world. Gulls turned and swerved and plunged, their squawking strident against the soft hiss of the sea. The tide rode high, sparing only a narrow stretch between the breaking waves and the stone wall that lined the front. Brent inhaled, savouring the tang so typical of a seaside town, and sprang from the wall onto the wet sand. His footprints were the first of the day as he walked away from the mouth of the river where both the port and the university lay. In the distance he could make out the lighthouse and the keeper's lodge perched on the Head. The Keeper. His mind turned to Lucie, the young woman he'd left in that other world. When he first met her, she'd been the Keeper's Daughter and he'd taken the form of a young girl. Later, in troubled times, she'd become the Keeper herself, the head of her town. He had loved her like a sister, like a mother, like a sweetheart. An irresistible urge to skip and dance and jump in the puddles broke upon him. He longed to burrow into her arms. Only when he was with her could he quell the restlessness that drove him ever onwards. At the end of the weekend he promised himself, and lengthened his stride, forcing his stiff limbs to move faster until he broke into an easy run. A startled seabird rose from amongst the tufts of grass that bordered the beach and skimmed nearby. Brent halted to watch, admiring the curve of its wings as it swerved skywards. A part of him soared with the bird, winging its way upwards and as he did he looked down on his body forlorn at the water's edge. "What do you want?" he cried out across the waves, venting his frustration. "Will I ever be at peace?"

Chapter 1 ~ Whirlwinds

Truant

The policeman planted himself in front of An, blocking her path.

"Shouldn't you be in school, Miss?" he asked, glancing at his watch.

An laughed. How absurd. She had adopted the form of a teenage girl during her stay in Avan. Outwardly she looked a slender, fourteen or fifteen year-old with long blond hair and graceful limbs. It was the form she preferred, affording most freedom of movement, behaviour and thought. How could she explain to this man in his strange dark blue costume with a funny round hat that where she came from such institutions didn't exist? That 'school', from what she'd heard, was the last place she'd go to learn? And, what's more, that she was not just a school-aged girl, but also a wise-woman, a fighting Amazon and much more?

"You wouldn't be being impertinent, would you?" His features crinkled in the warning signs of annoyance, clearly misinterpreting her laughter.

Don't shock the natives, her sister Sally had said. Easier said than done. Despite all Sally had told her, she didn't always know what shocked and what didn't. How could she have guessed that walking through town at her age at that time of day would get her accosted by a policeman?

Sally had good reason to be concerned. A band of weirdoes, led by a bureaucrat from the University, was trying to discredit the

Theosophy Department where Sally and her friends worked. To counter these attacks and win over public opinion, the Department was organising festivities to show-case their work the coming weekend. Any additional trouble with the authorities or the press could destroy everything.

"Not at all, Sir. I am new in town. I know nothing about schools here."

"And where would your parents be, young lady?"

They were in the world she came from, seeking help against the wild men whose rampage made the countryside unsafe to travel. Her parents knew full well she could fend for herself. What's more, the notion of child didn't make much sense when you could be both child and adult.

"My parents are busy, far away. I am staying here with my older sister, Sally. She works at the University."

Taking out a tiny notepad, the policeman extracted a pencil from the binding, licked the lead and jotted down a few notes. "Where does your sister live?"

Flushing with embarrassment, An admitted, "I don't know the exact address."

Since her arrival the day before, she had always gone with Sally and her friends, paying no attention to the names of streets. She hadn't imagined it would be important.

"Runaway?" the policeman mumbled to himself.

An wasn't sure what the word meant, but, judging from the policeman's tone, she guessed she could not ask without raising further questions.

"Come with me, Miss. We'll sort this out at the Station."

The 'Station', which was not so far away, was a reasonable-sized house built of red bricks that contrasted with the other buildings around, made as they were from a grey-green stone. A blue fluorescent sign over the door announced: 'Police'.

"Step inside, Miss." The policeman held out his arms to herd her inside as if he were expecting her to bolt.

The entrance hall led to a large room in which a young woman dressed much like the man but without the hat, stood behind a long wooden counter, gesticulating with her free hand as she talked on the phone.

When the call was finished, the policeman asked, "Can you handle this, Mandy?" jerking a thumb in An's direction. "We might have a runaway on our hands," he added quietly, but not quietly enough to stop An hearing. What was wrong with these people that they repeatedly talked about her in her presence as if she weren't there?

"OK Jock," Mandy replied, her eyes lingering on him.

Mandy led An to a tiny room that was bare except for two wooden chairs and a small table. Indicating that she should sit, the policewoman closed the door and sat opposite her.

"What's your name, Miss?"

"An."

"Would you like some tea, An?"

"I'm not thirsty. Thanks." Despite Sally's encouragement, she had not acquired a taste for the strong dark liquid these people drank all day long.

"Where do you go to school?"

"Why do you people keep harping on about school?" An was perplexed at the insistence with which these people reduced everything to a question of school.

The woman frowned. "Because school is compulsory."

Even though she had a pretty good idea what a school was, An decided it might be fun to tease the woman a little. She wouldn't have done so, if the woman hadn't been so apparently easy-going. "Where I come from," An explained, affecting the naïveté that pleased her so much about being a young girl, "we don't have these things you call schools. What do people do there?"

A look of exasperation crossed Mandy's face. She straightened her back and fixed An with no-nonsense eyes. "They go there to learn."

"But why go to a place to learn when you can learn everywhere?"

"Enough! I need to verify your address. Where are you staying?"

"I don't know the address, but I can find my sister's flat easily enough."

"Maybe you have a phone number?"

"Yes. My sister did give me her number." She fished the paper from the depths of her coat pocket and handed it to the policewoman.

Mandy pulled a phone out of her pocket and dialled the number. "No answer."

Of course. Sally had planned to visit the Rector about Mae. Mae was the secretary of the Department. She had been the victim of a scheming man called Frick who was trying to have her sacked. "Sally must have gone to see the Rector," she explained, grinning.

"You don't take this very seriously, An, do you? It can be

dangerous for young girls like yourself to wander the streets unaccompanied, even during the day time."

An couldn't help laughing. Compared with some places in her world, Avan was a peaceful haven.

The policewoman shook her head. "Only the other day a young woman from the local library disappeared leaving no trace despite all our efforts to find her."

Sally had shown An the newspaper article relating the so-called disappearance of her friend Keira who worked in a library. She hadn't really disappeared: she had been on an adventure in the Reaches.

"We're going to have to keep you here for a while till someone comes to fetch you."

No way! She had no intention of staying with the police. She fidgeted in her chair and blushed. "I need to go to the loo."

Still irritated, the policewoman stood and led her down the corridor and showed her the door. "Hurry up! I haven't got all day."

The woman would surely stand guard outside the door, so she hastened into one of the two cubicles and closed the door. There was no window through which to escape. She hastily transformed into an old lady, and, wedging one of the cubicle doors closed, she shuffled out of the toilet and walked passed the waiting policewoman who eyed her suspiciously but said nothing.

First contacts

Mae strode across the bridge that joined the main university campus to the island in the River Avan on which the Theosophy Department had been built. She hadn't been to her office for over a week. The thought of the immense pile of post awaiting her had her groaning. It might be a small department, but as its secretary she was inundated with correspondence. When she had rushed off after Professor Rafter who was gravely ill, she hadn't thought to close her office, let alone ask anyone to sort the mail. How was she to know she'd travel to another world?

The thought had her touching the gold pendant that hung around her neck, concealed beneath her blouse, a present from D'rick the head of the Litt'l People. It conferred the ability to travel between worlds.

She had managed to bring back Sally and her friends just in time for the final preparations of the Department's celebrations planned for that weekend. The other members of staff didn't know it yet, but these young people were to be the stars of the festivities that she fervently hoped would save the Department. That meant, however, there would be a lot of modifications to make.

She wasn't sure how the Professors would react to such last minute changes. Uppermost in her mind, however, was worry about Professor Rafter. Would he be fit enough to give his talk the following morning? Two of Sally's friends, Keira and Jenny, were doing their utmost to improve his health.

The moment Mae entered the Department she was assailed with requests.

"Have you seen Professor Rafter? We've absolutely got to discuss the programme with him," Professor Enquist asked.

Mae took a deep breath and, trying to conceal her agitation, she explained to Lyra Enquist: "The Professor will only be here tomorrow morning. I will be coordinating the preparations. Can you tell everyone we'll meet in the small seminar room in ten minutes?"

Lyra stared at Mae. The woman knew her well. They had been friends for quite a while. So Mae wasn't surprised at the look of astonishment on the woman's face at her new found assurance. Lyra was about to question her further when Mae stopped her.

"Trust me, Lyra," she said cryptically before she turned away to answer Professor Trundle who'd also asked her a question.

"Gavin, Sally will be helping you. She'll be here in a short while. Let her know which sites you want to visit."

"But Sally was never interested in history," he countered.

"You'll see."

He looked at her, unbelieving, but she had no time to explain further. She turned back to Lyra who had taken several steps away and was observing her. Mae grinned. "Lyra. I forgot to tell you, I'll introduce you to Jenny Tay. She'll be demonstrating the use of earth magics for farming and healing on Sunday morning. I thought we could use Hoyt Park or the botanical gardens. Do you know any farmers who might be interested?"

Seeing Professor Dryman enter the Department, she called out to him. "Chris! Do you think we need permission to use the ring of standing stones to hold a celebration at dawn on Sunday morning?"

"I'll check," he said, as usual taking everything easily in his stride. "Will Professor Rafter be leading the ceremony?"

"No. Keira will be singing for the sunrise. I just hope her concert Saturday night doesn't go on too long."

Mae was caught up in such a whirlwind of action that it was only then that she realised everyone was staring open-mouthed at her. She burst out laughing and entered her office calling out over her shoulder, "See you all in ten minutes."

The seminar room was just big enough to seat the twenty members of staff now crowded into it. Mae hesitated on the threshold, trying to gauge the atmosphere. Professor Greenacre, the oldest of the professors, was complaining to Martina.

"... I thought we'd got the programme fixed," he said, shaking his head, making his long white hair sway from side to side. "I don't see how we can possibly change things at this late stage. It starts tomorrow."

Martina, who was professor of occult sciences, didn't agree. "What we had planned was rather fad. Surely even you can appreciate that, Wolf?"

"Don't get me wrong. I'm not against change, Martina. It's just that we need time to do things properly, especially if they are new. And we have no more time."

Gavin Trundle sided with Greenacre, patting his friend knowingly on the shoulder, while Chris Dryman supported Martina, laughing as he did.

Mae had heard enough. She stepped into the room and wove her way between those people still standing, encouraging them to be seated, till she reached the computer at the front. Flipping the switch to turn the machine on, she faced the assembled staff and greeted them.

"I'm so glad you could all attend at such short notice." She glanced at Greenacre who nodded in agreement, presumably at the lateness of the convocation. "As I mentioned to some of you, Professor Rafter will join us only tomorrow for his talk."

"Can we know why he can't be here now?" Lyra asked.

"I won't hide the news from you, although it would be better if no one outside this room were to know. Professor Rafter has been taken ill and is undergoing treatment."

"How serious, is it?" Lyra asked, alarmed.

Mae hesitated a moment, fighting back the tears that threatened to flow. "It is extremely grave. There seems little chance of recovery."

A worried hush fell as Mae bowed her head, rubbing her eyes with the back of her hand. "He will give his talk as planned tomorrow..." her voice broke and she was forced to stop for a moment "... but otherwise he will not be present. He has asked me to oversee the organisation of the event."

A buzz of conversation rippled through the room as people speculated on the implications of the Head's illness and absence.

"Colleagues. Friends," Mae called out, using Rafter's own words to address them. "The Professor would not want us to spend time discussing his health. He would want us to make a resounding success of this weekend."

The talking ceased and all heads turned towards Mae. Seeing that Chris Dryman was seated next to the door, Mae asked him to open it. "We are to receive unexpected and very valuable help in our work," Mae continued as Sally and her friends filed into the room and came to join her, "from a group of young people some of whom you know."

She waited till all were settled then pursued.

"The people you see before you have just returned from a voyage that has taken them to places that most people could hardly imagine, even in their dreams."

"Don't underestimate dreams," Professor Lettrot interrupted.

Everybody laughed. Professor Liam Lettrot taught dreams and dream travelling.

"We don't all dream like you," Chris Dryman joked.

People laughed again. They need to laugh, Mae thought. This is going to be very hard for them.

"Let me introduce them to you," Mae suggested. "Sally you all know," she began, adding as an after thought: "or you think you know."

She saw Lyra smile. Yes my friend, Mae thought, many things have changed. Not just me. "What I am about to tell you must be kept a secret. If any of you have difficulties with that, I ask you to leave now."

Nobody moved.

"You will probably know that Sally took part in an experiment financed by a Swiss entrepreneur that involved travelling to the dream realm. I won't go into the details of that mission which turned out to be extremely dangerous and from which Sally was lucky to escape with her life. The outcome was that all the people standing here before you, including myself, journeyed to another world called The Reaches."

Several people gasped, others looked incredulous. So much for their extensive experience in the transcendent and the occult.

"And in the course of that journey many of us have developed skills that we can put to good use to make the coming weekend a resounding success."

Mae paused for a moment, expecting people to challenge or question what she'd said. And sure enough, Prof. Greenacre cleared his throat and spoke, addressing his colleagues rather than her.

"Here we all are, worried about our public image and trying hard to do something to improve it. But I can't help wondering what people will think when they know that it is a secretary who is coordinating these festivities. Shouldn't it be a professor?"

A number of the professors looked at each other, ill at ease, as if they had been found guilty of an unforgivable oversight.

"Without going into a long debate about the relative merits of professors and their status in universities," Lyra responded, "it is clear that the organisation of these festivities requires skills and leadership that only one person in this room possesses. And that person is Mae."

"You may be right, Lyra" Gavin Trundle conceded, "but as Wolf said, it's a question of image and the continuing status of professors."

"I was not aware we were talking about the status of professors," Martina put in, not bothering to conceal her irritation, "but about the organisation of an event, which I remind you Professor Rafter himself delegated to Mae."

A tense silence filled the room, broken only when Sally stepped forward and spoke: "We all work in the Department of Theosophy. We study and practice transcendence, the occult and healing, amongst other things. If you want to question Mae's credentials you should know that in addition to her brilliance in organisation she has the gift not only to travel between the worlds, but she can also transport other people between the worlds. She saved the lives of a whole town in the Reaches by using her gift to transport the women, children and elderly as well as many of the men to safety. How many of you could transport thousands of people solely by the power of your mind?"

"Wow!" Lyra exclaimed.

"Amazing!" Martina added, so excited at the idea that she was unable to sit still.

"Professor Greenacre, Professor Trundle and any of you who may have had doubts, are you prepared to accept Mae's leadership for this weekend of festivities?" Sally asked.

"I accept," Professor Trundle hastened to agree.

"So do I," Greenacre added. "And I apologise for bringing this matter up, although I am glad I did because now we know what talent we have amongst us."

"The Theosophy department is really special," Lyra pointed out, a broad grin on her face. "If we were in any other university department, someone like Mae would never be entrusted with such a responsibility."

Mae laughed, relieved. "Thank you for your confidence," she said. "But I warn you, Professor Greenacre, you haven't heard the last of the unexpected talents that are in this room today. When I mentioned Sally earlier, I didn't tell you what she could do. Apart from the ability to travel and to transport people between the worlds, she has developed a way to transform the world around us so as to reveal the forms it once had. That was why I suggested she work with you, Professor Trundle, when you take people on a guided tour of the historic sites in and around Avan."

"Of course, we'll have to figure out how far to go and how much people will be able to take without panicking," Sally put in.

Mae made no mention of the other things Sally could do. Nor did she mention Vee, the mysterious voice in Sally's head that accompanied her and guided her. It wasn't necessary and probably wouldn't be wise.

"Let me introduce the others to you," Mae continued. "Most of you will know Keira who is already quite a celebrity with her singing. She used to work at the Avan library."

"So that's what happened to her," Chris commented, chuckling. "So much for the reliability of the press."

"In the Reaches she has been working on the use of singing and sound for healing. It may mean little here, but she is an honoured member of the Sisterhood of the Stones. She's also worked intensively on developing simples and potions. She will give a concert at the Arena on Saturday evening singing songs in Gran, the dialect in Granwich, a town in the Reaches. And she will celebrate the rising sun in the circle of standing stones at dawn on Sunday."

Keira bowed theatrically, grinning.

Mae almost expected people to applaud but they all seemed in a state of shock. Couldn't blame them really.

"Brent, you may also have met in Avan. In the Reaches he worked on transformations, being able to take on several different forms. He also underwent the rite to become a fully-fledged shaman, but that's another story. Rest assured that we won't be demonstrating transformations during the weekend."

"We must talk," Chris Dryman said, gazing intently at Brent.

"Think you've found a fellow soul?" Martina asked, grinning.

"But the most important gift that Brent has is story telling," Mae told them.

"His stories are so captivating," Sally told them, "that his listeners have the impression they are really living the story."

"We thought we might have a session of story telling during the weekend, but we haven't decided when to put it yet," Mae explained. Brent made no comment, apparently embarrassed at being the centre of attention. Sally had told Mae that he was still having difficulties adjusting to being a young man again after a prolonged period as a little girl.

Mae continued. "Martin and Fran you may have already met around the Department this week. Martin is Swiss and Fran German. In the Reaches they learnt the art, or should I say 'magic', of cooking and have been working with Lyra's students to prepare a giant buffet for Sunday midday. Before that they'll hold a workshop on the use of herbs and wild flowers in cooking."

"Anju you may recognise. She's Professor Outman's granddaughter. She accompanied him for his conference about Chaos Theory here in Department a while ago. With her friend Dieter, who comes from Germany, they have developed spectacular forms of unarmed self-defence, that were tried and tested in real life combat in the Reaches."

No need to tell people that Dieter was a former police inspector who had investigated a mass murder, one of the dead being Tyrell, Professor Rafter's late assistant.

"It's more like an aerial dance, that is very effective in combat," Anju explained, full of enthusiasm.

"Anju invented it all," Dieter put in, chuckling. "I'm just one of her students."

Anju playfully pummelled his shoulder then slung her around him and pulled him in a tight embrace.

"They'll be giving a demonstration followed by a master class at the end of the afternoon Saturday," Mae explained.

"Jenny is an artist from Switzerland. In the Reaches she discovered she has a talent for earth magic. She can rebalance the energies of the earth and encourage plants and trees to grow. She also works with the earth's energies to anchor people and heal them."

Jenny beamed. "It's a bit like painting. Just as Sally works with musical vibrations to transform the world around her, so I work with the colours and forms I perceive in the energies."

"Wonderful!" Lyra exclaimed. "You must teach us how to do it."

"I'd love to," Jenny said with her delightful French accent. "But that will have to wait. We all have to return to the Reaches straight after the weekend."

Mae glanced around the room. She had the impression that all these weathered academics looked like a bunch of children being told a fairy tale and Brent hadn't even used his magic on them, yet.

"Jenny will give a workshop about earth energies to farmers and amateur gardeners on Sunday morning," Mae told them. "And last but not least, meet Tom, Jenny's boyfriend. He was a journalist in Switzerland. In the Reaches, he was working on what you might call surveillance techniques, but a terrible accident almost took him from us."

Tom adjusted his wheelchair as he turned to Jenny and held out his hand to her.

"It was the combined efforts of Jenny, Keira and our dear friend Ma'gina that saved my life," he told them. "My spine was broken but they managed to get it to knit back together."

Mae could see that Lyra was bursting with excitement at the prospect of such healing abilities. "Tom has been in contact with press here and abroad, organising coverage for our event this weekend," Mae concluded.

"So there you have it. I have prepared a revised programme for the weekend…" and she lent over the beamer to switch it on and project the programme on the screen. It was then that the door opened and an old lady sauntered in.

"I'm sorry lady. This is a private meeting," Chris said, about to lead her by the arm back out the door.

Mae had no idea who the woman was, but apparently Sally did because she burst out laughing. "Let her in, Chris. She's with us." Sally continued to chuckle. "You really know how to make a spectacular entrance," she said to the woman. Then turning to the others she presented the woman. "Meet my sister An from the Reaches."

Well that will put the cat amongst the pigeons, Mae thought. Here was a woman from the Reaches, who, in addition, Sally claimed was her sister.

"Excuse me," Professor Trundle, said perplexed. "But judging from this woman's age, she can't possibly be your sister."

Others seemed to agree with him.

"One of An's abilities," Sally explained, taking An by the arm, "is to transform into different shapes. This is not her usual form."

"May I?" An asked Sally.

"Only if you're good," Sally giggled.

An transformed into the young girl she often was. Several people gasped. Professor Trundle fainted into the waiting arms of Martina. Keira went swiftly to his side and administered a small quantity of a liquid from a vial she extracted from her pocket.

"Extraordinary!" Trundle muttered as he recovered his senses.

"So you two are sisters?" Martina asked.

"Half sisters," Sally clarified.

"We have the same mother," An added.

"So you lived in the Reaches?" Martina pursued. "I didn't know that?"

"Neither did I!" Sally laughed. "Apparently I spent the first few years of my life in that world. So my mother told me."

"Excuse my curiosity," Martina went on. "It's just that I'd heard you were an orphan."

"That's what I thought too till quite recently." Sally sounded embarrassed.

Mae could see that Martina was full of questions but this was neither the time nor the place.

"OK. Now that the show's over," Mae joked, "we need to get down to some serious work."

An stopped her. "There is one more thing. I caught sight of a tall, thin man with a black moustache snooping around your offices."

"Frick!" Mae gasped, suddenly feeling weak at the knees. The man was a plague she couldn't seem to shake off.

"We'll check," Anju said, nodding to Dieter. "Should we bring him back here?"

"No take him next door," Sally suggested. "We can observe what happens there from here through this one way mirror."

Once they'd left, Dryman asked: "Isn't that the man from the University Council who's behind the audit?"

"It is indeed," Mae explained. "He's also trying to get me sacked, saying I am incompetent."

Lyra scoffed at the thought.

"As I was leaving to fetch some medicine for the Professor, he tried to stop me." She pulled back the sleeve of her blouse revealing a deep blue bruise around her wrist. "That was a week ago! When I ordered him to stop, he put his hands around my neck and tried to strangle me." She pointed to the finger marks on her neck.

"What did you do?" Lyra asked, leaning forward in her seat, gripping the arms of the chair.

"I laid him out with one of the moves I learnt in self-defence classes for women."

"Well done," Martina said, applauding.

"He must be mad," Greenacre put in. "His behaviour doesn't make any sense otherwise."

Several people muttered their agreement.

Through the one-way mirror, Mae could see Anju and Dieter lugging in Frick, unconscious between them.

"How are we to deal with Frick?" Mae asked, pointing to the window. She was unsure what to do and cautious of trusting her own judgement when she disliked the man so much.

"Let me talk to him," Brent said. "I'll tell him a story and ask him a few questions."

"OK!" both Sally and Mae said together.

"Why did he say he'd tell him a story?" Martina asked once Brent had left.

"His stories are so compelling, he can make people react the way he wants."

"Sounds a bit like hypnosis to me," Liam Lettrot said.

"In a way, yes," Sally replied, "except that he doesn't actually need to speak for the person to hear the story."

Mae caught a worried look on Greenacre's face. She wondered how many others might be concerned about the extent of Brent's power and the thought of how it might be abused.

"Can you wake him?" they heard Brent say to Anju.

She touched the man's neck lightly and he stirred. The moment he opened his eyes, he started shouting at Brent and the others. "I'll make you pay for this. You are doing filthy black magic ..." Frick took a step towards Brent and raised his hand to hit him but his hand remained suspended in mid air as his eyes glazed over.

Brent stood silent, intently looking at Frick for a minute or two, then sat down saying: "Please take a seat Doctor."

Frick lowered his hand and seated himself awkwardly as if finding it difficult to coordinate his movements.

"Please voice you complaint, Doctor. And keep it succinct," Brent said.

"There are subversive elements in the University, operating from within the Theosophy Department. One of them is that secretary. She physically attacked me the other day. What's more, the Department is a complete waste of money. We'd be much better off without it."

"What are you going to do?" Brent questioned him.

"As for that horrible secretary, the University has decided to sack her. The hearing took place this morning."

Mae gasped in horror and fury. "How dare he!" she exclaimed. She couldn't say more as everyone wanted to hear what Frick was saying in the next room.

"…The audit will prove I'm right. But the procedure is far too slow. I'll use other methods to discredit them and reveal what they are up to. Their backers will withdraw and the university will close the Department by the end of the academic year."

"Tell me, Doctor, how many of you are carrying out this work?" Brent asked.

"I have the backing a powerful group who will help if necessary."

"Thank you, Doctor. You may leave now."

They could all see that Frick hadn't left as prompted.

"Did something go wrong?" Lyra asked, worry in her voice.

Mae could sense growing fear filling the room. The fairy tale had moved on to a more sinister phase. People were no longer smiling as they watched Brent at work. He had resumed his intent silence in front of Frick whose eyes were glazed over again. Then suddenly, to their general surprise, Frick stood and left without acknowledging anybody. Several people breathed a deep sigh of relief now that the man was gone.

When the door opened, a number of people jumped nervously, maybe imagining that Frick was about to enter and catch them in a secret meeting. They were relieved to find it was only Brent followed by Anju and Dieter.

"Will he remember anything?" Chris asked.

"He shouldn't remember our meeting," Brent informed them. "Although he probably will remember that he visited the Department."

"What are we going to do about him?" Mae asked, feeling the ambient fear gripping her.

"Brent, Anju, Tom and I will keep an eye on his activities. We'll try to find who he is working with or for," Dieter said.

"Dieter used to be a police detective," Mae explained.

"How could he discredit us?" Martina asked.

"That's for you to tell us," Dieter replied.

Nobody had an idea.

"Will he try to disrupt the festivities?" Mae asked.

"It's possible," Sally said. "It would be one way to try to show we are incompetent."

"Maybe Tom could work with the assistants, rather like the Watchers in the Reaches," Jenny said. "Keeping a constant eye on them."

Seeing people's incomprehension, Tom spoke up: "The Watchers were a group of citizens in the town of Granwich whose job was to be aware of everything that happened so as to prevent trouble. I worked with them for a while."

Several assistants present said they'd be delighted to help. "We could even enlist help from some of the students," one of the assistants suggested.

"Let's be cautious about whom we choose," Tom concluded.

"And what about Mae?" Lyra asked. "We can't accept this! It's totally unjust."

"I don't think they can sack her so easily," Chris mused. "I'll ask a few friends from the Law Department."

"Whatever happens," Martina added, "you should know, Mae, that you have our fullest support!"

"Hear, hear," everybody said. Lyra came forward and hugged her and Chris gave her a friendly tap on her shoulder. Mae couldn't stop herself shedding a tear or two.

"But what about our backers?" Professor Greenacre asked. "Didn't he say he would get to them?"

"Can you organise a meeting with the people from the Blavatsky Foundation, Rolf? We need to talk to them urgently," Chris asked. "I think they should meet Mae and Sally and her friends. They are our strongest card."

"I'll try to organise a meeting this afternoon or tomorrow morning," Rolf said. "Where should we meet?"

"Not here," Mae said.

"I'll ask Alo if we can commandeer his house. It's not far from the centre and we can direct operations from there," Sally said.

Yes. They could trust Alo, Mae thought. He was a shaman who had helped them prepare their trip to the dream realm and beyond to the Reaches.

"Good. Now we have to work on the festivities," Mae said. "We won't need Frick to discredit us if we don't prepare properly."

Everyone agreed.

"I'll send out for sandwiches," Mae suggested.

"You don't need to bother," Fran told them. "Martin and I prepared lunch for you." The two of them carried in a number of heavy wicker hampers and opened then on a table in one corner. The moment the containers were open the smell of food was irresistible.

"OK. Let's pause to eat," Mae announced, giving in to the desire to eat and drink.

"That was wonderful," Mae said, thanking Fran and Martin on behalf of everybody once the meal was over and the hampers removed. "Sally, you have something to say?"

"Yes. Thanks Mae. I had Alo on the phone and he's delighted to let us use his town house as a centre for our operations during the weekend. I told him we'd probably move there during the afternoon."

"Excellent," Mae said.

"I have news too," Prof. Greenacre said. "The representatives of Blavatsky Foundation have agreed to meet us. If it's OK with you, we can meet them early this evening. I could call them and suggest we meet at Alo's place."

"Could you dim the lights a bit, Chris?" Mae asked as she pulled up the programme for the weekend on the screen. "I'll go through this rapidly and then we can split up into groups and continue to work on the details. We begin on Saturday morning at ten o'clock with Professor Rafter's talk. His talk is ready."

"What do we do if he's not fit" Lyra asked.

It was Jenny who answered. "We've managed to improve his condition considerably but there are some things that we can only contain but not eradicate. Keira and I believe he should be able to give his talk, but it's probably better if he doesn't have to answer questions."

A thoughtful silence followed Jenny's words.

"As we want to get out into the town and meet the people," Mae continued, "Prof. Rafter's talk will take place in the reading room of the main Avan library. Keira organised that and we have sent out word as widely as we could."

"Your guided tour, Professor Trundle, will begin at two o'clock on Saturday afternoon, if that is OK with you. It looks like the weather will be good. You told me you planned to start from the Cathedral, so the posters we've put up invite people to meet there. Tom has managed to get a spot on the radio later today so you can talk about what you plan to do and why you are doing it. Is that alright?"

"Excellent. Sally, I suggest we walk around the tour together this afternoon and see what you can do to illustrate our collective history."

Sally nodded. From his choice of words, Mae guessed the professor hadn't really grasped the extent of what Sally was capable of.

"It might be wise not to announce your itinerary on the radio," Dieter suggested. "Just in case anybody seeks to disrupt the visit."

Mae shuddered, as did several others. Dieter had an uncanny knack of reminding people of the difficulties and dangers ahead of them.

And so they continued for more than an hour as Mae presented the programme, event by event, and people made suggestions and proposed improvements. Towards the end, Fran slipped out to fetch drinks and homemade cake that she and Martin handed round, much to everybody's delight.

"We have to leave now," Fran told them a while later. "Lyra's students will be waiting for us and we still have a lot of things to prepare for the buffet on Sunday. We'll see you all at Alo's place this evening where we'll cook the evening meal ."

"If the people from the Blavatsky Foundation are still there, you might like to invite them to join us," Martin suggested. "Don't you say in English, 'the way to a man's heart ...'?"

Everybody laughed.

As they left, the meeting broke up, people going off in different directions in twos and threes to continue their preparations. Tom left with a group of assistants to a secret destination they'd fixed with Dieter and Anju while other assistants went to enrol students from the Department.

Only Mae and Chris were left in the deserted Department. Mae welcomed the calm and quiet after the whirl of activity. Despite the inevitable difficulties that lay ahead, she felt confident. She could feel her pendant vibrating peaceably on her chest and she said a silent prayer of thanks. Prof. Dryman accompanied her to her office along empty corridors.

"You did an excellent job, Mae. You should be proud of yourself. And even if you are not, I am proud of you."

"Thanks."

He stood in the doorway watching her gather all the material she needed to organise the weekend. As a precaution she also took all the files about the staff. You never know what might happen, she told herself. "Can you grab my laptop for me and that hard disc. I may not be able to get back in here if Frick has his way. It wouldn't surprise me if he didn't get an injunction preventing me from entering the campus."

Dryman chuckled. "You may well be right. What a block-head!"

Mae turned off the lights and locked the front door to the Department as the two of them left.

"I can't help seeing this as a symbolic act," she confided. "Frick may well get what he wants but the energies here are too strong for him to be able to stop us moving forward and doing something even better."

Warehouse

From the shadows of his vantage point in a recess, Tom watched.

One by one, or in twos, people slipped into the building through a small door concealed in a narrow alley. They crossed the wide, empty space of the giant warehouse, their steps echoing off the walls, entered a long dusty corridor that seemed interminable and climbed several flights of stairs till they reached the disused conference room on the top floor. From there, had the blinds not been pulled, they would have had a postcard view over the rooftops of Avan.

The warehouse had once been used to store bales of cotton when transatlantic trade by steamer had been in its heyday. Many years later, an aspiring entrepreneur had had part of the building transformed into large offices at great expense, mistakenly believing that enough businesses would prefer to trade near the port, but a subsequent slump had put an end to his dream.

One relic of an earlier occupation was an immense assortment of oiled ropes and reinforced cords of all lengths and colours, along with fixations to hold them in place. The former owner had apparently planned to map out a future city in the New World. New surveying techniques however had undermined his project causing him to go bankrupt and his stock had been abandoned since then.

Ownership of the building had shifted often until it ended up in the hands of the father of Kean, one of the assistants. His father, who currently had no use for the place, had loaned it to him on condition he made no structural changes.

The former user must have left at short notice, abandoning most of the furniture, which lay scattered around the conference room.

Much of it remained usable. Dieter and Anju were busy righting chairs with the help of several assistants, as more and more young people arrived. Not knowing what to do, some offered to help, but most stood alone or in small groups chatting quietly or glancing furtively at each other. It was hard to believe that they attended the same small Department together.

Tom made a mental note of who mixed with whom, who talked most, who just stood and observed. He delighted getting back into the feel of being a Watcher, an activity that had brutally ceased in the Reaches after his accident. He counted thirty-five people present when Anju closed the door. Rolling his wheelchair forward, he greeted everybody. "Welcome. Do take a seat."

A number of people jumped, few had seen him watching.

"A Watcher has three key qualities," he began as he wheeled his way around the table. "One is to melt into his or her surroundings: inconspicuous at all times; always on the move; never predictable. Another is the meticulous observation and memorisation of what happens. And finally, a Watcher knows how to communicate the essential of what he or she has seen to the other Watchers."

Both Dieter and Anju grinned. They knew him well.

"We have asked you to join us because the Theosophy department is threatened by one or more ill-intentioned people and we think it is likely they will try to disrupt the festivities this weekend. We also know that they plan to try to discredit the Department. Our job will be to understand their mind-set and to be aware of, if not to anticipate their every move. Nobody is forcing you to help, so if you are not where you thought you were, I suggest you leave. It goes without saying that all you will hear in this room is confidential. If that is a problem, you should also leave."

He paused a moment as he looked around the group, most of whom had now sat at the large conference table. Nobody moved. No one spoke.

"Thank you. My name is Tom and I have been trained by some of the best Watchers that exist. And this is Anju and Dieter. Amongst other things they are experts in unarmed combat. You shouldn't need to fight, but just in case ..." He noted that several of the students grinned at the prospect. "We have very little time. The festivities open tomorrow at ten o'clock with Professor Rafter's talk. I suggest we fill you in on the situation. That should take about thirty minutes. Then we'll split the group in two. I will work with one group on techniques for Watchers for an hour and Anju and Dieter will work with the rest of you on self-defence. Then we'll swap for another hour."

Anju and Dieter explained about Frick and what he planned to do. "Dr. Frick is affiliated to a secret organisation and is counting on the support of its members. We urgently need to find out who that might be," Dieter told them. "As soon as we've finished with our crash course here, some of you will have to gather information about all the clubs and organisations he's belonged to."

When the students heard that Professor Rafter was seriously ill many of them expressed their concern. All knew him personally. Many had had seminars with him. For all of them he was the central pillar of the Department.

Anju then unrolled a large detailed map of Avan and its surroundings on the table. Most people stood to get a better look. She went on to explain the weekend's programme and pointed to the places where things would be happening. She also told them of the radio broadcast and the later meeting with the Blavatsky Foundation that evening.

"Before we split into groups, I have one more thing to tell you," Tom said. "We have to cover a much wider area than the Watchers and that could put us at a considerable disadvantage. So I have got hold of a series of tiny walkie-talkies that my friends and I use when we go potholing. We have enough for each team to have at least one. I'll show you how they work."

Several hours later, almost all of the students and assistants had left on various missions. Anju and Dieter had gone with them, but Jenny had come to fetch Tom accompanied by Professor Enquist. A laptop lay open on the table next to the map.

"Look!" Kean was saying, excited at his discovery. "It's called the Starless Square. There's not much about them, but Frick was a leading member when he was a student. From the little written here by a former member who turned against them, they are linked to the ultra conservative wing of the church."

"I've heard of them," Lyra said. "They were suspected of manning witch hunts. There was a scandal a few years ago. Several young women were badly burnt when someone set fire to their house. Some members of The Starless Square were taken in for questioning, but no proof could be found and they were released."

"Attacking the Theosophy Department sounds like something the Starless Square would make a point of honour about doing," Kean said.

"Do we know where they meet?" Tom asked.

"I have an idea," Lyra said. "Anyone for a drink in the pub across from the Cathedral?"

"Hold on a moment," Tom said. "We can't all just walk in there. Kean, I suggest you and the others take up positions in and around this place and watch while Lyra and Jenny go for a drink. If one of you students can drive me to the radio station, I'll go and keep and eye on Sally."

Dark Pub

"Look!" Lyra exclaimed, pointing at the sign of the pub. Swaying gently in the breeze, it was pitch black and devoid of any marking lest it be the three words: The Starless Square.

Jenny shivered despite the warmth of the late afternoon air. She glanced over her shoulder. The cobblestoned square stretched from the darkened door of the pub to the majestic walls of the cathedral. Hurried figures crossed the open space, not one of them lingering in the shadows.

"Let's get inside," Jenny said. "This place is sinister."

They were the sole customers in the pub apart from an old man slumped in an armchair near a fire. The two women chose two stools at the bar and ordered drinks.

"What a puzzling name this pub has," Jenny said to the bartender. "Have you any idea how it came about?"

The bartender planted two glasses in front of them and poured out the white wine.

"You ain't from around 'ere," he remarked and went about his work.

Charming, Jenny thought. So much for a warm welcome!

"Let's go sit over there," she suggested, pointing to a corner with armchairs. They had been chatting amiably about this and that when the old man, who'd been sitting nearby, stood up with difficulty, a glass of beer in his hand, and sidled over to them.

"I couldn't help hearing your question," he said. "May I join you?" And not waiting for an answer, he sat opposite the two women.

Taking a swig of beer, he wiped the froth from his mouth and leant closer to them across the low table. "The Starless Square! Makes you wonder, hey?" he said in a conspiratorial whisper. "The pub got its name at a time when this square had a sinister reputation. The Bishop had a thing about witches. He liked to see them burn. Called it God's good work. There," and he jerked his thumb over his shoulder towards the door, "out in the square, right in front of the church."

He took another swig, looking intently at the women over his beer glass. "In the end, rumour has it, he was cursed by a witch, and a dark cloud has hung over this place ever since." He chuckled.

"What was the Bishop's name?" Lyra asked.

"No idea," the old man said, struggling to his feet.

"Thanks," Jenny said, watching him shuffle back to his place and sink into the armchair as if nothing had happened.

"Let's get out of here," Jenny said. "This place gives me the creeps."

Radio

When you look behind the surface, Vee was saying in Sally's head, it's amazing what you discover.

Sally smiled. He'd been quiet since she had returned to Avan. She missed his voice in her thoughts.

You did well not to show him too much of your ability, Vee continued. It would have frightened him.

Sally appreciated his advice. Although he was in many ways a part of her, his perspective on the world was different and he spotted things she hadn't noticed.

"That's extraordinary," Sally said to Professor Trundle as they neared the radio. "I hadn't realised how much this town was steeped in its past."

"Not half as extraordinary as your ability to …"

Professor Trundle was interrupted by a young man who staggered drunkenly up to them and asked: "You gotta light, mate?"

Trundle shook his head disgusted, clearly annoyed at the interruption. But the young man swayed forward and whispered just loud enough for both of them to hear: "Tom says mind what you say in public." And then he staggered off down the street. Trundle was frozen in mid step, his mouth fallen open.

Sally took him by the arm and led him on. "It's over here, Professor."

The radio was housed in a large Victorian mansion that had once belonged to an important family who'd made and then lost their fortune buying and selling raw materials shipped from America. The receptionist asked them to wait while she called the journalist. From where they sat Sally caught sight of a girl making signs at her from the door of the toilets.

"Please excuse me a second, Professor, I have to visit the loo."

She walked casually to the door marked 'Women's' and entered. The girl was waiting, a finger pressed to her lips. Having made sure there was nobody in the cubicles, she whispered: "Tom asked me to tell you that Frick is part of a conservative religious group called the Starless Square. They are known to carry out witch-hunts against anything to do with the occult or magic. Be careful if the journalist tries to get you onto talking about black magic or the like. It might be a trap…"

The girl broke off at that moment, hearing two quiet knocks on the door. She hastened into one of the cubicles and locked herself in just as the door opened and a woman walked in.

"Are you Sally?" she asked. "I'm the journalist."

Sally made a show of washing her hands and followed the journalist out of the room.

The studio was small, seating three at a tiny round table on which three microphones were placed. Behind a thick glass window a technician gave a thumbs up and spoke over the intercom asking them to test the levels of their microphones. The journalist donned a set of headphones. There was no way Sally could warn the professor of what she'd heard. Taking out her notebook she scribbled: AVOID OCCULT AND BLACK MAGIC. COULD BE A TRAP. Showing it to the Professor she hoped he wouldn't react too strongly.

"Yes. I agree," he said.

Relieved, Sally smiled at him.

"We will have about five minutes," the journalist told them, asking them to stay quiet now, it was almost time.

When the red light came on the journalist introduced her two guests as a Professor and an assistant from the Theosophy Department and briefly mentioned that a series of events was being organised in the town that weekend.

"Maybe you could explain why you are organising a public event this weekend, Professor?" she asked.

"We want to show the town's people the work we do and explain why it is relevant for them."

"And what sort of work do you do Professor?"

"I'm a historian. I teach the history of religions."

Sally was relieved he hadn't mentioned paganism that was also part of his work.

"And how do you plan to show the people of Avan that your interests should interest them?"

"You'd be surprised how much both the town of Avan but also the way we live in it and work here have roots that can be traced back to religious practices hundreds if not thousands of years ago."

The journalist was about to interrupt him with another question, but the Professor pushed on.

"That is why we have planned an itinerary around Avan tomorrow morning, beginning at ten o'clock by the cathedral, to show some of the history that is still present amongst us. Everyone is welcome."

"And you?" the journalist asked, turning to Sally. "What does your work as assistant involve?"

Sally suddenly felt a wave of panic grasp her. Most of what she had done could hardly be talked about on the radio.

Tell them what you are interested in, Vee suggested.

"I am particularly interested in the way quite simple actions like singing or dancing or story telling or cooking can improve the world around us."

"I'm not sure I understand. That sounds a bit like magic or wizardry. Is that what you do?" the journalist said.

Careful Vee whispered. Don't go into details.

"The best way to explain would be to demonstrate. That is why we are organising the events this weekend. There will be singing and dancing and storytelling and the most delicious cooking, so people can judge for themselves."

The journalist looked a bit peeved at the answer but time was up and they had to stop. "Thank you both for coming," she said and the red light flicked off. The journalist shook hands with both of them and scuttled away without another word.

Once outside, a wave of relief washed over Sally. The whole experience had been much more stressful than she had expected. She glanced around wondering if she would see Tom or one of his Watchers, but nobody was in sight.

"Well done," Trundle said quietly.

"Don't thank me. Thank Tom and his team for warning us."

The Professor chuckled, much to Sally's surprise. She had never seen him so relaxed and at ease. "I think we have another important meeting to attend," he said, taking Sally by the arm. "Let's hope we do as well there."

Chapter 2 ~ The Witch-Hunt

Meeting

"Are you all right Doctor?"

What a stupid question! Of course he wasn't. "Do I look all right?" His hands were shaking, his heart fluttered dangerously. He could hardly breathe, such was the weight on his chest.

"It's true, you do look pale."

Hardly surprising. He'd been through a nightmare. "How would you look if you'd been bewitched?" Maybe even worse! Who knew what they'd done to him while he'd been held captive.

"White, probably. Bleached of blood. I'm not sure. Confused too, maybe."

The thought made him shudder. But he certainly wasn't confused. Everything was crystal clear. Too clear.

"Have they left any marks?"

The idea revolted him. It was the first thing he'd checked. "Nothing." At least, nothing that was visible.

"That's a relief."

It didn't make things any better. They might have scribbled invisible signs all over him for all he knew. He could be damned forever. "The worst is, I can't remember a thing." A whole hour of his life had gone up in smoke. All he could remember were the two who had overpowered him; a deceptively pretty-faced girl with oriental perfume and a muscular man with a moustache like his own. Those faces he wouldn't forget.

"They could have done anything to you!"

Thanks for reminding me. "Isn't it time the others arrived?" he muttered, grinding his teeth, impatient to get his revenge. The filthy Satan worshippers! May they burn in Hell!

"It's true. They should be here by now."

"Did you warn them to come in the back way?" he snapped.

"Yes. Doctor. They know the drill."

A quiet knock heralded their arrival.

At last!

They filed in, nodding wordless greetings and took their places in a long rehearsed ritual. The Starless Square was the scene of their regular meetings.

"Gentlemen," he welcomed them. He could feel his fury ready to brim over, but he reined it in. He had to. Now was not the time. Clenching his fists till his knuckles turned white, he forced his voice to remain level and calm.

"The devil workers in that Theosophy department have struck again." He paused to let the shock sink in. "I was victim of a cowardly attack by a group of them."

Several gasped.

"As I delivered word of the sanctions of the University Council against their foul secretary, I was set on by a whole gang. I fought back with all my force, knocking several down, but they unleashed their witch's spell leaving me powerless. When I finally came to, an hour had gone by and I was alone in the corridor, drained and feeling dreadful."

"This is ghastly," one of the group said.

All agreed.

"How dare they?" another said. "Attacking a distinguished member of the University Council in broad daylight!"

Frick let them rant and rave for a few minutes, revelling in their indignation.

"We must go ahead with our plans," he insisted, bringing the meeting to order. "We must hit hard and drive them to their knees before this goes any further. We must rid Avan of this nest of black magic and sorcery."

He had the impression that those around him were glowing with enthusiasm. He certainly felt warmth suffuse through him at the idea. Pulling a crumpled piece of a paper from his pocket, he held it up, saying: "Before they attacked me, I managed to get hold of a copy of their programme for the weekend."

"Excellent!" several people exclaimed, drawing close to get a better look.

"They begin at ten tomorrow morning with a talk by their guru, Rafter. It will take place in the Avan Central Library and is open to the public so it will be easy to get our people in to heckle." He didn't need to go into details. They already knew who was to do what. "But the real fun comes at two when they take people on a tour of the town beginning from the entrance to the Cathedral." He cackled, his wide grin echoed by several of those present. One of the members looked worried. "You're not afraid they wheedled our plans out of you while you were in their hands?" he asked.

The possibility had crossed his mind, but he was determined to go ahead. The situation couldn't go on any longer. "They might have, but I doubt it. Just in case, though, I think we should alter our plan. We'll bring forward the big show we'd planned for the evening so it greets them when they arrive at The Square in the morning. It'll be just like it used to in the good old days."

"What a wonderful idea, Doctor, so exquisitely refined," one of the members exclaimed. "The Square will once again be starless."

Old People's Home

The avenue was lined on both sides by a row of ancient lime trees, reputed to induce peace and calm in those living nearby. A load of superstitious nonsense, Frick thought. None-the-less many of the mansions that had once housed the richest families in Avan had been bought up and were now occupied by old people's homes. Like every Friday afternoon, he hastened along the quiet road, past shuffling pensioners and misshapen codgers in wheelchairs pushed by foreign nurses, on his way to visit his mother. She was not so old that she would normally need to be placed in a home, but at the death of his father she had broken down, rapidly becoming incapable of catering for herself.

When he spoke to her, something that happened more and more rarely given her precocious senility, they never mentioned his father. The man's erratic behaviour had terrified both of them for years. From good humour, he would suddenly wax violent, lashing out at all around. Frick had never been able to figure out what provoked the change. All he could do was keep out the way.

He'd plunged himself in his studies. Not that he was a particularly good student, he had no illusions about that, but he worked hard and it had paid off, ensuring him a place at university. Unfortunately he couldn't always avoid his father. He'd suffered many a beating. Even when he was locked away in his room, his textbooks open around him, he couldn't block out the screams of his mother as his father's temper got the upper hand and he sent her flying across the kitchen.

The receptionist greeted him with a smile. "Your mother is in the lounge, Dr. Frick."

The pale woman had been there as far back as he could remember. He found her unfailing presence reassuring. Nodding a greeting, he strode into the lounge. At this time of the day, he generally found several inmates seated here and there, each alone and silent. Today they had deserted the lounge in favour of the gardens. A number of magazines were scattered unread across a low table and the television droned away in one corner. His mother was sitting in an armchair in the bay window staring in the direction of the trees, her eyes vacant. She made no sign that she'd seen him arrive.

"Mother," he began, laying his hand on hers to attract her attention. "How are you today?"

She jerked her hand away, avoiding his touch and continued to peer out the window. He was used to her silences, but he still wished she'd show some sign of recognition.

"Good news," he told her. "We finally managed to get rid of that secretary I told you about." Taking a seat opposite her, he glanced out of the window noting that they had recently been cleaned. He wondered how much it cost to maintain such a place.

The two of them had developed a ritual that dated back to his childhood. When his father was out with his cronies, young Frick would settle at the kitchen table while she did the cooking and he would tell her his plans and schemes. She never commented. He preferred it that way. As a child, he had taken her silence to imply approval. Now, of course, her silence had a different meaning, but he still enjoyed telling her his ideas, even if she understood nothing of them.

He was about to tell his mother of their plans for the weekend, of the delightful prospect of marring the festivities planned by Rafter's acolytes, when an uncomfortable feeling of being watched made him cautious. He glanced around the lounge, but they were alone. He despised superstitious people and couldn't stand the thought that he might be succumbing to superstition. He briefly wondered if his untoward feelings could be the result of a spell cast on him earlier in the day. But the feeling persisted, if anything getting stronger, so he decided to act on it.

"Mother," he began, "do you remember that evil professor I told you about?" He didn't wait for her to answer. He would have been alarmed had she done so. "He's giving a talk tomorrow morning at the library. I really don't understand why the local authorities let him get away with it. There's far too much laxity in this town. Well our little group has planned a surprise for him."

He laughed at the thought that he, of all people, should be spinning such a story. It was so unlike him! He shuddered. Could it be a spell at work? Surely not. "We plan to make it impossible for him to continue spreading his filthy lies."

It wasn't true, of course, their main action was planned for later, but if anyone was listening they'd be misled. He smiled at the idea knowing that his smile would be misinterpreted. He decided he would attend Rafter's talk after all, so he could see what the fools did to try to prevent the promised 'surprise'.

He stood and leant forward till he was very closer to her. They never kissed each other on the cheek as some families did and she didn't like him to touch her either. Instead he whispered: "I'll tell you all about it next time." It was only a game, but it made him feel a little better. "Goodbye Mother," he said as he straightened up and turned to go.

She hadn't ceased staring out the window the whole time. For all she cared, he might not even have been there. A wave of red-hot hatred flamed brilliant within him. His hands clasped into fists, his teeth ground together. How he hated his father! How he hated being like him!

The Foundation

The doorbell chimed and Sally hurried to open the front door. The representatives of the Blavatsky Foundation were punctual. Standing on the doorstep was Professor Greenacre accompanied by a man, a woman and a girl, all dressed in grey suits and overcoats. Sally had imagined them more flamboyant.

It's a disguise, Vee joked.

Sally gave him a mental nudge.

The man and the women were the same age as Greenacre and smiled to see Sally. The girl must have been several years younger than Sally and looked severe and tense.

This is not going to be so easy, Vee whispered.

"Do come inside," Sally invited, stepping aside to let them in. Once she'd taken their coats and hung them in the entrance, Professor Greenacre introduced Sally. "This is Sally Sarri, Professor Rafter's assistant and one of the bright lights of the Department."

The image made Sally smile.

"Sally, I'd like you to meet Moira Campbell, President of the Blavatsky Foundation and John Draycott, Administrator." Greenacre paused a moment as they shook hands and then turned to the girl and said: "And this is Irina, rumoured to be a descendant of Madame Blavatsky herself."

Sally shook her hand, surprised at how cold and bony it was. "Pleased to meet you all," Sally said. "Do come into the sitting room."

They had decided that the people from the Foundation would be received by only a small group. Then, should they accept the invitation, they would meet the others at the evening meal.

"Professor Dryman, you probably know already…" Greenacre said, presenting his colleague, "… and this is Mae Owen, Administrator of the Department."

Interesting that he gave her an instant promotion, Vee noted. I wonder what they'll think if they know the university has sacked her.

Shhhh! Sally thought.

"Where is Professor Rafter?" the President asked.

"He was unable to attend," Sally replied, "but sends you his greetings."

Once all seven were seated in Alo's armchairs, Chris began. "I'm very glad you were able to come at such short notice."

"We were planning to attend the events you have organised this weekend, so we were already in town," the President explained.

"We asked you here this afternoon," Chris continued, "because the Department is currently in a strange situation and we feel it is important to present that to you."

Sally glanced at their visitors; only Irina showed any sign of concern as she frowned.

"For many years, under the leadership of Professor Rafter, the Department grew and developed, while the university environment in which it existed changed very little. Now modifications in society are beginning to have a profound effect on academic institutions. In particular, the emphasis on market logic with such notions as 'return on investment' has an ever-increasing influence. Our department is not exempt from such forces. The Council has decided to carry out an audit as part of a drive to streamline the university and improve response to the demands of society, and industry in particular," Chris informed them.

"I wonder how they could possibly audit a Theosophy Department," the President laughed.

"That's exactly what Professor Rafter told them," Chris said, "but to no avail."

Then, as they'd planned, Mae took over from him.

"The audit would not normally be a cause for concern, we should get high scores despite the questions being heavily skewed against us. But a small yet very vocal faction of the Council seeks to manipulate the audit to get the department closed down. From what we can tell their opposition is ideological."

Mae paused a moment before continuing.

"Even that we could handle. Our event, amongst other things, was aimed at getting wide support from the local population. But earlier today we discovered that this group doesn't intend to stop there. They are planning to disrupt the events organised this weekend and will try to discredit some members of staff. We were able to interrogate the leader of their group and he confessed to their plans."

"Are you sure of this?" John Draycott asked, incredulous. "The whole thing seems a little farfetched."

"That group has already managed to get Mae dismissed by the university without any consultation with the Department, on the basis of false evidence," Sally told them, thinking the fact would illustrate her point.

Careful, Vee warned her, this could get tricky.

"But what were the grounds for the dismissal?" Moira Campbell asked.

"We are not aware of all the grounds," Sally told them. "We have been caught up in preparations for this weekend's events and there was another project we had to finish."

"It sounds like a typical conflict between two people to me," Irina said, her face almost a sneer.

Sally instantly disliked her. The girl's voice was sharp and piercing, verging on discordant. It grated against Sally's nerves, making her want to grind her teeth.

"We certainly can't get involved in such petty quarrels," Irina added dismissively.

Moira didn't seem surprised at Irina's outburst, although her words clearly disturbed her.

Chris made a sign to Mae not to respond, and went on to reply himself. "When false accusations are brought against a very valuable member of our staff as part a wider campaign to discredit and finally destroy the Department, the word 'petty' is perhaps not appropriate."

Sally watched the girl's face become even harder. Out of the corner of her eye she saw Greenacre shifting in his seat. He'd been silent until then and she was worried what he might say. Had he not opposed Mae during their meeting?

Coughing to gain their attention, Greenacre adopted a professorial tone that Sally noted had even Irina attentive. "Our department is dedicated to exploring and deepening the experience of transcendence. Sally and Mae and a group of their colleagues have taken that exploration to a startling new level that I'm sure would have delighted and fascinated Madame Blavatsky. If I understand correctly, your Foundation has supported our Department over the years for just such work. Now a group of fanatics are trying to render our work impossible in the most base and sordid way by personally destroying the reputation of those who have worked so hard. We invited you here, this afternoon, because we wanted to inform you of this situation and because we believe you will support our efforts in these difficult times. If you wish we can provide you with more information, but we need to be assured that you will support us and not unwittingly contribute to what is tantamount to a witch-hunt."

At the mention of witch-hunt, Irina began to tremble violently and fell shuddering to the floor, her mouth flecked with spittle. Her back arched upwards in a wild spasm then she collapsed inanimate to the ground.

"It's one of her fits," Moira explained, getting down on one knee next to the girl without actually touching her. "She hasn't had one for ages. She used to have pills against such attacks, but she stopped carrying them around."

The girl was extremely pale. A thin trace of blood flowed from the corner of her mouth.

She must have bitten her lip or tongue, Vee told her.

"Mae, can you get Jenny and Keira. They are our best healers," Sally explained to Moira and John as she sat down next to the girl on the floor holding her hand. It was absolutely icy. "Chris, can you ask Alo or Mrs. Martin, the housekeeper, for a blanket? Irina's dreadfully cold."

"Thank you for your words of clarification, Professor Greenacre," Moira continued, getting to her feet, her worried eyes riveted on Irina. "You did well to remind us what this is all about."

Keira and Jenny entered at that moment and went straight to the prostrate girl. Keira took her pulses and rolled back her eyelids to examine the whites. Then she poured a drop of a pungent smelling liquid on the girl's lips causing some colour to return to her cheeks.

"The young lady is in very capable hands," Greenacre said. "Maybe we should withdraw to the library to give Keira and Jenny some peace and quiet in which to work."

Moira hesitated about leaving what was clearly her protégé. Jenny turned to face her.

"I will work the Earth's energies to try to get to the bottom of this trouble. You are welcome to stay if you wish, but I can work better if I have no distractions."

Moira shifted her attention from Irina and looked at Jenny. "Thank you. Please take care of her, she's very dear to me." Moira's voice faltered.

Jenny stepped forward and took one of Moira's hands in both of hers. "Rest assured, we will give our very best to make her better."

"… so you see," Sally said, bringing the explanations to a close after over an hour of intense discussion, "we had our hands full with the expedition to the Reaches and the preparations for the festivities here."

"Extraordinary," John exclaimed.

"And is Professor Rafter's illness so serious?" Moira asked, her voice full of concern.

"You should ask Keira and Jenny, they have been working on healing him."

As if they had heard their names mentioned, the girls entered the library accompanying Irina. It was Jenny who spoke. "May I talk about it Irina?"

Irina nodded.

"Irina has a very strong presence that shines brightly, but there is a tight web of tendrils that bind her energy. I have been able to ease their strangle hold but I cannot remove them. In fact, I doubt it would be a good idea. Irina has to work on it herself. I think she will discover she has considerable talent if she does. We will be able to help her, should she wish. I suggest she joins us in the Dream Class? I am sure her potential would be very much appreciated."

Moira invited Irina to sit next to her. The girl seemed reluctant to leave Keira's side.

Have you noticed the authority the woman has over Irina? Vee commented, almost as if she were her mother.

Maybe she is, Sally thought back.

"Dream Class? Is that a new part of the curriculum?" Moira asked perplexed but intrigued.

Both Chris and Greenacre looked quizzical. Sally couldn't help laughing.

"No. It's what the words say: it's a dream of a class, our dream of a class," she said. "It was Jenny's idea, if I remember rightly. There are about ten of us who have all travelled to Reaches and in doing so we have been able to develop skills or talents. Jenny works with earth magic, Keira uses song for healing, Mae travels between the worlds, I transform the world around me, … Others do other things. The idea of the Dream Class is simple really: we share what we have learnt with each other and learn from each other's experience. Of course, we still have to work on the concept, but we haven't had much time for that."

"It's a wonderful idea," Irina said as she turned to Moira, speaking for the first time since she'd returned from her fit.

Amazing, Vee whispered. Her voice has completely changed. It's not so tortured.

Sally agreed. The girl's voice was almost pleasant.

"Can I join them?" she asked Moira.

The President looked torn between giving in and holding on to the girl.

"There's no hurry. You don't need to decide now," Sally said. "Why don't you stay with us for our evening meal and then you can meet all the Dream Class and get to know them? Fran and Martin are cooking for us. They're real magicians in the kitchen.

Irina was urging Moira and John to accept.

"How could we possibly refuse such an offer," Moira said laughing.

Fits

Irena cursed. The fits were back and far more virulent than before. So much for being rid of them. Neither the specialist treatment nor the costly therapy had done any good. What a waste of time and money. A heavy cloak of lassitude settled over her.

"I wouldn't do that," Jenny warned.

The girl's words were gentle and encouraging, but Irina was annoyed that Jenny could sense her so well. If only she could block her out.

"You are feeding the web that imprisons you," Jenny said.

Keira, who had been massaging Irina's neck and shoulders, lay her head back on a cushion and stood. Irina intensely disliked being touched, especially by women, but Keira had such a winning way she'd accepted and had been surprised at how much she'd enjoyed it.

"Would you like to talk about it?" Keira asked.

Irina felt a stab of resentment. She couldn't stand being 'treated'.

"No!" she snapped, immediately regretting her reaction. She felt confused. These people had her reacting in ways that were unfamiliar. She was on the verge of tears, she who was so proud of being strong and resistant.

Keira sat down in one of the armchairs and, crossing her legs under her, hummed a weird and unfamiliar melody. Her voice was the only sound as the three girls sat thoughtfully watching the flames flicker in the fireplace.

The strange melody embraced Irina, carrying her along. Then Keira added words in a language she did not recognise. The music was rich and appeasing. Irina closed her eyes and felt her jaw relax. She hadn't realised she was clenching her teeth. Tears welled up in her eyes and she let them flow. Her chest heaved and, for an alarming moment, she was worried a new fit was beginning, but instead she sobbed as the tears flowed more and more freely.

When Keira's song ended, Irina sighed. "I have nightmares," she began, her voice barely audible. "I have had them almost every night for ages."

She halted, hesitant, afraid. She'd never talked of it. Not even to her therapists. Not even to Moira. Keira began humming the melody again, much more quietly. Irina found the sound deeply comforting. It was as if Keira's voice protected her, but it wouldn't be enough. Nothing was ever enough. She sobbed again and tears burst anew from her eyes.

"I hate it! I can't stand it!" she said clenching her fist. Then she relapsed into silence.

The screaming was only a hair's breadth away. She could feel it growing in strength, like a dreadful storm about to break. That was how it always began: the unbearable screaming of a woman burning at the stake. She shuddered violently, tensing her whole body against the imminent onslaught. Her nostrils flared anticipating the sickly smell of burning flesh. There was no way she could stop it.

"Help ... her!" she whispered desperately, her voice coming in strangled bursts. "For God's sake ... save her... I can't bear this!"

But she was forced to watch the skin blacken and crinkle with the intense heat as the image burnt its way into her brain, forced to listen to the woman's terrifying shrieks that shook her to the core, forced to breathe in the cloying stench that suffocated her.

Like the woman tied to the stake, she could not escape. With all her force she willed the nightmare to end and her prayer was answered as silent, formless blackness swept over and she lost consciousness.

Irina came to with a start and sat up causing her head to spin. She lay down slowly.

"Was I out long?" she asked, her voice high-pitched and trembling.

"About a minute," Jenny replied.

She gingerly thrust herself up on her elbows and turned to sit on the settee. Both Jenny and Keira were looking at her, concern in their eyes. Steeling herself against the horror of the memories, she forced herself to speak.

"It's always the same. There's a young woman..." her voice broke but she forced herself to continue, "... burning at the stake."

Feeling the nausea rising in her throat, she tried to stave it off by clenching her fists and gritting her teeth.

"I am condemned to watch, knowing I am responsible for her death."

Her words came out as a hiss between clamped teeth. She was so tense, she was on the verge of snapping. One thing was sure, if she let go this time, she would fall apart and never be whole again. It was then that the trembling started. If only she could hold on, she might make it through intact but the more she fought against it, the more she trembled.

Keira tried to give her some medicine, but her teeth and lips were clenched so tight that nothing could get by. Instead the girl held the tiny bottle under her nose. The pungent odour irritated Irina's senses and she wanted to cough, as if resisting its action, then she relaxed a little.

Keira prised open her mouth and shook a few drops on her tongue. The effect was unlike that of the doctor's pills. Instead of making her drowsy, Keira's remedy made her muscles relax but did away with none of her awareness of the situation.

"Better?" Keira asked.

She nodded, not trusting herself to speak. The trembling had almost stopped and the nausea was receding.

"What you need is to work on your dream," Keira told her. "I have travelled extensively in the Dream Realm, but I am not really an expert. We should ask Alo. He's a shaman. This is his house. Would you agree to meet him?"

Irina thought she'd had enough for one day. She was exhausted and wanted to be left in peace. "I'm so weary." Her voice was almost inexistent.

Jenny looked at her in a strange way, as if she were seeing through her, then she asked: "How do you feel?"

She did feel better, as if she'd got her second wind. "Yes," she said, realising that Jenny must have done something to her. "Thank you." Did she want to go further? Yes. She wanted to put an end to the nightmares. She wanted to be normal. "Ok. I'll meet him."

The man was tall and muscular, but what struck Irina most was his face. He had an infectious smile with sparkling blue eyes set in a clean-shaven, weather-beaten face under the shiny crown of his balding head.

"I'm Alo Marli," he said, his voice deep and rich.

He inspired confidence, she thought, as she shook his hand. It was warm compared to hers, his grip firm but not imposing.

"I'm Irina."

"Shall we talk here, or would you like to go to my office next door?"

She glanced at the fire, longing for warmth and comfort. "Here is fine."

"Would you like us to talk alone or do you want Keira and Jenny to stay?"

"They can stay. They've been so good to me."

"I generally don't try to interpret dreams," Alo explained when Irina had finished describing her dream. "I leave that to others who are better at it than I am." He smiled. "Of course, that doesn't mean dreams cannot be bringers of messages or they don't need to be understood, but I approach them more as journeys we make or adventures we have. In your case, though, I have the impression that you are undertaking somebody else's journey, probably someone from the past. What do you know about your ancestors?"

The question took her by surprise. She hadn't ever thought her dream might be linked to a real event or someone her ancestors had known. The idea gave her hope. Maybe she needn't be a prisoner of her nightmares.

"Well, Moira – she's my guardian – always introduces me as a descendant of Madame Blavatsky."

"Moira Campbell is President of the Blavatsky Foundation," Keira explained. "She's in the library with Sally, Mae, Chris and Professor Greenacre."

"I don't know if I really am a descendant. I was told that my parents died when I was very young and that Moira offered to look after me. It's a subject both of us have always avoided."

"Do you think she would agree to answer a few questions?" Alo asked.

"She might, if she thought it could put an end to my fits."

"Could you go and see if she's free for a moment, Keira?" Alo said.

"Hallo, Moira," Alo said. "Haven't seen you in ages."

Irina's was unaware they knew each other. Surely Moira would have mentioned it when they arrived at Alo's house.

"Hallo Alo," Moira said, kissing him lightly on the cheek.

"You know each other?" Irina couldn't help exclaiming.

Alo chuckled. Moira blushed.

"We have some similar interests that have made our paths cross more than once," Alo responded somewhat evasively.

It was not just her own past she was uncovering, it would seem.

When everyone was seated, Alo explained the situation to Moira. "Irina has been telling us about her nightmare."

"I didn't know you had nightmares," Moira said, casting a worried look at Irina.

"I didn't want to upset you," Irina said, embarrassed. "I cause you enough difficulties without that."

Moira was about to react, but Alo spoke first. "Would you like to tell Moira your dream?"

Irina took a deep breath and told the dream a second time. She was astonished to find that it got easier with telling. It wasn't easy for Moira, though. She gasped in horror and hid her face in her hands.

"We suspect the dream may have something to do with her fits," Jenny explained.

"Alo thinks the dream might have a connection with Irina's ancestors. Do you know anything about them?" Keira added.

All four of them looked expectantly at Moira.

Moira sat for a long moment in silence, her breath coming in short bursts, her eyes fixed on the carpet at her feet, her hands raking through her grey hair.

"Oh Irina!" she began, her voice distraught. "I had hoped I would be able to keep this from you."

Moira's behaviour alarmed her. Her guardian had always been a steady pillar that she could cling to when she felt she was going to bits. Without that support, she felt fragile and exposed.

"Your mother did not die in an accident as I led you to believe."

Irina could feel the trembling coming on. She looked desperately at Keira who must have understood because she came and sat next to her, putting her arm around her.

"She was haunted by terrible visions. She came to me for help but there was nothing I could do. She was unable to live normally and had to undergo intensive treatment, all to no avail. In the end, she threw herself into the river and was found drowned several days later."

Irina couldn't stop herself sobbing in Keira's arms.

"Your father was broken hearted. He loved your mother and you dearly. Shortly afterwards he had a fatal car accident. You had no near relatives. I offered to look after you and the court agreed. You were two years old at the time."

"Do you remember the nature of the visions Irina's mother had?" Alo asked.

Moira groaned and cast her hands up in desperation. "Exactly those Irina has in her nightmare."

Irina couldn't help it. She could feel the spasms coming on. She was about to have a fit.

"Don't fight it," Keira whispered in her ear. "Let it come."

What stupid advice! She had to fight it, to hold it at bay. What else could she do? She wouldn't give in. She had to win. She shook her head.

"Breathe," Keira ordered.

Irina let a rush of air into her lungs with a gasp. She was drowning.

"Again," Keira insisted.

Irina forced her clenched teeth open and sucked in more air.

Keira, who was holding her hand, shook it gently. "Breathe again!" Air gushed into her lungs.

"Make a noise as you breathe," Keira instructed.

Irina didn't understand. It was all she could do to stay afloat.

"Growl!" Keira ordered.

She could not. She would not.

"Growl!" Keira repeated.

Impossible. How could she? She was not an animal.

Keira pressed hard against her stomach as she breathed out. A sinister growling sprang from her mouth. She tried to silence it, but Keira pressed her stomach again. A deep blood-curling growl filled the room. She no longer needed Keira's help. The growl growled of its own accord. Wild. Dreadful. Frightening. But so full of life. When the growling finally subsided she burst out laughing and couldn't stop. She rocked backwards and forwards, holding her sides that hurt from laughing so much.

"Mama mia!" she exclaimed when the laughing was finally done.

"Mia is my name in the Reaches," Keira explained, a broad grin on her face.

Irina flung herself into Keira's arms and hugged her.

"Well now we can go and eat," Alo said, standing. "I think Martin and Fran are ready for us."

Everyone laughed.

Watching

Tom sat in the shadows of the empty meeting room. Night had fallen outside. The headlights of the occasional car flickered across the dusty windows causing eerie shapes to race around the room as dockworkers wound their way home for the weekend.

The apprentice watchers would soon be returning. Tom rolled his wheelchair closer to the table and studied the map. He didn't like using the same meeting place more than once, but they had little choice and no time. Watching was much more difficult than in Granwich. They didn't have the support of the population, for a start. You couldn't go up to the bartender in the Starless Square and expect his help as they might in Granwich.

In addition, they had much more ground to cover with far fewer watchers. And people moved about much faster in Avan making them hard to track. The walkie-talkies helped and some watchers were using bicycles to get about town. The more he thought about it, the more Tom was convinced that something new was called for. But he didn't know what.

Hearing a distant noise in the corridor below, he shifted into the shadows to wait and watch. The first to arrive came quietly into the room and settled in chairs waiting. One or two of the younger ones were noisier, laughing and chatting on the stairs as if they were on their way to a pub. Only Kean noticed Tom waiting but made no sign.

Once all had arrived, Tom rolled forward out of the shadows. "Being a watcher might be exciting at times," he said startling more than one. "But it can be extremely dangerous. Lives are at stake. Yours amongst them! So you need to be more careful. Some of you make too much noise. This is not a pub crawl! A watcher watches but is never seen. So who will report first?"

"Shortly after Lyra and Jenny left, Dr. Frick arrived at the Starless Square." It was Kean that spoke. "He entered by a backdoor and went up to the top floor. He went into one of the meeting rooms where he met a man who was waiting for him. The bartender brought them drinks and told Frick that two young women had been enquiring about the name of the pub. I heard what he said because he left the door open. Frick had the bartender describe the women. The doctor was able to identify Professor Enquist, but he didn't recognise the other woman. A quarter of an hour later, six men arrived, one at a time, furtively, and made their way to the top floor. They clearly knew their way about. I guess they meet there regularly. They shut the door and spoke quietly. I could hear nothing. They left after an hour. We split up and followed those who were on foot."

Tom asked questions, lots of questions. He encouraged others to ask questions too. A lot of details had got lost through inexperience, but he was pleased at the result. They now knew the identity of four of the eight members of Frick's group and could find out the names of some of the others from their car registration plates.

"I followed Frick. He went to see his mother in an old people's home on Lime Street. He must be a regular visitor because the receptionist recognised him. He spent half an hour with his mother. She's not so old, but she doesn't seem right in the head. She paid no attention to him. She didn't even greet him. Her behaviour seemed to upset him. I saw him clenching his fists as he spoke to her. He started to tell her his plans. But he seemed nervous and kept glancing over his shoulder as if he knew someone was watching. He said they were going to disrupt Professor Rafter's talk tomorrow. When he left he went to the university and stayed in his office for several hours."

Tom agreed with those who thought that Frick might have been lying about his plans, but they couldn't risk ignoring what he said. What with the Professor's ill health and the number of people expected, they had to prevent any disturbance.

"I followed one of the Starless Square group. A man called Cary

Green. He's a builder. He walked to a disused building that he apparently employs as a warehouse and loaded his lorry with a number of those shoulder-high barriers they sometimes put around building sites. He then drove out of town. He was too fast for me to follow. I lingered around hoping to see him drive back but, if he came, he didn't use the same road. On my way here I saw his lorry parked not far from the Starless Square. He must have loaded something else because there was a thick tarpaulin stretched over the back. I tried to look underneath but could only see a pile of sand."

Most people thought Green's activities had nothing to do with the Starless Square group. The difficulty with Watching was that events made no sense at the time only to become screamingly obvious with hindsight.

"I tried to follow a man called Gerald Twine but he drove too fast for me to keep up. He's a farmer. I checked him in the directory. His farm is just outside town. He raises pigs. I went there later. The place stinks. He was nowhere to be seen."

So each person described what he or she had seen. When they had all finished, Tom moved on to plans for Saturday. "I suggest we concentrate on the first two events: Rafter's Talk and the Guided Tour with Sally and Professor Trundle. If there is a disturbance at the library, it may not be caused by the people we have been following. They may have supporters or helpers. Some of you will have to be in the Library and others will be stationed outside..."

They went on to discuss details.

"I have misgivings about the Guided Tour," Tom told them. "It begins from Frick's own territory, close to the Cathedral. If I were him, I'd want to make a symbolic stand. Although I have no idea what they might do."

Various people made suggestions, but none seemed likely.

"We'll have to keep the place completely covered, just in case."

Shortly afterwards the meeting broke up having planned to meet for breakfast the next morning. Kean drove Tom to Alo's house so he could confer with the others.

Dinner

Moira took her seat at the table next to Professor Greenacre. Whoever had prepared the table, which had been laid for more than twenty people, had done so with great care. Between the glasses and plates and cutlery, the table was festooned with twisting ivy leaves bedecked with brightly coloured flowers along with tiny fruits and nuts. She had expected Irina to sit next to her, but the girl had abandoned her in favour of Keira. The two were in animated conversation about music.

Once everyone was seated, Sally stood and addressed the group. "Before we begin there are two things I'd like to do. First, let me introduce everybody."

Sitting next to Sally were John and Alo who were both smiling at something one of them must had said. It was good to meet Alo again. He hadn't changed much, still the charmer who made her heart flutter all that time ago. Then came Keira and Irina. She felt a pang of jealousy to think that Keira had so easily eclipsed her in Irina's attentions. Irina must have felt her eyes on her because she glanced in Moira's direction and smiled. It was a relief to see her relaxed and happy for once.

Then came two people Moira had not yet met. "This is Dieter and Anju. Anju is the granddaughter of Professor Outman who recently gave a conference here about chaos theory. Dieter, who comes from Germany, used to be a police detective. Now the two of them are our experts in self-defence," Sally informed them. The tenderness between them was heart-warming. Given the difference in age between the two, you might have thought they were father and daughter although they didn't look alike. But they had a way of touching each other, albeit fleetingly, that hinted at much more.

Jenny she had already seen at work with Irina but the young man in a wheelchair sitting next to Jenny was new to her. "Tom is our eyes and ears," Sally had said enigmatically.

"Are you a detective too?" Moira asked, causing Tom to chuckle.

"No, I'm a Watcher. I work with a group of young people to make sure that nothing disturbs our celebrations this weekend."

Moira wanted to know more, but Sally moved on. Between Jenny and Greenacre at her side were two Professors from the department: Liam Lettrot who taught dreams and good old Gavin Trundle, a fountain of knowledge about the history of religion and paganism.

When it was Moira's turn to be introduced, Sally said: "And this is Moira, President of the Blavatsky Foundation, who, if I'm not mistaken, is a former student of our department."

It was Moira's turn to laugh. "That was a long time ago. Few of you were around at the time. It was before Professor Rafter came here."

"That reminds me," Mae said, who had just sat down to Moira's right, "Professor Rafter sends you all his warmest greetings. I've just come from his country house."

"How is he?" Sally asked, barely concealing her worry.

"As much a joker as ever," Mae grinned. "He's resting, getting up his strength for tomorrow."

Next to Mae were two other Professors from the Department: Lyra Enquist that Moira always consulted when she needed help with healing and Chris Dryman an expert on shamanism. She liked Chris. He made her feel at ease with his relaxed, jovial manner and his clever mind.

Finally, there was a small Asiatic woman with long pitch-black hair.

"This is Naniu. You may have heard her singing. She's a good friend of the Department."

Moira had indeed heard of Naniu, she even had one of her records.

Across the table, next to Sally's seat sat Brent. "The Storyteller" Sally called him. When Sally added that he went under other names, he blushed like a little girl. Moira wonder what that was about. This 'Dream Class', as they called themselves, already had quite a history, she realised.

Next to Brent was a young girl. She couldn't have been more than fourteen but seemed quite at home talking to adults. Sally introduced her as "… my dear sister, An." And went on to explain: "An lives in the Reaches, that other world we told you about," she said addressing Moira directly. "She's just here for the weekend." Moira wondered if she'd let her daughter travel to another world at that age.

Finally, next to An was Martina Aschlyman, who taught occult sciences.

"We were talking about the battle between good and evil," Martina told them, nodding to Brent and An.

"I'm thinking I should invite An to talk to my students about the subject," Martina mused.

"She'll corrupt them all!" Sally exclaimed laughing, causing An to blow her a kiss.

Two seats at the head of table next to Martina, those nearest the kitchen, were vacant. The cooks, Moira imagined. And sure enough, as if summoned, a young woman opened the door so a man could push a heavily laden trolley though into the room.

"And these are our magicians in the kitchen!" Sally announced with a flourish, "Fran and Martin."

Everyone applauded.

"In a former life Fran was a molecular biologist and Martin an expert in explosives, amongst other things."

The most startling thing about Fran was her shaved head. Rather than being reminded of sinister stories about concentration camps, Moira was surprised to see how beautiful Fran looked, what with the striking contours of her head free of hair and her bright blue eyes.

"The second thing I have to do," Sally continued, "is to ask Keira to sing grace."

Moira was surprised that they should maintain such a ritual in a group most of whom had no apparent religious affiliations.

"There's a long story behind this grace," Keira explained. "I learnt it from a young woman whose name is Grace." Keira chuckled at some private memory and then went on. "She is the head of the Sisterhood of the Stones. I am very grateful to her for accepting me as a member of that Sisterhood."

Moving towards Fran and Martin, she placed her down-turned hands outspread above the trolley and sang a short but poignant song in a language Moira didn't recognise.

"Bon appétit!" Martin said as he and Fran began placing the food on the table.

Martin and Fran had prepared many different dishes, but the dish that pleased Moira most was the fritters made with leaves and flowers. Each one was different and the taste was exquisite.

"All the plants come from here," Martin explained. "We collected them the other day with Lyra's students and then had a great time trying them out with the students."

"They were delighted," Lyra put in. "I've never had such a satisfied class!"

By the time they'd reached the desert, a delicious sorbet made of berries from the fields and forests, many people had drifted into the next room where coffee and tea were being served. Moira wanted to ask Tom a question so she seized the occasion when Dieter went out to sit between Anju and Tom.

"What exactly do Watchers do?" she asked.

"They watch," he replied laconically and then laughed. "I suppose in a way our job is to help anticipate the future by paying attention to details in the present."

"A bit like planning you mean?"

"Not really. Planning tries to dictate what's going to happen. To be honest I don't think planning works so well in our complicated world."

"How do you know what to watch?" Anju asked.

A very good question, Moira thought.

"That's the problem," Tom replied. "There is so much to pay attention to and any part of it could be significant. Take this wine glass," he explained, picking it up and turning it in his fingers. "You probably would dismiss it as unimportant. After all, there are more than twenty similar glasses on the table. But who knows, the fact that it is here is this very position," and he placed it back on the table next to his plate, "may be a signal to an accomplice that a murder is to be perpetrated."

"I wish my grandfather were here," Anju said. "He'd have a field day. He loves this kind of discussion. He'd say it was a question of complexity."

"What do you mean?" Tom asked, eager to know more.

"Have you ever heard of emergence?" the girl asked.

Moira was astonished at the extent of Anju's knowledge. It was not something you'd expect a girl of her age to talk about.

"No. It was never mentioned in my journalism classes," Tom joked.

"Well," Anju began, running her fingers thoughtfully through her pitch-black hair. "In complex systems, like the human body or parts of society, for example, new things emerge spontaneously from the complexity itself. If you were to take the system apart and look at the bits and pieces that make it up, you'd find no evidence of what is about to emerge. All attempts to predict the future in complex systems by analysing the parts of the system, have only a limited chance of success."

"Hold on," Tom said, obviously grappling with Anju's concepts. "Does that mean that even if we could watch everything happening in Avan, which of course we can't, we still couldn't satisfactorily predict what is going to happen tomorrow at the library?"

Oddly enough, rather than putting him off, the challenge of that impossibility stimulated him.

"Obviously there are many situations that are predictable, but we are not interested in them," Anju pointed out. "What worries us are the unpredictable situations like the reactions to Professor Rafter's talk tomorrow."

"When I learnt the art of Watching in Granwich, a town in the Reaches," he explained for Moira, "Watching was much easier. The situation was less complex. Although I realise now that the problems we have here were also present there too, to a lesser degree."

"Maybe you are watching the wrong type of things," Anju mused.

"What do you mean?" Tom asked, clearly excited that they might be on the verge of a breakthrough.

"If things really do emerge from complexity, then you'd need to look for signs that something is about to emerge and that might indicate the hitherto unidentified future possibilities."

Tom looked puzzled, screwing up his eyes as if trying to see what Anju was talking about. "What might emergence look like?"

"I don't know," Anju admitted.

Brent, who'd been listening to the conversation from the doorway came forward and sat next to Anju. "When we first met in this very room with Professor Rafter before we went to the Reaches, I had a strange vision. It was as if lines of force crossed the room joining people together. The lines shifted and changed in strength as people spoke or something happened. I only saw them for a moment then they were gone."

All were turned to him waiting for more.

"Well maybe emergence looks like that," Brent said, "like complex lines of force in the present. And where they join together and form strong nodes, that is where the future is likely to emerge."

Anju hit the palm of her hand against her forehead, saying: "Of course. Topology."

Nobody understood.

"Yes. That's how we describe the force fields in chaos theory."

Brent chuckled. "All you have to do now Tom is to get to see those force fields."

"Thanks," Tom replied sarcastically.

Their conversation was interrupted by Mae inviting them into the room next door, apparently Keira was going to sing. When everyone was comfortably settled in an armchair or on the thick carpets on the floor, Keira explained: "In the area around Granwich the Commoners speak a dialect called 'Gran'. This song is an ancient lullaby sung in their dialect."

Moira closed her eyes when the first notes rang out and as the music unfolded, she had snatches of a vision of pitch-black houses sparkling in the moonlight, an enchanted town. Magic was the only word for it. How else could you explain that Keira's voice could bewitch you so. When the lullaby was over, everyone applauded and Keira bowed theatrically.

Naniu rose from her seat and embraced Keira. "Amazing!" she exclaimed. "Your voice has changed and improved so much. The quality, the depth, the feeling … it's wonderful!"

Keira nodded her thanks and went on: "During the concert tomorrow evening, Brent and I will take it in turns to be on stage. He will tell a tale after each song. We thought we might try out the idea this evening. So Brent …" and she held out her hand to him.

Moira hadn't noticed how tall and slim Brent was when he had been seated at the table. Standing next to Keira near the fireplace, the contrast between the two was striking. She was all curves and sensuality, accentuated by the provocative way she dressed with a tight T-shirt, a flouncy short skirt and brightly coloured tights.

Brent, in comparison, was stiff and angular. He seemed ill at ease in his body and that discomfort was visible in the way he dressed. The colours jarred and neither the baggy trousers nor the thick sweater flattered his figure. To be honest, she could hardly imagine him alone on a stage in front of thousands of people.

"The night was moonless and cold," Brent began without the slightest warning or preamble.

Moira was startled to find she was shivering. Several people wrapped their arms around themselves as if to ward off the cold.

"An unending line of thousands of refugees, children, women and a smattering of men, straggled out along the road, some riding in carts but most stumbling silently forward, weighed down with worry and fatigue, …"

Extraordinary, Moira thought, as she was carried along amid them. She could literally smell the sweat and the dust and the scent of exotic night flowers. When, later, Mae abruptly appeared out of nowhere amongst the refugees accompanied by a most beautiful young woman called Lucie, Moira couldn't help gasping. Lucie, who was the leader of the people of Granwich, seemed to glow with a bright light that reminded her of pictures she'd seen of saints.

Amid confusion and indecision, Moira hears Mae suggest she transport all the refugees to a place called the Lost Meadows. Although people seem sceptical, Moira is buoyed up by the strength and determination radiating from Mae. Moira feels the strange wrenching feeling as Mae travels between the worlds taking them instantly to the Lost Meadows to find D'rick, the head of the Littl' People. She feels her heart swell with pride when D'rick greets Mae as a princess and presents her with a gold pendant to the accompaniment of the chorus of Littl' People. Moira feel's Mae's ever-increasing exhaustion as she transports wave after wave of refugees to the Lost Meadows until she can go no further. Moira shares Mae's ultimate effort to return to Avan bringing back with her a young woman called Mia who looked remarkably like Keira.

And just as abruptly as it had begun the story was over, leaving the listeners stranded in Alo's sitting room. Moira was both delighted and disturbed. Looking round the room, she realised she was not alone having difficulties returning to the present.

Brent stood quietly by the fireside, his eyes half-closed,. How could she possibly have mistaken him for a misfit? What a wonderful gift. Everyone burst into applause. And some of Brent's discomfort returned as he bowed stiffly and returned to his seat next to Sally.

"Don't you think you overdid it a bit with Lucie?" Sally as she put her arm around Brent's shoulder.

"That's how I see her," was all Brent replied, his face flushed with pleasure.

Chapter 3 ~ Transcendence

A walk and a talk

Brent laced up his walking boots, looking forward to wandering the abandoned streets on the outskirts of town. He loved being out at night. A hesitant knock sounded at the door of the room he'd commandeered at Alo's place. It was late for improvised visits. Opening the door, he found Sally standing in the doorway.

"Would you mind if I slept in your room tonight?" Her look was almost pleading.

Brent invited her in, but she held back on the doorstep.

"What happened to Keira?" Brent asked, realising with embarrassment that it probably wasn't the most diplomatic question.

Sally grimaced. "She's sleeping with Irina," she replied, biting her lip, unable to disguise her irritation. "The spoilt little brat insists she'll have nightmares if Keira is not with her."

Brent chuckled. "That'll teach Keira not to go around saving damsels in distress. That's supposed to be the man's role."

She punched his shoulder playfully. "You can talk!" Both of them laughed.

"I'm off out for a walk before I go to bed. Make yourself at home. There's a second bed over there. I'll be back in an hour." He hoped his words might alleviate some of the embarrassment of sharing a room but not a bed.

"Do you mind if I come with you?"

"Of course you can. I just thought you might like to settle in while I was out."

Sally giggled uncharacteristically. "Embarrassing isn't it!"

"I suppose we'll survive, whatever happens."

"Have you got sturdier shoes and a coat?"

She shook her head.

"I've got a cape. It ought to keep you warm," he said spreading a heavy cape around her shoulders. "And Alo has boots in the garage. Maybe we'll find a pair that fits you."

Once they were kitted up, they stepped outside to discover that the wind had got up, chasing clouds across the starlit sky. They walked in silence along the road away from town, thoughtful.

"I love to walk, especially late at night," Brent said. "The world comes awake with a wild sort of life at this time of the night."

Sally said nothing. She just sighed. Silence fell again, broken only by the wind in the branches and the occasional screech of a nearby owl. It was Brent's turn to sigh as his heart winged to the Reaches.

"Do you miss Lucie so much?" Sally asked, presumably understanding what the sound of hooting would mean to him. He had been trapped in an owl's body when he first met Lucie who looked after birds.

He hesitated before replying. Life just wasn't the same without Lucie. She was his light. She had managed to coax him back when he was lost and confused. It was with her that he had discovered his gift for storytelling. He felt his breath shudder as if he were about to sob.

"Terribly." His voice was unsteady.

Sally took his hand in hers and continued walking in silence. He was astonished at the wild confusion of feelings he felt at holding Sally's hand.

"Have you always told stories?" she asked.

He had never given the question much thought. "Well, yes. When I was younger I used to wander the night streets imagining all sorts of stories." The memory sent a thrill through him. "See that house over there," he said, pointing to a house set back from the roadside in a large garden. People must have still been up because light from the living room flooded out onto the lawn and lit the trees and bushes. "I would imagine what those people were up to, developing quite a tale. That's why I find the night so exciting: it's full of stories."

Sally tugged gently on his hand, forcing him to stop. Then she took hold of his other hand and pulled him closer. Leaning up on her tiptoes, she pressed her lips to his and kissed him cautiously.

"I love you, Brent," she whispered, her sweet breath caressing his lips, and she slid her arms around his waist and pulled his body against hers, laying her head on his chest. Part of him wanted to push her away, to protest, but part of him felt like he had been longing for this moment for ever and now that it had come about it was only natural they should be together.

He stroked her shoulder length auburn hair, and then slid his hands under her hair around the nape of her neck, cupping her head in his hands. He didn't trust himself to speak. So he returned her kiss, lightly brushing his lips against hers. Both of them sighed.

"I love you too, Sally," he said, feeling her tighten her hold around his waist as she pressed her breasts against him. "But my feelings are confused."

Sally burst out laughing, hurting his feelings, causing him to stiffen and draw back.

"Don't misunderstand me," she hastened to explain, pulling him closer again. "I'm not laughing at you. It's just that I sympathise with your confusion. Can you imagine what it is like to have a man's voice in your head all the time? Luckily Vee is sensitive. He wouldn't make comments, for example, when I am kissing you. But I do feel that he is jealous."

The perspective was both extraordinary and alarming.

"Both of us are intimately linked to someone else," Sally concluded. "Yet despite that fact, I am sure we were made for each other."

He shared her conviction. He had already known it when he'd first seen her that time in Alo's house. She'd been asleep in an armchair, her suntanned legs laid bare by her dress that had ridden up her thighs and he had not wanted to disturb her but he couldn't tear his eyes away.

"I think you might be right," he said cautiously. To his surprise she tickled him.

"You're always so cautious!" Then she kissed him again, longer this time and more passionately, pressing her lips hard against his. He pulled her closer and forgot his doubts as he responded to her passion with his own growing excitement.

"It's time for bed," he said his breath coming hard.

"I believe it is."

Breakfast

As Brent and Sally made their way down the stairs en route for breakfast they could hear Irina chattering in the dining room.

"It's remarkable how much the girl has changed," Sally said, not disguising her disgust. "I preferred the taciturn version!"

Brent stifled a yawn. Sleeping with Sally had turned out to be demanding. He chuckled at the thought and felt desire rising again as he remembered some of their exploits. "She'll get over it, once the novelty has worn off." He wasn't sure he could say the same for himself with Sally.

As they reached the bottom of the stairs, Sally halted to give him a kiss, lacing her arms around his waist and pulling him in a tight embrace. Keira stepped out of the dinning room carrying a teapot. All three of them blushed.

"Thank heavens you've come to my rescue," Keira said, waving the teapot in the direction of the dinning room before she disappeared into the kitchen.

They found Irina downing an immense slice of bread laced with butter and honey. She replied to their greetings with a garbled "Good morning!"

"You seem particularly hungry this morning," Brent quipped. "The country air must be doing you some good." Sally made a face at him when Irina wasn't looking.

"I'm so happy," she said having finished her chunk of bread. She looked towards the door, a troubled look on her face.

The dining room door opened, although it wasn't Keira but Jenny. "Bon appétit," she said. "Tom's gone to a breakfast meeting with the Watchers and I came to tell you what they have learnt. Tom had no opportunity to talk about it yesterday evening."

"Where's Keira with the tea?" Irina asked, her tone irritated.

"I suspect she got lost in the kitchen, maybe you should go and save her," Sally suggested, affecting a worried face.

Irina glared at her and stomped off to the kitchen.

"What was that about?" Jenny asked.

"Lover's tiff," Sally said dismissively.

Brent chuckled and gave her a playful shove, but she grabbed his hand and pulled him closer.

Jenny looked intrigued. "Don't you have an expression in English," she asked, "something about a cat being away ...?"

Everybody laughed just as Irina entered, hauling Keira after her.

"Anybody for tea?" Keira asked, making an exasperated face.

"One of the Watchers heard Frick say he planned to disrupt Professor Rafter's talk this morning," Jenny began, once she'd closed the door, "but Tom suspects the doctor was trying to lead us astray. He thinks Frick will concentrate on the guided tour, especially as it begins directly from the Starless Square."

Mae entered the room at that moment and poured herself some tea. "I'm off to fetch Professor Rafter. What have Tom and Anju planned for the library?"

"Watchers will be posted both outside and inside the library. Anju and Dieter will stay close to the Professor, if ever there is any trouble," Jenny told them.

"I plan to do the same," Mae said. "I can always transport Rafter to safety, if necessary."

Jenny looked worried. "You should only do that if all else fails. I suspect that such transport might put too much strain on his heart..."

Mae looked dejected.

"I'll be there too," Irina said, surprising them. The young girl clearly considered she was part of the group, even though her presence could in no way help protect the Professor, Brent thought.

"That will be very useful," Sally said.

Keira shot her a filthy look. Mae looked perplexed, clearly wondering what was going on.

"We'll all be there," Brent added trying to allay the tension.

"Sally," Jenny asked, "could we talk a moment in private? I'd like you to tell me the itinerary for your guided tour." Sally gave Brent a kiss that he suspected was also meant as a message to Keira, and the two left.

"We should talk," he said, turning to Keira who still looked annoyed, "about our performance this evening." As they rose to go, Mae also took her leave on her way to fetch the Professor, abandoning Irina alone, lost and put out.

Emergence ...

Tom yawned. All night long he had dreamt he was wandering a maize, unable to get out and the feeling of being rudderless lingered.

'Did you find a solution?" Anju asked as she arrived in the deserted warehouse with Dieter.

He couldn't immediately figure out what she was referring to. "Ah, emergence! No, not yet."

Anju was carrying a large bag of bread rolls and bars of chocolate and Dieter brought two thermoses. The apprentice Watchers had not yet arrived.

"I talked to An about it," he told them. "She's staying with us at Sally's flat."

In fact they had spent several hours discussing the subject before going to bed. Maybe that was why he had slept so badly.

"She thinks it might be like Jenny and the earth energies, but instead of revealing the forces flowing in the earth, I would need to reveal, at least to my inner eye, the forces driving towards the future."

Tom rolled his wheelchair across to the main table where Dieter and Anju had placed the food and helped himself to a roll and a hunk of chocolate. "A real Swiss breakfast," he commented, laughing. "I asked Jenny to describe how she does it and I tried myself, but I couldn't get it to work."

Their conversation was interrupted by the arrival of the Watchers.

"What's new?" Tom asked, once everyone was seated around the table.

"I've been investigating another of the Starless Square called Jeremy Nohan," Kean told them. "He's a chemist's assistant, he's single and in his late thirties. Works in one of those chain stores down the high street. Nothing spectacular about that," he said grinning. "But rummaging through back numbers of the local newspaper on the Internet I found that he was called in for questioning by the police along with a man named Peter Glat in the investigation of a fire that badly burnt two women. The men were later released due to lack of evidence." Dieter whistled through his teeth.

"That must be the rumour Lyra told us about involving the burning of supposed witches," Dieter guessed.

"I could find out nothing about Glat, he's not in the telephone book," Kean continued.

"I've discovered something too," Ben told them.

He was one of Lyra's assistants, Sally had told Tom.

"You remember those crash barriers I saw Cary Green loading onto his lorry yesterday. He must have stolen them. It was on the radio this morning. Someone took five crash barriers from a warehouse in town, the reporter said. The theft might have gone noticed, but they were to be used for a match this afternoon."

"That might mean the Starless Square plan to use them," Dieter speculated. "If they are stolen, it is more difficult to trace who put them up."

Tom poured himself a coffee, saying: "So everyone should keep a look out for crash barriers. They might be the sign they are up to something."

As nobody had any more news, they tidied up, not wanting to leave evidence they'd been there even if they had the permission of the owner, and set off separately for the library except for a small group that was to keep an eye of the Square next to the Cathedral.

The main reading room in Avan Central Library was old fashioned, with its high ceiling and its dark oak panels and shelves. Most of the books were stocked in rooms off the main area and the children's section was further away down a long corridor. The room was often used for poetry readings as well as a conference from time to time. It was there that Rafter was to give his talk.

When Tom arrived with Anju and Dieter, Keira was in deep conversation with some of the library staff. "Can you loan me your key to the back door?" she was asking. "The Professor has been a little under the weather so we want to bring him in and take him out that way rather than via the main entrance."

Keira apparently got the key she wanted because she slipped it to Dieter when she came over to speak to them. "Let me show you around," she said.

When they returned to the main reading room, a number of Watchers were helping the library staff clear away the armchairs that were a familiar fixture for those who were regulars, storing them in a depot out the back and returning with trolley loads of foldable chairs for the audience. Tom had suggested the Watchers give a hand, both to be less conspicuous but also to casually gain information from the library staff.

The main room could seat up to a hundred, but nobody was very sure how many people would turn up. Keira went to help with the chairs while Tom, Anju and Dieter moved off down the corridor to the children's library that was deserted. Kean joined them there.

"This place would be an easy target for a fire," Dieter remarked.

The thought sent a shudder of horror down Tom's spine. It had been in a fire started by a band of assassins that he had lost the use of his legs and probably would have died if it hadn't been for Jenny and Keira.

"Keira told me the wood had been specially treated against fire," Kean commented. "How about smoke or stink bombs?"

"We can hardly search people as they enter," Anju responded.

"Why not?" Dieter said. "We could set up a desk at the entrance."

It would be so easy to disrupt Rafter's talk, Tom realised, but they couldn't take extreme measures to try to prevent it.

"These events are supposed to bring the Department closer to the people," Tom pointed out. "It would be counterproductive to set up barriers around us when people come to see us."

"What we need are barriers people can neither see nor feel, like an invisible shield" Anju mused.

"None of us have such a gift," Tom pointed out, noticing that Kean was looking at them strangely.

"Well maybe we should think about acquiring it," she replied.

Tom winced. He knew something about trying to acquire gifts. Maybe you just couldn't wish for something like that. Perhaps it was a gift and not a skill to be learnt or acquired deliberately.

Judging from the voices down the corridor, people were beginning to arrive. The group split up and Tom rolled his wheelchair into a quiet, out-of-the-way corner of the main room and settled in to watch. The room was already almost full and people were lined up along the back, leaning against the bookshelves. He was surprised at the wide variety of those present: men and women in suits who looked like they came straight from their office; younger women who must have left the baby at the nursery for a few hours; eager students, notepads at the ready; even the elderly, trembling slightly as they waited.

... *and transcendence*

Sometimes it was useful to be an outsider, Tom realised. You could get a better insight into people's relationships and habits, unhindered by pre-conceived ideas. Many people seemed to know someone, but greeted each other with some distance: a nod, a wave or a couple of words. It was as if an invisible force hampered their coming together. When people arrived together, mostly in twos, they stuck together and didn't mix much with others, even if they knew them. It reminded him of an experiment they'd done in school with iron filings and a magnet. There was nothing to align the people or galvanise them. Their energies were scattered and separate, cancelling each other out.

What a contrast with the small group gathered around Keira. They were all vying to get closer, to attract her attention, to speak to her. He chuckled realising that she was like a magnet. It gave the group much more force and attracted even more people till a small crowd had gathered. Everybody was pleased to see her. People elsewhere in the room were craning their necks to see who was causing the commotion.

If he tried to explain it, it was as if her energy was spreading infectiously till the whole room was caught up in her sphere of influence.

The situation changed the moment Professor Rafter entered, accompanied by Mae on one side and Sally on the other. The interest in Keira subsided as heads turned one after another in the direction of the professor. The atmosphere changed too. From electric and sensual and – what was the word for it? – bodily, maybe, it transformed to expectation and somehow 'ethereal', fragile and almost unearthly. If people ended up breathing deeply when Keira became the momentary centre of interest, they now held their breath. It was as if the room was suspended. It reminded him of a French expression: 'suspendu à ses lèvres', literally people were suspended from his lips. Wasn't the English equivalent that people were 'all ears'? The words didn't do justice to the feeling of suspension that accompanied the moment.

Mae settled Rafter in an armchair placed on a low podium while Sally addressed the audience. "It is with great pleasure that we'd like to welcome Professor Rafter this morning. For those of you who don't already know him, he's head of the Theosophy Department of the University of Avan and has written a number of major works about shamanism, amongst other things."

Tom noted that although she held the attention of the audience, she did not create such a forceful centre as Keira. It was as if people's attention was only through their ears but not their guts. People's guts, if you could say such a thing, were concentrated on Professor Rafter.

"His talk this morning," Sally continued, "heralds a weekend of events organised by the Department that continues with a guided tour of the old town led by Professor Trundle and myself. You are very welcome to join us in front of the Cathedral at two this afternoon. The remainder of the programme is posted in the entrance to the library. But enough from me! Professor," she said turning to him.

"Thank you Sally. Theosophy," Rafter began, "is the study of our direct relationship with that which is beyond and above the normal range of human experience. Now, that might sound like a contradiction. How can we possibly experience what is beyond our experience? The key word here is perhaps 'normal'. But let's leave that till later, if we have time."

Tom could sense that Rafter's words were putting a strain on people's attention as they sought to grasp his meaning. Rafter had created something akin to a vacuum in the middle of the room that many people were struggling not to be sucked into.

"So how do we experience what is above and beyond? Well music is one way. To illustrate what I mean, maybe Keira would agree to sing one verse of a song for us."

Judging from the look on her face, Keira hadn't known he would ask her. "Of course." She stood and shifted into the aisle next to her at the back of the room.

Many people turned their heads and those who resisted the urge to look could hold out no longer the moment she began to sing. And as she sang, the vacuum that Rafter had created was filled with her voice in more ways than one. It was not just her voice, but her whole being that had the room vibrating. When she finished the audience erupted in applause. Tom had never realised before how much applause was a limited expression of the movement the audience felt at listening to a performance.

The experience of Keira singing was so strong and moving that many people had some difficulty switching back to Rafter when he began speaking.

"It is hard for me to compete with Keira's singing," Rafter continued, laughing. "Her voice, or more precisely her whole presence, moves us in ways we find difficult to describe. Don't we say, when talking of such an experience, that it is beyond words? In comparison, the ideas I am expressing, for all the food for thought they might provide, cannot move you in the same way. But words can move us! Story telling is an ancient art that has suffered at the hands of books, but there are still people who can use words to tell a tale that takes us beyond and above what seems normal. Sarah," he said turning to address a young girl sitting next to Keira, "could you tell us a very short story?"

Once again people craned to see whom the professor could be talking to. Sarah rose and strode down the passage between the rows of seats till she reached the podium where she stood next to Rafter. People were clearly intrigued. Here was a girl who couldn't be more than ten years old and yet she was so self-possessed that it was uncanny. It was as if their curiosity transferred a great store of energy to Sarah, who seemed to glow with it.

"The young woman stood alone by the riverside, staring down the river, a deep ache in her heart."

Tom, like many others in the room, couldn't help clutching his chest to try to alleviate the pain he felt there.

"She remembered the scene as if it had been yesterday. A whistle had filled the air as the boat pulled noisily away from the landing stage and chugged down the river towards the sea. Many people had been laughing and shouting final farewells. She stretched forward as far as she could, pressing against the railings, trying to keep her love in view as long as possible. Tears streamed down her cheeks, blurring her vision. Her love waved from the deck and she waved frantically back. Why had the Lord insisted her love travel with him on this quest? That had been five years ago and no news had come of their expedition which everyone deemed lost at sea…"

With an enormous effort, Tom pulled himself back from the story and watched what was happening in the room. The whole place was vibrating, rather like it had with Keira's song, but instead of sparking movement, Sarah's words, created a sort of suspended stillness. Even Sarah seemed still and unmoving as if balanced on the breast of a wave about to break. And when the story came to an end, the wave came crashing down whirling people around leaving them confused and wondering why they had tears flowing down their cheeks and their chest ached so.

Sarah sat down unobtrusively at Rafter's feet, folding her hands in her lap and waited for the applause to die down and for Rafter to continue. Rafter's whole talk struck Tom as if it were a choreography in which the movement shifted from the professor to others and back again.

"Music, storytelling, dance, delicious food, walks in nature and ritual, are some of the doors that open the way to that which is above and beyond. All of you have no doubt had such an experience. You might even argue that it's normal. So why bother to make such a fuss? Why have a whole university department dedicated to the subject?"

"Here I reach a crossroads. If I turn to the right I could explain why that experience of transcendence, which is what we call it, is extremely important not only for our individual health and happiness but also for the balance of society at large."

At that moment Tom spotted Frick standing in a doorway at the back of the room peering over the heads of a large number of spectators who'd gathered there. He had just arrived. Tom felt the staff of the Department and the company of Watchers stiffen at the sight of him. An undercurrent of fear crisscrossed the room, making his hair stand on end. Unseen by most of the audience, it unsettled them as several people fidgeted unknowingly in their chairs and some looked around, distracted.

"The accumulation of material goods and facts and figures is not enough to nourish humanity. The pursuit of such a goal alone would leave the world flat and lifeless. Without transcendence we would become just as bland and monotonous. Transcendence is the essence of life, its specialness, its joy, its magnificence, ... And the search for transcendence gives our lives a much deeper meaning," Rafter said, in what was akin to a private duel with Frick that could be seen only in the energy in the room and that lasted the time Rafter gave it his attention. Then the moment was gone and the fear with it as Rafter turned his attention elsewhere.

"But if I look the other way at the crossroads then I discover a wild but magnificent garden that stretches far beyond what the eye can see. Forgive me if I prefer to choose that direction, but exploring that garden is my life's work and that of the people around me in the Theosophy Department. We explore how we can use such practices as music or dance or story-telling or dreams to go further, stretching out beyond the limits of the material universe, rediscovering forces that the ancients were aware of, forces that are the motors of our world and many others too."

Out of the corner of his eye, Tom saw a whirlpool of activity gathering around Frick but when he looked in that direction nothing moved. Each time he looked back to Rafter, the impression returned. Pulling out his walkie-talkie, he intended to whisper a warning to Dieter, but changed his mind, unsure as he was of his intuition.

"It would be wrong to indulge in a romantic dream in which those lost times were so much better than today."

Tom couldn't help thinking that Rafter was aware of what was happening and was directly addressing Frick again.

"But the loss of that essential knowledge, or rather our estrangement from that knowledge, has left us stranded, confused and unable to understand the wider picture of the world we live in."

For the first time since he'd begun his talk Rafter halted and taking a glass of water that Mae offered him, he drank deeply. He appeared tired all of a sudden. Both Mae and Sally looked worried. Across the room, near the corridor to the children's library Tom saw Jenny standing, her eyes closed, leaning against the wall, a frown on her face. She must be feeding Rafter energy. Maybe he was being influenced by what he knew of Rafter's condition, but he had the impression that the Professor was loosing control of the situation and the collective energies were shifting away from coherence and harmony towards disorder and discordance.

Then Rafter handed the glass back to Mae, straightened up in his chair and continued with renewed vigour.

"The knowledge and the gifts that come from exploring transcendence, like the masterly singing of Keira or the magical story telling of Sarah or the skilful cooking of Fran and Martin whose delicious dishes you will taste tomorrow at midday, are part of our birthright as human beings. We have much more potential than we think. But stepping beyond the limits, awakening that potential and striving for excellence is not without hard work and considerable risk."

Rafter looked directly at Frick as he paused before going on. And in the unseen battle that opposed them, although Rafter was by far the strongest, his concentrating on Frick seemed to give the latter more strength.

"In 1632 a man called Galileo Galilei was tried and condemned by the Inquisition for pushing back the limits of the known world. But it was not just institutions like the Church that hounded the seekers of transcendence. A considerable number of the witch-hunts that haunt our history had their origins in the fear and jealousy of the everyday man or the woman in the street confronted with the gifts of the few. Make no mistake, the ability to harness transcendence is a gift. To some extent, art in the widest sense has offered an acceptable channel for such gifts to express themselves. Healing too, in certain forms, is also socially acceptable. But other gifts, whether real or imagined, like those you can read about in novels, have often been associated with evil and relentlessly attacked as diabolic."

Rafter looked drained, his face blanched, as if the whole history of persecution had rolled over him in that second, crushing him. Unobtrusively, Sally took his hand by way of encouragement. It was as if the whole Dream Class and the members of staff of the Department present were all saying in chorus: "You are not alone!"

Rafter smiled wistfully.

"Isn't it paradoxical," he continued, although his voice had lost some of its strength, "that a society that values learning so much, should be so frightened of the knowledge and the skills born of the will to push back the limits of our world and go beyond the self-evident. We applaud when a man is put on the Moon, but I wonder how many people would applaud if the papers were to announce that man had travelled to parallel worlds or other universes?"

A scuffle broke out in one corner of the room. Anju was trying to restrain a man who was wildly waving his arms around. The place was packed and panic spread rapidly as people struggled to move away from what appeared to be a brawl.

"Let the man speak, Anju," Rafter said with authority, getting unsteadily to his feet.

Anju released the man and stepped back causing him to collapse to the floor. He refused her offer to help him get up, cringing away from her outstretched hand as if she had the plague.

"It's not science you're talking about," the man shouted, furious, spittle forming around his mouth "But black magic and devil worship!"

"Thank you for so convincingly illustrating what I was saying," Rafter said.

The man wanted to continue haranguing the Professor, but the people around him refused to let him.

"Listen to me, young man!" One woman said waving her fist at the furious individual. "We didn't come here to hear you spreading your hatred. You're stopping us listening to what the Professor has to say."

The man moved threateningly towards the woman and might well have attacked her if Anju and Dieter hadn't forcibly accompanied him to the door amidst hearty cheers from the audience.

Rafter sat down heavily in his armchair and drank more of the potion Mae had handed him, his eyes closed, as the audience quietened down.

"Thank you for your support and your interest," Rafter said wearily.

Tom could see that the Professor would not be able to continue much longer. "As you enjoy the music and the story-telling and all the other events Mae and Sally and their friends have planned during this weekend," he said, indicating the two young women standing on either side of him, "remember that those events are all the fruit of our work in pushing back the limits of the world around us and our passion for going beyond what is deemed normal in the quest for the ineffable."

He stood unsteadily, supported by Mae and Sally, with Sarah still seated at his feet, as the audience rose to applaud him. He smiled happily although his shoulders sagged and his head hung slightly forwards. During the short time he had been talking he looked as if he had aged twenty or thirty years.

When people began to press forward to congratulate him personally, Sarah rose and spoke while Sally and Mae ushered Rafter to the exit at the back of the library.

"Professor Rafter has been a little unwell these last days and is very tired," Sarah said, causing the people to stop in their tracks, overcome with concern for the Professor. "He thanks you all for your well wishes and your support, but he needs to rest. Please leave by the main entrance. We look forward to seeing you again later today or tomorrow at one or another of our events." Ceasing to talk, she released the audience who turned and filed thoughtfully out the door, through the hallway and into the street beyond.

Tom sat unmoving in his wheelchair amid the bustle of people heading for the exit. The whole talk and what he'd seen of the interplay of forces in the room had left him flabbergasted. One image stuck in his mind: Sarah holding sway over the crowd solely with her words as Rafter stumbled out almost unnoticed by a back entrance heavily supported by Mae and Sally. Something extremely important was happening, but nobody seemed aware of it, as if the actual happening of things blinded them. He was reminded of the expression that you couldn't see the wood for the trees. What he saw however was quite clear: here was power changing hands. At the same time, here were life and death walking hand in hand. He felt a shiver run down his spine and he shuddered.

He glanced back across the room expecting to find most of the audience still seated discussing the conference only to discover to his surprise that the reading room was almost empty. The last stragglers were filing out as the caretaker and library workers began piling up the chairs and stacking them on trolleys. It was time to move, but something held him there. His indecision troubled him. There were things to be done. He couldn't just stay there unmoving. Inaction was so uncharacteristic of him. But he couldn't bring himself to wheel his chair to the entrance.

He pulled out his walkie-talkie and stared at it for a moment as if it could answer his unspoken questions. Then, on an impulse, he called Kean who was leading the team of Watchers outside the library. "Any sign of Frick?"

"Nope."

That didn't surprise him. Frick had only just left the library. "Anything else?" He realised he willed Kean to tell him something was happening. It would have explained the sickening feeling he had.

"All's quiet. Looks like you were right. Nothing's going to happen here."

Tom should have been relieved, but instead he felt more uneasy.

Apart from the solitary heckler everything had gone off far too smoothly. His uneasiness continued to grow and anxiety gripped his belly. He felt like they were all on a rollercoaster, suspended momentarily on the cusp of a curve about to plunge recklessly into the depths. The slightest movement and the whole thing would kip over. He could almost hear women's screams in anticipation. The sound of them took his breath away.

"Don't speak too soon," he warned. "It's still coming. I can feel it."

"Where?" Kean demanded, anxious too, now.

"I don't know."

Commotion

Frick hastened down the steps and hurried along a narrow alley heading for the back of the building as the crowd spilled out of the library. He was annoyed. The distraction they had planned had misfired. Instead of galvanising the audience against Rafter, it had had the opposite effect. He hadn't expected support for Rafter to be so strong.

At least the haggard appearance of Rafter gave him some satisfaction. The man was clearly not well. He rejoiced in that fact. Any weakness in the Professor constituted a weakness in the Department. One thing troubled him though: the number of under-aged groupies hanging around Rafter's gang. Not all of them were mere hangers-on. The girl that told the story couldn't have been more than ten years old yet she clearly had the power to bewitch her audience, unless someone else was doing it for her.

He couldn't help wondering if that bewitching hadn't had a lasting effect on him because each time he closed his eyes he saw her face, serene and self confident, with her short gingery brown hair tied up in plaits pulled back behind her ears and her piercing blue eyes staring at him. Ever since he'd seen her, he knew she would be the ideal subject for the little attraction they planned for later in the day.

A dreadful commotion erupted at the back of the building, shattering the silence. The wild barking might have been mistaken for the noise of a dog kennel at feeding time had it not been for the women's screams. Twine must have let the pit bulls lose.

Frick rounded the corner, taking care not to be seen. A pack of large dogs were snapping at Rafter who had fallen to the ground. A number of women flapped their arms at the dogs, trying to fend them off. From his vantage point hidden in the shadows, Frick saw a man and a young girl burst from the back door of the library. He would recognise them anywhere. They were the two that had overpowered him in the Department the day before.

The two set about the dogs and in no time the barking stopped and the screaming along with it. Several dogs lay dead on the ground their heads set at curious angles to their bodies, while other dogs slunk away down nearby alleys. Nobody bothered with them. All attention was riveted on the professor who lay unmoving at the foot of the steps.

Frick took note of the people present. Kneeling next to Rafter was that horrible secretary and one of Rafter's pretty assistants along with a young man and woman he didn't recognise. Standing protectively over the group were the tall man with a black moustache and the young girl with the short, pitch-black hair who had been his assailants.

Nowhere in sight was the ten year-old that he'd been sure had followed Rafter out. He couldn't understand where she could have disappeared. Maybe he should go back to the library and search for her. If she was to be the star of his little show he needed to get his hands on her.

At that moment, the girl with the dark hair abruptly pulled a walkie-talkie from her pocket and placing it to her ear, listened briefly. As she did so, she scanned the courtyard until her eyes fixed on the place where he was hiding and nodded, presumably to whoever was talking to her. She leant over to the tall man with the moustache and whispered a few words. He too glanced in Frick's direction and she set off towards him.

No way! He wasn't going to let himself be caught twice by the same people. He hurriedly retreated down the alley, narrowly avoiding tripping over a dustbin lid, till he reached the road and was able to mingle with the people who lingered on the library steps discussing Rafter's conference.

Not far away a couple stood in earnest discussion. A young girl lounged next to them twiddling her thumbs. She looked quite bored, if not a little irritated. He had never seen them before. Judging from their accents they were not from Avan. He had to strain to hear what they were saying as they clearly didn't want to be overheard.

"... His health is worse than they led us to believe," the woman was saying.

"I don't think they deliberately tried to mislead us," the man commented. "But if Rafter is no longer able to head the department, we will have to discuss the situation with the Foundation and assess if we should continue providing our support."

Bingo! These two must be from the Blavatsky Foundation, Frick realised. What good luck.

At that moment he saw the girl who was tracking him emerge from the alley. Turning to the couple, he said: "Excuse me for butting in, but I couldn't help overhearing what you were saying about poor Professor Rafter. He did look so ill. He really aught to get proper medical treatment."

"The people looking after him are amongst the most competent," the girl snapped.

"I dare say," Frick replied, quelling his distaste for the insufferable brat. "But some illnesses need specialised medical care and the infrastructure that only a large hospital can provide."

The man nodded vaguely in approval and then asked: "You are from Avan, aren't you?"

"I am indeed."

"Could you recommend a good pub where we can have a snack before the guided tour?"

Frick made a show of thinking things over before replying. "The easiest solution would be the Starless Square. It's right next to the cathedral. I'm going in that direction, I can show you the way."

"That's really kind of you," the man replied.

The girl didn't seem very happy. "I'd like to join my friends," she told the woman.

"They'll be busy taking care of Professor Rafter," the woman reasoned. "And they have to get ready for the tour."

The spoilt brat looked like she might rebel against them and go off on her own. Frick didn't want that. He was beginning to think that this girl might take the place of the other one.

"They will surely go to the same pub," he lied, knowing full well that none of the Department people would set foot in the Starless Square. "It is so convenient for the cathedral and the beginning of the tour."

The girl hesitated then capitulated. Frick led them across the road away from the library and as he did he threw a quick glance over his shoulder. There, standing in the alley stood the dark-haired girl watching him as she talked into her walkie-talkie.

"Wasn't it spectacular, the way they dealt with that heckler," Frick ventured, thinking he might be able to find out something useful. "I didn't recognise the man and the girl who escorted the heckler to the door."

"The man's German," the girl explained, clearly happy to have found a role in the conversation. "He used to be a police inspector."

"Really!" Frick said.

"And the girl comes from India."

The chatterbox had no notion of restraint and would surely tell him all he needed to know. The couple didn't seem to be paying any attention to their conversation as Frick slowed his pace so that he and the girl fell a few paces behind.

"She seemed so young. You are surely older."

"I am. She's only fifteen whereas I'm almost seventeen." The girl ran her fingers through her hair and pushed out her chest.

Interesting. Underage! He'd file that fact away for future reference.

"That's odd." He tried to sound confused. "I must have been wrong. I thought they were a couple."

The girl giggled. "They are."

Their conversation had to end there because they were nearing the cathedral. Frick pointed out the Starless Square and took his leave. He had several urgent things to do before the show began at two.

Once he was round the corner and out of view, he pulled out his mobile and dialled Glat. "Peter?" he asked. "You are good at photos, aren't you? Well I have a mission for you." He went on to explain what he wanted.

"Excellent. See if you can get something we can use by this evening. It's urgent."

He dialled Nohan's number. "Do you remember that substance we used on those two witches?" He paused for Nohan's reply. "Well can you get hold of some and bring it to the Starless Square in half an hour. Good. I'll be there."

Collapse

Brent covered the professor with his coat and Sally folded her pullover and eased it under his head. He put an arm around Sally's shoulder both to keep her warm and to comfort her.

"I've called an ambulance," Dieter informed them, kneeling down next to the others.

Rafter had not regained consciousness. His breathing was shallow and uneven, despite Keira's potion and Jenny's magic. "It's as if he were beyond my reach," she said.

"His hand is so cold," Sally murmured as she rubbed the professor's hand gently in hers. "Hold the other one, Brent, it must be cold too."

He shifted to the other side of Rafter and took hold of his hand. Their little group made a strange tableau, knelt or crouched around the prostrate figure, their heads bowed, their features drawn in anxiety. No words broke their silent vigil.

The distant siren of an ambulance announced the arrival of help and hopefully relief. Dieter stood, muttering that he would guide the ambulance to the place. He was joined by Anju who had just returned. His help was not needed however, because the vehicle came to a halt only a few feet from them. The two ambulance men bustled out, opened the double doors at the back and pulled out a stretcher on wheels.

Sally, Brent and the others stood and moved away to leave room for the men to do their job. Brent could see that Sally had found it difficult to let go of the professor's hand. He was surprised to discover that he had too. As he stood huddled together with his friends, he couldn't help feeling that these two men with their white coats and their efficient, professional manner were an intrusion. One of the men rapidly took the professor's pulse and checked his wounds. The blood on Rafter's arm where the dog had bitten him looked downright nasty to Brent.

"It's only a superficial wound," the ambulance man told his colleague, to the relief of everybody.

The Professor was lifted onto the stretcher and placed in the back of ambulance. Sally climbed in next to the stretcher and beckoned to Brent to join her. Tears were streaming down her cheeks.

"We'll meet you at the hospital," Keira said as the ambulance door closed. The vehicle drove off and the siren rang out again as they gathered speed.

Sally broke down and sobbed on Brent's shoulder. Her emotion brought tears to his own eyes. He placed his arms around her and kissed the crown of her head. When she finally calmed, she murmured: "He has come to mean so much to me. I couldn't bear to loose him."

They pulled apart and turned to look at the unconscious professor. His face was pale and tense. Sally leant forward and took hold of Rafter's hand.

"When my foster parents first brought me to the university as a teenager to help me decide what to study," she said quietly, "I attended an introductory conference by Rafter. He described Theosophy in such vibrant terms that I was captivated. My mind was immediately made up. No other subject interested me. I enrolled in the Theosophy department straight away. In my early days as a student, I was full of admiration for him, convinced that I had met a truly great man. Later as I came to know him better, my admiration didn't diminish but I discovered a very sensitive man who remained approachable. He had his foibles, but I found them endearing. I had the impression he had something of a weakness for me, although he was not one for favouritism. I will always remember what he said when he offered me the post as his assistant. He told me I was very good, much more so than I could possibly imagine. He always encouraged me. He believed in me and never gave up on me…"

She began to cry softly as she stroked the Professor's hand.

"Please don't give up on me now!" she whispered.

The ambulance came to a halt and the back doors swung open revealing two male nurses who rolled Rafter's stretcher into the waiting hospital. Dazed by the speed with which things happened, Brent and Sally followed slowly through the sliding doors and into the bustling casualty department. They were just in time to catch sight of Rafter being rolled into a cubicle made of curtains suspended from rails in the ceiling.

Access to the cubicle was barred by one of the nurses who pulled the curtain closed, leaving Rafter alone. There was nowhere to sit, so Brent and Sally stood across the corridor, holding hands, leaning against the wall. When a nurse came by, Sally waylaid her.

"We are with the patient in there," she asked, pointing to the cubicle, "is there any reason why we can't sit next to him?"

The nurse peered into the cubicle before replying. "Not at all ducky. Go ahead and make yourselves at home. Sorry about that. We've been so busy. It's always like that before a match. The intern will be here as soon as possible. I'll be back to tend his wounds."

Drawing aside the curtain, Brent let Sally enter the cubicle and followed her in. There was only one chair. Sally pulled it close to Rafter's bed and sat down. Brent stood behind her and placed his hand on her shoulder. She inclined her head and kissed the tips of his fingers and then turned her attention back to Rafter. She cradled the professor's hand in hers. "He's so cold."

Brent looked around for a blanket, but nothing was available. Poking his head out of the cubicle he spied the same nurse as before and asked for a blanket. She pointed to a cupboard and hurried away down the corridor. Brent opened the cupboard and pulled out several blankets. Returning to the cubicle, he spread one over Rafter, the other he laid over Sally's shoulders.

"Thanks," she said, not taking her eyes off Rafter. "What time is it?"

"Twelve-thirty."

"I'm going to have to leave soon for the guided tour."

Brent pulled a cell phone from his pocket and dialled Keira. "Keira says they'll be here in a few minutes."

At that moment the curtain was pulled open and a man dressed in a knee-length white jacket, unbuttoned down the front, strolled casually into the cubicle.

"I'm Dr. Slate," he said, shaking their hands. "So what happened here?"

"He's been ill for some while," Sally told him. "I believe he was being treated here in this hospital but I don't know what was wrong with him. This morning as he left the library, he was attacked by some dogs in the street and he collapsed."

Brent thought the doctor's examination of Rafter was rather skimpy, but then Brent wasn't a doctor.

"He's exhausted and needs a good rest. According to his hospital records he ought to be taking medicine for cancer but from what I can see of his condition I think he must have forgotten to take it."

Rafter was not a forgetful person. It seemed more likely to Brent that if he didn't take the medicine, it was deliberate.

"What would have been the effects of such medicine?" Brent asked.

The doctor didn't seem willing to reply, but Mae entered at that moment and she knew him well, having worked in the hospital for a number of years.

"I was just asking the Doctor about the medicine Professor Rafter had to take," Brent told Mae.

"Well John?" Mae asked.

"It would probably have caused nausea and possible giddiness, amongst other things."

"Maybe he chose not to take it, especially as he had to give a talk this morning," Brent ventured.

"That would be unwise. One of its effects is to slow the growth of the cancer."

Jenny and Tom and Martin and Fran were all peering round the curtains of the cubicle enquiring about the Professor's health. Lyra and

Chris were also there. As was An. When the head of clinic arrived, he had to push his way through the crowd to get near Rafter.

"This won't do at all," he told them. "There are far too many visitor's. Not only are you disrupting the service but the patient needs rest and quiet. You will have to limit your numbers to two at a time and only during official visiting hours. Now I must ask you all to leave. I need to carefully examine him, I want to have some X-rays done and he will certainly sleep for a couple of hours at least."

Looking from face to face, Brent could see everybody was distressed at not being able to remain near Rafter but there seemed little they could do about it.

They all filed out till the whole group was congregated outside the main entrance.

"I don't like this situation at all," Sally said.

Judging from the nods of agreement, she was voicing the opinion of the majority. "My feeling is that the Professor would rather be at home surrounded by friends than alone, stuffed full of drugs in a hospital ward."

"You should go to the Cathedral," Mae said to Sally. "And Anju and Dieter want to talk to you, Tom urgently. They haven't been able to reach you on your walkie-talkie." Then turning to everybody, she said: "I will stay here. They won't try to stop me. I worked here for a while. When the Professor awakes I'll ask him if he would prefer to be at home. If he says yes, then we can plan what to do."

Chapter 4 ~ The Guided Tour

Preparations

From the top floor window of the Starless Square behind half drawn curtains, Frick observed the crowd gathering in front of the west porch of the Cathedral. There must have already been more than fifty milling around like sheep. Goodness knows why such a rabble was interested in their pathetic guided tour. There was nothing to see in Avan. But then again, the more people there were, the bigger the audience for his grand attraction. He recognised Professor Trundle chatting with Rafter's assistant and a tall young man he'd seen tending to Rafter in the backyard of the library. He noted there was no sign of the little storyteller. She seemed to have disappeared completely.

Nohan was late, curse the man. Where could he be? If he didn't arrive soon, they'd miss their chance. He glanced at his watch. It was almost two. He couldn't wait any longer. He hurried down the stairs and peered through the window that communicated with the bar to make sure the girl was still there. She wasn't. Blast! He rushed out of the back door, paying little attention to where he was going, and bumped straight into her, knocking her to the ground. Could she have been waiting for him? Of course not! There must be another explanation. He helped her up. Tears were streaming down her face.

"Are you all right?"

"No!"

"I'm sorry I knocked you over."

"It's not that," she muttered, sobbing. "They don't want me. They won't let me be part of their nasty little group."

Dim-witted witches. They'd excluded the girl. Didn't surprise him. Such a self-centred brat. Might come in useful, though. All that mattered for the moment was keeping hold of her. Easier said than done. If only Nohan had been there.

"You've had a serious shock." He took her by the arm and led her into the pub through the back entrance. "You need to rest a while. Untreated shock can cause all sorts of complications."

She followed, sniffling, but compliant. "It's kind of you. But I really aught to attend the guided tour." She glanced over her shoulder towards the door.

"Are you sure you are really wanted there?"

She broke down in tears, laying her head against his shoulder. He patted her back, father like, and took a deep breath. How good her perfume smelt. She was young and thin and smaller than him. His mouth watered. Pulling her tighter in his arms, he felt a stirring of desire.

Over her shoulder he spied Nohan. Waving him closer, he held up a finger to silence him. Nohan ginned. He drew a small bottle from his pocket, unstoppered it, poured a small quantity on a cloth and handed it to Frick, who held it firmly over the girl's nose. She clawed at his hands as she struggled to get free, but he held on tight. Fortunately, her resistance was short-lived. When she collapsed, the two men lugged her up the two flights of stairs and laid her on the broad table in their meeting room.

"Are the others ready?" Frick asked as he went to look out the window. The crowd had considerably grown and would soon be leaving. He wasn't sure of their exact itinerary but he did know they would return to the Cathedral.

"Everybody is ready."

"Good. We'll use this one." He prodded the girl's back with his forefinger. It was then that he saw the congealed blood on his hand. "Off you go and help the others." He licked the traces of blood. "I'll get her ready for the ceremony."

Nohan chuckled. "She shouldn't give you much bother. That drug will keep her out for a while. Have fun."

Setting out

Sally turned to see who was tugging at her sleeve.

"You haven't seen Irina, have you?" Moira asked, her face pinched in worry, John at her side.

Sally had been fixing the final details of their tour with Trundle. She held up a hand for a pause then turned to Moira. "I thought she was with you."

"She was. But we had a row and she stamped out in a huff."

"I'm a bit tied up now." What a pest of a girl, always getting in the way, even when she wasn't there. "Brent, could you let Tom know? Maybe the Watchers know where she is." That would have to do for the moment.

She cast an eye over the crowd. There must be nearly a hundred people chattering quietly in small groups or standing attentively, waiting for them to begin. They hadn't anticipated such a success. The Cathedral clock struck two. It was time. Trundle raised the megaphone to his lips and spoke.

"Ladies and gentlemen, on behalf of the Theosophy Department, we'd like to welcome you this afternoon. How good of you to join us on our tour of some of the ancient places of Avan. Sally and I are to be your guides over the next hour and a half. During that time we will visit half a dozen historical sites, ending back here at the Cathedral."

"Avan, as most of you will know, was one of the key centres of Celtic civilisation both for its trade but also as a place of worship and celebration...." And he went on briefly to explain some of the activities at that time. They had decided to keep the talking to a minimum, concentrating on explaining the sites that Sally was to reveal.

"Our first port of call, however," Trundle went on, "is a more recent site. It's less than five minutes from here." He set off across the Starless Square and round the back of St. Bride's Cathedral with the group trailing after him.

The site they wanted to show people had been a supermarket, but now stood in ruin in the middle of a deserted car park. They'd chosen the place, mainly because Sally could transform part of it without passers-by being able to see.

Trundle led the group across the car park to the back of the ruin. "During our visit," Trundle explained, "we are going to use a special technique to give you a glimpse of how things were many years ago. The effect is quite surprising the first time you see it and might be alarming for some of you. So I suggest you close your eyes when I tell you to and then open them again on my signal. I also ask you not to take photos, however tempting that might be. OK? Good. Now close your eyes." He nodded to Sally who sifted back through the past looking for the scene she'd discovered there earlier. Having found it, she gently eased it into the present, being careful to leave the façade of the more modern building as a backdrop so that it concealed what she had done.

"You may open your eyes," Trundle told them. A number of people gasped, but no one fainted or ran off screaming. Most people stood wide-eyed, their mouths open in shock. The first time was clearly going to be the most difficult. Sally was relieved. She wasn't sure they could cope with mass hysteria.

The building was little more than a low hovel. Bent tree branches formed the main structure, lashed together with cords and covered with smaller branches interwoven to provide a dense web on which clods of mud had been dried. There was no door, but a space in the wall covered by a dull cloth indicated the entrance. Dried flowers and leaves were spread out on a rough wooden bench that stood against the wall of the hovel.

"This was once what you might call an apothecary. It is difficult for us to imagine, because we are so used to organised commerce. At the time, there were no shops, but most people dedicated their lives to a particular activity, like healing for example. They would learn the trade from an older person who was often a member of their family. The woman who lived here spent all her time preparing simples and potions that she then used in healing the people of her community or gave to others to use. In return, she received food and drink and help."

"Can we look inside?" one woman asked.

Trundle looked questioningly at Sally.

"You can. But be careful, the structure is rather fragile."

One or two people ventured forward on tip toes as if afraid it was a mirage and would suddenly disappear taking them with it.

They've seen too many films, Vee chuckled.

"Phew. It stinks," one boy said, holding his nose.

"There's not much room inside," a woman pointed out. "It's full of hanging herbs and dried plants and seeds and tree bark." She shook her head. "The bed is tiny and made of straw. Not much room for two."

Several people laughed.

Trundle nodded to Sally who let the past slip away, leaving them standing behind the ruins of the former supermarket once more. Several people looked around trying to figure out what stage mechanism had been used.

A man commented: "That's a neat trick. I thought at first it was a hologram. But seeing people go inside I realised it couldn't have been. How do you do it?"

In their discussions they had anticipated such questions and had opted for a pseudo-scientific answer. "Imagine that all times exist at once. With considerable practice and a good deal of skill you can shift from one to another. But let's not get caught up in the technicalities. Our next stop will be in Hoyt Park."

He and Sally set off at a brisk pace leading the enormous group towards the main road and the bridge over the River Bree.

Struggling

Jenny ran a hand over the map willing her mind to go beyond the lines and symbols and sense the forces of the land itself. All she could feel was paper.

The snap of Tom's walkie-talkie closing brought her back to the present. "What's up?"

He stared thoughtfully at the outspread map as if it might have the answers to a host of questions. "Irina," he replied, wheeling his way round the table to look at the map from a different angle. "She's gone missing."

"When?"

"Just before the guided tour." He was clearly exasperated. "We are spread so thin."

She had never seen him so frustrated.

"There are over a hundred people on the guided tour. Far more than we expected."

She had always known him to be such a calm man.

"And this evening at the Arena we will have more than a thousand for Keira and Sarah, judging from advanced ticket sales."

Instinctively, she wanted to comfort him, to take him in her arms and kiss the nape of his neck, but instead she moved away to the window, to give him more space, and to get a better view of his energy field.

"It's all too much!" he sighed. "I feel like I'll explode trying to hold all the threads together."

He was arched over the map, his elbows rested on the table. She let her eyes go out of focus and concentrated on the energy. She studied his familiar form. It was agitated; short spurts of colour splayed out in many directions. If he went on like that he would end up exhausted. Deeply worried, she let her attention slip. She too was tired. In the overall blur that the energy field had become she caught sight of an odd flickering over the map. Snapping her attention back into focus, the flickering disappeared. She let go once more and the glimmering began again. Try as she would she couldn't get it into focus.

"Something's happening just above the map," she told him, excited at what she'd discovered. "It's not the usual energy and I can't focus on it properly."

He lifted his head which he'd laid on the map and gave her a tired look that seemed to say: so what? "I've tried looking for your energies before," he reminded her. "I couldn't see anything."

She shook her head. "It's not MY energies, as you call them. It's something different." She was beginning to get irritated, and that wouldn't do at all. She took a deep breath. This was a riddle, and they'd almost found the answer. She was sure of it. "You're almost there."

"It doesn't feel like it. I feel cut off from whatever it is I'm searching for."

It was the words 'cut off' that gave her the idea. How silly not to have thought of it before. The words reminded her of how she healed people who were cut off from the world, like newcomers in the Reaches. She coaxed energy to flow in and out of the person along lifelines connecting the person to the world. Here things were different. It wouldn't be so easy. The energy that floated above the map was of a completely different nature. She wasn't sure she could even work with it. But there were probably similar lines connecting Tom to the vision he sought and that vision might well reside above the map.

"I have an idea." She came to stand next to him, placing her hand on his shoulder and planting a kiss on the top of his head. He looked up at her, despair in his eyes.

"I can't …" he began, but she pressed her forefinger against his lips.

"Listen. When I see the earth's energies, I sometimes visualise them as a grid map superimposed on the countryside. Maybe the energies of the future, if I can call them that, can also be visualised as a map. I don't need a map, but maybe a map would help you. At least to begin with."

He clearly didn't grasp what she was getting at.

"I can see a different sort of energy circulating above the map as you look at it. I can't see it very well but maybe if I can strengthen the link between you and the map, you'll be able to see it."

"I'm game," he said wearily.

"OK. You concentrate on the map, or rather a space just above it and let your eyes go slightly out of focus."

As he did so, she quickly focussed on the earth's energies and first used them to boost his energy. Then she searched for a link between him and the map-space. She was frustrated to realise that she could find nothing. Shifting her attention away from the earth's energies, she was just able to perceive the shimmering she'd seen earlier. She held that image and looked for something similar in Tom's energy field and sure enough she found it. The excitement caused her to loose her concentration and she had to start over again. Once she had the shimmering in both Tom and over the map she tried willing them together. It didn't work.

"I must be doing something wrong. I can see the shimmering over the map and I can see it in you too, but I can't bridge the two."

Tom chuckled. She was delighted to see that he had got some of his colour back and didn't seem so tense. "Don't you remember what Brent said about trying too hard?"

She laughed too. "Maybe that's it."

She reconnected with the shimmering but this time, instead of willing a bridge into existence, she just helped the energy flow were it wanted to.

"Wow!" Tom gasped, a great grin on his face. "It's like different sized whirlwinds over the map." Then he sighed. "But I can't make head nor tail of it."

"Don't despair!" she told him, giving him a kiss. "You're getting there!"

The walkie-talkie buzzed. "Yes!" Tom answered and listened for a moment. "And there's nothing inside?" Only to add a short while later: "OK. Thanks."

Jenny looked at him questioningly.

"Workmen have put up the crash barriers in the Starless Square. But there is nothing inside them. Not for the moment at least."

Jenny shared his frustration. "What are they up to?" she mused.

He clearly had no answer. It wasn't easy to experiment when lives might be at stake.

"Well we've got somewhere," Tom admitted. "Mostly thanks to you." He blew her a kiss. "But not enough that I can neglect traditional Watching methods."

On the way over the bridge, a charming man in his mid thirties, calling himself Collin, had waylaid Sally and plied her with questions in his smooth voice about how she'd changed the physical world as she'd done with the hovel.

He's a talent scout, Vee whispered in her head, laughing silently.

For all Collin's charm, she couldn't help feeling uncomfortable with his inquisitiveness. She kept her answers vague. From other conversations, she had learnt that most of the spectators were not sure who was actually making the changes. But the man had no doubts.

If you let him, Vee continued, he'll have you performing in a circus.

Luckily Brent came to the rescue. Throwing his arm around Sally's shoulders, he apologised politely to the man and drew her away saying they had important questions to discuss.

"Thanks," she whispered, relieved.

Once the whole group had come through the main gates into Hoyt Park, Professor Trundle assembled them on a large tarmac area that was sometimes used to disembark coach-loads of tourists. The Park was immense, covering an area equivalent to nearly a third of the town of Avan.

"Hoyt Park, which is now the home to the University, was once the focal point of the whole district for spiritual activities. Some signs of those practices persist today, but most of them are long gone. Right next to us, for example," and he pointed to a flat grassy meadow by the side of the path. "Who would guess that there used to be a burial mound right here."

This was Trundle's sign for her to transform the place. The grassy mound, which was more than thirty yards across, was considerably higher than the one near An's house in the Reaches. When she had prepared the tour with Trundle, they had not been able to explore inside.

Vee, she asked, could you check inside? But don't be too long I'll have to change it back in a short while and I don't want you caught inside.

She felt him slip away as she turned to gauge the reaction of the spectators. Many of them had been standing much closer when the transformation occurred and the proximity had startled them.

"We know very little about this burial mound which we only discovered as we were preparing this visit," Trundle told them, apologetic.

In the mean time, Vee had returned and had managed to tell Sally one or two things about the inside of the mound.

"I know a little more," Sally told them. Unlike Trundle she didn't need the megaphone because she had learnt how to project her voice. "Part of the burial mound was used for a whole lineage of Celtic chieftains."

Trundle looked astounded at the news and appeared impatient to ask her how she knew.

"But another part of the mound is an underground temple built with a very special form to focus sounds and magnify them. Sound played an extremely important role in worship as you will see when we reach our next site."

Trundle seemed to have got over his surprise because he invited the people to follow him to the standing stones.

Keira was waiting for them there as planned.

"I'd like to welcome Keira," Trundle said as the crowd came to a halt next to the first of the stones. "Many of you will know her as a singer. She's giving a concert this evening in the Arena. But you may not know that she is an expert in stone circles and standing stones." He invited Keira to talk.

"As Sally told you, sounds and music, in particular, were key parts of Celtic worship. They used sound to renew the sacred energies of the earth. And such standing stones helped modulate and magnify sounds."

She moved closer to the ring of stones and then turned to the crowd.

"I am going to show you how it works. This is only a demonstration. If you want to attend the full ceremony for the rising sun, I invite you to join me here before sun up tomorrow morning. The functioning of the ring depends on the exact position of the stones. Now these stones have been moved over time and it would be impossible for me to make them ring as they should." Keira glanced at Sally. "But if we roll back time."

Sally transformed the site to its earlier form.

"Then it becomes possible."

The original shape of the ring had been majestic. The stones were higher, there were more of them and they seemed to exude a silent harmony that was extremely moving.

"You are now standing on a sacred site," Keira told them. "I must ask you to respect it and refrain from talking or entering the ring. You may well feel a deep urge to sing along. That's normal, but I must ask you not to do so."

She bowed to the audience and moved inside the ring, placing herself slightly off centre. She closed her eyes and sang a single note softly. At first almost nothing could be heard from outside the ring. Then little by little, as Keira modulated the sound, the ring began to respond to her voice sending eddies of sound around the ring and beyond. It was as if several hidden choirs were singing counterpoint in an eerie language. A wave of excitement rippled through the crowd. Some people even had their hair standing on end.

When Keira finished, she remained standing silently amongst the stones, communing with them. Then she made her way back outside and came to stand in front of the crowd. They were unsure what to do, finally following the lead of some of their number, they all applauded.

"How did you learn to do that?" a young woman asked, full of admiration.

"I was taught by a very dear friend whose mother and grandmother and great grandmother all sang for the stones and the earth."

"Could you teach me?"

"That is something only the future can tell. But if you really want to learn, I'm sure you'll find a away and who knows, maybe that way will be me." Keira laughed.

"Thank you, Keira," Trundle said. "See you tonight at the Arena and tomorrow morning before dawn here at the standing stones. Now we must be off. We have several more things to see."

Cursed

Frick pursed his lips as he drew a small black square with his indelible, felt-tip pen. It was not easy, even if the skin was flat and smooth. Once he'd finished, he sighed with relief and applied himself to filling in the square till it was an even black. A glance at his watch showed him he still had time.

He unbuttoned her blouse, one of those flimsy foreign things, and, struggling with the cumbersome weight of her unconscious body, managed to remove it and unbutton her kid's bra. Nothing sexy there! Her breasts were so small that they fit snugly in his cupped hands. He pinched her nipples, slowly increasing the pressure between his thumb and forefinger till the girl stirred and moaned. Her moan sent ripples of excitement through him. Better not persist. He didn't want to wake her. Not yet, at least. He opened the bottle Nohan had left him and applied a small amount of the liquid to a cloth that he held over her nose, just in case.

Her shoes and socks were easier to remove, but her trousers were so tight he had some difficulty yanking them down her spindly legs. He tossed them into a paper bag along with her blouse and bra. She wore a tiny gold bracelet around her ankle that he decided to leave. Her skimpy panties were black and lined with laced. How incongruous! Under such an apparently sexless exterior lay this treasure. Slipping his finger under the waistband, he slowly pulled them down revealing a blond bush that smelt of the sweet perfume of a well-known brand of women's deodorant. He leaned closer and filled his lungs with it. The mixture of odours made him giddy. The cathedral clock solemnly struck three. He counted to be sure. No time for more. Stripped of her clothes, she lay as pale and as still as death on the dark table.

He grabbed the white sheet that Nohan had dumped in a heap on the floor. Phew! It wasn't very clean, he thought, holding it at a distance, but that was of little importance. It would do. He pulled out his flick knife and released the catch. With a swift movement he slit the middle of the sheet and then returned the knife to his pocket. Lifting her head by her hair, he pulled the hole in the sheet around her neck. Then, heaving her up into a sitting position, he shoved the sheet down over her body and bound it around her waist with a rough cord that he pulled as tight as he could.

With one arm around her neck and the other under her thighs, he lifted her and dumped her into an armchair. Her head lolled to one side and dribble oozed from the corner of her mouth. He hit her with all his force across her face causing her to jolt upright in shock. She whimpered but did not wake. The shock of the blow shot through him too filling him with a sensation of omnipotence. A trickle of blood mingled with the spittle on her chin. She looked the perfect portrait of an urchin child.

Gathering all his strength, he hit her again, causing blood to spurt from her mouth. Her eyes snapped open and she stared at him with utter hatred.

"I curse you!" she spat in a deep masculine voice that couldn't possibly have been hers.

Frick didn't dare move. He was so terrified that he began to tremble violently.

"I have waited so long for this moment," the voice snarled,

pointing an accusing finger at him. "Thrice I curse you! I curse you for all those innocent men and women you burnt! I curse you for killing my loved one! I curse you for killing our girl child!" the voice spat the words at him like arrows, each one sinking deeper into his flesh. "Your life will be short but will be full of unending pain. Your death will be much slower and your suffering will be atrocious!"

He felt a strong hand seize his heart and squeeze it tighter and tighter, till he thought it would burst in his chest. He screamed, but no sound came from his mouth. He shook his head trying to free himself, to no avail. The pain continued, unabated, excruciating. Then suddenly her eyes rolled back, leaving only the whites visible and her back arched over forming a rigid arc with her body. And just as abruptly she collapsed on the floor, shaking wildly as spittle sprayed from her blood-flecked mouth. Finally the spasms ceased and she lay completely still and silent.

Frick fell to his knees, his hands clasped to his chest gawking at the girl's body in horror. She really was possessed. The tension in his chest tightened. This was no game. The devil had cursed him. Its filthy hand had reached inside him and soiled him from within. He wanted to rip open his chest and tear out the curse. But there was nothing he could do. A fire raged in his chest and there would be no quenching it. He sank forward till his head reached the floor and he moaned in agony.

"I didn't do that," he pleaded. But no one heard him. "It wasn't me! I swear it." But he knew it was too late. Judgement had been passed. A stab of pain shot through his chest and he gasped. Was this the end? A second stab followed the first. The agony was so great that he fled the only way he could: he blacked out.

"Hey! Frick! What the hell are you doing on the floor?" Nohan asked, his voice alarmed, as he shook him.

Frick groaned. The flames continued to burn in his chest. It was almost as if he could smell the burning flesh.

"Pull yourself together. We've got to get the girl outside on the pyre."

Frick cringed at the word. He tried to talk, to beseech Nohan not to do it, but no words came from his mouth.

"If you don't come now Frick, you'll miss the fun."

Frick fell back on the floor, rolling face down, his whole body wracked with sobs. "It burns!" he managed to say. "It burns!"

But Nohan had no patience left. He stood and, grabbing hold of the girl, he shoved her into a large sack, tossed the sack over his shoulder and strode out of the room.

"No! No!" Frick tried to scream. "Please!" But no sound crossed his lips. And the fire burnt on.

The village

The crowd crossed the long footbridge that spanned the River Bree, walking from Hoyt Park in the direction of the centre of town. The tide was out and the river had shrunk to a sinuous waterway amid the mud flats. A light breeze blew off the sea bringing with it the distant sounds of gulls.

He's catching up with us, Vee said, interrupting her reverie.

Who is?

Why smooth Collin, of course.

Sally looked around to see if Brent was anywhere nearby to save her again, but he was deep in conversation with the young woman who'd asked Keira to teach her how to sing.

"You walk too fast for me," Collin huffed and puffed as he finally reached her.

"You need to get some regular exercise, Collin," Sally retorted, her eyes fixed on the far bank of the river that was to be their next stop.

"My work doesn't leave much time for sports."

Except when he's running after future attractions, Vee quipped.

"What work do you do?" Sally asked casually.

"I run a company that creates 3D effects for cinema."

I told you so, Vee triumphed. He's going to harness you to one of his machines.

You're all doom and gloom today, Vee, Sally teased him, smiling inwardly.

Suddenly she realised she hadn't been paying any attention to Collin.

"... so you see, it's quite a demanding job."

They had reached the end of the bridge and had to climb down a set of steps to the riverbank.

"Please excuse me. I have work to do."

I think you got yourself a fan, Vee muttered.

If Brent had made such a remark, Sally would have given him a friendly punch, but Vee, having no body, couldn't be punched. What's more, he could hear all her thoughts.

Take me as having been punched in a friendly way, he commented.

She chuckled silently in her head.

Sally didn't wait for everyone to climb down from the bridge before she shifted the whole riverside village into sight. The waterway had been much narrower then, causing the village to appear as if it were on a sharp bend in river.

We are lucky it's not high tide, Vee commented. If the river as it is now had to flow through such a narrow estuary I'm not sure what might happen.

You're right, she thought. That swift current could be dangerous.

"Please do not go near the water's edge," Sally warned. "The bank might not be stable."

The small wooden houses with thatched roofs were built on stilts and connected to each other by narrow suspended walkways.

"As you can see," Trundle explained, "the town or Avan or Aefvan as it was then called, was much smaller."

Several people laughed at the comparison.

"To tell you something of the tale of Aefvan, I've asked Sarah to join us. Some of you may have heard her tell a story this morning during Professor Rafter's talk."

Sally wondered how Brent had managed to transform unnoticed by anyone, for, sure enough, there was Sarah standing on one of the high-flung walkways. Trundle offered to hand her up the megaphone but she declined.

"A cruel wind blew in from the sea as the longboat rowed up the estuary towards the village," Sarah began.

Everybody shivered, of course, Sarah being Sarah!

"They navigated skilfully around the pointed stakes driven into the river bed and docked by the nearest house. The whole village of Aefvan had gathered to greet them. In the forefront stood the druid, dressed in a long speckled robe of many colours, and next to him was the chief of the clan, ..."

Sarah's story was cut short when one of the youngest of the children on the visit slipped and fell into the river. Screams went up from the audience as the child struggled to keep his head above water with the strong current sweeping him away.

As everyone's attention was on the child, nobody noticed Sarah fling herself off the walkway and transform in mid-flight into a majestic eagle. In one easy swoop, she plunged on the child and grasping him by the waist in her talons she lifted him out of the water and dropped him on the bank where he sat dazed and dripping wet. His parents rushed up to console him. The rest of the audience cheered and clapped thinking this had been a part of the show. When they finally remembered they had been listening to a story they were astonished to find an eagle pruning its feathers exactly where Sarah had stood earlier.

Brent's been keeping secrets from us, Sally thought to Vee.

Better move on, Vee replied, before anyone asks any questions.

"Let's move on," Sally called out. "We can get the child to warmth and the rest of us can finish the visit."

She led the way along the narrow path that ran from the footbridge to the road that would become the High Street and take them back to the Cathedral. Hardly had she set out than Collin was at her side.

"Remarkable! How the hell did you manage that transformation? It would cost us a fortune and months of work to do that."

"What transformation are you talking about?"

"Come off it! You know exactly what I mean. Stop playing with me. I wonder what other things you people can do?"

He'll wet himself if he gets any more excited, Vee commented.

Sally burst out laughing. She couldn't help it. Sometimes Vee caught her off guard.

Collin must have taken her laughter as confirmation and was literally dancing beside her. "I really must make a film with you all. A film tailor-made for you and your gifts."

Sally laughed again, this time at Collin's suggestion. "It's an interesting idea. I will talk to the others about it. But you will have to be patient. We are leaving right after the weekend on urgent business and we have no idea how long that will take."

"Can I come with you?"

He's afraid he'll loose you and his film, Vee thought.

"You wouldn't want to come, you'd be terrified." Sally struggled to stay straight-faced.

He looked seriously taken aback and was about to complain when Sally stopped at the corner of a little-used street, as this was to be their last halt before they returned to the Cathedral. When most of the group had gathered around her, she let the wasteland shift to its earlier form, revealing a giant oak tree that cast its shadow over the crowd.

"From what we know this was the home of the druid. Or rather the place he withdrew to when he wanted to meditate or confer with the forces of nature."

Jenny was waiting for them there as planned.

"We've asked Jenny to talk to us briefly about the earth's energies at this place," Professor Trundle said, pointing to Jenny. "She's a foremost expert in those energies and healing. She'll be giving an open seminar for farmers and gardeners and people who like nature tomorrow morning at nine-thirty."

Jenny climbed up onto a small hillock next to the oak tree. "Good morning! Bonjour! Guten Tag!" she greeted them with her delightful French accent. "The Earth is crisscrossed with a web of energy currents. Those currents are essential for the wellbeing of both the Earth and everything living on it. One such line," she said, pointing in one direction towards the footbridge and the standing stones beyond and in the other direction to the cathedral, "runs through the most important places of Aefvan: the standing stones, the burial mound, the village, this tree and the site where the cathedral was later to be built."

She moved closer to the oak and laid her hand on its trunk. Leaves began to sprout in a wild profusion from its branches, thickening the living canopy above their heads. Several people gasped, others applauded.

"This tree grows right on a hub of the earth's network, meaning that the druid could have tapped into those energies by sitting at the foot of the tree. One of the main tasks of druids was to maintain the balance of the earth's energies. Sadly we have few people capable of doing that today."

"Thank you, Jenny. Remember, if you want to know more, you can attend her seminar tomorrow at the botanical gardens in Hoyt Park at nine-thirty."

The crowd applauded.

"And now we move on to our last port of call, the Cathedral," Trundle concluded.

At the hospital

"A hundred and twenty people! That's excellent," Mae said, adjusting the position of the walkie-talkie so she could hear Tom's voice better. "Where are they now?"

Tom had asked Kean to bring Mae a walkie-talkie so she could keep in touch during her vigil with the Professor. She glanced at Rafter, but he still had not regained consciousness. He had been moved to a private room in the oncology department shortly after the others had left. He was more comfortable there and the atmosphere was much less hectic.

"So they'll soon be at the Cathedral."

The idea of involving Keira, Brent and Jenny during the guided tour had been hers. They had had little time to promote the events. This way people got a taste of what was to come and would surely talk about it to others.

"I heard about the eagle," she told Tom, chuckling. "I am glad Brent saved the child but I just hope we don't get into trouble for making our gifts too conspicuous."

When she had argued in favour of the weekend festivities for the Theosophy Department and had travelled to Reaches to return with Sally and her friends, it had never crossed her mind that their abilities might provoke anything but praise and wonderment. Now she had misgivings about people's reactions, but it was too late. She'd just have to advise the others to be more circumspect. It wasn't easy. These were truly wondrous gifts and they were delighted to share them.

"Any news of those crash barriers?" Maybe they were quite unconnected with Frick and his sinister gang. "Could they be a distraction from something happening elsewhere?"

Tom seemed sure that Frick would strike in the Square. She hoped his intuition was wrong.

Signing off, she turned her attention back to Rafter to discover that his eyes were wide open and fixed on her.

"Mae?" he asked, sounding confused. "What happened?"

She moved closer to his bed and sat on the only chair. "Someone let a pack of wild dogs lose on you. They didn't hurt you much but you lost consciousness."

"How long have I been out?"

"A couple of hours."

"And where are all the others?"

"The hospital kicked them out. The doctor was concerned that such a large group would be a disturbance both to the hospital and to you."

"What rubbish."

"Well they had to go anyway because of the guided tour."

"How's that going?"

"There are over a hundred and twenty participants." She went on to explain the episode with the child falling in the river.

"An eagle, hey!" Rafter chuckled.

"You certainly sound in better form Professor. How do you feel?"

"Much better. I didn't think I would make it through that talk. I had to cut a large part. I hope people weren't disappointed."

"Judging from those who went on to the visit, your talk must have been a roaring success."

Rafter's lips curved in a hint of a smile. "Your optimism, Mae, is one of the things that has kept us all going, you know."

Thank heavens he had no idea of her growing anxieties about the whole group and what they were doing.

The head of clinic arrived at that moment followed by a bevy of assistants in a flurry of starched white coats. "So Professor, you are back amongst us," he began, glancing at the chart suspended at the end of the bed. "How do you feel?"

"Much better, although a little nauseous."

"That will be the pills against the growth. I heard you'd stopped taking them."

Mae thought she saw a sheepish look cross Rafter's face, but his words were in no way remorseful. "I am not afraid of the growth as you call it, doctor. But I intensely dislike feeling befuddled and having my stomach do back flips every time I move."

"You realise the dangers you will be taking if you cease the medication."

"I am quite aware what the outcome of this will be." Rafter was clearly at peace with himself. "I thank you for your efforts, but I will make the necessary arrangements to return home. If I am to die, I want to do so surrounded by my friends."

The doctor shifted uncomfortably at the bedside, looking down at his shoes. "You know we really can give you the very best attention if you stay here with us, Professor, and you will be in less pain."

Mae glanced at the Professor's face, but it showed no signs of suffering. Not that that surprised her. She was sure he was excellent at concealing his feelings, however extreme they might be.

"Know that I have nothing against you, Doctor, nor against your staff, who are all charming." He smiled at the blank faces that hovered behind the doctor. "But if I am to die, and that seems to be the likely outcome, then I will do so where I want. Luckily I still have the possibility to choose. And, as I said, I want to be at home with those I love."

He glanced at Mae, smiling. She couldn't help the tears that crept into her eyes and overflowed down her cheeks.

"I'll organise it for you, Professor," she told him, a lump in her throat as she fought back her tears. In her time in the Department, she'd come to love and admire this man as if he were her father. If he were condemned to die in the near future, she would make the time remaining as satisfying and as rewarding as possible.

"I believe we can help a little with that," the doctor offered. "At least, let us loan you an ambulance to take you home, Professor."

Rafter nodded his assent. He looked as if this negotiation had tired him and Mae was anxious to get it over with. The doctor shooed the assistants away and took a step closer to Rafter.

"I have been very proud to know you, Professor. And if ever you should change your mind or if you need me, don't hesitate to send me a message."

Rafter thanked him and offered his hand, which the man took, clasping it between his own two hands and shook it solemnly.

"May God be with you," the doctor said almost in a whisper and, his head bowed, he left the room.

"He means well … but what a tragic lot!" He pulled a comical face in a way that was so typical of him. "I'm not saying it's going to be all fun, far from it, but at least we don't have to go around with such grave faces."

He leaned forward and stretching out his hand he brushed the tears from her cheeks. She inclined her head lightly against his hand and turned her lips to kiss it. He gently stroked her hair and then withdrew his hand.

"There is one thing I absolutely want to do before I go."

She knew that he was not talking about going home but that other going from which he would not come back. She ran her hand over her face to conceal the new tears that flooded her eyes

"I will need your help to make sure I manage."

She wondered what he could want to do.

"I want to tell a tale, a tale about myself and my life and I need to tell it to Sally and I would like you and all her young friends to hear it."

"I promise you, Professor, that you will have every opportunity to tell your tale. We will return to your house as soon as the ambulance is ready. Then once you are settled you can rest and get your strength back while I arrange for everybody to join you after the guided tour."

She was already making a list of everything she had to do in her head and those people she'd have to phone and what supplies to get in at Rafter's place.

"You needn't worry about money. I have plenty and not much use for it." He chuckled at his own joke. "You can use my card to buy the necessary things…."

He became thoughtful and she wondered if he was about to fall asleep but he spoke again. "We may never have a moment like this again, just the two of us together. I know it's not yet the time for farewells, but I want you to know how much I have appreciated working with you. I always knew that you had much unrealised potential and I am so happy to know that that is beginning to surface. You will go far, Mae, I'm sure of it."

He paused, to catch his breath. Talking, even for such a short time, taxed him.

"One thing would give me great pleasure. But that is up to you to decide, when the time comes."

Seeing him close his eyes and his head sink into the pillow, she was afraid he would forget to tell her. "What is that?"

"That you offer Sally your support and assistance as you have to me. She will have a lot on her plate when I am gone."

His words left her perplexed but she would willingly do as he asked. She liked Sally, as she did all the members of the Dream Class. "I will do my best."

A close thing

As the crowd entered the High Street, they might have been mistaken by a casual onlooker for a silent demonstration. The visit seemed to have left many participants pensive and distant from the bustle of everyday life that characterised the town centre. Passers-by eyed them with curiosity if not suspicion. There was a latent hostility in the air, Sally thought.

It's partly because they feel left out, Vee guessed.

And they don't understand, she added.

Their thoughts were interrupted by Moira and John who were waiting for them in the High Street.

"Any news?" Sally asked. Judging from the grim faces they were making, the news couldn't be good.

"We went to the police, but they had no news of her." Moira rubbed her red eyes.

"I have heard nothing from Tom and the Watchers either," Sally said. To be honest, she'd been so involved in the tour she hadn't given it a second thought. "As soon as the guided tour is over, we'll all help you look for her."

The way back to the Cathedral led down a short alley off the High Street. It was strikingly silent compared to the turmoil of the Saturday shoppers. Once the whole group had flowed out into the square in front of the Cathedral, Trundle halted and addressed them.

"Our guided tour ends with the Cathedral and its Square. Compared to the other sites we have shown you, this one is much more modern. Despite that fact, this place is steeped in history, a very unhappy history at that."

He paused for a moment glancing rapidly over the mass of faces looking expectantly at him.

"Do any of you know how this Square came to be called the 'Starless Square'?"

Heads shook here and there. One or two people said "No!"

"It got it's name because of the witch hunts that took place in this area in the sixteen hundreds. A small group of enthusiastic local traders put a great deal of effort and energy into tracking down anyone and everyone that neighbours would denounce as witches…"

Sally felt the walkie-talkie vibrating in her pocket. She whipped it out and opening it, held it to her ear. It was Tom.

"A lorry has just dumped a heap of firewood around one of the smaller trees at the far-end of the Square. They're going to build a pyre, I'm sure of it. A real-life reconstruction of their witch burnings."

Sally gasped in horror.

Surely they wouldn't go so far, Vee said, trying to reassure her.

Both of them thought of Irina at the same moment.

"No!" she hissed.

Several people turned to stare at her, surprised if not irritated by her behaviour. She pushed her way through the crowd till she reached Brent.

"Get Moira and John out of here, as fast as possible," she whispered in his ear. "Use any excuse. Then come back. We'll need you."

He didn't wait for explanations, but left immediately to find Moira.

She spotted Jenny standing on the cathedral steps.

I just hope we are in time, she thought to Vee, as she ran across the Square.

"Can you make it rain?"

Jenny looked at her quizzically.

"No time for questions, do it now, do it as fast as you can, a real downpour."

As she ran back to the group she saw Brent leading Moira and John out of the Square. Trundle was still explaining the history of the square.

"So it is called Starless because the black smoke from the pyres on which they burnt the witches filled the sky and blocked out the stars."

At that moment, as if it had been programmed, a lorry drove away across the Square and out the back entrance revealing a flaming pyre in the form of a large circle around a sapling to which a girl had been attached. Her head slumped forward on her chest. She seemed to be dressed in a white gown. Catching sight of the scene several people screamed. Others applauded, presumably imagining it was one of their 'attractions'.

"This is not our doing," Sally shouted. "This is the work of the same evil forces that made this place as dark as it is."

Then she turned her back on them and ran across the square only to find her way blocked by the crash barriers. So that was what they were for! Heavy drops of rain began to fall. Jenny had done her best. But it would not be enough.

She'll suffocate before she burns, Vee informed her. They've built a ring around her, so she's not on fire yet.

What can I do, she thought desperately.

Transform the fire, he told her.

I've never done anything like that.

Do it! Vee shouted in her head. Do it now!

It was hard to concentrate as she gripped the crash barrier, staring in horror at the growing flames. Pandemonium had broken out in the crowd behind here, but she had no time for it. The flames now danced all around Irina, making her image shimmer in the heat like a mirage. The rain was falling harder, but the fire burnt on.

Petrol probably, Vee speculated.

Sally was furious at Frick and his cowardly gang of men who'd picked on a helpless girl. She let her energy rip through the air as she transformed the roaring flames into climbing plants that scuttled upwards at a furious rate spouting a multitude of flowers on the way up as if desperate to reach the light above, forming a brightly-coloured bower concealing and protecting the unconscious girl.

Sally clambered over the barrier and ran flat out towards Irina. As she did so, she heard the distant voice of Brent rising over the noise of the crowd. He must have made it back to the group. He was telling them a story, the details of which were lost in the panting of her own breath.

He'll keep them happy and captive till we can sort this out, Vee said.

Sally forced her way between the flowering branches and knelt at Irina's side. The girl was still unconscious, her makeshift robe and her skin blackened with smoke.

She looks almost serene, Vee commented. As if she were having a pleasant dream and not a nightmare.

Keira and Jenny arrived at that moment and helped her remove the cords that attached Irina to the tree. Keira administered a small amount of a potion from her bag while Sally pulled out her walkie-talkie.

"Tom. It's OK. We've got her. Irina was to be the victim. Can you ask your watchers to help Jenny get Irina away from here?"

Tom told her that everyone was to go to Rafter's place.

"Good. Have her taken there." She snapped the walkie-talkie closed. Keira bent to help Jenny carry Irina away. "No. Let Jenny carry her. We need you here. You should sing for everybody."

Keira must have grasped what Sally had in mind as she turned to go back to the waiting crowd.

"Can you give us a rainbow and some sun?" Sally asked Jenny.

"Sure," she replied with a grin and staggered off towards the back of the Cathedral where Kean and several Watchers were waiting for her.

Most of the people in the crowd were glassy-eyed with Brent's story, including Professor Trundle.

"You can bring it to a close," she whispered to Brent. "They tried to burn Irina but she's unhurt. We were just in time."

Brent looked relieved as he wound up his story with a flourish. It had been a happy one apparently, as most people were beaming, untroubled by the last drops as the rain ceased and the fact that they were soaked. They seemed to have completely forgotten the appalling drama that had just played itself out right in front of them.

"Oh look," a little boy said, pointing at the sky above the Cathedral. He looked remarkably like the one who'd fallen in the river. "A rainbow!"

"Wonderful," several people exclaimed.

Keira didn't wait for Sally to announce her song, she just sang. She chose the lullaby she had learnt in the Reaches. She had first sung it for a little girl that had been abused by a man. It seemed an appropriate choice. And the people swayed gently too and fro in time with the music as the warm rays of the sun burst between the clouds.

People drifted away slowly, unwilling for the most part to leave, thanking Keira profusely, shaking hands with Sally and Trundle, swearing they'd tell lots of people about it and promising to attend other events during the weekend. Collin was one of them.

"Those climbing plants were extraordinary!" he whispered conspiratorially. Then he slipped her his card as if it were a secret message, saying: "For when you all get back."

Brent shot her a quizzical look.

"He wants all of us to make a film with him."

He snorted.

Once the last of the crowd had left, she was finally able to enquire after Moira and John.

"In a tearoom," Brent told her, grinning.

"Well done."

Trundle looked somewhat confused. "Thank you, Professor. The tour was wonderful," Sally told him. "We are going for a drink with Moira and John. Would you like to come with us?"

Trundle shook his head as if trying to clear it. "A tea would be a good idea. All this excitement has left me feeling a bit drained." Brent and Sally linked arms with him and headed down the narrow alley to the High Street.

"I had no time to find a better place," Brent apologised, making a disgusted face as he pointed to the shabby snack bar in which he'd planted the two representatives of the Blavatsky Foundation. Once inside, they made their way alongside the counter on which plastic containers held such delights as mashed potatoes, Shepherd's pie, garden pees, steak-and-kidney pie, ….

No wonder foreigners are so sure you eat badly, Vee thought with mock distaste.

Sally gave him a mental pinch and chuckled. When they reached the cash desk she ordered a pot of tea and Trundle carried it to the table at the back where Moira and John sat looking extremely worried.

"Tea anybody?" Trundle asked as he placed the tray on the Formica table and slid along the plastic bench leaving room for Sally and Brent. Moira and John declined, motioning to the empty cups in front of them, but Brent and Sally readily accepted.

"I have good news for you," Sally told Moira as she sipped her tea. "You've found her?"

Moira exclaimed, drawing odd looks from the group of chattering mothers huddled together at the next table.

"Yes!" Sally said with a grin.

"Where was she?"

"In the Square, in fact." A desperate image of Irina in flames crossed her mind but she forced it aside.

"Silly really. She was right where she got lost," Brent commented.

"What happened?" Moira asked.

"We don't know yet," Sally replied. "She was unconscious and very strangely dressed. It is possible she has suffered a very traumatic experience. It might be better not to ply her with questions."

Judging from the scared look on Moira's face, she was imaging the worst. Tears welled up in her eyes and she clenched her fist.

"Was she …?"

Sally knew immediately what she meant. "I don't know. I don't think so. She was unconscious when we found her, but she had a smile on her face."

Moira stood up, saying: "Can we go and see her? I can't wait any longer."

Brent and Sally gulped down their tea and stood to join Moira and John who were already on their way to the exit.

"See you later, Professor Trundle," Sally said seeing that he was going to take his time about his tea.

Chapter 5 ~ Combat Dance

Hell's Fire

Oh the agony of it! Scorching tears stung his eyes, but brought no relief. It hurt beyond imagining. Frick let out a strangled cry somewhere between a moan and a whimper. A raging fire was consuming him from within. If he were to cough he was sure smoke would burst from his lungs. He struggled to his knees in an attempt to stand but a searing pain shot through his chest causing him to gasp for air and buckle over onto the floor, crashing headfirst onto the bare boards.

He lay there unmoving, absolutely furious: furious at himself, furious at that accursed girl, furious at the world at large. It was all so bloody unjust. Why him? He wanted to stomp his feet and hammer his fists, but he didn't have the strength. Gritting his teeth, he heaved himself up using the chair until he managed to stand, holding on to the table-top, fearing that he would be struck down once again from within.

There, inches away, was a carrier bag lying on its side, its contents half spilled across the table: a training bra, flimsy black lace panties and a silk blouse. Nohan had forgotten to dispose of the girl's clothes. Frick gagged twice then threw up copiously over the table and onto the floor. His throat burnt red-hot each time he retched. When the spasms ceased, he let go of the table with one hand and wiped his mouth. He couldn't stop trembling. Compared with the fire burning inside him the room was freezing cold. He staggered to the cupboard in the corner and, wrenching the door open, he pulled out a dark grey blanket that he draped over his shoulders. It made little difference.

He had to get out of there. Fast! Once the police found the girl's carbonised body ... The image of it, the whites of her eyes staring out of the charred mass, had him retching again. He staggered to the door and clutching the banisters, made his way down to the ground floor, his knees threatening to give way at each step.

Stumbling into the men's, he closed the door behind him and splashed cold water on his face. Unrelenting, the scorching heat burnt on in his chest. He swilled water around his mouth and gingerly tried swallowing some, and when that worked he swallowed more, but no matter how much he swallowed it couldn't quench his thirst, it couldn't extinguish the fire in his chest.

It was then that he made a serious mistake: he glanced at himself in the mirror. The old man's face that stared back at him was barely recognisable. Dark lines circled his eyes, his forehead was creased with deep furrows and the skin around his mouth hung flaccid in a look of disgust. And there, planted in the middle of his forehead, was a small, black square identical to the one he'd etched on the girl's face. The sight of it sent terror through his guts.

He remembered the voice that had cursed him and realised that he had been branded like a monster. He growled in rage and hammered with all his force on the mirror with his clenched fist causing it to splinter into many jagged pieces. Surprisingly, the mirror hung in place taunting him with a grotesque mosaic composed of a myriad of images of his distorted face.

He turned his back and, pulling the blanket up over his head like a hood to hide his face, he made for the back door. The Square was empty. There was no sign of the people from the guided tour. He sidled along the wall that led from the pub to the west wall of the Cathedral.

He'd made it almost to the porch when a police siren rang out. Terrified he made a rush for the door and slipped into the church. The smell of incense immediately assaulted his nostrils causing him to cough. Each time he coughed it was akin to a shock of fireworks bursting from his lungs. He clutched his chest in a vain attempt to contain the pain.

Then he remembered the police. Using the pews for support, he staggered down a side aisle and managed to reach a small chapel in which candles were burning in votive offerings. Slumping onto a wooden chair in a dark corner, he closed his eyes.

When he awoke, a choir was signing nearby. Had he died? A searing pain in his chest belied the fact. The sound of shuffling feet alerted him to the presence of people. Maybe it was a burial. Could it be that girl's funeral? What rotten luck!

Peering round the curtains that partly concealed the chapel, he saw two rows of choirboys carrying candles, moving rhythmically forward as they sang. It was the beginning of choral evensong and he would be stuck there for at least an hour. A considerable congregation had gathered on either side of the central aisle, where they stood following the advance of the choir with their heads turned.

Frick shifted his chair even deeper into the shadows and leaned back till his head rested on the cold stone of the cathedral wall. Directly in front of him was a small altar above which a painting of the Madonna and child hung behind a wooden cross. He couldn't take his eyes off the Madonna. His mind must be playing tricks on him because he could have sworn she looked like the girl who'd cursed him. The more he looked, the more she stared back at him, till he could bear it no longer.

He was about to scream and bolt in terror, when some semblance of reason halted him. He would attract too much attention. He stood, with difficulty, tearing his eyes from the painting, and pulling the blanket up until it covered most of his head and shoulders, he shuffled slowly along the side aisle till he reached a small door leading to a narrow alley that went to the back entrance of the Square.

Around the hearth

Laughter greeted them as Sally, Brent, Moira and John crossed the threshold of Rafter' town house. Merriment was the last thing Sally expected, what with Rafter gravely ill and Irina recovering from a vicious and surely traumatic attack. They hung their coats in the entrance and went into the sitting room where they discovered Professor Rafter installed comfortably in a large armchair with a blanket wrapped over his knees. His eyes sparkled and he had a smile on his lips.

A blazing fire burned in the hearth and a buffet was spread out on an improvised table nearby. Clearly Fran and Martin had been at work. It smelt delicious. At Rafter's feet sat Irina on a large cushion. It was her that had been laughing, the traces of it could still be seen in the wrinkles around her eyes and in the upward curve of her mouth. Keira and Jenny sat across from the Professor on chairs brought in from the dining room. Lots of other chairs were scattered around the room begging to be used.

Mae entered from the study at that moment, carrying a bunch of papers in one hand and a glass in the other.

"This is for you," she told Rafter, handing him the glass. "Tom will be here soon with Kean, and Anju and Dieter will drop by for a short while. They're busy preparing their demonstration for the end of the afternoon."

Sally glanced around the room and realised she hadn't seen An for ages. "Where's An?"

"She's got some project of her own. Something to do with schools," Mae replied.

She's an odd one, Vee commented.

She's just curious, Sally retorted.

"What sparked that off?" Sally asked.

"Apparently she got arrested yesterday by a policeman who insisted she should be in school," Mae told her. "Well she managed to give the police the slip, but she's intrigued by the idea of school as they don't exist in the Reaches, so she's gone to find out more about it."

"Irina," Moira said kneeling on the floor next to the girl, taking her hand in hers. "I'm so sorry about earlier..."

"Here, have my cushion," Irina interrupted.

"We were so worried about you. We thought something terrible had happened..." Moira halted in mid sentence staring at Irina clothes. "Where did you get those?"

Irina was wearing a tight black tea-shirt on which was printed 'I like it!' and a long grey skirt.

"I've never seen you dressed like that."

"Keira loaned them to me. Good aren't they."

Sally had to admit they did suit her.

Something's changed about the girl, Vee told her. And it's not just her clothes.

"So what happened to you?" John asked.

"I have no idea," Irina admitted. "I vaguely remember leaving the pub, but after that everything is blank. When I awoke I found myself here. I suppose I should be worried as I was only wearing a dirty sheet wrapped around my body, but I felt so good, as if I had shed a great weight. No more headaches, no more tension, and no nagging fear that I might have a fit."

She grinned at Moira and then at everybody. Her grin was so infectious, Sally was sure everyone wanted to grin back. She certainly did.

What a change, Vee noted.

Sally was wondering whether they should tell Irina what had happened, but couldn't make up her mind. It was then that Rafter spoke for the first time.

"Maybe you others should tell Irina what you know. I think she is capable of hearing it."

Jenny began. "Tom had the Watchers keeping an eye on the Starless Square and the Cathedral. He was convinced Frick would do something terrible there. The Watchers told Tom that someone had built a pyre around a tree in the Square."

Then Sally continued. "When I heard what the Watchers had seen I suddenly guessed that Frick planned to immolate someone like in the witch burnings of old. And because you had disappeared, Irina, I had a horrible suspicion that you were to be the victim."

Moira gasped in horror.

"I wanted to spare Moira and John the sight of that so I asked Brent to take them to safety."

"I'm sorry about that squalid snack bar," Brent added, "it was all I could find at such short notice."

"We were completely perplexed" John said. "You rushed us away and then you ran off almost immediately abandoning us."

"Even before I saw the pyre had been lit," Sally continued, "I asked Jenny to make it rain, just in case, which she did extremely quickly."

"It was weird," Jenny told them. "I had no idea why Sally wanted rain, but her request was so urgent and compelling and desperate that I just did it."

"But the rain couldn't stop the fire," Sally went on. "They must have put something on the wood to make it burn better." Sally was afraid Irina might have a fit at the mention of it, but instead she listened enthralled. "They had built the pyre in the form of a ring at some distance from the tree to which you were tied."

"That was quite common," Rafter put in, and went on matter-of-factly: "It generally caused the poor woman to die of suffocation before the fire reached her."

Sally cast another furtive glance at Irina, but the girl was serene. "Well anyway, there was no way I could get to you in time, so I transformed the flames into growing plants which put a stop to the fire and helped replenish the oxygen around you. The plants grew so quickly, spurting upwards like flames, with flowers budding everywhere. You were soon hidden from view in a fragrant bower."

Irina clapped her hands, a great grin across her face. Knowing the story of Irina's nightmares about witches burning, everyone looked at her startled.

"That was brilliant, Sally, absolutely brilliant."

"Indeed!" Rafter agreed, an unmistakable look of pride on his face. Sally blushed.

"The watchers helped me carry you to safety and bring you here," Jenny added.

"And Brent and Keira dealt with the crowd," Sally chuckled. "I don't think that even Professor Trundle had any idea what really happened."

Rafter raised his eyebrows at her in mock criticism, then smiled winningly and she smiled back. It felt so good to see him happy.

"Everybody left delighted," Brent concluded, "and lived happily ever after." At which everyone laughed.

"Well," Irina began, somewhat pensively, "my side of the story is much less exciting. I really can't remember anything that happened after I had that row with you, Moira."

Judging from the look on her face, she clearly regretted having fought with Moira.

"I have no idea how I came to be on the pyre dressed only in a makeshift robe. Apparently I had a black square marked on my forehead, but that had disappeared by the time I arrived here and regained consciousness."

"The Starless Square," Tom said, wheeling his chair into the room at that moment, followed closely by Kean.

Several people looked perplexed, so he explained.

"A square without stars would necessarily be black."

"The square on your forehead just faded and disappeared." Jenny told them. "I don't know how, because whoever drew it used indelible ink and we hadn't been able to scrub it off."

"The only thing I can tell you," Irina concluded, "is that I feel I have been healed. It's hard to explain. I feel completely different. I don't think I have ever felt so free before. It's as if years of nightmares had been lifted from me."

Open day

An stood in front of the main gate next to a sign bearing a coat of arms and the inscription: 'Saint Mary's Grammar School for Girls'. Up the drive she could see a number of large two-storey buildings that looked quite new. She hesitated about entering. A sign said: 'Pupils and staff only'.

"Wanna have a look round?" a voice said behind her.

She turned to find three girls who must have been more or less her age.

"It's open-day so you can go in. I'll show you round, if yer like," one of the girls said. She was the tallest of the three. All of them were wearing identical clothes: light grey trousers, a white blouse and green tie, and a dark green blazer on which she could see the same coat of arms.

"Is this your school?" An asked.

"Yup! The best school in town," the tall girl said, clearly proud of it.

"Where d'yer go to school?" one of the other girls enquired.

"I don't," An told them.

"Ah. Home schooling aye?"

An wasn't sure what home schooling meant. "No. We don't have schools where I live," she admitted, hoping she wouldn't get into trouble again for saying so.

"Cool!" the third girl said.

"Yer only saying that 'cause you haven't got good marks," the second girl said.

Marks? This wasn't going to be so easy.

Their discussion was interrupted by the arrival of a group of older boys.

"Hey! Tricia," one of the bigger boys said to the tallest girl. "Give us a kiss!"

She turned her back on him, pretending to ignore him. An could see the girl was frightened. They all were. The boys was not wearing a uniform like the girls, instead they wore shoddy jeans and various tea-shirts with words in gothic print plastered across their chests. The boy grabbed Tricia by the shoulder and forced her to turn and face him. Lacing his fingers around her neck he pulled her closer and closer to his mouth while she struggled wildly to keep her distance.

"Enough!" An said. She stepped forward and, much to his surprise, shoved the boy away. "Why don't you pick on someone your own size?"

"Someone like you, squirt," he laughed and the other boys chuckled. "Maybe you want a kiss instead."

It was An's turn to laugh. They looked perplexed, but the boy must have taken it for encouragement because he stepped closer.

"I warn you," An said, "You aren't going to like what is about to happen. You still have time to turn round and go away."

The boy puffed up his chest. "Enough of yer empty words, slut. Gimme that kiss." He lunged at An, but she sided-stepped and knocked his feet away from under him causing him to fall flat on his face.

"I warned you," she said as he rose to his feet, furiously clenching his fists.

"Give us a hand lads. This one's playin' 'ard to get," he said to the other boys.

He didn't get any further, finding himself on the ground again, his nose bleeding. He staggered to his feet, and wiping the blood from his face he snarled at her. His colleagues held back. The three girls had also withdrawn to a safe distance. He started towards her again.

"You really like making the same mistake over and over again," An said calmly.

He pulled up short and stared at her. "What d'yer mean?"

"What's yer name?" An asked.

"Bruno," he replied begrudgingly.

"You misjudged you opponent, Bruno. You thought you'd picked on a weak and defenceless girl. But that girl had you on the floor twice in no time without the slightest effort. She stands here in front of you unscathed and your nose is bleeding profusely. And yet you still come back for more. I don't want to hurt your pride any more, Bruno. Why don't we call it a day?"

"What's yer name?" he asked.

"An."

"OK An, but I still want a kiss."

"You'll get a kiss from me, Bruno, when I decide I want to and not before." She turned her back on him and walked over to the girls, linking arms with Tricia. "You promised me a guided visit."

Once they were out of ear shot, Tricia said: "You were brilliant. If you don't go to school, wherever did you learn how to fight like that?"

"I have two very good friends who taught me unarmed combat. You should come and meet them. They are giving a demonstration in

Hoyt Park this afternoon. But now it's time for that visit."

They showed her the physics room and biology lab and the gym and the computer room and finally they took her to their classroom. They were all in the same class. Low tables were scattered around the room, each with a couple of chairs next to it. The walls were covered with maps and drawings and texts written in large letters. At one end of the room there was a board that was all black. Tricia explained it was used for writing on.

"I don't understand," An told them, seating herself cross-legged on one of the desks while the others gathered around her. "What do you learn?"

"History, geography, English language, economics,..." Tricia told her. "Normal school subjects." As if that explained everything.

"And what do you learn from?"

The three girls looked incredulously at her. "From books, of course," the second girl, whose name was Maria, said.

An burst out laughing. "How can you possibly learn everything from books? If I want to learn about a country, for example, I go and visit it and ask questions, like I'm doing now. I'm learning about school, for example."

"But how could you do exams?" the third girl named Beth asked.

"Exams? What's that?"

Beth looked at her as if she was dim. "Exams! They're things you have to do to check you've learnt what the teacher told you."

"What form do these 'exams' take?" An asked.

"Mostly written tests where you have to answer questions you're asked," Beth replied.

"So you mean that to see if I could fight well I'd have to prove it by writing a text?"

"Put like that it does sound absurd," Tricia said. "But we do have practical exams, too. For example, to see how well we can use a language."

"I'm hungry," An told them. She hadn't eaten at midday. "I have two friends who are preparing a giant banquet for tomorrow midday with a group of students from the university. Do you want to come with me and sample some of their food? They won't mind at all. They love cooking."

"Where are they preparing this food?" Tricia asked.

"In a community hall, next to the Cathedral."

"I know the one. Sure I'll come."

Maria and Beth both agreed.

When they arrived at the Hall, which was a large, open, indoor space off the Starless Square used for meetings or large meals, Fran was just decorating some cakes.

"Hi Fran," An said. "I'd like you to meet Tricia, Maria and Beth, friends of mine."

"Grusse!" Fran said.

"Fran is German," An explained, "but her English is excellent."

"Here, try this," Fran said, thrusting a full tray of pastries into An's hands.

An handed the cakes around and the girls all ate.

"What do think?"

"Mmmm! Delicious," seemed about all anybody could say.

"I thought as much," Fran said chuckling. "Do you girls want to give me a hand? I've got behind with the cakes. People keep eating them," she laughed as she took back the tray. "I'll show you what to do."

So they all followed Fran to a series of trestle tables in one corner on which many bowls were laid out with different ingredients in them. Fran told them what to do, occasionally explaining why she used such and such an ingredient and not another.

"So you see, Tricia, you don't necessarily need to go to school to learn cooking," An commented.

"Why does Fran have her head shaved?" Beth whispered. "Is she ill?"

"Ask her," An suggested. "She won't mind."

So Beth asked Fran next time she came by.

"That would be a very long story," Fran said smiling. "But the short story is that I like it like that and so does my man." She came closer to Beth and said: "Touch! You can feel the form of my head."

Beth went extremely shy but Fran caught hold of her hand and stroked it across her bald head.

"Well?" Fran asked, letting go of the girl's hand.

"It feels strange. It makes me go all shivery."

Everyone laughed, except Beth who blushed.

"Hey, Martin," Fran called out as he came in carrying more supplies. "When you touch my head does it make you go all shivery?"

"Every time," Martin said, giving her a kiss.

"Stop teasing my friend," An said.

"Once you've finished, take a look round," Fran said to the girls. "And if any of the dishes catch your fancy, let me know, I'll tell you how to make them."

"I've seen several dishes already," Maria said looking in the direction of a number of students preparing food.

"She's not talking about the boys, silly," Tricia said, making a show of being exasperated. "What a one-track mind!"

Early years

The meal had been delicious, but Fran and Martin had already left to continue their work at the Community Hall, so people showed their appreciation simply by licking their fingers and looking content, some even yawned, maybe anticipating a short siesta. They were likely to be frustrated, Rafter thought, unless of course he managed to send them to sleep with his story.

"Why don't you all take a seat and make yourselves comfortable," Mae announced. "I believe Professor Rafter would like to tell a story."

"Thanks Mae," he began. "It all sounds so grandiose when Mae announces it. But I simply want to tell a tale that will contain some surprises, and with any luck might be entertaining if not instructive."

He looked around the room before going any further. Sally, Brent, Keira and Jenny were all installed in armchairs, watching him attentively. Moira and John had left to deal with a problem at their hotel, but Irina was still there seated on the floor, but now at Keira's feet. Anju and Dieter were away, busy preparing their demonstration. Tom had rolled his wheelchair into a corner and listened unobtrusively from the shadows, as was his way. Kean was about to leave when Rafter stopped him.

"If you wish to stay, Kean, you are very welcome."

"Thank you, Professor. I'm honoured." Kean found himself a chair near Tom.

"There were no Theosophy departments anywhere when I began my studies," Rafter explained. "I was interested in shamanism and ritual magic, at the time, but they could only be studied at university from the angle of history or anthropology or possibly psychology. Not at all as a living practice."

He hadn't really wanted to take any of the subjects but his father had insisted he get a university degree. For people of their standing, that was the done thing.

"So I was forced to take anthropology and I studied the practice of magic and shamanism elsewhere."

It hadn't been easy to learn magic. Nobody wanted to admit dappling in it. The serious wielders of magic never made themselves known. People kept to themselves.

"I was lucky to meet Alo and Naniu. They introduced me to others. Without their help, I would never have discovered the workings of magic. It's a very secret world. They don't call it 'occult' sciences for nothing," he chuckled.

"I was never very good at magic. I wasn't so hot as a shaman either. But like you, Brent, circumstances forced my hand."

There were so many things he could tell of his life, but he might not have forever to tell them. Some things he had to share, others were more like luxuries that he allowed himself.

"When I finished my degree, with honours, I seemed set for a brilliant career in anthropology. At least that's what my professors thought. They saw in my excellent marks the promise of a future light in anthropology. But I was listless. I didn't want to spend my life researching tribes in the Amazon, which was the Department's speciality at the time."

He'd once travelled to the Amazon and observed a tribe there. He'd really enjoyed meeting the people and had learnt a lot from them, but the return and all the analysis of the data he'd gathered bored him.

"Now we get to the part I'm sure you've all been waiting for," and he winked at Sally. "It was at that moment, when I couldn't decide how to go on, that I met a beautiful, young woman called Tess."

Sally laughed. "Inevitable!"

"The Professor is only human, after all," Brent quipped.

Rafter chuckled. He liked these young people. He only wished he had more time to spend with them.

"You know," he said, "you are very lucky. You have embarked on the journey I tried to go on, but you have each other. Look at you, more than ten people, some of you already with prodigious gifts. You will be so much stronger and better because of it."

He was thirsty, and, as if anticipating his needs, Mae handed him a glass of water. He thanked her and went on.

"You can't imagine how important it is not to be alone."

He fell silent for a moment. He was beginning to feel tired, but he insisted on pushing on. He needed to get to the end of this before the weekend was out. He might not have more time.

"What happened to the woman, Professor?" Keira asked.

"It was love at first sight. We were instantly attracted to each other. I had no idea where Tess came from or what she did for a living. She never mentioned them."

They'd often gone for walks together in the countryside around Avan, and when they got to know each other better, they made love in out-of-the-way places. The pleasure and joy of it made him smile.

"Then one day Tess was gone. I could find no trace of her anywhere. I was devastated. I threw myself into my studies in an effort to forget. I had chosen to write a thesis on shamanism seen from an anthropological perspective. Not shamanism in wild countries but shamanism as it was practice here in England. My professors were not very happy. It was not serious enough for them, but I insisted."

He could remember hours of discussions during which the Head of the Department had tried to dissuade him and, when that had failed, the man had turned to threats, saying he'd refuse to caution such a subject. Luckily one professor offered his support and said he'd take Rafter on as a doctoral student.

"Just after I finished my thesis and was once again faced with indecision about whether to continue my academic career or not, I received a small packet that had been delivered by hand by a messenger I didn't meet. Inside was a small gold ring."

Mae gasped. "Is that the ring you loaned me?"

Rafter nodded. "It is indeed. The ring left me perplexed. I had no idea who had sent it, nor what I was supposed to do with it. It certainly wasn't meant for me to wear because it was far too small."

"So you travelled to the Reaches?" Mae asked, excited at the prospect.

"Not so fast, Mae. I was not a genius like you!"

She blushed. He took her hand, saying: "I told you that you were much more than - what did you call yourself? - a simple secretary." He released her hand letting her wipe the tears from her eyes. He took a deep breath and continued.

"It took me a long time to figure out how to use the ring. And when I did, I found myself in the Reaches."

That had been both a wonderful and a terrible time. A wave of tiredness swept over him as the pain gripped him with renewed vigour. Sally must have read the signs on his face because she suggested they stop there for a while.

"You should rest Professor," she said. "You can tell us what happened in the Reaches later today before we go to Keira and Sarah's concert."

He nodded and closed his eyes, letting himself slip into oblivion.

On to something

"I think I'm on to something," Anju said. The tips of her fingers brushed whatever it was, but each time she tried to get a hold of it, it slipped beyond reach.

"Attack me!" she ordered, turning her back to him.

Dieter must have hesitated because the attack didn't come immediately. His thrust flung her forward onto the grass before she could react. She rolled over and stood up.

"Are you all right?" he asked, taking her in his arms and kissing her.

"I'm fine," she said pulling away and turning her back. "Attack me again."

Once more she had no time to react before the blow sent her sprawling. She rolled over anew and sprang to her feet, a grim look on her face.

"Again!" she said.

Once again he had her flying. She lost count of how many times he attacked her. She ached all over.

"Maybe we should stop," Dieter said. "You need to be fit for the demonstration."

She took a deep shuddering breath. "Give me a minute, then we'll try again, one last time."

She closed her eyes and relaxed. An image sprang to mind. One of the first lessons they'd given in the Reaches. She'd been teaching balance. She had the women stand on one leg, poised, trying to feel their centre. She felt for her own centre like her trainees had done. From there she reached out till she could feel the space around. She could feel Dieter waiting. She felt his tension, his concern, and she felt the way he held himself, most of his weight on one leg, his arms folded across his chest. A wave of joy flowed through her as she realised she'd found the answer.

She stood up straight and smiled at Dieter. "Ok. Attack me."

She closed her eyes, concentrating on the energy field around her. His foot shot out to knock her legs away from under her, but missed when she sprang in the air, her eyes still closed.

"You have to do better than that." He rolled over on the ground and tried to attack her as he passed, but she saw the movement coming and stepped aside. Despite her closed eyes, she found she could anticipate his every move. He tried to sneak up on her from behind and grab her, but she ducked and swinging her leg around sent him flying onto the grass.

"Extraordinary!" he exclaimed, joy in his voice, as he rolled over and stood up. "How do you do that?"

"Give me a kiss," she said, opening her eyes, "and I'll tell you."

Some while later, Dieter had still not mastered the technique although he did feel her field as she moved around him. "Let's take a break," he suggested.

He sat on a park bench and she sat on his lap, her arms swung around his neck. She liked the feel of his body next to her. She had no need to say anything; she just revelled in his warmth.

"Hey! Anju!" a voice called out.

They both turned to see An skipping across the grass accompanied by three girls her own age.

"Anju and Dieter," An said, "meet my new friends, Tricia, Maria and Beth."

They stood and shook hands.

"I had a bit of a fight with some boys," An told them, a grin on her face. "One of them got a bit of a shock when he found himself lying on the ground after he tried to grab me."

Anju and Dieter chuckled. "They could hardly have known they were up against an Amazon." Anju saw An's warning look and did not pursue the point.

"Look we've got something new to show you," Anju said and pulled Dieter to his feet as he'd taken refuge on the bench. "With my eyes closed," Anju said demonstratively.

Dieter tried all his best moves but he couldn't catch her out. When she'd had enough, she laid him out. The four girls clapped, An with them.

"Wow!" Tricia said in astonishment. "How do you do that with your eyes closed?"

"I can feel him coming. I sense what move he's about to use."

"Could you teach us to do that?" Maria asked.

"It's not easy," Dieter warned. "I haven't managed yet."

Anju looked at the three schoolgirls. "You can't combat dressed like that."

"We've got our sports kits with us," Tricia told them. "In case we had to play basketball."

"OK, go change over there in the bushes," Anju suggested.

The three came back dressed in shorts, tea-shirts and sneakers. They looked quite fit.

"How often do you do sport?" Anju asked.

"Well," Tricia replied, "apart from basketball twice a week we also go swimming often and jog together most mornings before or after school."

"I suggest I do the work-out," Dieter said. "You really need a rest."

Anju went and sat on the bench. She could see that Dieter was taking them through the dance they'd developed for the women in Granwich.

"I will begin a dance made for combat that we taught some women. It looks more like a dance than combat as they needed to conceal the fact that they were training to fight the men."

The girls threw themselves into the exercise and within half an hour were very good at it.

"Excellent," Dieter told them. "But now we should rest because we have to give a demonstration in a short while."

"Let's go to the Community Hall and get a snack," Anju suggested.

"We just came from there," An told them with a wicked grin, "but I'm sure Maria would be delighted to return, she's got her eyes on a boy down there."

Maria aimed a playful swipe at An who avoided it with ease.

"Let's go then," Anju declared.

Supermarket

Aisles of empty shelves one after another dragged on for an eternity. A thick mantle of dust shrouded everything, blurring contours, softening angles, dulling sounds. The deserted ruin was akin to a surrealistic painting that overflowed the contours of reality and leaked across the floor.

A searing pain shot through Frick's chest. Bent over double, he clutched his flaming chest. After a while the pain abated allowing him to straighten up. Each shuffling step forward threw up a cloud of fine particles that swirled around him: his own personal cloak of unreality masking him from the world. Being lost to his fellow humans didn't mean he could forget.

A scream ripped through the silence causing him to clap his hands over his ears. It was not his scream. That much he was sure. It was a woman who howled in his head.

"Help me!" she hurled. "It hurts!"

His nostrils, which had become accustomed to the clouds of dust, sensed something new: smoke. There was a fire nearby.

"It burns!" The woman's screaming set his teeth rattling.

The odour solidified and took form, smelling increasingly of burning flesh. He tried to block it out, wrapping the filthy blanket over his mouth and nose. But the stink got round such feeble defences. An inarticulate scream tore him apart, wrenching at his guts, its sound cruel, unbearable, inhuman, till the noise subsided and stopped with an ultimate whimper, his own.

When he resurfaced he found himself on his knees, his forehead pressed on the filthy tiles. He spat out the dust that had worked its way up his nose and into his mouth and tried to wipe it from his eyes, but his hands were so dust-ridden that he put more in his eyes than he was able to remove. The stench of burning hung sickly in the air. He heaved himself up with the help of a nearby block of shelves and staggered on.

It was a silly hope, really. He knew it. But maybe there were still some beds abandoned in the furniture department. When he finally rounded the end of the interminable aisle, bereft of all the shining products that had once garnished its shelves, no comfy bed awaited him, not even a second blanket. At best, there was a pile of folded cardboard, tied up loosely with a length of string. He leant forward and let himself tip over onto the pile. Then he rolled over on his back, pulled his blanket tight about him and closed his eyes.

"I know nothing," the child protested, fear in its eyes.

He'd had her tied to the chair by her wrists and ankles. "Your mother is a witch," he told her, spitting out the word that was so distasteful to him. "She admitted it." He remembered the long hours of torture he'd needed to extract the confession. "Surely you must have known."

"I know nothing."

"Do you know what happens to witches?"

She shook her head, but her terrified eyes belied her gesture.

"They burn at the stake!" He delighted at the sound of the words that were so final and binding. "Now if you were to help us…" He played with his riding crop. "You might escape burning yourself."

She remained silent, cowering, no doubt expecting him to hit her.

Then all of a sudden, as if struck by a bolt of lightning, she sat upright and stared at him, her eyes boring into him.

"Your time is nearly come, Frick," she said, all fear gone, her voice thick with menace.

He raised his crop to hit her, more out of fear than anger, but his crop was no longer in his hand. Instead a writhing snake had wrapped itself tightly around his arm and sank its fangs into his wrist. He screamed, smashing his arm against the wall in a desperate attempt to free himself of the brightly coloured beast. His arm had gone a lurid colour and felt numb.

"You witch!" he screamed. "I'll have you burnt!"

But the venom was slowly creeping up his arm and into his shoulder and neck. The right side of his body felt leaden and lifeless. His right eye twitched, his mouth misshapen by the poison, began to drool.

"I'll make you pay for this," but he didn't get any further because his legs gave way and he rolled over onto the floor. A great cloud of dust rose up about him and as it sank over him, he too sank into darkness and despair.

Headless

"Anybody seen Frick?" Glat asked, troubled by the disappearance of their leader.

They were meeting in an outhouse of Twine's pig farm. No other venue had been available at such short notice. Glat hated the place. It stank. He might never rid his clothes of the stench. Twine seemed oblivious to the filth. Maybe he'd been around pigs too long.

After their aborted attempt to burn the girl at the stake, going to the Starless Square was out of the question. For one thing, Nohan had forgotten to get rid of the girl's clothes. For all they knew, the packet was still sitting on the table waiting for a would-be detective to stumble upon it. Glat had been unable to find out whether the incident had been declared to the police. Better to be cautious.

And then there was Frick.

Nohan had told them about the man's weird behaviour. "I checked his office and flat, but he wasn't in either. And he doesn't answer his phone."

"Maybe the girl bewitched him," Green suggested, lowering his voice.

A shiver went down Glat's back. He remembered the last time they'd tried to set fire to two women. They'd been witches all right. What happened left no doubt. Getting the fire started had been a nightmare, even with a jerrycan of petrol. Once the women realised their house was ablaze, a hoard of bees swarmed out and attacked Glat and his friends. He shuddered at the thought. Within moments, the stings had swollen and become infected. It had been excruciating and had taken weeks to heal.

"We'd better find him," Green said. "We can't afford to have him blabbering to the police."

Stupid bugger, Glat thought. If Frick had been there, he would never have dared. Now they were all vying for his place. Everyone agreed they needed to find Frick as soon as possible and they made plans to search for him. In the silence that followed, Glat reckoned it was a good moment to reveal his photos.

"Frick asked me to take some pics of that tall guy with the moustache that attacked him in the Theosophy Department. He had a hunch that the guy was having - what did he call it? - an illegal affaire with a minor."

Green chuckled. "Right up your street, hey Glat?"

Everybody laughed except Glat. The implication that he had anything in common with such a slug annoyed him. Not that he was embarrassed about what he did. He was proud of his sexy pictures, they were quite artistic, and the younger the people photographed the more money he could get.

"So what have you got?" Green asked eagerly. The question didn't surprise him. Green was a regular customer.

Glat pulled out a small wad of photos he'd printed from his computer. "Here's one of the guy kissing the girl on a park bench. I touched it up a bit to make it look like he's got his hand between her thighs."

"Excellent," Green said.

"That should do the trick," Nohan added.

"I've got lots more," Glat told them laying out a picture of the girl sitting astride the man's legs facing him as they kissed. "But that's not all. I got lucky. Four schoolgirls turned up and started some sort of weird combat practice with him. Look."

He displayed a photo in which the guy was standing with his hands on one of the girl's buttocks. "I made one or two adjustments," he admitted. He was good at that sort of thing. Even an expert would have a hard time telling the difference. "The best thing, though, was that the girls changed right there and then."

He laid a postcard-sized photo on the table in which three schoolgirls were busy undressing in the bushes. His own pictures didn't usually excited him. He liked to keep business and pleasure separate. But this was special. Having them right under his nose had really got him worked up.

"Have you got any more?" Green asked, staring at the picture. When Glat nodded grinning, Green asked: "Could you make me copies?"

"Enough of your business," Nohan exclaimed, disgust in his voice. The man seemed unmoved by the photos. Glat couldn't understand him. Most men would give good money to get their hands on such a set.

"What are we going to do with these?" Nohan asked, jerking a thumb in the direction of the photos.

"I thought of handing them anonymously to the police," Glat replied.

"I have a better idea," Nohan said. "We could hide them in that Professor's office and tip off the police. If we write the address where the guy is staying with the girl on the back of one of the photos, we'll kill two birds with one stone."

Everyone was delighted and took it in turns to congratulate him and Nohan.

"Glat, can you find out where they are staying?"

Even better, he thought. Nothing would please him more than snooping around the place where the girl slept.

"Would it help if they were on TV?"

It was Dylan who spoke. He was a recent addition, brought in by Frick. He worked for the local TV from time to time. For a man from the media he had very little to say and when he did speak what he had to say was often confused.

"I mean, wouldn't it make more of a scandal if they have been seen on TV together?"

Nohan looked perplexed and somewhat annoyed. "I don't understand."

As Glat understood it, the idea appealed to him. It might even bring in more money from selling pictures anonymously to the sleazy tabloids. "I think Dylan means we'll make a bigger splash if the scandal breaks after they've figured on TV."

Dylan nodded with a silly grin, happy to have been understood.

"Why not?" Nohan said. "How will you do it?"

"I'll call some guys I know, independent cameramen, always on the look out for something good to sell the TV companies."

"And what about the rest of the weekend programme?" Twine asked, returning to the Theosophy people. "Isn't there to be a concert at the Arena tonight?"

"Couldn't we have that singer of theirs arrested for taking drugs?" Clyde suggested, speaking for the first time.

He was the youngest and newest member of the Starless Square. Frick had introduced him recently. Glat suspected he was a small-time drug dealer. A shifty sort of guy with filthy black hair. Glat wouldn't trust him an inch. Why ever had Frick brought him along? It didn't make sense. Lest it be that Frick was one of Clyde's customers.

"I can get hold of some good stuff real easy, dump it in her dressing room and then tip off the police."

Nohan didn't look very happy at the idea. "It's far too risky," he said. "Security is tight around such a big event. If you get caught you'll be in serious trouble. And us too."

"I agree," Twine said. "The Arena's pretty well guarded."

So they refused Clyde's idea and moved on to discuss the next day. Out of the corner of his eye, he noticed Clyde smiling a twisted smile. Glat guessed he would go through with his idea all the same. Clyde was stubborn like that. It would be a challenge. Glat didn't care. He disliked Clyde. They'd be better off without the scum.

Impromptu

"Hey, Burt! Pull that cable over here!"

Anju was dismayed to see that the corner of Hoyt Park in which they planned to hold their demonstration was swarming with TV technicians pulling cables, setting up cameras, wiring mikes, installing lights and generally making a nuisance of themselves in an efficient but self-important sort of way. The place was all the more cluttered as intrigued bystanders watched on and people were beginning to arrive for the demonstration.

"Could you stand over there, Miss, so we can check the lighting?" a man asked her. She ignored him.

"It's a real invasion!" she complained, pulling Dieter to one side.

"Well. We wanted publicity, didn't we?" He seemed resigned to the way things were.

"How did they find out about this?" She was sure Tom had not organised it. He would have told them. Dieter had no answer. She turned to An, who had just arrived with her three friends, and asked her: "Could you find out how they knew we'd be here?"

As An went off to question technicians, Dieter greeted the girls. "Are you three still game to take part in the demonstration?"

"Sure," Tricia said, although she didn't sound so certain as she glanced at the cameras.

"And did you ask your parents if it was OK?" he added.

"Our parents encourage us to do sport and we often have tournaments and competitions, so they are used to it," Maria told him.

"I hadn't realised we were going to be TV stars," Beth giggled, "I would have had my hair done."

Anju could see she was joking, although the nervousness seemed real enough. Most girls of her age would be hyperventilating or swooning at the thought of being on TV.

"Someone tipped them off about your demonstration," An reported. "And the big boss liked the idea. That's why he sent a whole crew from national television. They'll be broadcasting live part of the time, apparently."

Anju took a deep breath. She wasn't against being on TV, but she didn't want to be the subject of a TV show.

"Do you know which one of them is the boss?" she asked An.

"The tall one over there with the leather jacket."

"I'm going to talk to him. I will need support. Can you see if you can get Sally, Brent and Keira to help me?"

"They're already here. I'll go fetch them," An said weaving her way between the TV equipment.

Anju wanted to play this her way. It was her demonstration, not theirs. Judging from the way they barged in, you'd think they had initiated the whole thing.

Sally, Brent and Keira arrived, laughing at something An had said.

"So you want to do battle with the TV?" Keira asked, grinning.

"No," Anju said, taking hold of Dieter's hand. "I just want us to be able to do our thing the way we want and not have everything dictated by the needs of television. Will you help me?"

"Of course," Brent said.

"OK. Let's go and see this boss. I'll do the talking, but if ever I'm in difficulty, I count on you to help me. Is that all right?"

They agreed.

The boss was busy giving instructions and ignored Anju when she tried to talk to him. After several unsuccessful attempts she shifted to combat mode and sent the man flying in a spectacular move that caught him completely off guard. She didn't let him get up, but instead planted herself on his chest, blocking his hands and arms with her feet.

"What the hell do you think you're doing?"

"I'm giving a demonstration of unarmed combat. Is that not what you came to see?"

As he struggled to get free, she rolled over forcing him to roll too and sent him flying a second time, this time landing with a sharp thud that winded him. She took up her position sitting on his chest again.

"You have no right."

"I'm only giving you what you wanted," she replied, ignoring his protests and vain attempts to free himself.

By now a considerable crowd had gathered around them, forming a dense circle that Dieter and the others made sure was kept at a distance. A couple of the TV crew came to watch, but most of them manned their posts by their cameras and microphones and lights, watching from there. Some found it funny to see their boss handled in that way. Others sought to help him, shouting out things like: "Leave him alone you bully!" or "I'll call the police if you don't let him go."

Anju ignored them. "If you agree to listen to me till I've said what I have to say, I'll let you up."

The boss continued to grumble. In the mean time a couple of burly technicians were easing closer to Anju from behind. She couldn't see them, but with her new-found intuition she felt them coming and anticipated their moves. She rolled off the boss, cart-wheeled out of reach and spun round in time to bang their two heads together. Both men collapsed to the ground, unconscious. She resumed her seat on the boss's chest while Dieter dragged them out of the circle.

"How the hell did she do that?" one of the on-lookers gasped. "She couldn't possibly have seen them coming."

Anju slid her hand along the boss's neck and, finding the pressure point, she put him out. Leaving him unconscious on the grass she stood and addressed the audience.

"You are surprised that I knew they were attacking me even though I couldn't see them. We have other senses than our eyes. In fact, each of us is surrounded by a field of energy and if you practice you can feel that field and know where it is going. Let me show you."

As she glanced around looking for the girls, she noticed that the TV crew were busy recording what happened. Good. She had got what she wanted: they were concentrated on her and what she did and not on making television.

"Tricia," she called out. "Can you give me a hand?"

The girl shifted into the middle of the circle.

"Attack me from behind."

Tricia sprang at her, without allowing Anju a second's respite. Anju stepped aside, anticipating the move and Tricia fell to the floor. Anju offered her a hand to get up. She called in Maria and Beth too and all three attacked her, but she was able to anticipate their moves. Each time she avoided their attacks, people applauded.

"Tricia, Maria and Beth are all new to combat," Anju pointed out, "so maybe we should give them a round of applause for taking the risk." Everyone applauded and some even cheered. The three girls bowed.

"You are maybe imagining that I would fare less well against a well trained man. Let's see then. Dieter!" she called out and he came forward into the circle. "Your turn to attack."

She immediately recognised the energy of one of his most spectacular moves. She saw the lines of it traced out in space and could see exactly where he would go and when. Instinctively she knew what to do, causing his strike to miss her completely. There was a roar of appreciation from the crowd. Dieter caught his breath and tried again, hoping to defeat her with speed, but in her head his speed was no advantage. It was as if his whole series of moves were in slow motion allowing her plenty of time to respond. He was incapable of touching her.

"Thanks Dieter," she said, bowing to him.

The audience applauded whole-heartedly.

"It must take ages to learn to do that?" a young woman in the front row commented.

"I don't think so," Anju replied. "I myself only discovered how to do it this afternoon."

"You're a fast learner," a man called out.

"Maybe," Anju replied, smiling. "But we have taught many women unarmed combat and you'd be surprised how fast they learn."

"Could you teach me?" the young woman asked.

"And me?" several others said.

"We do not have enough time, but I will teach a few of you a combat dance we taught some women who had to hide the fact that they were learning unarmed combat. We developed a way to teach poise and anticipation and fluidity of movement without raising any suspicions."

She called ten of the women forward and took them through the first steps of the dance they'd developed in the Reaches. Some had difficulties, others found it easier, but all of them were delighted with what they managed to do.

"It's like feeling where you are in the world," one woman commented.

"I've never felt so aware of my movements before," another admitted.

When the short demonstration was over, Anju had the women bow to receive applause and bowed herself as people cheered and whistled.

"Now we have to awaken sleeping beauty," she said with a chuckle.

The boss was still unconscious on the ground.

"Let's hope he's not in too much of a bad mood for having missed the show. At least he'll be able to watch it on TV."

Everybody burst out laughing.

She applied her finger to the pressure point and felt the man stir. Once his eyes flicked open, his face was livid.

"How dare you?"

"Be careful what you say. You're on national television."

He glanced around only to see several cameras pointed in his direction and a boom mike suspended above his head.

"Hey boss," a voice called out. "I've got the programme manager on the line. He said the programme was wonderful."

The boss looked perplexed. Anju held out her hand to him and helped him get up.

"No hard feelings?"

"Apparently you've done a good job in my absence."

"All I did was give a demonstration of unarmed combat which is what I came to do. Thank the men and women who work for you, if the film they made is good."

Chapter 6 ~ For the Love of a Woman

Framed

"Jock. What did you think of that?" Mandy asked switching the television off in the back office and turning the screen towards the wall.

The Chief Constable didn't like his officers watching TV on duty, but he wouldn't go so far as banning the box. She'd found the girl's performance remarkable, literally running the TV show without any preparation or help. And her skill in self-defence was just as stunning. Such a girl would take no nonsense from the likes of Jock.

"Spectacular!" Jock granted not without irony, donning his helmet and fixing the strap under his chin.

"They should teach us techniques like that," she continued.

He laughed. "If every young girl we crossed in the street could fight like her, we'd have a serious problem!"

Typical, she thought. Just like him to belittle what women did. "You wouldn't be being sexist by any chance?"

"Who me? I'm all for women."

"That's not what I meant." She couldn't decide if he exasperated her or amused her.

"You coming?" It was time for them to go out on the beat.

"I'll just get my hat," she told him. The phone rang at that moment. "Can you answer that?" she shouted over her shoulder from the hallway.

"What was that about?" she asked when she came back.

"Odd," he replied, still holding the receiver in his hand.

"What do you mean?" She took the receiver from him and put it down.

"It was a tip off. The bloke reckoned we should check out the office of a professor at the university."

"Sounds like he's trying to frame someone," she said, fitting her hat squarely on her head.

"Well, it's on our way. You never know it might turn out to be a lead. We should check it out."

Easier said than done. It was half an hour later when they found the caretaker and asked her to open the Theosophy Department. They spent the wait arguing about why anyone would want to harm the reputation of an ageing professor close to retirement. Jock was inclined to suspect the professor, but she insisted that they didn't have the slightest evidence to doubt the integrity of the academic.

The caretaker, who looked the perfect caricature of a witch, was not happy at being hauled from her TV set on a Saturday evening. She complained all the way to the Theosophy Department. Jock let Mandy do the apologising. She knew he intensely disliked cantankerous old women. Not that the woman was old, she just acted as if she were.

Once the caretaker had let them into the Professor's office, Mandy asked: "Who has a key to this room?"

"The Professor, the cleaning staff and myself. That's about it."

"Do people in the Department normally lock their doors?" Jock asked.

"No. Not normally. It's the first time I've seen Professor Rafter's door locked."

"Do the cleaning staff come in over the weekend?" Jock pursued.

"Sure. Saturday is their big day. During the week it's difficult to do their work properly. I'll leave you. Pull the door to after you. The main door is easy to open from the inside. Just turn the latch. It will lock automatically behind you."

Mandy glanced around. The room was big, with bay windows overlooking the river and lots of armchairs and a tidy desk in one corner. Nothing was out of place. The only objects on the desk were a small pile of books and an unmarked buff envelope. The latter looked quite incongruous, laying as it was in calculated disordered that jarred with the orderliness of the rest.

"I bet you anything that what we are looking for is in that envelope," she said. "These people are really naïve! Who do they take us for?"

Seeing Jock moving to pick up the envelope, she stopped him. "Maybe we should have this fingerprinted."

He sighed. The contents of the envelope clearly intrigued him and he was impatient. "But what if it contains nothing out of the ordinary, we'd look pretty stupid calling in the forensic chaps."

"OK. Let's have a look."

He eased open the envelope and emptied its contents onto the desk.

Both of them were astonished at what they saw: a series of photos of young girls with a man who must have been in his thirties. None of the girls could have been more than fourteen or fifteen. Although the girls were not naked, the photos were lewd. In one, the man had his hand on the crutch of one of the girls. In another he was kissing the girl who sat astride his legs, his hands making free with her breasts. There were also photos of other young girls getting undressed in the bushes presumably nearby.

"Hey! This is really interesting." Jock exclaimed, examining the photos more closely.

His reaction disgusted her. It was as if the photos turned him on. Typical man.

"Isn't that the girl who was on the TV this evening?" he asked. It sure was. "And the man with the moustache was on TV with her."

"We've stumbled onto something very odd here, Jock," she mused. "Good Lord! Isn't that one," and she pointed at one of the pictures, "the girl who gave us the slip the other day?"

Jock leant closer to get a better look. "It could well be." He whistled through his teeth. "Wow! We don't often have such a case here!"

Mandy sat down in the Professor's chair and turned on the flexible light over the desk, directing it on the photo of the man touching the girl's sex. Something was odd about the angle of his hand and the way the light caught it. She wished she had a magnifying glass.

"You don't have a magnifying glass by any chance?"

"Sure!"

She thought he was kidding, but he pulled out his new Swiss army knife and sure enough there was a small magnifying glass folded up in it.

"Useful!" she told him, turning to look at the photo through the small lens. As part of her on-going training in the police force, she'd recently followed a course about digital photography. They'd been shown how crooks faked photos. So the moment she saw the position of the man's hand in the photo she knew what was wrong.

"It's a fake. Look at his hand," she said, handing him the magnifying glass.

"I'm not so sure." Typical. He always found fault with her judgement! "They look genuine enough to me."

She dismissed his reticence as one of his frequent manoeuvres to gain control. "Whoever it was who planted these photos was not very good at it! And he imagined he could discredit not only the Professor but also the man with the moustache in the photos and the girls as well."

Jock shook his head as he took the photos from her, piled them up and pushed them back in the envelope. "I wouldn't be so categorical. We should get an expert opinion."

She gritted her teeth. So much for team work.

A full house

"How's the Professor?" Sally asked Mae as they entered Rafter's house.

"He's fine," the voice of Rafter called out from the living room.

Contrary to what he said, he looked drawn and worn out when she went in to see him. "Did you manage to sleep at all?"

She could see that he'd prefer not to answer, trying to hide how he really felt, but the pain was clear to see. She pulled up a chair next to the makeshift bed Mae had set up and took hold of his hands. It was something she would never have dared do before. He had always been an approachable sort of person, but there had been a professional aura about him that kept people at a safe distance.

Two things had changed. First there was the trip to the Reaches with the development of their gifts and the eruption of the Dream Class in his life. The fact that they were now camped out in his house, almost as if it were theirs, was surely the most tangible sign of the change. And then there was the illness that left him vulnerable and dependent in a way he would never have accepted before.

"Your hands are cold. Would you like a hot water bottle?"

He laughed, or at least he tried to laugh.

It must be difficult to laugh when the pain has you in its grips, Vee said.

"You and Mae are like real mothers to me!"

"We like to be of use." She rubbed his hands in an attempt to warm them. "But we'd much prefer it if you were well and didn't need our help, at least not like this."

She looked away, using the pretext of the arrival of Keira and Brent, to hide the tears that welled up in her eyes.

"I appreciate your efforts," he said, lowering his voice. "You can't imagine what a pleasure it is to have you all here. You're so full of life. It gives me hope."

Keira and Brent joined them and Mae, Tom, Dieter, Anju and Jenny came through from the next room followed by Fran and Martin. Irina had gone to talk to John and Moira in town and An was still out with Tricia and the other girls.

Rafter greeted them all. "This house has been empty far too long. Seeing you all here makes me think that I had turned into an old bachelor without even realising it."

Nobody laughed, which was probably all the better because he was clearly very serious. Sally would never have called him a solitary person, but then she'd seen him mostly in his role of professor surrounded by staff or students.

He glanced across the room. "This place should have had children running around it."

The image seemed incongruous. Sally could hardly see Rafter bouncing children up and down on his knee or playing football with them.

Vee snorted at the idea.

They knew him only as a figure of authority with a good sense of humour.

"So did you go to the Reaches?" Keira prompted.

"I did indeed. I'll tell you about it. I don't have Brent's magic but I will endeavour to transport you with me on that first and last visit."

I had expected the ring to take me to Tess but it did no such thing. When I opened my eyes I found myself sitting on a tree trunk surrounded by trees as far as the eye could see. There were no discernible paths and no signs of dwellings or human life. Everything was silent. Everything was still. Only the distant rustle of a breeze in the treetops indicated that this was not a picture I was sitting in.

As I got to my feet I sent a couple of rabbits scurrying away through the undergrowth. They must have been watching me, but I hadn't noticed. I had no idea where I was. I felt a bit light headed. I suppose I should have been worried about how I was going to get home but I didn't care. I had an appointment with the Head of Department the next day about getting a post in the university as lecturer. To hell with it! My adventure was more important.

Clearly I couldn't just sit there and wait. So I headed off in the direction I was facing, weaving my way between the trees and bushes, trying to keep to a straight line. I wasn't at all sure if I would get anywhere like that. For all I knew the forest might go on forever. In a book on Shamanism I discovered in the local library, I'd read about people following their inner eye when they were lost. But I didn't have an inner eye, and even if I did I had no idea how to open it.

As I plodded on, getting more and more weary, I thought over all I had done: my studies, the university and my meeting with the woman I hoped to find. I couldn't help feeling it had all been futile, as futile as wandering through an immense forest with no idea where I was going. I was hungry and tired and thirsty and foot-sore and despondent and my head was beginning to spin.

When I stopped for a rest, I took out the ring, which hung around my neck on a silver chain, and examined it. I had the silly idea that it might tell me where to go or transport me somewhere else. I even tried closing my eyes. But when I opened them I was still in the same place. I got to my feet and stumbled on.

Within five minutes I found myself entering a clearing in the middle of which stood a low wooden house surrounded on all sides by a covered terrace. It looked deserted and when I got inside I found it was. But at least there was running water and a stock of food in the kitchen. Once I had eaten, I lay down on a bed, exhausted and sweating profusely. I couldn't fall asleep despite my fatigue. Instead I tossed and turned, feeling confused and desolate.

Tess was sitting next to me when I awoke, holding my hands. I felt so cold, I couldn't stop shaking. I had gone from one extreme to another. I tried to sit up, but my head began spinning.

"Lie still," she told me, her soft voice calming me. "You've been ill and still are."

She gave me a spoonful of a potion to drink. I must have fallen asleep because when I opened my eyes night had fallen and I no longer felt so cold. In the dark I could hear her moving about in the next room, singing quietly to herself. I didn't recognise the language nor the songs she sang. Then the door opened and I could see her silhouette against the candle light from the room next door.

"How do you feel?"

"Pleased to see you again."

"You caught the sickness that people from your world catch when they come here."

"Where's here?"

"The Reaches. You are in my world."

Of course I'd read about people travelling to other worlds, but that was only in books. I suppose I should have been excited or concerned, but I couldn't grasp what it meant. The only thing that mattered was that I had found Tess and she was sitting next to me on the bed. I put my arms around her, pulled her close and we kissed, cautiously at first then more passionately. In a way, it was as if we'd never been apart. But we had been separated and that I couldn't forget.

"You suddenly disappeared," I said when we finally pulled apart. "What happened to you? I was so worried and upset…"

"I didn't feel well. I was afraid I was suffering from the same sickness you have now. I had no medicine with me and I was afraid if I told you the truth, you wouldn't want me any more."

At which Tess began to cry. I took her in my arms. We stayed like that for quite a while, long after her sobs had ceased, just relishing in each other's warm presence.

"I made the wrong choice," she went on, as I wiped the tears from her cheeks. "I regretted it every day, but circumstances stopped me from returning. I often imagined coming back and explaining everything. Those were happy dreams. Then the situation changed and I might have been able to visit your world again, but I was afraid. I imagined you had found someone else. So I had the idea of the ring. The way I saw it, the ring would give you a chance to come, if you wanted to … And if not, you could ignore it."

I pulled her close and she nestled her head on my shoulder.

"I never forgot you. I just didn't understand. As time went on, I began to doubt both you and myself. I thought maybe you hadn't loved me, or that you had someone else. I felt confused and empty."

Tess kissed, running her hands through my hair and I realised my fears had been unfounded. I had been so silly. I went on to describe how I plunged into my studies but how I felt restless as if there was something else I had to do but didn't know what.

We stayed in that house for almost a week. We made love, of course, and we talked a lot as we walked hand in hand through the forest. Tess explained her world. She taught me how to do many things I wouldn't have thought possible. And she showed me how she could transform into a bird. The first time I saw her do so I was terrified.

With time I got used to it. But, despite her lessons, I never managed to transform. This bothered her a lot. I didn't understand why and finally got up the courage to ask.

"I am part of the ruling class, what we call the Patriciat," Tess explained. "One of the distinguishing features of the Patriciat is that we can transform. As I am only allowed to marry a man from the Patriciat, if you cannot transform, we would never be able to marry."

So what! Being with Tess in that house was all I wanted. Although she was delighted to be there, she didn't see things the same way. She was bound by tradition. In our world we pay less attention to customs. Maybe that was why I misjudged her reaction. When I suggested we return to my world, she was uncomfortable. She told me that would no longer be possible, but wouldn't tell me why.

I got jealous, thinking she had a husband, which would explain why we never left the forest. It was silly, I know, but I got angry and insisted she explain. It was with tears in her eyes that she told me.

"Shortly after I returned from your world, my father forced me to marry a man from the Patriciat. I had no choice. The guy was kind and understanding. I told him all about you and he accepted what I said..."

I was astonished and hurt. "So he knows you are here!"

"He does."

I felt confused and angry. In one way I had what I wanted, but in another way I could never have it. I didn't think in terms of possession as some men do when they think of marriage and women, but all the same, that she lived with a husband seemed like an insurmountable barrier. Tess must have seen my bewilderment because she advised me to take a long walk and think things over. I didn't want to leave her. Maybe she would be gone when I returned. But she reassured me she would stay.

I walked for hours, chewing over everything that had happened but I couldn't decide what to do. When night fell, I used the ring, as she had shown me, to guide me back to the house. I was relieved to find her waiting for me. I couldn't help feeling that these were our last hours together. We made love that night, but our lovemaking was tainted with a sadness that gave our embrace a desperate feeling.

The next morning, Tess announced that she had to return to her house. "I will be away for a week or two, but if you agree, I would like you to stay here and wait for me. While you were out yesterday I fetched food and I have also brought a selection of my father's books about magic and transformation. You could also use the time to practice the things I taught you."

I don't think Tess was sure if I would stay. I certainly hesitated a long time. But finally, my mind made up, I said: "I will stay for a while. Who knows, maybe we will be able to find a solution." I didn't believe my words, but a part of me wanted to. So I stayed on and read the books she'd brought me and practiced the magic she'd shown me.

The books were fascinating and I devoured them. I had never found the like in our world. The authors clearly stated what they knew and didn't try to hide their knowledge in arcane terms. Despite the clearness of the words, it wasn't always easy to understand. The concepts were complex and the world vision quite unfamiliar.

The days went by and days turned into weeks and she didn't return. Instead I found that new books had been left for me in what had become my study and the larder was always full. As I had done before, I plunged into my studies, fascinated by what I found. Here was a completely different view of the world that threw my earlier studies of Shamanism into a completely different light. I could see how to extend my research along new avenues that came closer to my desire for a more practical approach.

It was at that time I had the idea of setting up a unit in the university to continue my work. As the idea evolved and developed I began to want to return to my world and carry it out. I calculated that I must have been in that house for nigh on twelve months and it was time to go home. I had no way to communicate my resolve to Tess so I decided to leave a note on my desk guessing that someone must bring me the new books when I wasn't there or was asleep and that person would take my message to her.

Two days later I found a note scribbled on a paper on my desk. It said: I haven't been able to come and I regret that greatly. Now I can travel again and will come and see you tomorrow morning. xxx.

I wondered what had stopped her coming. Had Tess been seriously ill? Or had her husband finally decided he didn't like her being with me and locked her up? My head was full of wild stories. The turmoil was so great that I was sure I wouldn't be able to sleep, but in fact I slept profoundly all night.

"Talking of sleep, maybe you should have a rest," Sally said. "I'm sure we can wait a few hours to hear what happened next."

Rafter looked confused, as if he had been immersed in the story. He was very pale and his face was pinched with pain. Mae came forward and offered him some medicine. Then he closed his eyes and lay his head back on the pillow.

"Let's all go next door," Mae suggested and one by one they filed out, leaving only Sally sitting next to the Professor, holding his hand.

"A most wonderful story," she whispered, more to herself than to him. Looking up she saw he'd opened his eyes again and was looking at her.

"It's all for you," he said then closed his eyes and slept.

A locked door

When Sally joined the others she found everybody clustered around Mae. What was going on? Then she heard Mae sob.

"What's the matter?" she asked.

Mae was such a dependable, solid sort of person. To see her helpless and bewildered, it was as if someone had removed the support Sally had unwittingly been clinging to. She too felt helpless.

Mae was seated in one of the dining room chairs with Keira on one side and Brent on the other. Jenny, Martin, Anju and Dieter were also there but Fran and Martin had gone off to the kitchen to prepare a snack. Sally crouched in front of Mae and laid her hands on the young woman's knees, looking up at her.

"This story is going to end tragically," Mae said. "I'm sure of it."

"Do you mean that Rafter's lover will die?" Brent asked.

Mae shook her head. "I don't know. I just feel there is a great sadness and loss coming."

"Here. Try this," Fran said handing Mae a large slice of chocolate cake. "Martin says it's a good remedy for sad stories."

Everyone laughed.

Mae wiped the tears from her eyes and took a bite. "Mm! Delicious!

"Maybe we all need a slice of your magic cake," Keira told Fran.

"You're just hungry because you've got nerves about the concert tonight," Brent joked.

"You can talk, you silly little girl!" Keira replied, prodding him in the ribs.

"I wouldn't make fun of Sarah, if I were you," Jenny said. "She might work you into one of her stories."

Everybody laughed.

There's some truth in that, Vee commented.

You're just jealous, Sally retorted.

Martin emerged from the kitchen, pushing a trolley loaded with tasty snacks.

"I didn't expect you to start with the desert," he commented. "But why not."

Once again everybody laughed. Things seemed back to normal.

Mae got to her feet saying that she had some work to do and left the room. Unsure that Mae had properly recovered, Sally followed her.

"Mae," she said, seeing the young woman put on her coat. "Where are you going?"

"To the university. I've forgotten some important papers."

"Do you mind if I come? I can drive if you like."

Mae agreed.

She looks relieved to have company if you ask me, Vee said.

Sally felt uncomfortable with this new, weaker side of the woman.

"Where do you want to go on the campus?" Sally asked once they had settled in the car Rafter had loaned them.

"The Department." Mae lapsed into silence as they drove into town and across the bridge over the River Bree. "I feel like I am being sucked into something that I didn't choose."

"You mean the Dream Class?"

"No. The Dream Class is a part of my life. No. There is something new coming. Something big. I can feel it. And it's going to break over us like a tidal wave."

A premonition, Vee said, putting a word to it.

"Vee says you have a premonition."

"I suppose you could call it that. But I don't want it to happen. I can feel myself shaking inside even though I have no idea what is coming."

Sally laid a reassuring hand on Mae's knee as she brought the car to a halt near the tiny footbridge that led across to the island on which the Department had been built.

"Let's go find those papers," Mae said, freeing herself from Sally's hand.

At the main door to the Department they met the caretaker who was locking the main door.

"What a busy evening!" the woman commented, clearly irritated by the fact.

"What do you mean?" Mae asked.

"Well before you, the police were here."

Mae glanced at Sally as if to say: is this the trouble I'm expecting to happen?

"Amazing. What did they want?" Mae asked.

"They wanted to investigate something in Professor Rafter's office. They didn't tell me what. Nobody ever tells me anything. So if you two don't need my help, I'll be getting back to my series. I've already missed more that half of it."

"Good night," Sally and Mae said, and they entered the Department.

Both of them must have had the same idea because they hurried up to Rafter's office taking the stairs two at a time. The door was locked.

"He never locks his door," Mae commented, pulling out the spare key Rafter had given her. Stepping inside and switching on the lights, nothing seemed out of place. "Odd. I wonder what the police were looking for."

Maybe they have already taken what it was, Vee suggested.

Sally walked over to Rafter's desk, remembering all the times she'd had seminars in that room. A wave of nostalgia rolled over her. How strange to be there without him. She sat down at his desk and glanced through the small pile of books standing there, while Mae walked around the room looking for clues. All the books bore familiar titles except the last one. It had been covered in crumpled brown paper. She pulled it from the pile and flipped it open. To her shock it was full of pictures of naked children in suggestive poses. Her gasp caused Mae to join her at the desk.

"Where did you find that?"

"Under this pile of books." Sally couldn't help putting two and two together and coming up with a very uncomfortable sum.

It's a plant, Vee announced, very sure of himself.

"Someone must have put this here to incriminate the Professor," Sally said, voicing Vee's thoughts.

Mae took the booklet from her and flipped through the pages. A postcard-sized photo fluttered out and landed under the desk. Sally reached down and picked it up.

"God Lord!" she swore. "Look at this!"

She laid the photo on Rafter's desk. In it Dieter was kissing Anju. That in itself was not so worrying, but the photo depicted his hand firmly pressed between the young girl's legs.

It's a fake, Vee said.

"Vee says it's a fake," she told Mae. "It was taken this afternoon in the park when they were practicing with An's friends."

"I wonder why the police didn't find this booklet if they searched the place?" Mae asked.

"Because they found something else instead, Vee suggests."

"So this is how they planed to discredit us," Mae exclaimed, clasping the back of Rafter's chair with clenched fists. "The bastards!"

"Let's get out of here," Sally suggested, "in case the police come back."

She stuffed the compromising book and the photo in her coat pocket. They hurried to Mae's office and picked up the papers she needed and headed for the exit. From the shadows of the unlit corridor they could see a man fumbling with a bunch of keys outside the main door. Neither of them recognised him. They both had the presence of mind to remain concealed as the man gained access to the Department and hurried up the stairs. Mae and Sally tiptoed after him, just in time to see him opening Rafter's door.

If the man had closed the door, there would have been no way to get inside without him knowing, but he'd left the door ajar and hadn't switched on the light. Whoever it was, was in a hurry. Peering round the door, Sally saw the man searching Rafter's desk. When he didn't find what he was looking for, he got down on his hands and knees and searched the floor.

Both Mae and Sally stood in the shadows at the back of the room, concealed amongst the many armchairs. Mae pulled out her phone, alarming Sally who thought she might try to phone someone. Instead she prepared to take a photo. When the man emerged from under the desk he sat down heavily in Rafter's chair putting his chin on his hands.

"Where could it be?" he muttered. "Bloody hell. What if the police got hold of it?"

While he spoke, Mae managed to take several photos.

I hope it works in low light, Vee commented.

The man was getting more and more agitated. What can we do? She asked Vee. I don't have Brent's talent, she thought.

Why not use transformation to scare him?

Why not indeed!

She made a sign to Mae to keep quiet and she transformed Rafter's desk lamp into a snake. The man didn't notice at first till the snake slithered across his hand and started to wind it way around his neck. He screamed and jumped back, but the snake held on to him. He fell to his knees and started praying out loud.

"Mary, Mother of God, protect me!" He repeated the phrase over and over to no effect. The snake happily wound its way several times around his neck.

Sally stood up and switched on the light causing the man to scream again. When he caught sight of her he began frantically making the sign of the cross in front of him.

"Keep away from me, witch," he said in a strangled voice.

"I think we've caught an adept of the Starless Square," Mae commented as she stood up too. "How is Dr. Frick?"

"What have you done to him?"

Sally ignored his question and transformed the power cable to the lamp into another snake and had it wind its way around his leg. He screamed again.

"I ain't done nothing," he pleaded. "Let me go."

His words made Sally furious. "Do you call burning young women doing nothing?"

To her surprise she found she could control what the snake did. She made it wind its way further up his leg so that its fangs got closer and closer to his groin. He desperately tried to push it away but he didn't want to be bitten either.

"So what are you doing here?" she asked. "Tell us and we might let you go unharmed."

He remained stubbornly silent. She had the snake bite into his trousers at the top of his thigh. He screamed again.

"Why did you leave that dirty book here?" Mae asked.

"It was just a joke."

"You call that a joke?" Mae said taking a step forward. Sally put out a hand to hold her back.

"What else did you leave?" Sally asked.

"An envelope with photos in it."

"Like this one?" Sally asked, brandishing the photo of Anju and Dieter.

The man looked relieved. "So you've got the book?"

"I have indeed," she said, her voice filled with determination. "Why do you want it so badly?" Sally asked.

"It's got my name in it."

"Well I am going to give it back."

Mae looked shocked. "That's evidence against him."

"Don't worry," Sally reassured her.

Sally glanced at the name scribbled on the inside of the back cover, laid the little book open on the desk and took several cautious steps back. The man must have thought he was reprieved, although the snake was still wound around his neck. But the book began to tremble on the flat surface as Sally willed the transformation to take place. Out of the dog-eared pages of the book burst tiny replicas of the children depicted in it.

The sight was extraordinary. She could hardly believe she had caused it to happen. The children tumbled out of the book, rolled over on the desk and jumped to the floor. By the time their little feet hit the carpet they had grown to their full size and each stepped forward, leaving room for more to follow from other pages of the book.

They might have been small and naked, but they had teeth and nails and strong fingers. Snarling and cussing with rage, they flung themselves at him, ripping at his clothes, tearing out his hair, biting into his arms and neck and legs. He screamed as he tried to fend them off, but more and more children tumbled out. Some went straight for the man's sex, which he desperately tried to protect, but there were too many of them. They sneered at him as his sex hung limp and shrivelled in front of him and mocked his inadequateness.

More than twenty children in various stages of undress strove to get their revenge. In the confusion he managed to wriggle free of the seething mass of bodies, but only to find he was cornered in one of the bay windows. The children advanced on him, claws outstretched.

"Look what you have done to us," one of them growled.

"It wasn't me!" he pleaded. "Please!"

"Do you think it made any difference when we pleaded with you and your like?" a young girl spat. "You never paid attention to our pain and suffering!"

He cowered back against the window that was slightly open.

Careful. He's going to jump, Vee warned.

"Wait!" Sally shouted, pushing her way through the children trying to reach him.

The fetid, fishy stench almost made her gag. The man must have thought she was going to attack him too because in desperation he flung himself out of the window before she could get to him. She expected to hear the splash when he hit the water as the river flowed right under the window. But all she heard was a muffled sucking sound as if he'd been swallowed whole by some slimy monster.

She clapped her hands, causing the children to disappear, although the stink continued to hang in the air. A glance at Mae showed how terrified the young woman was. She was shaken herself. Her arms and legs were trembling. It was not just what she'd seen that shocked her. Above all it was what she'd done. Her abilities had never seemed so

144

alien and frightening.

"It was just an image," she said hoping to reassure both Mae and herself.

Sally crossed to the window and leant out trying to see what had happened to the man. At first she could make out nothing in the dark along the shaded riverside, but little by little her eyes adjusted. It was low tide and the man had landed feet first on the mud flats. She could see him struggling to get away, hampered by the mud that clung to his feet and legs as he sank deeper and deeper with each step. Good riddance, she thought, although she had some qualms about the fact that he might drown if he continued wading towards the centre of the river.

Mae went over to the desk and picked up the booklet gingerly with her fingertips, trying to touch it as little as possible, as if some of its filth might rub off on her and stain her forever. Sally couldn't help worrying that the children might come tumbling out again. But nothing happened. Mae flung the book out of the window, trying to throw it as far away as possible. Quite by chance, it hit the man on the head and fell right in front of him. They were both deeply relieved to see it gone.

Checking that she still had the photo of Anju and Dieter in her pocket, Mae said: "Let's get out of here!" and they hurried out of the building, using one of the side doors in case the main entrance was being watched. "We have to inform the others," Mae said as they hurried back to the car, keeping to the shadows all the way.

Fake

"So what do you think, Chief?" Mandy asked, sure he'd side with Jock.

"If it really is a fake," her boss replied, "I'm not so sure that it is a simple case of trying to frame someone. It just doesn't add up."

It wasn't his fault, but the Chief Constable had a lisp and was very self-conscious. He'd developed an unfortunate tic: he was continually putting his hand in front of his mouth making it difficult to understand what he said. Meetings with him were a real strain. You had to listen carefully to be sure you understood. Mandy wondered how he'd managed to get into such a position of authority. Not that he was bad at his job. He was a proficient policeman and the station was well run.

"I can't understand why anyone would bother to take the risk? This professor must have something to hide."

Jock grinned with evident satisfaction.

The phone rang. The Chief answered. "It's for you," he said surprised, handing Mandy the receiver.

It was the caretaker at the university. She'd been walking her dog along the towpath, when she'd heard screams coming from the Theosophy Department or maybe the river beyond. No she hadn't been to check. She was too afraid. Mandy promised they would investigate and hung up. The Chief looked at her questioningly.

"A new lead at the university. The caretaker heard screams coming from the building or maybe the river nearby."

The Chief rose from his desk and donned his cap. "Let's go and check this out."

The caretaker was waiting for them when they arrived. She let them in and trailed behind as they climbed to the Professor's office.

"Somebody must have been here," Jock pointed out. "The door was locked. Whoever it was must be trying to cover something up."

Why did Jock always jump to conclusions? She wanted to point it out, but she didn't dare in front of the boss. Instead she looked around the room. At first sight, nothing was out of place. Then Mandy noticed that the light over the desk was missing. She looked around, but found it nowhere.

"How odd," the caretaker said. "It's hardly worth stealing. They're quite cheap."

Mandy went and looked closer at the desk. Several books had slithered off the pile and lay at odd angles across the desk. "These books have been moved."

"Was the window open?" the Chief asked.

"What did you say?" the caretaker asked cupping her hand behind her ear.

"I think the window was open," Mandy said, trying to cover for her Chief.

The Chief leaned out of the window, looked down and then popped his head back in. "Either of you got a torch?"

Jock produced his and handed it over.

"There's somebody down there stuck in the mud," the Chief informed them in a matter-of-fact voice. "The tide is rising and the person will drown if we don't act. Jock, call the station and have them get a boat out." He turned to the caretaker. "When did you hear the screams?"

"Eight-thirty. I was walking the dog by the river during the commercials."

"Get a full statement, Mandy, and we'll meet back at the station in thirty minutes."

The men left together.

When Mandy returned to the station she went straight to the Chief's office. The man was on the phone, but indicated she should stay.

"That was Jock," he said putting down the receiver. "He is by the river with the people in the boat. They've rescued the man. He was lucky he didn't fall on his head in the mud when he jumped from the window."

Mandy wonder how the Chief could be sure he'd jumped. Maybe the man had been pushed.

"The odd thing is that his clothes were all torn and he was bitten and scratched all over. He was covered with lots of tiny, bloody marks. Whatever happened to him it has driven him stark raving mad. He kept gibbering on about being attacked by a hoard of naked children. Jock could get no sense out of him. Jock told me he thought it might be witchcraft."

This whole case was so weird. It reminded her of stories about black magic and voodoo. Surely not in Avan. An involuntary shiver ran down her spine.

"We found one more thing," the Chief informed her, embarrassed. "He had one of those flexible desk lamps wrapped around his neck with the electric cord tied around his leg."

Mandy burst out laughing, she couldn't help herself, maybe it was her nerves. She had some difficulty stopping her giggles when her Chief stared at her disapprovingly.

"This is hardly funny." He looked furious. "The man was grasping a small book in his hand full of pornographic pictures of children. Inside the back cover was a name: Glat." He asked her to check the records for the name.

"I don't need to," she told him. "I know who he is. He is Peter Glat. We hauled him in on a possible arson charge. Two women almost got burnt alive in their house. But we couldn't press charges because there was not enough evidence. I believe he's also being investigated for running a porn ring, buying and selling dubious pictures some of which are of children. We've never been able to catch him red-handed."

"Well we've caught him now, although there's not much left."

Mandy felt very uncomfortable about the whole case. It was beginning to frighten her and she'd never been frightened before. She wanted to confide in the Chief, but hesitated. He wasn't tolerant of signs of weakness, especially in women. She didn't want to appear stupid or, worse, superstitious.

"I have an odd intuition about this case," she told him, taking the risk. "It gives me the creeps," she admitted. "The way Glat was treated reminds me of things I have read about witchcraft and black magic. Maybe Jock is right." She didn't like admitting it. "When those two women were nearly burnt alive, someone suggested it might have been a witch hunt and the fire was meant to be a pyre."

He laughed. "You've been reading too many novels, Mandy." He patted her on the shoulder in what was supposed to be a fatherly way. Instead his gesture was dismissive, if not insulting. She had expected as much, and although she suspected he might be right, she still felt disappointed.

"Go find out where this Glat lives and I'll get a search warrant. See if you can find out where that young girl lives and the man who was in the picture with her. Maybe they know something."

Doubts

"Did you know that predicting the future was classified as witchcraft and was punished by burning at the stake?" Keira was telling Tom when Sally and Mae arrived back. "Professor Trundle told me. He's quite an expert on the subject."

"Thank heavens I haven't managed to foresee the future," Tom replied.

Despite his attempt at humour, he was clearly peeved at his inability. Most of them, Sally thought, had developed their gifts spontaneously and had not had to work to develop them. Tom had no such luck.

"Not only do I not know what to look for, but I haven't figured out how to understand it. Jenny suggested thinking of the present as a map. Brent said I should see it as potential stories and look for those that were the most promising. Anju told me about the force fields she sees in combat that enable her to anticipate people's moves. But none of these metaphors work for me."

Sally patted Tom on his shoulder. "Well I have something new for you to struggle with," Sally told him and she went on to describe what had happened at the university, keeping quiet about the episode when the children attacked the man.

Anju was shocked to hear about the photos of her and Dieter and how they were being used against them.

"I was always afraid something like this might happen." Dieter sounded resigned. "People refuse to understand the love of an older man for a younger girl. They readily twist it into something ugly and then lash out with their judgements."

"Maybe because many older men are enamoured of young girls, if the truth were known," Tom put in.

"That maybe so, but it is not at all the same thing," Anju said vehemently. "They are often in love with an image, something they feel they lack and believe they are not allowed to have, not a real person they want to be with."

Anju slung her arm around Dieter's neck and leaned over to kiss him, but he pushed her away. Sally could see Anju was hurt by his rebuff. She was about to say something, but Anju beat her to it.

"Dieter, do you love me?"

His suffering was clear for everybody to see. "I do. But I don't want our love to hurt you. This sort of thing is liable to get very messy and painful."

Then Anju did the most startling thing: she hit him. He staggered back under the blow. A tense silence filled the room. Everyone was astounded and shocked at her behaviour.

"What do we learn in combat?" she asked fiercely, as he rubbed his shoulder where the blow had landed.

"To go with the energy of the strike and use it against the person who attacks," he replied, looking perplexed at her question.

"Then why did you let me hit you?"

He hesitated, thoughtful, then replied: "Because maybe I thought I deserved it. That you were angry at me for getting you into this mess..."

"You feel guilty," she summarised. "Do I love you?"

He rubbed his shoulder again. "You do."

"And do I blame you for us being in love?"

He hesitated. "No."

"Then why do you stand there paralysed when others try to make you feel guilty if you are not?"

He didn't answer.

"Should you not try to see how you can use their energy to your advantage?"

He remained silent.

"Didn't you implicitly invite them to attack you because you yourself thought you were guilty?" And she abruptly burst into tears. "I'm sorry," she apologised, wiping her eyes. "I too am accusing you. It was not my intention."

"There is nothing sordid or degrading about your relationship," Sally observed. "Neither of you dominates or abuses the other."

"Only in unarmed combat," Dieter teased, half-heartedly.

"You never forced yourself on me," Anju pointed out. "In fact, you were extremely cautious, too much so for my liking."

Everybody laughed.

"When I first met you," Dieter said, "you exasperated me, but you fascinated me too. I will always remember that first combat in the basement. I just couldn't understand how you could get the better of me, but I agreed to let you teach me. When I realised I was in love with you and that you loved me too, I wanted to run away. The perspective terrified me. You were less than half my age. All my education told me that loving you was wrong. I suspected myself of all the basest motives, even though it wasn't true. I believe I was also frightened of being in love. The feelings I had and still have for you were so strong that I was afraid they might carry me away. The time we spent together in the Reaches helped a lot, especially because we worked so well together teaching those women. I had no time to worry about what our being in love meant. The people there accepted our relationship as quite natural. When we returned to Avan, I made up my mind that I was prepared to face whatever happened so we could be together. But this malicious photo business caught me off guard. I'm sorry."

Anju, who had been silently listening to his speech, took his hands in hers and pulled him into a tender embrace. "I love you," she whispered.

"And I love you too."

"Love is a very strange thing," Tom said, looking at Jenny. "I have known Jenny since we were at school. She just seemed the right person for me. There was never any doubt in my mind that we would spend our lives together."

Jenny chuckled and nodded her head in agreement.

"And even though my parents, who were real snobs, wanted me to study medicine and tried to separate us, saying she was a bad influence because she was an artist, we stayed together. And I'm really glad we did."

"It wasn't easy," Jenny added. "We had nearly no money. Luckily you were able to get a job as a journalist and I sold some paintings so we managed to live simply but happily together. And Martin, my brother helped a lot."

Martin was standing in the entrance to the kitchen next to Fran. "I had long seen that you two were hopelessly in love. Your being together was the most natural thing in the world but, at the same time, I couldn't help feeling jealous because I had nobody."

Fran ruffled his hair and snuggled up close.

"Then I got lucky," Martin said with a broad grin. "I met a delightful German girl who was on the run and I fell head-over-heals in love with her. The only person who tried to come between us was an evil man called Leuchtli, but we managed to give him the slip," he said running his hands over her shaved head.

"You think you've had a hard time!" Brent said as if he'd been the victim of a profound injustice. "I have three women in my life and they keep wanting me to choose between them."

Everyone burst out laughing except Keira who looked a bit put out.

"Even now, if I mention one before the other I am likely to be in serious trouble. So I'll mention first the one who isn't here: Lucie, the Keeper's Daughter. She saved my life and brought me back from desolation. My love for her is complex. She's like a mother and a sister to me and although we were never lovers, I know we love each other. Maybe we will never be lovers. Maybe we'll never be a couple like you all are," he said, looking at Dieter and Anju. "But I still love her."

"And then there's Keira or Mia as she was called in the Dream World. We had a torrid love affair in which she coaxed me out of my timidity and taught me all manner of things about sensuality and sex. I could probably write a practical manual based on that experience."

Everybody laughed again.

"In a prophetic sort of way, she prepared me for the transformation that occurred when I became Sarah." He paused to take a breath.

"I'm sure there are more things I can teach you if you want," Keira invited, sucking her thumb in a most suggestive way.

"I am still drawn to you," Brent admitted, smiling at her jest. "There are many times when I would like to forget myself in your arms."

"What are waiting for?" Keira asked.

"It's complicated," he said and he glanced at Sally.

"I love Sally," he told them. Hearing him say it in front of everyone made her heart flutter. "I must have been a bit blind not to have realised it before. Now I can see I was in love with her ever since the very first time we met at Alo's place, even if I showed no signs of it then."

Keira shook her head in disbelief. "You may not have known it, but everybody else could see it. I remember thinking you were going to steal my Sally away and that the only way to stop you was to make a play for you myself."

Brent looked astonished. Dieter chuckled.

"Looks like we are not the only ones with problems," he said to Anju.

Sally took hold of Brent's hand and, pulling Keira closer, she kissed them both.

"I think we are going to need some more chocolate cake," Martin said, "if this goes any further." Everybody laughed.

It was then that Sally noticed Mae curled up in an armchair, her head in her arms. "What's the matter?" Sally asked, placing her hand softly on the nape of Mae's neck.

Mae burst into sobs. Everyone gathered round. "I've never had anybody," she complained between the sobs. "I spent all my life caring for others and I completely forgot myself. Even when I was little, with my foster parents, I tried my hardest to stop them fighting. They were always arguing and shouting at each other. I hated it. I just wanted to be surrounded by people I loved and who loved each other and me."

Sally handed her a handkerchief. She was surprised to discover that Mae was an orphan like herself. Mae had never mentioned it.

"I enjoy being with you all because there is such a strong bond between us. I love being able to do things for you and to make everything work out. But I deeply wish I had a love of my own. OK. I love the Professor. I love him like a father, almost. It's a tender sort of love that almost hurts. But it's not the same."

"I think we all love the Professor," Sally said. And looking at those gathered around Mae she could see them nodding in agreement.

"I may not be able to read the future so well," Tom said, "but my crystal ball tells me you'll have someone very special in your life quite soon."

Mae laughed as tears ran down her cheeks. "Thank you, Tom. I couldn't ask for more." And everybody hugged everybody in a swirling mass of bodies.

It's like New Year's Eve, Vee commented. By the way, he added, nobody bothered to ask me whom I love!

Sally broke from the round of hugs and kisses and clapped her hands to get people's attention. "Vee wants me to speak for him. All the other men have spoken and he wants to have his say."

Now you've got me embarrassed, Vee said.

Just get on with it, she said, teasing him.

"To most of you, there is no difference between me and the person I love," Sally said for Vee. "In the beginning that was not the case. I was the most hateful thing to Sally. All she wanted was to be rid of me, whereas I couldn't live without her. A bit like Anju was saying about images, only far worse: each of us was an image to the other. Sally saw me as a filthy voyeur who was always prying into her most intimate moments. And I saw her as my impossible shining salvation that I felt deeply guilty about wanting."

Sally felt a bit odd about being Vee's voice. "You have to realise," she clarified, "that the view on things that Vee is expressing is new to me too. I don't know everything he thinks. We are not just two facets of the same person."

Having said that she returned to being Vee's mouthpiece. "With time we got to know each other better. You might say that the two-dimensional photos we had of each other took on other dimensions and became more alive and real. Yes, we were lovers, but only briefly. Most of the time, our being close was more like brother and sister. Then that fateful day in the Lost Meadows my body was blown away and all that was left of me was this voice in Sally's head."

Sally was finding it quite a stress to relay Vee's thoughts. Just a little while longer, he pleaded.

"You think you have problems. Imagine I am inside Sally's body as she makes love to Brent. I who care more for her than anybody else. I have to feel her love for him burning through me. I once told Sally I was not jealous. That is not strictly true. Thank heavens I have no control over her voice or her movements because I might be tempted to do something drastic. Having said that, I know I never would. I love Sally too much to hurt her, even if my being with her all the time, hurts me sometimes."

Sally was exhausted and sank onto a chair.

"It's time to go," Keira said, pulling Brent gently out of Sally's arms. "Sarah shouldn't be late for her moment of triumph," she joked, grabbing hold of Sally's hand too and pulling her towards the door as well. People were donning hats and coats in the hallway, but Mae hung back, a sad look on her face.

"Why don't you go with them, Mae," Fran said. "Martin and I will look after the Professor till you get back."

"Come on Mae," Brent encouraged. "You might meet that man you are looking for!"

Mae pulled a face, but began putting on her coat. "Thanks Fran. Thanks Martin. Look after the professor for us."

Chapter 7 ~ Two Stars

A hunch

"I've brought along Professor Trundle. No need for introductions, I suppose. You must know him much better than I do. I think he might be able to help us," Tom said once all the Watchers were seated around the table in their familiar warehouse. "Thanks for coming Professor despite the fact you had no idea what we wanted from you."

"You had me intrigued," Trundle said.

"I'm following a hunch, so I might be completely wrong, but it's worth a try." Tom wasn't even sure he could explain it to himself, let alone to anyone else. "The future can often be unpredictable, and in our present case that seems to be so. How could we possibly have known they planned to try to set fire to Irina? And what possible connection could there be between that and the child pornography they tried to plant in Rafter's office? Despite appearances, I suspect there is a logic to it that I will call 'associative', for want of a better word."

This really must seem confusing, he thought. It certainly was to him.

"Please excuse me if I'm not clear. I'm reaching out for something that is just beyond my grasp."

"Don't worry about us," Kean said. "Reach ahead!"

"What if all the strategies these people use against the Department and its events this weekend are loosely linked to one central element?"

"And what might that be?" one of the Watchers asked.

"The Starless Square! I mean the witch-hunts and the burning of witches. What if everything they do is related in one way or another to a constellation of elements to do with witchcraft and witch-hunts?"

"I begin to see why you asked me to help," Professor Trundle said. "But tell me more, so I can get a better idea of where you want to go."

Tom handed Kean a long roll of paper who unrolled it on the table, covering most of the map, and then he handed him several felt-tipped pens.

"Let's jot down our central idea." He had Kean draw a black square in the centre of the paper. "We've had four of what might be called 'attacks' so far. There's the heckler during Rafter's talk who accused the professor of devil worship."

Kean wrote 'heckler' on the paper.

"Then there's the pack of wild dogs that were set on Rafter."

Kean added 'wild dogs'.

"Then there was the staging of a burning at the stake. And just a short while ago, they attempted to discredit us using lewd pictures of children."

Four ideas were grouped around a central black square.

"Now let's see if we can make the connections between these 'attacks' and witchcraft or the accusations against witches."

Trundle got to his feet and walked part of the way around the table. "One thing is obvious," he began. "Witches were accused of sacrificing babies and little children to the devil in their black masses. That would seem to tie in with the pornography part."

Tom was delighted and he had the impression the professor was too. The man certainly was enjoying himself.

"Then there's the devil worship that the man accused Rafter of. Worshipping the devil became the central accusation in many witch-hunts. And of course the pyre is obvious." He scratched his head. "I'm not sure about the dogs, though."

"So where do we go from there?" a Watcher asked.

"Maybe you should tell us, Professor, what the witches were accused of doing," Tom suggested.

"It changed over time and depended on who was accusing, but ordinary people mostly accused witches of souring crops, causing possession by the devil, starting fires, cursing people, bewitching them, making them ill, causing women to get pregnant or to loose their baby, sacrificing babies, flying through the air, attending orgies with the devil, being drugged, telling the future, … For the more learned, the main accusation was devil worship, the organisation of covens of witches and attempts to undermine the church."

Tom suggested Kean write a word or two on a small piece of paper for each accusation and place it on the table.

"Now the question is: which if any of these directions might inspire them this evening at the Arena?" Tom asked.

"Well they might try to set fire to the place," one of Watchers suggested.

Tom shuddered at the thought. It was his worst nightmare.

"And what if they tried to drug everybody?" someone else asked.

"Or they could let off stink bombs," another put forward.

"Most of the other things seem improbable," Trundle commented, "unless of course they cause an orgy by drugging the whole audience."

Everyone laughed.

"I don't want to eliminate any feasible suggestions, we should watch out for them all," Tom said, "but up to now they haven't attacked anyone else. They've always aimed at one of us."

There was a moment's silence then Kean said: "Well they could try to drug Keira or Sarah." Tom had an odd feeling about the suggestion. It did seem to fit. But how could he possibly be sure?

Dieter had not said a word so far. Tom wondered if he was still preoccupied by what had happened with Anju, but he looked neither absorbed nor absent.

"Your approach is interesting," Dieter, said. "I think it could add a more global and creative perspective that might go some way to thinking the unpredictable. In detective work we generally concentrate either on the individual or the context. Let me give you an example. If you were to investigate the man who tried to plant porn in the Professor's office, I bet you'd find he had some connection to porn himself either as a consumer or a seller or a producer. In many cases, people's knowledge and skills plus their connections and social background dictate what they do. If you know all about them, their behaviour is rarely unpredictable. But as we generally don't know who we are dealing with, what happens appears incomprehensible."

"Are you suggesting we profile all the members of the Starless Square?" Kean asked.

"If we had plenty of time and lots of money, we might do that."

"But aren't there criminals who deliberately set out to do the unpredictable to throw people off their trail?" Tom asked.

"Sure!" Dieter agreed. "But that requires a level of sophistication we don't have here. The guy who planted the pictures was clearly an amateur."

"So what do we know of the members of the Starless Square?" Tom asked.

Everyone put forward ideas: only one was an intellectual who'd been to university; another was a chemist, or at least worked in a chemist's; and then there was the builder who had a couple of people working for him; not to forget the pig farmer with his small, stinky farm; and someone who had something to do with pornography.

"Of course, we don't know all the members of the group," Tom pointed out. "But if we put together what we know already about the people and the ideas we had from the Starless Square, things like drugs or the fire or some electrical failure or even the stink bomb, might all work."

Tom glanced at his watch: it was time to leave. "Well let's go to the Arena and watch out for these things in particular. And thanks to you, Professor. Are you coming with us?"

Trundle laughed. "I think I might be a bit too old to go to such a concert. It'll be packed with young people like yourselves!"

"Of course you're not too old Professor," Kean said. "We'll find you a place at the Arena where you won't be bothered but you can follow the whole thing."

"Ok, then," Trundle agreed.

Before the show

Tom studied the entrance hall of the Arena. It looked somewhat forlorn with its bare concrete walls and arching steel pillars. The doors would open in an hour, so the audience had not yet started arriving. Only the technical staff and the security guards walked the wide corridors.

They were greeted by the head of security that took them on a guided tour. The man explained that the concert hall had been built ten years earlier and could seat up to two thousand. "The concert's sold out," the man told them. "For a last minute event, that must be a record!"

The building was wedged between the railway line and the seafront, close to the estuary of the River Bree on one side and, a little further away, the opening to the port on the other. The site had been chosen so that concerts would cause as little nuisance to the town as possible.

The stage had been reduced in size because Keira and Sarah didn't need much space and by doing so they could squeeze in several hundred people more. The girls were examining the sound system. A heated discussion seemed to be going on. Tom shifted his wheel chair closer to hear.

"We don't need microphones," Sarah was telling the technician.

"Nobody can sing in a place like this without a microphone," he insisted. "And you're not even going to sing. They'll never hear your voice at the back."

Sarah ginned at Keira. They must have anticipated this difficulty.

"You go stand at the back and see if you can hear me," Sarah suggested.

But the man turned his back on them and stormed off.

"Let it go," Keira said, and Sarah shrugged.

Tom waved to them and then followed the security man who was heading for the wings.

"Where is the fuse box?" Dieter asked.

There were several of them: one for lighting, another for the sound system and a third for the general electric system. All three were in different places. Not very easy to keep an eye on, Tom thought.

"Is there anyway someone could cut all the electricity in one go?" he asked.

The man gave him a puzzled look. "Are you folks expecting trouble?"

"We don't know. Maybe," Tom said. "We are just trying to be careful," hoping his words would reassure the man.

"Well there is a transformer outside the building close to the railway line. But you'd have to be a qualified electrician to switch that off."

Or maybe a builder, Tom thought.

There was very little that could burn in the building so a fire seemed unlikely, but Tom still asked about fire escapes and alarms. The place was linked to the fire station. If an alarm were set off, the fire brigade would come immediately. He also asked about smoke extraction, thinking of smoke bombs and stink bombs. There were large fans and an adequate ventilation system. It struck him that if anyone managed to cut the electricity the smoke extraction wouldn't work.

"What happens if there is a power cut?" he asked. "Will the fans still work?"

"Sure. They're on a separate circuit."

Well that was a relief.

"Have you ever had to evacuate the Arena in panic circumstances?" Dieter asked.

"No. But the architects were obliged to calculate the exits to allow everyone to get out in a hurry. It was one of the requirements of the building committee."

Their next port of call was the dressing rooms. As the only performers, Keira and Sarah had a whole corridor of dressing rooms. In reality they were sharing one of the smallest. That was were he and the others found them. The two girls were discussing their wardrobe, debating which colours to wear.

"I say we should wear black," Keira insisted.

Sarah turned up her nose. "I prefer bright colours."

"It might not be a good idea to wear black," Tom butted in.

"Why?" the girls asked in unison.

"We have a hunch that the Starless Square will try to take out the electricity. And if they do, the audience will see you better if you are dressed in white."

Sarah chuckled. When everyone looked at her for an explanation, she said: "That would sort out our argument with the sound technician. We simply won't have to worry about the mics."

"Maybe we should get in some candles to put on the stage," Keira suggested.

"As long as they can't be used to start a fire," Tom hastened to add.

The security man, who was still with them, had a suggestion too. "If you see the properties manager, I think you'll find we have see-through, fire-proof containers for large candles. In that case, you might want to rethink the stage design."

"Have we got time?" Sarah asked, clearly excited at the idea.

"If you come with me, we can see what props we've got available," he replied heading for the door. Sarah follow him.

"I have an idea for the lighting too," Sally mentioned.

She'd been huddled in a corner of the dressing room with Jenny. Tom had not noticed them on arriving. "But it won't need any props," she added with a laugh.

"If this goes on like this," Anju joked, "we'll have to turn off the electricity ourselves."

Everybody laughed and Tom wished they were right in their assumption. He shuddered at the thought of what else they might have to endure.

On the balcony

Sally wanted to get a closer look at the ceiling and walls of the

Arena, just in case. She wasn't sure her idea would shed much light, but at least it would be spectacular.

It's an enormous surface, Vee commented.

If I can turn fire to flowers, I can do this.

As long as you don't start turning water into wine.

You're exasperating, she told him, mentally giving him a shove.

She turned to Jenny who had accompanied her. "I've been thinking. We should combine our abilities more often, like when you and Keira worked to save Tom."

Jenny didn't look too happy about being reminded. Tom had almost died trying to save others.

"Why do you say that?"

"Because we'd be much stronger that way: not just individual stars, but a constellation."

"Sarah and I have planned to do a number together," Keira, who had joined them unnoticed, said.

"That's good news," Sally said, delighted. "All this talk of power failures has given me an idea of what I can do to add my own contribution. How about you, Jenny?"

"It's funny you should ask. I was just wondering if I could work on the overall energy of the Arena and the audience once they arrive. Maybe if I raise the energy level, the concert will be more of a success, or at least the audience will be more receptive to Keira and Sarah's work."

"And there is less likelihood of trouble," Keira put in.

"Maybe I should have done something similar for Rafter's talk. The idea just didn't occur to me," Jenny mused.

"You'll need a place to stay during the concert," Keira said. "You can't just stand in the middle of the audience."

Sally laughed at the image of her working magic from the middle of an unsuspecting crowd.

"There's a small balcony that overlooks the hall," Jenny informed them. "Tom's put Professor Trundle up there. I thought I might join him."

"Then I'll come too," Sally added. "It will be our centre of operations."

Keira started to move away saying: "I have to go back to the front of the hall to see what surprises Sarah has prepared for me."

All three laughed at the thought of Sarah's creativity unleashed on the poor property manager.

"Good luck," they both called after Keira.

"You too," she called back.

Sally greeted Professor Trundle.

"Any news of Professor Rafter?" he asked, concern in his voice.

"He was resting last time I saw him. He's in a lot of pain, but he tries to conceal it. He doesn't want to take too much medicine because he says it makes him drowsy."

"Do you think he would appreciate a visit?"

"I'm sure he would. Maybe you can drop by tomorrow afternoon."

He nodded and Sally turned to Jenny, but the young woman had closed her eyes and was clearly meditating. Tom arrived at that moment, wheeling his chair out onto the balcony.

"There's a ramp up to this floor, so I can get around without having to use the lift," he whispered, apparently not wanting to disturb Jenny. "I don't want to be trapped in here if some idiot decides to cut the electricity."

"I wanted to talk to you about that," Sally said moving closer. "The idea of us being without light gave me an idea for a transformation I could do and Sarah is staging a candlelight concert, so maybe we should make sure the light does get cut."

Tom chuckled. "If I were risking my life to cut the electricity, I'd be a bit put out to discover that it had already been done before I got there."

Jenny came and joined them.

"So?" Sally asked.

"There is already quite a high level of energy here. This place seems to resonate with the ring of standing stones on the other side of the river. I don't know why."

"I can maybe help there," Trundle told them. "Early writings point to a second ring of standing stones that stood here, close to the estuary. Maybe that is what you can feel."

"I can check if you like," Sally said. "Although I won't let the transformation occur as we are sitting right in the middle of it."

She closed her eyes and let the successive layers of history flash by in her mind's eye. "You are right Professor. There was an immense ring here, much bigger than the one in Hoyt Park." She closed her eyes again and focussed on the ring. Its centre was right in the middle of the concert hall.

"Jenny, can you see anything particular over there?" Sally said

162

pointing to what must have been the centre.

"Wow!" Jenny exclaimed. "I hadn't noticed that. It's like a giant fountain of energy."

Sally and Jenny glanced at each other and grinned. Sally guessed they'd both thought the same thing. "We're going to have to persuade Sarah and Keira to change some things," Sally said and she hurried away with Jenny in tow.

Their first stop was to examine the exact spot where the energy surged up out of the ground. There was a trap door in the floor nearby.

"Where does that go?" Sally asked the property master who was walking nearby.

"There's an underground passage to the dressing rooms. Occasionally we do theatre in the round and the passage let's actors get onto the stage unseen."

"Perfect," Jenny said and they ran over to the stage where Sarah was putting the final touches to her decorations.

"Sarah! Keira! We have discovered there is a great deal of energy shooting upwards in the middle of the Arena and we'd like to suggest you shift the stage there. The audience will be all around you, but that could add to the effect."

Keira looked a little unsure. "How do we get to the stage? We'd have to walk through the audience."

"Not at all," Jenny explained. "There's an underground passage that leads from there to the dressing rooms. Come and have a look."

Keira asked the property master to open the trap and they all went down to examine the passage. It was quite spacious and was lit by tiny emergency lights that a technician told them worked even if the electricity was cut.

"You want to put the stage here?" the property master asked.

"Yes," Keira said. "Would that be possible?"

"Sure. Easy. It's on wheels. All we have to do is to jack it up and roll it over here."

"And can we conceal the trap?" Sarah asked.

"No problem," the man told them. "Especially if you are working with very little light."

"What about the seating?" Keira asked.

"That's not so easy, but we should managed to change it in time."

In the dark

It was pitch black. How odd. The lights were all out. The place was deserted. Clyde stopped and cocked an ear. Nothing. Just a faint humming, far, far away. Weird. Had he got the wrong day? Typical. He glanced at his luminous watch. No. The day was right. See. I'm not so stupid. Must be a power failure.

He had only half an hour left. Maybe he shouldn't have taken the stuff. Seeing it there, it had been so tempting. Nobody would notice if a little was missing. Just a little. Well a bit more than a little. Half of it, actually, almost three quarters in fact. Why waste all that on the police? They wouldn't appreciate it. And anyway, it kinda got under your skin like that. Sort of irresistible itch!

Why not! Indeed. Why not? He hadn't taken any for a while. Surely he deserved a reward for being so adventurous. None of the others would have taken the risk. Lilly livered bunch! All of them! Didn't want his idea, did they? Typical. No taste. No sense of a good thing.

Blind, he felt his way down the corridor. Not so easy, damn it. The walls and floor kept pulsing despite the dark. He tried to will them to stay still, to no avail. The stuff was like that. Always made things go a bit strange. Good stuff too. Strong! Bloody strong! He giggled. Insane laughter bounced back off the naked walls. The sound startled him, setting him swaying in the darkness.

He promptly bumped into a half-open door sending up a resounding crash. He scuttled away along the corridor like a frightened insect and hid in one of the deserted dressing rooms. Shit. His heart was hammering. He'd have a bump on his forehead. He could feel it swelling.

Must be that twit Green. He wasn't supposed to cut the electricity. Couldn't trust him with anything. A growl behind him had him spinning round in terror. A tiger. He flung himself out of the way. And with a flash the lights came back on. Jesus! It was only a costume. Idiot!

Back out in the corridor he flipped the light switch. Dark again. He exhaled in relief. Safer that way. Dark? Well not completely. Four or five doors away, light flooded from a half open door. That must be the one they'd be using. He leaned against the wall. Thank heavens it had stopped pulsing. He listened.

All was still. He moved to tiptoe forward. But something was out of keel. So he tiptoed on the flats of his feet. He giggled at the idea, the back of his hand wiping his mouth. Giggling made him dribble.

He peered cautiously around the door. Small room. Large mirror. And the reflection of his own ugly face. A bright red bump filled the middle of his forehead below a shock a greasy black hair. His eyes were pitch black, the pupils wild and dilated. Satan's henchman he thought. Hold on. He was getting things muddled. It was the others that were meant to be with devil. He was on the side of good. He smiled. But his image leered at him.

Two white dresses hung on hangers. One small. The other larger. He wished he had his felt pen. To splatter them with his filthy thoughts. Dirty words. And bulging cocks. Anything to defile their virgin purity. But enough of that. Time was running out. He had to hide the goods. There were several drawers in the work surface below the mirror. All were empty. He slid the small packet to the back of one. What a waste. No really. He hesitated. Why not take a little more? Traces would be enough to incriminate the girls. Nah! Better not. Come on, Clyde, he told himself. Time to get out of here and call the police.

He glanced up at the mirror, alerted by a movement. Over his shoulder in the doorway stood the kid. She was leaning against the doorframe watching, her head cocked to one side, smiling. He didn't like that smile. It was frankly malignant. Terror twisted his guts. Daft twit. Get a grip. She can't be more than ten.

Wild stories spun themselves out in his head. He could force her to eat the stuff. She wouldn't know what'd hit her. He imagined kissing her little lips, forcing them apart, pushing his tongue into her mouth. He imagined his knee easing its way between her thighs. He couldn't help it, he was dribbling at the thought. He wiped his mouth clean and turned to face her.

She showed no fear. That was not right. Something was out of joint. Shouldn't she have run? Or screamed? Could he be imaging this? She seemed real enough. She continued to observe him, her piercing eyes making him ill at ease. She stood still, relaxed and confident, saying nothing. He took one step towards her. A threat, he thought, that ought to do it. But she didn't flinch. Instead she smiled, a vague look of concentration around her eyes.

"The heat was unbearable," a deep voice whispered in his ear. He turned to see where it came from. Nothing. Nobody. "Sweat poured down his brow…" And it did, indeed. He was soaked with it. He ripped off his jacket and tore at his shirt, popping the buttons as he did. He wiped the sweat from his eyes with the crumpled garment and tossed it to the floor. He fumbled with his flies, breaking the catch in his hurry to get his trousers off. And there he stood, naked and uncomprehending. What was happening to him? The girl had not moved.

"And the weather abruptly turned, bringing icy gusts off the snow covered northern mountains..." the voice continued in his head.

He was wracked by uncontrollable shivering. His teeth chattered wildly. He wanted to get dressed. Anything to keep the cold out. He wanted to scream. Enough! But his jaws were locked shut.

"He traced the marks of shame across his chest and brow..."

His eyes snapped up. She had thrown him a large black felt pen. He caught it. God knows how. Unstoppering it with his teeth, he traced savage hieroglyphs across his chest and arms. The felt pen continued down around his sex in concentric circles and along his legs like snakes. And then he traced signs on his face, a line from forehead to chin down his nose divided him in two. Incomprehensible squiggles below his eyes completed the design. He dropped the pen.

"Then he turned slowly towards the upheld mirror and looked into his own unfamiliar eyes...."

No! He wouldn't. No! No! But his head turned despite him. And there in the mirror stood a vile figure. The devil's henchman. Haggard. Hunchbacked. Hideous. He stepped back, repulsed, his teeth clenched tight against the bile that rose in his throat.

"Now take what is yours."

He knew exactly what the voice meant. He fought against it. But his hand stretched out and opened the draw. Reaching right to the back, he fumbled for the small packet. With trembling fingers he undid it, opened his lips wide, stuck out his tongue and emptied the contents into his mouth. It tasted foul. He closed his mouth and swallowed. His mouth was dry. Some of the powder clung to his tongue and lips.

"All of it!" the voice commanded.

He licked his lips and ran his tongue against the roof of his mouth till all had gone.

He could feel the first rush as the stuff began to work. Surely he'd taken too much. Panic burst into his brain like wildfire. Black spots danced before his eyes.

"Don't panic or you really will die."

He tried to relax but his chest was so tight he could hardly breathe. The black spots faded but the anxiety clung on.

"Now find yourself a quiet place and pray that you might be saved."

He staggered towards the door, only to realise that the girl had gone. Had she ever been there? He wasn't sure. Turning he grabbed the pile of clothes he'd thrown on the floor and staggered away down the corridor till be found a fire exit.

Outside the air was cold but somehow refreshing. He could hear the waves as they broke on the nearby beach. He shuddered, not with terror, but with joy. He couldn't comprehend what was happening. He crossed the road, dodging several cars and jumped down onto the beach. Casting his clothes into the waves, he ran naked along the sand, singing nonsense verses at the top of his voice. He flung himself onto the ground and rolled in the sand. It was still a little warm from the day's sun. It felt good. He wanted to curl up in it. But he had to go on.

He got to his feet and followed the beach, running bare foot on the wet sand till he could see the chapel that served to bless new boats. It had an immense door facing the sea. He tried it. It was unlocked. He heaved the thing open just enough to squeeze inside and fell to his knees in front of the altar. Angels swirled about him, but darker figures lurked in the shadows, their predatory eyes on him. Thank heavens the angels kept them at bay.

He closed his eyes and leaned forward till his forehead pressed against the cold flagstones. The swirling masses grew thicker and thicker till he felt like he was floating in a sea of spirits. He clung on for a long time, but, exhausted, he finally let go and drifted away.

Streaker

Jock's phone rang.

"Jock. Is that you?" the voice said.

"Yes chief," he replied, motioning to Mandy to wait for him.

"You two still on duty?"

"We were about to go off. What's the problem?"

"Some nut has been seen streaking across the Seafront Road near the Arena. Several motorists phoned to complain. Said it was a safety hazard!" The Chief could be heard chuckling over the phone. "Could you take a quick look?"

Jock glanced questioningly at Mandy who shrugged.

"Ok Chief. We're not far from there." He hung up. "A streaker! Haven't had one of those for a while."

"I thought they'd gone out of fashion." Mandy chuckled.

A streaker would bring some light relief after the business with Glat, Jock thought.

There was to be a big concert at the Arena, but the audience hadn't yet arrived. An immense poster hung above the entrance proclaiming: Two stars in concert! Two giant stars topped the text, white against deep blue. No names. No pictures. A cryptic message that, according to the radio he'd listened to earlier, had attracted a full house. He couldn't understand why so many people would flock to an amateur performance connected to the university.

The area along the seafront next to the Arena was relatively quiet. They crossed the road and looked along the beach. It was deserted. Only a dark heap broke the water's edge. A body? They hurried their pace, only to discover a sodden pile of clothes.

"The streaker?" Mandy grinned.

They fished the rags from the water and laid them over a bench at the edge of the beach. Buttons had been ripped from the cheap shirt. The trousers were torn around the zip. There was no underwear. In the pockets he found a phone that dripped seawater. He shook out as much as he could and wiped it on his sleeve before pocketing the phone.

"Left or right?" Mandy asked.

He had no idea. They stared in both directions. Some way along the front stood a small chapel. It was a familiar sight but tonight it's shape looked odd in the failing light.

"One of the doors is open," Mandy pointed out.

They only opened the doors when they wanted to bless a boat, Jock knew. "Let's go and have a closer look."

The two of them strode along the beach in the direction of the port. Jock took a deep breath of sea air. He loved this place. He glanced at Mandy out of the corner of his eye. He liked the sexy way she swung her hips. She seemed deep in thought. They'd known each other for a number of years. In the beginning he'd tried to flirt, but she'd made it clear she wasn't interested. So he kept his distance waiting for an opportunity. They were both single. Maybe she'd change her mind and he'd get a chance.

"I was right," she said, jerking him back from his reverie.

One of the two doors was open, moving gently too and fro in the breeze. All was dark and still inside. There was enough light for them to make out the altar. There were no pews. Jock pulled out his flashlight and sent the beam deep into the corners. The chapel appeared empty. He turned the light on the altar, a flat slab of marble supported by two vertical stones.

A dark form was huddled around the wooden cross. On closer inspection it turned out to be a man, his back turned to them, curled up in a foetal position with the cross between his knees and stomach.

Judging from the wheeze of his breath, the man was still alive. Jock shook his shoulder. The man was freezing, but didn't stir when touched. Jock rolled him onto his back to see if there were any wounds.

To their astonishment, the front of his body was marked with weird cabalistic signs. The wide circles around his sex reminded Jock of photos he'd seen of Australian aboriginal paintings. Snakes had been traced down his legs and arms. On his chest they could see strange words in characters and a language they didn't recognise. His face was a mess. He must have been hit on the forehead because a giant bump rose red and blue in its middle. A vertical black line divided his face in two, following the bridge of his nose, and each of his cheeks was tattooed with the same hieroglyphs as on his chest.

"Black magic!" Mandy exclaimed, clearly afraid of what she saw.

Jock had to admit she was right. The sight gave him the creeps. The blight seemed to be spreading.

He pulled out his phone and dialled the station. "Chief? We've found your streaker." He described the man lying in front of them. "You should send an ambulance. He's probably suffering from exposure."

When he hung up he saw that Mandy was hunting in the cupboards. "Trying to find something to cover him," she explained. "We don't want him to die before they get him to the hospital."

She came back carrying a white altar cloth and stretched it over the man. It was an odd moment. Here was a naked man, tattooed like a devil lying on an altar covered with a holy altar cloth, watched over by a couple of police. Jock wouldn't have been surprised if a witch had stepped out from behind the cross and greeted them.

"Hallo" a soft voice said, causing Jock to jump.

Mandy shrieked grabbing hold of Jock's hand.

"Don't be afraid. It's only me." The man on the altar slowly sat up and took stock of his surroundings. "Have the angels left?"

Neither Jock nor Mandy replied. They just stared. She was still holding his hand. He wasn't going to shake it off.

"They protected me, you know. Kept all those black things away." He got unsteadily to his feet, winding the long white tissue around his shoulders like a robe of office.

"How did you get here?" Jock asked, recovering first. He reluctantly let go of Mandy's hand. Having two police officers standing there, holding hands might not be appropriate.

"I was told to come."

"Who told you?"

"An angel. I think. I'm not so sure. Things are a bit blurred."

"And what's your name?" Mandy asked, apparently over her shock.

"Clyde. Clyde Marre."

A siren rang out in the nearby street.

"Come on Clyde," Mandy said, taking him gently by the arm. "Let's get you to a warmer place where you can tell us all about it."

The concert

A small, round podium stood raised above the surrounding seats in the middle of the giant hall. Four large cream-coloured candles in narrow glass containers stood alight at the four cardinal points of the stage. They reminded Sally of the candles that burnt in the cathedral. The house lights had been lowered to their minimum creating a hushed atmosphere such that the first arrivals whispered as they took their seats. From her vantage point on the small balcony she had a clear view of almost all the hall. Next to her sat Professor Trundle who was deep in discussion with Jenny.

"Yes, Professor. You were quite right. There used to be a ring of standing stones right here where the Arena is now…"

Tom was also there. He'd rigged up a microphone and earpiece so as to communicate with the Watchers and still have his hands free.

"Amazing! Drugs then," he whispered. When he'd finished he told everybody what Sarah had told him.

"Your guess was almost right then," Trundle congratulated him.

"I know. But he still managed to slip through unseen," Tom replied. "This place is too big for the number of people we have available."

The hall was filling rapidly, but the atmosphere remained hushed and expectant as people discovered the dimly lit auditorium with its four giant candles.

It makes people think they're in a church, Vee commented.

Sally spotted An who had arrived with her three young friends. They'd managed to find seats quite close to the stage, next to Anju and Dieter. Mae was there too with them, having taken time off from caring for the Professor. She also saw Irina with Moira and John as well as several of the younger members of the Department scattered here and there with friends.

There's your Collin, Vee said.

Are you going to annoy me about every man that takes an interest in me? Sally asked.

No. It's just that he's craning his neck in every direction looking for you, so if you don't want to be seen I suggest you sit back.

Her relationship with Vee had become strained since Brent had publicly declared his love for her. She wondered ruefully how life would be having an ongoing fight with someone in your head.

The doors were being closed and lights had been dimmed, leaving only the four candles to illuminate the space around the stage. That was Sally's cue. She shifted her attention to the ceiling, having it gradually transform into a bright starlit sky as it could only be seen from mountaintops. The Milky Way was clear to all, threading its path across the night sky.

The audience let out a collective gasp as they saw what had happened. Some even applauded. Sally felt for the standing stones and using their forms, she transformed the walls of the Arena, encircling the audience in a giant ring. A second gasp went up. They really hadn't been expecting anything like it. Sally concentrated on the sky again and had a crescent-moon rise majestically over the stones in the East. As a final touch she scattered a handful of shooting stars across the sky.

That was Keira's cue. Sally could see that she had already taken up her place on the stage next to Sarah, unnoticed as yet by the audience. Keira let out a faint sound that immediately found its match in the stones, setting a series of whirling choruses spinning around the Arena over the heads of the audience. From her vantage point, Sally could see people looking in every direction wondering where the music was coming from.

Glancing over her shoulder, Sally saw that Jenny was deep in concentration. She must be driving up the energy in the room, letting it cascade out from the central fountain. As Keira continued to feed the choruses, Sarah began speaking. Her voice carried crystal clear throughout the auditorium.

"In the beginning was the Word," she said, "and with the Word came the voices and through those voices reigned the music, bringing life to the world. Then, as now and for ever more."

Keira must have been calling on the women of the Sisterhood of the Stone, a group she had been invited to join in the Reaches. They could unite their voices over great distances and sing together even when they were worlds apart. At intervals around the ring, one by one other women's voices joined that of Keira's, calling and replying to each other with phrases of music that set off the responses of the stones. The effect was astonishing, even to Sally who had already heard Keira sing with the Sisterhood.

Sally caused the moon to grow as it rose in the sky till it was almost half full.

"A light breeze blew between the stones as the sisterhood joined in song, each from their respective world," Sarah said. And she made the call of an owl.

Professor Trundle jumped in surprise. The sound was so life-like, Sally wondered if Sarah had transformed into an owl. But no! She was standing upright next to Keira who continued to sing.

"Outside the ring a hoard of savages stalked closer, clubs and axes in hand."

A ripple of fear shot through the audience as the owl screeched again.

"Let us in!" Sarah shouted using a deep masculine voice.

As one the audience turned to look back at the ring behind them, trying to catch sight of the threat that was approaching.

"We know you are in there, witches. We've come to get you."

Something in Sarah's voice had caused the temperature to drop. People's breath hung before them in dull clouds caught in the starlight.

A violent hammering rang out from several places around the ring. It was Sally's turn to be startled. They hadn't planned this, yet it fit alarmingly well with the story Sarah was telling. She could see that Keira and Sarah were frightened too although they were concealing it well. Had they managed to conjure up something they couldn't control?

Tom rolled forward in his wheel chair and, tapping her lightly on the shoulder, whispered in Sally's ear. "It's the people outside in the foyer trying to get in. They are alarmed because they can't open any of the doors."

"It must be the ring that is blocking them," Sally said. She motioned to Jenny to come closer. "If we raise the energy even higher can we cut this whole place off from the noise of outside?"

"I'll try," Jenny replied, sounding dubious.

"You lift the energy and I'll do the rest."

She sent Vee to warn Sarah and Keira what was happening.

Both Mae and herself could transport people to other worlds, but they had never shifted more than fifty at a time. There were over two thousand people seated in the Arena. The immensity of the task was staggering. Thank heavens it wasn't necessary to transport them, just isolate them from outer influence for a short while. She would have welcomed Vee's advice, but he was off warning the two performers.

It might be sufficient to create an intermediary space around the ring, a bit like a giant bubble. She had explored such neutral spaces as she prepared the others to journey to the Reaches. Travelling to such spaces was easier. Glancing back at Jenny, she saw the girl had her eyes closed and her brow was furrowed. Returning her attention to the auditorium, she surveyed the starlit sky and the ring of standing stones that circled the captivated audience and using Rafter's ring that she still had from her trip to the Reaches, she imagined surrounding the whole scene in a giant bubble.

The ground shuddered beneath them as if there had been an earthquake, causing several people to gasp in fear, and the whole place seemed to stagger sideways before steadying again. She glanced at Tom who shook his head.

"I've lost contact," he whispered.

What she had done must have blocked out radio waves. But at least the hammering had ceased. That was the important thing.

The Moon, which was nearing the zenith, was almost full now, and in its silvery light Sally could see that flowers had sprung up around the podium on which Sarah and Keira stood. She knew she had not done that. Could she be transforming things unconsciously? Then she glanced at Jenny, who was grinning as she saw what was happening.

It must be the result of Jenny strengthening the energies, Vee suggested, back from his trip to the stage.

Sally pointed out the flowers to Professor Trundle who was in raptures.

"Why do you persecute us? We do you no harm." Sarah said reverting to a female voice.

If before people had felt fear, they were now beset by a feeling of bewilderment and injustice. All the voices of the Sisterhood circled over the heads of the audience, moving round and round the auditorium in a spiral till they joined Keira on the podium forming a female choir that hummed softly.

"Our task is to balance the energies of the Earth."

Sally sent a cascade of shooting stars flying across the sky.

"Why are you afraid of us?" We give birth to you. We feed and raise your children and we nurture and protect your world. There is nothing to be afraid of. Put down your arms. Return to your beds. May your dreams be pleasant."

With which, the chorus sang the Gaelic lullaby that Grace, the head of the Sisterhood, had taught Keira. As they did, Sally pushed the moon forward through its cycle till it was almost new as it set on the horizon to the West. At the same time, the sun began to rise in the East causing streaks of orange and red to grow and spread above the ring and the enchanted audience.

When the lullaby reached its end, silence fell over the audience. On the stage, side-by-side stood Keira and Sarah dressed in their white dresses. Sarah, true to form, had also donned brightly coloured stockings. The two girls stood quite still, caught in the first rays of the sun. The raucous cry of an owl awoke the audience with a shock and they burst into applause. Many stood to applaud. Others whistled. Keira and Sarah bowed this way and that till finally the waves of applause ceased.

"Thank you," Keira said. "Thank you. As we prepared our concert here tonight we discovered that the Arena was built on a giant circle of standing stones that pre-dates the one you all know in Hoyt Park."

"Part of the music you have just heard was made by using those stones," Sarah explained.

Such was the magic of Sarah's voice that nobody was troubled by the fact that those stones no longer stood there.

"With the right sounds in the right place, the stones will answer your call," Keira continued. "I will be using this way of singing to celebrate sunrise tomorrow morning in Hoyt Park. You are welcome to join us."

"For most of the rest of our concert this evening Keira will be singing you songs in Gran which is the dialect used by the working people in Granwich. They have a long tradition of music-making and singing and meet regularly to sing and dance," Sarah explained.

"And between each song, Sarah will tell you the tale of the song and give you a glance at life in another world," Keira added.

Overtime

"Core blimey! What next!" Jock said.

He was not one for swearing, especially when on duty, but this was too much. Hardly had they packed the young man off to the mental hospital, when he received a call that there was a problem at the Arena. Would he and Mandy ever get off work? Well, at least they couldn't complain it was boring. When they reached the Arena, they were greeted by the manager and staff of the auditorium who were in a panic.

"We can't get in!" the manager said, gesticulating, his voice almost hysterical. "We've tried all the doors. Every single one is blocked. Even the underground passage to the stage is inaccessible. What if there was a fire...?"

They had hammered on the doors but got no response, a technician explained. "You'd think someone would open the door given the noise we were making. Nothing. It was as if there was nobody inside."

"How many people are in there?" Mandy asked.

"Two thousand four hundred people!" the manager exclaimed, pulling at his greying hair.

"Are you sure something has gone wrong?" Jock asked. After all, even if it wasn't his cup of tea, maybe everyone was simply enjoying the concert. If the noise was as loud as some concerts he'd seen on TV, they probably wouldn't even hear someone knocking on the door.

"No," the manager had to admit.

"But we never lock the doors. It's against the fire regulations," the man responsible for the security said. "I don't even think they can be locked from the inside."

Mandy looked perplexed. He'd spent long enough observing her to recognise the signs of fatigue. Did his own face look as worn and drawn?

"It doesn't make sense," she admitted. "Unless we've inadvertently walked into a horror movie. Why would anyone block the doors from inside. And certainly not all of them." She paused, screwing up her eyes in concentration. "Can you hear the concert through the doors?"

"Well, no. In fact we can't hear anything," the manager replied, clearly confused.

"That may not be so surprising," the technician pointed out. "There are just two girls singing and they aren't even using mics and they have no instruments. Even the people inside the Arena probably can't hear them."

Their conversation was interrupted by the arrival of two fire engines.

"I called the fire brigade to break down the doors," the manager explained, shouting to be heard over the wail of sirens.

When they'd explained the situation to the firemen they went inside to examine the doors. Maybe it was his tiredness, but the place looked unreal as it flashed blue in the lights of the fire engines. There were many entrances to the auditorium but the main access was through two large doors that faced the outside doors across the foyer.

Jock tried pressing his ear against the door to see if any noise could be heard from within, but there was such a racket in the foyer that he could not be sure. The firemen were discussing how to force the doors so as to do as little damage as possible. Jock wandered off on his own, following the hallway that led around the outside of the auditorium.

There were a large number of doors into the concert hall. Blocking them all must have taken a considerable effort. Surely it couldn't have gone unnoticed. Reaching one of the last doors that was furthest from the foyer, he tried opening it on a whim. They'd all look rather silly if the doors weren't blocked. To his surprise and amusement the door was not locked at all.

He pushed open the door, stepped inside and closed the door quietly after him. The place was pitch dark and as silent as a tomb. He didn't dare move in case he'd arrived at a silent moment in the concert when the lights had been dimmed. But the lights stayed dimmed and no sound came, either from the performers or the audience. A shiver ran down his spine and his hair stood on end.

He had seen some things in his work that would have turned the stomach of most people, but standing there in the dark with over two thousand silent people in a silent concert terrified him. He pulled out his torch but hesitated to switch it on. What if he discovered that everybody was dead, slumped on their chairs in a macabre mass murder? Come off it, Jock, he told himself, you need a good night's sleep. He flicked the torch on and cast about him directing the narrow finger of light into the immense darkness that filled the hall. There was nobody there. There weren't even any chairs or a stage. If this had been April Fools Day he might have understood. But how could they get so many people out unnoticed?

He retraced his steps to the small side door, having dismissed the idea of exiting by the main doors right in front of the firemen and the Arena staff. It would have terrified them. Despite the lights in the foyer, he couldn't shake the cold fear that gripped him. The firemen were still negotiating noisily with the manager when Jock arrived.

"Are you all right? You're white as a sheet," Mandy said. "Have you seen a ghost?"

"Wait till you hear," he said and made his way to the door. He tested the handle and found that it was not blocked. Turning to the animated group, he raised his voice. "Ladies and Gentlemen. I have made a discovery that is not going to please you."

The conversation spluttered to a halt and all turned to look at him.

"I suspect we have been the victims of a giant hoax." He turned back to the doors and threw the two open with a dramatic wave of his arms.

"But those were locked," the manager began, only to stop the moment he caught sight of the empty hall. The group moved forward into the auditorium, which was now flooded with light as one of the technicians had thrown a switch. All of them stood transfixed as they observed the scene.

"Where has the stage gone?" one man asked. "And all the chairs?"

"Not to mention the audience," Jock pointed out, wondering if they'd catch his irony.

The head of the firemen cut through the state of shock. "Well. I don't think we are needed here," he said, ending with a grunt. Jock wasn't sure if it was an attempt at laughter or a partly concealed groan.

Jock went up to the manager and asked: "Would you like us to open an investigation?"

The guy looked at a loss. "I have no idea what to think. It all seemed so serious. It was a university department that organised the concert."

Jock hardly dared ask which department, but in the end it was Mandy who asked. The Theosophy Department. He'd finally managed to shake off the shivers that had been running down his spine but they began again. Was there no limit to what these people could do?

Seeing the small cafeteria across the foyer he said: "I think we all need a hot drink. Could you open the cafeteria for us?"

The whole group traipsed out of the empty auditorium, the technician turned off the lights and closed the door behind them.

The cafeteria was tiny and there were few seats. People were expected to drink or eat standing. But they were all so shaken that each of them found somewhere to sit. Once they'd been served with drinks that the manager said were on the house, the discussion turned to possible explanations. The debate was passionate but not very productive.

"It's a hoax," the manager muttered several times. "If you want my opinion, this whole thing is orchestrated by a small group of influential people who don't like my programming policy." He continued to mumble about being a victim until a technician interrupted him.

"It can't be a hoax," he argued, trying to throw some serious light on the matter. "How could they possibly have moved all those chairs? They're far too heavy. I reckon it's some sort of illusion possibly using sophisticated holograms." Few were convinced.

One woman even suggested it might be a collective dream. "This can't possibly be real."

Jock was beginning to feel better after a good cup of tea and wondered if they shouldn't go home before something else happened when he heard what sounded like the auditorium doors being opened. The whole group turned as one to see what had caused the noise. Hundreds and hundreds of happy-faced people came flooding out of the auditorium blinking at the bright lights and one by one the many doors flew open.

The audience were bubbling over with excitement. Arm in arm, they laughed, many even embraced. Jock could hear some of what they said. The concert had been wonderful. One person even called it magic. No one seemed to have been hurt and no one acted as if they had been part of monstrous joke. Jock got wearily to his feet and went to talk to some of the people. Those he spoke to were full of praise. On closer questioning, however, they only had a vague recollection of what had happened apart from the fact that it was the best concert they'd ever attended.

Jock called Mandy over. They crossed to the main door and slipped inside. The auditorium was full of empty chairs and there, in the middle, stood a small stage surrounded by four giant candles that were still burning. A considerable crowd of fans and supporters were huddled around the two performers congratulating them. Amongst them he caught sight of several of the young girls he'd seen on the photos found in the Professor's office, but he didn't have the energy or the strength to go and question them.

Then Mandy pointed out the tall man with the moustache that had also figured prominently in the photos. A wave of exhaustion rolled over him and he sagged. For all he knew, they might just disappear if he tried to approach them. How he hated sorcery! He felt very odd standing there in that empty space that was no longer empty. He felt strangely buoyed up, as if he were floating on hidden waves.

"I'm not getting involved in that right now!" he said firmly to Mandy, astonished at his own resolve. "This story has no end. If we don't let go, it will swallow us up."

She glanced at him, a look of alarm on her face, presumably not so much at what he said but at the fact that he was saying it. To hell with it! He linked arms with her, something he'd never done before, and led her out of the Arena and into the fresh night air.

They walked in silence, arm in arm for a while. Then, once they were in the shelter of a large bush that overhung the path down to the sea, he turned to her, pulled her towards him and planted a kiss firmly on her lips. He was as surprised as she was at what he had done. Something odd had come over him. He was about to apologise when she leant forward and kissed him in return.

Magic had its advantages, he had to admit. Better make the most of it before one or both of them turned into a toad.

Chapter 8 ~ Loved Ones

Unexpected passion

Jock's flat was not large, but it was furnished with taste and impeccably tidy. He prided himself on that. He'd even read a magazine about interior decorating picked up in the flea market one Saturday. Not that he paid much heed to what he'd read, but he had to admit that using some of its ideas gave his flat a better look. It made the place more welcoming and comfortable to live in.

Somehow, bringing Mandy back there in the middle of the night made him acutely conscious of all his efforts. He hastily turned off the main light as if that would conceal what he'd done, preferring a small, more intimate lamp on the table. He'd often imagined bringing Mandy home, but those torrid fantasies were nothing like the real thing. Mandy didn't seem at all bothered by his flat, she simply laced her arms around his neck and pulled him in a tight embrace.

Shedding their regulation hats and jackets that fell abandoned to the floor amid more kisses, they fumbled with each other's shoes trying to prise them off their feet. Mandy giggled at their sudden clumsiness, but neither of them spoke. Were they to say anything, he imagined, whatever magic was at work would be broken and they'd unavoidably fall back on their longstanding professional relationship: two police officers going about their job. He shrugged off the idea.

Turning her back to him, he pressed himself against her as he undid her blouse and ran his hands over her breasts. She wore no bra. She sighed as he pinched her nipples and pushed back with her buttocks against him. He gasped at the pleasure of it. Breaking free, she undid his shirt and ran her hand across his chest, venturing down across his muscular stomach – he was proud of that too; all that work in the gym had been well worth it – till her fingers reached his flies and began unzipping his trousers.

How they managed to make it to the bed, he wasn't sure. He'd always imagined their lovemaking would be short-lived but passionate, a sort of brightly coloured firework display. In reality, it had been soft, tentative, exploratory, all fingers and lips and tongues and skin against skin. When they came it was like a long-awaited but inevitable encounter, overflowing in deep waves of pleasure. Once the tide subsided, they lay back and Jock pulled the covers over them. Mandy snuggled up close, kissing him as she did.

"What a surprise," she said. Her voice so tender, he hardly recognised it. He was unwilling to break the silence. Instead he wrapped his arms around her and delighted in her warmth.

"Did they bewitched us?" she asked, half seriously.

He wanted to groan at the idea, but instead he chuckled, surprised at the sound of his voice. "It was certainly magic!" he said, much as he disliked the word.

She pushed his shoulder with her nose in mock reproach. "I've never felt like that before. It was as if I'd lost control."

Part of him didn't want to mull over what had happened. Doing so might burst the bubble and expose what had happened as somewhat less than magical. The tenderness had surprised him. In the number of short-lived affairs he'd had, never had sex been anything other than a hasty relief. He felt an irresistible desire to tell her that he loved her, but dismissed the idea as stupid. If he were to say so out loud it would certainly ring empty and betray him. So he hugged her tight, hoping that would let her know how much he appreciated making love to her.

"What are we going to do about those people?" she asked after a long silence.

Work, he thought, unhappy about the intrusion. Well, they probably couldn't avoid it, but he'd have preferred to have left it till morning.

"It seems extraordinarily complicated," she went on.

That was for sure. The question was how could he put a stop to all this nonsense as quickly as possible.

"I don't think they're bad. It's almost playful and childlike."

He let her do the talking. It wouldn't do to disagree with her after what had just happened.

"But the result might not be so good."

More like evil, he said to himself as he thought of Clyde curled up around the cross and the man they'd found floundering in the river.

"Someone has to teach them restraint before their activities get out of hand."

She sounded so motherly that he had a vision of her as a giant mamma suckling the young girls and boys that hung around the Theosophy Department. The image reminded him of the pictures they'd found in the professor's office and his penis stirred again.

He chuckled at his reaction and when she looked questioningly at him, he replied: "I wonder if we are best suited to teach them the lesson?" Then he kissed her before she could reply. And all thoughts of criminals and investigations and magical children got lost in a flurry of kisses.

Girlfriends

An was surprised by Maria's voice. It was like a delicious caress that sparked a smouldering deep inside her. She struggled to ignore it.

"Let me show you," Maria said, sitting crossed legged on the bed. They sat on the double bed, imitating Maria's position.

"Now stick your thumb up in the air," Maria said.

Tricia and An did as they were told but Beth refused.

"Nobody's going to bite it," Maria laughed.

Beth gave in, but looked as if she felt very silly holding up her thumb.

"Now press your three thumbs together."

After some jostling in a mock combat between Tricia and An, all three aligned their thumbs, pointing upwards.

"Now close your eyes and no peeking!" Maria warned. "Keep still, Beth."

An felt something warm and wet touch the tip of her thumb, sending shivers down her spine. She heard Tricia gasp and felt the girl's thumb become tense against hers. Whatever touched her thumb and those of the others, it slipped and slid down around their thumbs till they were two-thirds of the way into a deep wet cavity. Their thumbs became wetter and wetter as they were sucked and licked.

She could feel the other thumbs exploring hers and the mouth and tongue that encased them, slithering wet and warm, in slow movements. Tricia's breathing came in gasps while Beth gave out little whimpers.

An couldn't help letting out a sigh of disappointment when Maria withdrew her lips. Opening her eyes, she saw Maria grinning at them.

"Did any of you come?" she asked.

Beth stuck her thumb in her mouth and nodded.

"It gets you off every time," Tricia commented, giggling.

So this was a regular game, An realised. She began to wonder why she'd had any qualms about seducing the girls.

"I felt so worked up, I thought I was going to burst," Beth said, pulling her thumb out of her mouth and shedding some of her shyness. "I've been like that ever since Fran had me touch her shaved head."

Maria chuckled. "You're always hot for girls!"

"And you An?" Maria asked, a coy smile on her face.

"You almost had me there," An replied, unable to conceal her regret. Although she wasn't sure if her regret was because she hadn't gone far enough or she'd gone too far.

"Most girls of our age don't approve of our little games," Maria commented, making a funny face.

"We tried them out on a couple from the basketball team but they ran off screaming," Tricia added and all three laughed.

An struggled to understand her hesitation. She didn't normally say no to an attractive girl. Maybe it was the apparent innocent playfulness of it. Her years of experience seemed out of place, especially as the girls had no idea what or who she was. It was their very innocence and playfulness that drew her to them. She wanted to partake of that, revel in it and somehow forget herself.

"You look sad. Is it because you didn't manage to come?" Tricia asked, placing a warm hand on An's thigh.

"You're right," An replied, taking hold of Tricia's hand and pulling it to her lips to kiss it. "I almost did and it was frustrating to stop so soon." She nibbled the tips of Tricia's fingers causing the girl to squeal with delight. "But that is not why I feel sad."

Tricia flung her arms around An's neck and kissed her. "Tell us then. We're friends, aren't we? Maybe we can do something to help."

An smiled. It was the smile of one of her other forms. She recognised it immediately: the wise old woman. "I am not what I seem."

"Wow!" Beth exclaimed. "Another story. I love stories."

"Shhh!" Tricia silenced her friend.

"I come from another world," An told them.

"Tell us something new," Maria said. "We'd guessed that already.

Who else but someone from another world would live in a place where there were no schools!"

They all laughed. Beth slung her arms around Maria and Tricia's shoulders and all three waited for more.

"Some people in my world are shapeshifters," An explained.

"What's that?" Maria asked.

"It means they can transform into a bird or an animal," Beth explained. "I've read several stories were it happened."

"You read too much," Maria reposted, nuzzling her friend behind her ear.

"Beth is right," An went on. "I can change into a bird."

All three sat wide-eyed, not with fear but with longing.

"Show us," Tricia insisted, licking her lips.

An changed into an owl, startling the girls. She flew to the armchair, and, perched on the armrest, she surveyed them through her giant round eyes.

"Can you understand what we say?" Beth asked.

An let out a gentle screech.

"I suppose that means yes," Maria giggled. "But we can't understand you."

An glided back to the bed and transformed into her usual form.

"But I don't understand why you should be sad. It's a wonderful gift," Tricia said. "I'd love to be able to do that!"

An looked long and hard at Tricia before continuing, wondering if she dared have some fun at their expense. "How old are you Tricia?"

"Fifteen," the girl replied, perplexed.

"Well, I am over three hundred and fifty years old," An said dramatically.

All three of the girls gasped as An transformed into her old woman form. The three girls instantly drew back and huddled together. An was no longer part of their group. Had she really been so old, their reaction would have saddened her, but it didn't surprise her.

"You look like my great grandmother!" Beth whispered, unbelieving.

"I know many, many things," An said remaining in that form figuring she would have more effect that way. "I am a wise woman with hundreds of years of experience. I have visited many worlds and talked to many people. I have many more gifts than shapeshifting. That is probably one of the least of my gifts," she said, struggling to keep a straight face.

Tricia, surmounting her fear and possibly her disgust, leaned forward and taking hold of An's fingers, all wrinkled with age, she pulled them to her lips and kissed the back of her hand.

"Thank you," An said, profoundly moved by the gravity and the beauty of what her friend had done. Her joke had gone too far, leaving her feeling guilty. Was she becoming flippant and irresponsible, a bit like the children of her age in this world. She hardly recognised herself in what she had done. "Thank you," she whispered, and freeing her hand, she transformed back into the young girl she preferred to be.

"So you are sad because you would like to be young like us?" Beth speculated.

"It's not that at all," An began but she immediately broke into a nervous laughter and then burst into tears.

Tricia was taken aback. "Are you laughing or crying?" she asked, sounding a bit peeved, no doubt wondering if An was making fun of her. Well, in a way she was, but An hadn't intended to upset her newfound friends in such a fashion.

"I'm sorry. I didn't mean to upset you. It began as a joke."

"Joke?" Tricia exclaimed.

"I'm sorry, Tricia. What you did was wonderful and extremely moving."

"You mean you are not 350 years old?" Beth asked.

"No. It's just that I have the ability to transform into the form of an old woman. It is a gift that very few people in my world have. Most people can only transform into animals or birds."

Tricia was still annoyed. "That was mean! You played on my emotions."

"I'm sorry. You deserve much better."

"You fooled us, all right," Maria laughed.

"What I said about a difference in age between our worlds was not completely untrue, although, by my silly behaviour to you Tricia, I have just given a counter example," An said enigmatically, taking Tricia's hands in hers. "As children, people don't react to you in the same way here as they do to the young in my world. There are many things you as children are not expected to do or to understand. Whereas, in my world we don't have any less responsibility just because we are young."

"You mean you don't have any children?" Beth asked, chuckling at the idea.

"Exactly! We only have young people. It's not the same."

Maria looked perplexed. "I don't understand? How can you not have children?"

An wondered how she could best explain. "In your world the words 'children' and 'young people' are more or less synonymous. Contained in the word 'child' is the conviction that young people need to be shielded from the world, protected from the hard reality of adult life, freed of many responsibilities that they are thought to be too young for. Here, childhood is a time for play and enjoyment and innocent discovery."

"And school," Maria added with a groan.

"Exactly. I know it is a gross oversimplification, but we could say that school is a protected place 'outside' adult life, as it were, where you are safe and free to learn."

"But surely you play too," Beth pointed out.

"We do and we enjoy ourselves as much as you do. But people in my world don't consider we have to be specially protected from the world around us just because we are young. We have our part to play... Does that make any sense?"

"Sort of," Maria conceded. "But I think I'd understand better if I could really see your world."

"Oh yes! Can you take us there?" Tricia asked.

"Can you teach us to shape-shift?" Beth asked, almost falling over herself in her desire to do so.

"I may not be able to teach you shape-shifting," An explained. "It is very much a question of individual ability. Most people in my world can't do it. And as for taking you to my world, I would willing do so, but there is a war on at the moment in the north and it might not be safe."

"I don't care," Tricia exclaimed. "If you can go, so can we."

"And what about your parents?" An asked.

"To hell with them!" Maria said.

"Listen," An said. "My friends and I will be returning to my world very soon. If we can find a good pretext that satisfies your parents, then I will take you with me for a short stay. And I will see if I can teach you shape-shifting. But do not be disappointed if you can't. As I said, most people can't. Now we should get to sleep if we want to be present when Keira greets the rising sun."

She lay back on the bed. Tricia cuddled up in her arms and closed her eyes. She could feel the girl's mouth close to her ear as Tricia whispered: "I love you." She kissed her back. Glancing over Tricia's shoulder, she could see that Beth and Maria were entwined together, cheek to cheek.

"Goodnight, my loved ones," An said.

Smouldering

Jenny took off her tee shirt and bra, hanging them behind the bathroom door. Then she stepped out of her trousers and pants. Tom watched her undress from his wheelchair, a smouldering fire burning in his eyes. He sat there patiently, naked but for his pants, waiting for her to help him wash. She bent forward to kiss him on his forehead, caressing his hair.

"Come closer," he whispered.

When she did, he slid his hands down the small of her back and over her buttocks.

"Lovely," he murmured, cupping their round form within his strong hands. Shifting one hand to her crotch, he ran his fingers through her pubic hair and eased his way between her legs. It was one of the things she greatly regretted: since his accident they had been unable to make love. To be honest, he had hardly desired it, as if the fire and his broken back had stamped out all trace of sexuality. Glancing in his eyes, she saw that desire had once again awoken.

"Let's get you undressed," she suggested.

The light touch of his fingers on her sex had set off an insistent pulsing inside her. She must have locked away such sensations, because it felt unfamiliar to be aroused. Pulling back, she slipped her arm under Tom's armpit and around his back as she took his weight to help him rise from the wheelchair. At first the task of undressing him had been extremely difficult, but with time they'd found ways to work together to make it easier. Rafter had left them his own bedroom that had an adjacent bathroom large enough to get the wheelchair inside. A special seat had been installed over the bath so that Tom could have a wash or a shower. With the help of his strong arms she managed to manoeuvre him onto the seat and slide off his pants.

She tested the temperature of the water with her hand and, climbing into the bath herself, she showered both of them. Then taking up a large bar of soap she began lathering his neck and shoulders. As she worked her way down, for the first time since his accident she saw he had an erection. Lathering the soap in her hands, she took hold of his sex, and running her hands up and down she felt it grow in her fingers. He moaned, his eyes closed.

"Wash the soap away," he suggested.

When that was done, he pulled her closer.

"Straddle me," he said, his voice imperative.

She knew exactly what he wanted. She wanted it too. Badly. Desperately even.

She lowered herself with great care onto his lap. It was not as comfortable or as agreeable as it should have been, but to hell with that, they were making love at last after such a long time. That was all that mattered.

Once they were both installed in bed, she rolled close to him and felt his naked body pressed against her.

"I love you," he said.

"I love you too," she replied.

After a long silence he added: "Sometimes it seems like a miracle that you should still want me when I am ..." and his voice broke and he sobbed.

She kissed away his tears. "I will always love you. You are the love of my life. How could things be otherwise?"

He sighed and both of them lay back looking up at the ceiling. A long while later, when she thought he had fallen asleep, he spoke again. "Why now?" he wondered. "Why should our passion be reawakened so abruptly."

"I have a hunch," she told him turning to face him. "All that energy I pumped into the Arena may have caused such excitement and arousal."

He chuckled, saying: "If that is the case, the town of Avan will have an inexplicable baby-boom in nine months."

Both of them laughed. She snuggled up close and closed her eyes.

Shocking fingers

Keira turned the visiting card over, studying it carefully. Amanda Stock, producer for National Radio at the BBC. The Nati, they called it. The woman had been in the crowd of well-wishers at the end of the concert. She wanted to record her and Sarah on Sunday in the local radio studio. Keira was flattered. There was a time when she would have jumped at the occasion, but now things were more complicated and she was having doubts about displaying their abilities so publicly.

She shifted in her armchair to get more comfortable, glancing at Irina who was seated opposite her dressed only in her underwear with a blanket draped over her shoulders. Ever since they'd retired to one of the attic rooms in Rafter's house, the girl had rattled on about the concert and what she'd experienced. Keira ignored her and returned to her thoughts.

She'd have preferred sleeping with Sally or Brent or even both of them rather than being bottled up with bubbly Irina who threatened to suffocate her with her babbling. It hurt to know that Brent and Sally were making love in a nearby room, without her. She couldn't decide which feeling was uppermost: anger or sadness. She must have caught Brent's habit. She wanted to pace the room. To fling open the door and storm out. To wander the countryside, walking without a goal or the hope of reaching one. The concert had left her completely relaxed. What a delight to sing in such an atmosphere. It had filled her with joy and longing. Now, cooped up and frustrated, she felt tense, painfully so.

"Let me give you a massage," Irina was saying as she lay her hands on her shoulders.

Keira hadn't even noticed Irina had got up and come to stand behind her chair. Why not? It might drain some of the tension. And if it did the contrary, she'd strangle Irina with her bare hands and fling the body in a river somewhere. She wanted to let out a blood-curling growl, but instead she said peaceably: "Why not."

"You'd be better on the bed," Irina suggested helping her get up and move to the bed.

Keira let her mind roam, forsaking her body to Irina's hands. She vaguely felt the girl undress her and, turning her on her stomach, apply oil liberally to her back.

Her roaming thoughts were not to be. The moment Irina laid her hands on her back it was like an electric shock. Every inch of her body was instantly alert, or maybe aware was the right word. She could see into every part of her body. Tensions dissolved one by one, muscles unknotted, troubled thoughts melted away, till she felt like her cells were humming. There was no other word for it: humming like a top. Suddenly she realised that Irina was silent. She must have stopped talking the moment the massage began. Keira hadn't noticed. She felt released of bonds she hadn't know were fettering her and the desire to run away had vanished.

Irina placed her two hands flat and unmoving on the small of Keira's back. They were pleasantly warm and their warmth spread through her making her sex tingle. A gentle pulsing began deep inside her and amplified till she had the impression her whole belly was caught up in it. She could feel her breasts harden and her nipples pressed down against the bed beneath. She couldn't help herself, she groaned. She was dribbling. She was sure of it. Becoming wetter and wetter. But she couldn't be sure if it was her mouth or between her legs. Her whole body had dissolved into wave after wave of pulsation that extended from the tips of her toes to the very end of each hair on her head. She knew she had to let go, the force of the waves would become unbearable if she tried to hold on much longer. So taking a giant breath she let out a long groan that sounded more like the call of an animal in the jungle and gave herself up to the waves which broke into millions of tiny water droplets and fell like dew from an early morning mist onto the bed.

She felt Irina cover her with a blanket, but she didn't have the strength to move. She had never experienced anything like it. For all her love for Sally, none of their lovemaking had ever produced such a violent and exquisite orgasm. Spasms continued to flutter inside her, making her shudder sporadically with pleasure as she slowly regained control of her body.

She turned on her side and looked at Irina who sat by her on the bedside, her hands folded in her lap. She still couldn't bring herself to speak, but Irina must have seen her quizzical look.

"I don't know," she replied to the unasked question. "I've never done that before."

The girl stared away into the distance as if searching for an explanation. "I could feel something rising and growing in me during the concert. There was a fountain of light bubbling up in the middle of the stage. It cascaded over the audience, filling the whole room with a bright light. Since then I see all sorts of swirling coloured lights around people."

She leant forward and placed her hand on the small of Keira's back. "Here for example."

Keira gasped as desire coursed through her veins again. "I don't think I could stand it a second time right away," Keira managed to say, forcing herself to move out of Irina's reach. "I think I would fall to pieces for ever."

Not alone

Mae sat hunched up beside Rafter's makeshift bed holding the sleeping man's cold hand in hers. She shivered. She felt left out in more ways than one. When she had returned from the concert she could sense deep desire hanging in the air. Everyone was bubbling with excitement. Except her. It was as if they moved in a different world. Theirs was filled with bright colours and warm feelings and togetherness and intense desire. While hers was grey and cold and flat and lonely. She hadn't been surprised to see them scurry off to bed, hardly pausing to talk. Even An and her three schoolgirl friends had hurried up giggling to their allotted bedroom. There was no other word for the state they'd been in: aroused!

Hadn't she been at the concert too? Why hadn't it had the same effect on her? She couldn't understand why people got so worked up about Sarah's stories. They were nothing more than pretty stories. What was wrong with her? What kept her from the joy and euphoria the others were feeling. Why was she not aroused? Silly me, she thought. I forgot. I don't have anyone to get aroused about! Enough! No use wasting her time spinning stories as an excuse for self-pity.

She straightened up and looked at the Professor only to find his eyes open and looking at her. His lips formed a weak smile that got lost in the folds of his wrinkled, pain-marked face.

"You should go to bed," he said. "It must be late."

Tears formed in the corners of her eyes. He studied her face for a long moment, his eyes as inscrutable as ever, till she began to feel uncomfortable. He raised one hand to her cheek and brushed away a tear.

"Did you ever love anybody else?" she asked after a long silence, setting aside her own sad stories. "I mean once you'd returned here."

He gave her question some thought as he eased himself up on the pillow. "No. She was the love of my life."

"But surely other women must have attracted you."

He smiled at her and shook his head.

"Sorry to disappoint you, but she was the only one."

"You must have missed her terribly." Mae tried to imagine how he must have felt being a whole world away from his love.

"I have a very good memory," Rafter startled her, leaving her wondering what he was getting at, "but I am also quite good at forgetting. It's useful if you don't want your life marred by unpleasant or even pleasant memories."

He chuckled, but his chuckle broke into a fit of coughing. When the spasms had died down and he was able to breath again, he said: "If I had continued to grieve, I would have buried my own life in grief. I loved her with all my heart, But I wasn't prepared to let that love destroy my life. I am sure she would have agreed."

It struck her as odd that he could be both indifferent and yet bound to the women for the whole of his life, but she accepted the contradiction as yet another one of those mysterious traits of the Professor.

There followed a long, thoughtful silence. She realised the house had quietened. She even had the odd impression the place was no longer so aroused. It was late and most people must surely be asleep. Then he spoke again.

"Is there anybody in your life?"

"Apart from you, you mean?" Her face twisted in a smile.

He smiled back. "You are too kind, Mae, but surely there must be someone else."

"I love you, Professor, a bit like I would have loved my father if I had known him." She paused to digest her own words and then continued. "But no! Otherwise there is nobody in my life. And that is a great source of suffering for me."

She suddenly felt embarrassed and must have blushed.

"I'm sorry, Professor. How thoughtless of me. To talk of my petty sufferings when you are continually in pain." Tears flowed down her cheeks again.

"Hush. Hush my little one. I can't promise that you will find the person of your love. That is beyond my power. But one thing I am certain of: you will always be greatly loved. All those people around you like Sally and Brent and Keira and all the others, they love you. And I love you too, Mae, more than you imagine."

She was quite aware that the others loved her and that she loved them in her own way. But it was still reassuring to hear Rafter confirm it. All the same, she couldn't help feeling left out.

"I feel different," she mused, giving voice to her earlier thoughts.

"Each one of the Dream Class is different It is just not always easy to live with that difference, especially when you don't understand its nature. How are you different, Mae?"

She told him about the concert and the way the others had reacted.

"Aroused?" he chuckled, managing to do so without breaking into coughing for once.

"But I seem to be immune to it."

"How do you know that?" he asked, serious again.

"Well, Sarah's stories don't seem to have the same effect on me. The others are carried away by her words, whereas I hear only pretty stories."

"What Brent does has many names. Some call it 'bewitching' others would call it compulsion. His voice forces others to submit to his will as expressed in the words of his stories. I don't think he fully realises what he does. It is possible that you are immune, as you put it, to compulsion."

She looked at him questioningly.

"That could be a very useful gift. Ill intentioned people can use compulsion to force you to obey them. Not that I believe Brent is in any way evil."

Mae sat up in her chair, straightening her back and breathing deeply. "So you think I might be naturally able to guard against compulsion?"

He nodded. "If I were you, I would keep the knowledge of such a gift to yourself. It might turn out useful sometime. I'll let you into a secret, though," he added, disregarding his own advice. "Brent's stories have no effect on me either. So that makes two of us."

It pleased her to have that much in common with the otherwise impenetrable professor. She wondered about compulsion and Brent's seemingly harmless gift. "I wish I had the gift of compulsion. At least I'd be able to get the man I want into my bed." She chuckled but Rafter remained serious.

"You wouldn't like that. Imagine how I would have felt if the woman in my life had been there only because I was able to compel her to."

She blushed at her silliness.

"Don't be ashamed, Mae. You all still have a lot to learn. I would have liked to be able to accompany you on that journey. But that doesn't seem likely." He coughed as if to prove it.

Mae hurried to pour some medicine and helped him take it. "Have a rest Professor. We can talk about all this later."

He closed his eyes following her advice and she helped him get comfortable. "Good night, Professor," she said.

"One last thing," he said as she stood to leave, "sooner or later, you young people are going to have to confront a big question: the nature of good and evil. Now there's a question full of pitfalls. The sooner you get a grip on it, the better it will be."

Forbidden curves

It hadn't been Dieter's idea to have a workout before going to bed. Anju had complained they'd been cramped in seats all evening and she wanted to move before retiring to bed.

"Come on Dieter! That's really half-hearted," Anju protested as she rolled over and sprang to her feet.

The air in the former table-tennis room in Rafter's basement was a little stuffy but they hadn't wanted to open the windows for fear of disturbing the neighbours. He turned to face her, taking up a defensive stance. She was right. His heart wasn't in it. She had him on the ground in seconds, knocking the wind out of him. He lay there, defeated, surrendering, unmoving, letting her straddle him as he tried to regain his breath.

"What's the matter with you?" she asked as she settled on his chest, her blue-green eyes worried as they scrutinised his face.

He looked up at her and as always, the sight of her tall, thin form with her spiky black hair and her smooth, sun-browned skin, touched him deeply. Was it love or desire? There was the key question. And it hurt. Love was acceptable but desire not. She pouted when he continued to lie there refusing to respond.

"It's those photos, isn't it?"

It was indeed. The moment he'd seen them, they had poisoned his life. Although they were the fabrication of a twisted mind, the photos were a perfect reflection of his worst nightmare, his deepest fears and doubts. He had no right to the intense pleasure he got from loving Anju and being loved by her. He loved every curve of her, he relished in all its little recesses and dark corners. The sound of her voice was a delight and her every movement was a pleasure to watch. And when they talked, he loved the way her mind worked: questioning, exploring, challenging and yet open and fresh. But to love her so much was wrong, terribly wrong. He knew it. Was he infatuated? Had she bewitched him with her youth? Had she become his drug? He certainly found it hard to imagine life without her.

"Maybe you should find a lover closer to your age!" he said in desperation, unable to keep the bitterness from his voice.

"Ah!" she sighed, making a show of thinking hard. "My puritan policeman." And she chuckled.

"It's not funny. Do you realise that the word Puritan was a slur used only by detractors of those who took the Bible seriously and who believed in leading a moral life?" Not that he adhered to the ways and ideas of his parents, but he had to admit they had left their mark. She knew that too.

He saw her eyes light up at what she must perceive as the challenge of his words. She loved a battle of wits as much as one between bodies, although he knew she would argue that the distinction between the two was an illusion.

"A moral life? You mean one in which women are singled out and condemned as the direct successor of Eve, the woman by whose weakness original sin entered the world? Sexuality, in other words. Epitomised by the way women entice men into sinning. A taint that only suffering and hard work can eradicate. Do you feel tainted by me?"

As always, her blows, whether verbal or physical, rarely missed the mark. She was right, he did feel tainted, but not so much by her, but by what the world would say of their relationship.

"It's not you." He felt desperately unhappy at being at odds with her, "It's what people will say and think."

She watched him silently for a moment, as if gauging her next move.

"I wonder if Genesis were to be re-written, given the current moral climate, Eve would probably be a young girl reaching puberty and Adam a somewhat older man."

He couldn't help being shocked. "You know I am not a practicing Christian, but it makes me uneasy when you blaspheme that way."

"Then I apologise for making you uneasy. That was not my intention. All I wanted to say was that the love of an older man for a younger girl has been stigmatised. It is seen as a vile sin by those same people who punched their Bibles in their crusade against the original sin as propagated by women. Like the men and women who tracked would-be witches. Who knows what dark thoughts were in their hearts behind their pious, starched-white façade."

She paused to see if he would react, but he remained silent.

"Do you love me, Dieter Drum?"

"Yes," he sighed. He'd been through that interrogation once before.

"Do you love me?" she repeated.

"I do," he reiterated, more firmly this time.

"Do you love me?" she asked for the third time.

"Yes. I love you with all my heart," he said with conviction, his whole body behind the words.

She startled him by imitating the sound of a cock crowing. Not once, but three times. "But unlike in the original story," she said, leaning forward to kiss him gently on the forehead, "you have not denied the one you love, on the contrary. You have asserted your love in the face of adversity."

Tears overflowed down his cheeks as he recognised the passage to which she alluded.

"If God is good, surely he would not have made a world full of sin. Surely he would reward those who love what is good. And sexuality, like love, is good. The two are intricately bound together. Only fanatics would try to tear them asunder."

He chuckled through his tears, and, pulling her close to him, he said: "You should have been a preacher..." But the rest of his sentence, not to mention all the ideas he had in his head, got lost in a flood of kisses.

Good and evil

Brent lay naked on the bed. He'd resumed his masculine form, not wishing to add more confusion by having Sarah make love to Sally. The concert had left him feeling electric and strangely elated. There was a heady, almost giddy, satisfaction to carrying over two thousand people away with his stories. No doubt the unusually high level of energy in the Arena thanks to Jenny's efforts also had something to do with his light-headedness. Sally was naked too. She lay next to him with her head rested on his chest, her auburn hair cascading over his shoulders and around his neck. He ran his finger through her hair, feeling how soft and sensual it was. Sally played idly with his penis, turning it this way and that. It was still half erect in memory of their earlier lovemaking.

They'd been so excited when they made it to their bedroom, they were trembling and febrile. Sally had forced him to take his time as they slowly undressed each other and when they were finally naked, she insisted he kiss her all over and she did the same for him. Instead of screaming in frustration, they both settled into a calmer mood of smouldering desire. Finally she had straddled him and had began slow gyrating movements that inflamed both of them till holding back was no longer possible.

She continued toying with him, as she asked: "How does it feel not to have a penis when you are Sarah?"

After the first shock of having transformed unwittingly into a young girl and the difficult apprenticeship getting used to her body, he no longer gave it much thought.

"It's a bit like being two separate people. The only thing that is common between Sarah and I is our memories."

She grasped his penis between her fingers and kissed it before turning to face him. "So you don't even get confused between the two?"

"Not physically. I don't feel like I've got both a vagina and a prick, if that's what you mean? But I do know what it is like to have an organism as a girl. That memory I retain. And vice-versa. What could get confusing are the relationships. I must admit I deliberately changed from Sarah to my present form. I imagine making love to you as a girl with a girl might be a strange experience."

She heaved herself up on one elbow and leant forward to kiss him. "You will never know till you try."

He chuckled and pushed her away playfully. "You're crazy about sex!"

"No I'm not!" she protested, laughing too. "I just enjoy making love."

He put his arms around her and she lay back, her head next to his. "I really love your sensuality. I suppose it resonates with Sarah."

"Are men not sensual too?" Sally mocked.

They lay there in silence for a while. He loved to feel the warmth of her body next to him; it somehow made him complete. He wondered for a moment if he didn't in fact wish he were both Brent and Sarah at once. But he had no time to explore the idea for Sally spoke again.

"To think I'd lifted the whole contents of the auditorium and over two thousand people right out of this dimension. I imagined I was just wrapping them in a bubble, to keep the hammering from disturbing the concert."

Brent chuckled. "Those police officers and the manager had a shock when people started flooding out of what they thought was an empty hall. I wonder how they managed to explain it to themselves."

"People cannot live with such a giant contradiction. Their mind necessarily invents a plausible explanation. That was why I wondered how you survived being both Sarah and Brent."

"Part of the answer is being clear about differences. But I also think Sarah is really a part of Brent and vice-versa."

Her smile gave way to a look of concern. "Some of the things we do are so immense, literally, that I begin to worry about possible unexpected fallout. What would have happened, for example, if someone had remained in the auditorium when I brought the whole audience back? Would they have been crushed? I feel like we know so little about what we do. A mistake could have disastrous effects."

He had to agree. "We are like children playing with powerful toys without the slightest idea of the consequences."

"How about you? How did you feel telling stories to so many people?"

"Both elated and worried. It's the power I suppose. I can sway so many people to my will …" and he fell silent in mid-sentence pondering what wielding such power could mean.

"At first I thought it was the strength of the stories. The idea appealed to me; to imagine I could tell such powerful stories that people were completely drawn into them. That would be the ultimate storyteller's gift," and he sighed, troubled at his own naïveté. "But then when that drug addict sneaked into our dressing room, he made me angry. He was trying to destroy us and I wanted to do him harm. I found it hard to hold back. I no longer told him stories. No! I gave him direct orders and he had no choice but to obey. It's called compulsion, Sally. That's not good. Not good at all."

She shivered and he pulled the blankets around them.

"Imagine if your love for me was not your free choice, but your obeying my will." He felt the room go even colder. "The thought is so disgusting and alien to me, I wish I hadn't had it." He hid his face in his hands. "I feel like a monster."

Sally placed her warm hand at the base of his neck and stroked it gently. He half-heartedly tried to resist, but she pulled him towards her and folded her arms around him.

"I love you Brent and my love for you is not the product of anybody's compulsion," she said firmly. "I am absolutely sure of that! Do you know why?"

He shook his head, tears streaming down his cheeks.

"Because your stories don't have the same effect on me they do on everybody else. They are just stories. I didn't want to tell you for fear I might hurt your feelings. No, Brent, I am immune to your compulsion, as you call it."

She kissed his forehead tenderly.

Her revelation was something of a relief. "I wonder how many others are immune." He could have kicked himself for asking the question. He'd suddenly become wary of his every motive. He shuddered. He really didn't want to travel down that road. "Do you think what we are doing is wrong?"

"We have assumed it isn't."

"You, yourself, said we were like children playing with our gifts. Perhaps we need to grow up."

"I'm not so sure. Our playfulness is one of our greatest strengths. It would be a shame to lose that. But maybe the time has come for us to ask ourselves the question," she pursued. "I only wish we could have asked Rafter about it. He would have been able to help us, I'm sure."

Brent got to his feet, surprising her by his resolve. "Maybe he's awake."

"I know it's selfish to ask him at such a time, but we need his help." She stood too. They hurriedly dressed and went down to the ground floor.

They peeked into the living room where Mae had made the Professor a makeshift bed. All was quiet. Mae sat on a chair nearby, her head resting on Rafter's bed. The Professor had one hand placed lightly on Mae's shoulder. He looked around when they walked in and greeted them with a smile.

"Good evening friends. Can nobody sleep in this house?" he asked.

Mae stirred and rubbing her eyes looked up to see who had arrived. Then she lay her head back on the bed.

"I know it is not the right time or place, Professor, but we have a very serious question and we need your help," Sally told him.

"Fire away," Rafter invited, settling back in his bed.

"Each of us has powerful gifts, Professor," Brent began. "We were delighted to discover them. They made us feel good. And it's been our pleasure and our joy to use those gifts during this weekend."

He was interrupted by the arrival of Keira with Irina in tow. Neither of the girls said anything, but just quietly sat at the foot of the bed and looked at Brent. Shortly afterwards Jenny arrived pushing Tom in his wheel chair. There must have been some magic at work, because within minutes Fran and Martin joined them along with Anju and Dieter.

Rafter chuckled, doing his best not to cough. "Only An is missing."

"No I'm not Professor." She edged around the door bringing the three girls with her. "May my three friends join us?" she asked introducing Tricia, Maria and Beth.

"Of course. Brent was about to ask an important question." He nodded to Brent to continue.

"I was saying that each member of the Dream Class has developed gifts that fit squarely in the realm of magic," Brent began, pacing the little remaining floor space in the living room between the reclining bodies. "Magic? Because they defy scientific explanation and go beyond our normal worldly experience. We have rejoiced in these gifts. They have saved the life of some of us," and they all turned to look at Tom who was embarrassed by their attention. "Those gifts have brought pleasure both to us and to many others."

Keira chuckled and looked at Irina. "You wait till you hear what Irina can do."

Brent ignored her. "We have used our gifts to do good, even if some people have suffered because of them. You might say that we have approached them as playful children discovering a new toy or a new friend."

Tricia gasped causing everyone to turn her way. "Sorry for interrupting," she apologised. "It's just that An told us it was our joyful innocence that attracted her to us."

Brent continued to pace. He was acutely aware that they had little time left. "Tonight I used my gift to punish a drug pedlar who was out to discredit us with his filthy habits. I didn't kill him, although I can assure you I was murderously angry. I sent him on his way, possibly to hell or if he is lucky to salvation. It was then I realised that what I do with my stories is nothing other than compulsion. And compulsion is evil," and he spat the word out, startling more than one. "So we need to ask ourselves: are we doing good or evil?"

To everyone's astonishment, Rafter burst out laughing. It didn't last long because he started coughing. Mae handed him some medicine and his breathing calmed again.

"I told you so," he said to Mae.

Everyone except Mae looked perplexed.

"The Professor told me this evening that we would have to address the question of good and evil," she explained. "And so here we are, Professor. Where do we go now?"

"I do not have the strength to give you a lecture on good and evil. I need my energy for other things that I must say before I go. But I will try to point to some possible paths you could follow."

Mae handed him a glass of water and helped him get comfortable in his bed. At that moment the clock in the hall struck one.

"In the beginning, contrary to rumours spread by the church, there was no distinction between good and evil. The words would not have made sense. Things just were. There was a natural order that made it that way. If you like, you might call that state of innocence and connectedness the Garden of Eden. However it was not Eve that changed things, nor the eating of the apple, but the coming of thought that wrought the fatal change. Thought made people separate from the world and from others and even from themselves. And in that separation they stepped out of the natural order. For a long time, a semblance of order continued to be given by the institutions they created like the church or the family or the local community. But that order was not the one inherent in the universe itself, but rather the order as thought out by men. Now many of the guidelines originally drawn up by those institutions have fallen into disuse in a world increasingly governed by the values of material wealth and individualism."

He stopped for a moment and looked around the room. Brent could see an intense look of pleasure on his face. This might be Rafter's last lesson, he thought with sadness.

"Now let's track back and follow another path. You might say that those who fight for good necessarily create and nourish evil. Some churches see their flock as little soldiers fighting for good and in doing so they only spawn evil. The dilemma of the origin of evil has always plagued the church. If God is omniscient and omnipresent then logically he or she must have created evil."

He took another sip of his drink, thanking Mae.

"We cannot return to the pristine naïveté that characterised the original garden when everything was at its rightful place. We cannot relinquish the gift of thought and the advantages that arise from feeling ourselves separate from the world. Yet thought will not give us the answer. It cannot encompass the complexity of the world. We could never anticipate all the possible ramifications of our actions, for example."

He paused again, looking tired despite the fervour in his voice and the brilliance of his eyes.

"So is what you do good or evil? It is, as you so rightly say Brent, a gift. A gift cannot be refused. Yet the word 'gift' in German means poison. So it has to be treated with care. Should you taste it only with moderation and restraint? Maybe not always! Sometimes excesses can be the most joyful expression of being. When Keira sings, she sings with her whole heart," he added looking in Keira's direction. "Just like Mae who organises things with all her heart and soul."

He ran his hand through her hair.

"Should you refuse to use your gifts? Surely not! It would be a dreadful waste. So what should you do? Maybe part of the answer lies in combining thought and a more pristine connectedness. You may say those are the words of a silly old man, but I truly believe the answer lies in a combination of separation and connectedness."

Nobody spoke. Brent wondered how many managed to follow the Professor's words. Not that what he said was incoherent, far from it, but he was no longer paying so much attention to tying his ideas together. Instead they fell jumbled in front of them as the Professor hurried to give them what he could. Somebody else would have to sort them out later.

"I told you I could only provide fragments," the Professor continued, confirming Brent's impression. "You must work on this yourselves. The question of good and evil may well be one of the biggest challenges you will have to affront. At least you're not fighting for a cause or defending a set of moral values so you won't be tempted to do evil to defend good. That's a common trap: think of the crusades, for example, or the inquisition."

Rafter's eyes flashed wildly as he glanced around the room. "Another thing, be cautious of those ideas that spring to mind spontaneously from your upbringing or your education. They might mislead you. Be careful of words too. They can betray you. Both 'good' and 'evil' are so bound up in strong cultural contexts, especially for us Westerners."

The Professor was becoming increasingly agitated. His hands were shaking too.

"And beware of those people who adopt extreme positions. By their polarisation, they will try to force you to the extreme too. Like the Starless Square: they will have won if you fight back with the same means they use."

Mae took one of his hands in hers. "Enough Professor. You've done enough," she said trying to soothe him.

"But I want to help as much as I can," Rafter protested, pleading, almost desperate.

"You've already helped us so much. Now you must rest. You still have things to do. So sleep and get your strength back."

Sally joined Mae and knelt down by his bed and took hold of his other hand. "Thank you Professor," she whispered. "Sleep now. You can tell us the rest of your story at breakfast when we return from greeting the dawn."

He finally closed his eyes as Keira began to softly sing a lullaby.

And one by one or in small groups people rose to return to bed for a few hours, each whispering "Goodnight" to the Professor as they left.

When Rafter's breathing slowed with sleep, Sally finally relinquished his hand and, giving a passing kiss to Mae, she joined Brent as they made their way upstairs to bed. Brent could tell she was upset, her head hung and her shoulders were slumped.

"We shouldn't have asked him," she said.

He wanted to reassure her, but he felt guilty too. She was right. They had been selfish. It hurt him to see the lengths to which the Professor was prepared to push himself to help them when they could do nothing for him in return. They climbed the stairs slowly neither saying a word and, once in their room, they prepared for bed. Sally lay down and pulled the covers tight around her neck. Brent didn't want to sleep.

"I'm going to make a note of what the Professor said before I sleep," he told Sally. "It would be a shame to forget something when he made so much effort to tell us." With which he pulled out his notebook and began to write.

The house was completely quiet, everyone was trying to snatch a few hours sleep before they left for the standing stones. Brent had reached the part about the church creating evil when Sally suddenly sat bolt upright and cried out, startling him. "He's gone!" She burst into tears.

Brent feared she'd had an intuition that Rafter had died and felt a wave of sadness wash over him. "Are you sure? He was tired but not so bad as that."

She looked at him confused, tears still streaming down her cheeks. "Vee has gone," she said, sobbing.

"Maybe he just wanted to leave us alone while we were making love."

She shook her head, a desperate look in her eyes and she flung herself into Brent's arms, shuddering. "He's gone!" she repeated, inconsolable.

"Well, he was jealous, you told me. Maybe that was his way of avoiding the conflict."

"You don't understand," she wailed, pulling back from Brent and hammering his chest with her fists. "He's gone ... forever!"

He took hold of her hands to restrain her, although there was no force in her blows. "How do you know?"

"Because the link is broken," she cried out and flung herself on the bed wracked with sobs. "He's no longer there. He's gone for ever."

When Brent tried to console her, she pushed him away. "You don't understand. He was a part of me. It's like having your heart ripped out."

Several people had come running, hearing the noise.

"It's Vee," Brent explained. "Sally says he's gone. That the link between them has broken."

Keira hurried away and came back with a little bottle from which she poured a few drops onto a spoon and, cradling Sally in her arms, she gave her the medicine. Jenny sat next to Sally and laid one hand on her shoulder no doubt using her gift to help. Keira sang softly using her gift too. But Brent could do nothing.

His gift had no effect on Sally and anyway, he didn't want to use compulsion on her. He stood there feeling useless and dejected. In a way it was his fault. He'd driven Vee out. How selfish of him. He was about to slip away when An stepped forward and took his hand.

"It's not your fault, Brent. Don't blame yourself. Sally needs you now more than ever."

She pulled him forward towards the bed. Jenny and Keira shifted to make room. Sitting next to Sally, he placed his hands on her shoulder, half expecting her to reject him. Instead she took his hand in hers and held it close to her chest.

"He was sometimes a pain in the arse." She made an effort to laugh. "But I loved him all the same. You have Sarah and I had Vee. What will I do? I feel so empty."

Chapter 9 ~ Dawn Chorus

Not again!

The streets of Avan were deserted. The Old Station lay in darkness, abandoned trains gathering dust in the sidings, disused railway sleepers lounging against the embankment still smelling of creosote. From the station forecourt, devoid of taxis at that late hour, Vee could just make out the lights of Avan Hospital, one of the few places where people were still be awake. There too all seemed quiet: no midnight emergency, no wail of sirens, no running nurses or hurried ambulance drivers and stretcher-bearers. No sense of urgency, not even there.

Vee moved on, his insubstantial footsteps betraying nothing of his passage. Even the dust that had settled around the upturned tables of the snack-bar chained together for the night, left no trace of his passing. Stepping under a streetlamp, the dog-eared light cast no shadow to indicate he had been there. He existed for one person and one person only. No empty rhetoric there, only pure fact: without her he was truly nothing, he was no one.

She'd nicknamed him Vee, Vee for voyeur, but in reality he had no more name than body. How could a bodiless being have a name? He'd begun and he would end a voyeur, he reminded himself. That he'd actually saved her life many times in the interim brought little consolation. Voyeur. A misnomer in many ways. For a start, it was not sexual excitement he got from watching her in those early days, even if she had believed it, but his very existence. All the more so when he later became a part of her: a voice in her head and the unseen eyes that enabled her to see elsewhere. In a way he'd already died at least once when the final blast had hit the Lost Meadows in the Reaches, shattering the vague echo of a body that only Sally had been able to see.

The absurdity of his situation was that he could do little else but watch and listen. He had no choice in the matter. If a voyeur were someone who got pleasure from watching others 'engaged in sexual activity' as the dictionary put it, then he was no voyeur, for it was precisely at those moments that he would have preferred to look away. Such was his attachment to Sally, he couldn't bear to watch her making love to Brent and to feel the intense pleasure she got from the other man's caresses. While he was a part of her, every touch, every odour, every emotion lay exposed, shared. He refused to believe he was jealous. It was just that he couldn't bear to be the unwilling witness to her most intimate moments. If fate existed, he had been dealt a most cruel hand.

He walked passed Sally's flat, midway between the station and the Market Place along a wide one-way street. In daytime, it was busy with traffic but at one o'clock in the morning, even on a Saturday night, the street was empty. The house was in darkness. Not surprising, Sally was elsewhere, having fun with her friends, and the other tenants went to bed at reasonable hours. Lights blazed in the police station further down the street, but, like the hospital, that was normal. The police were also workers of the night. Out of curiosity he could have slipped inside and spied on them, but it would be a senseless pursuit. He had no such urgent mission to fulfil. Those days were over.

Reaching the Market Place, several late night shops lay open, lights from their windows leaking out across the square. A number of shoppers slunk away into dark alleys, followed by the tell-tale clinking of bottles in tightly gripped carrier bags. He turned down the High Street, passing unnoticed next to a young couple that were discussing the concert earlier that evening at the Arena. He didn't wait to hear what they said. It no longer mattered.

Spotlights concealed on rooftops highlighted the spire of the cathedral, a bright finger pointed heavenwards. In comparison, the narrow alley that led to the Starless Square looked downright sinister. He hurried on in the direction of the footbridge across the River Bree. Not that he was late for an appointment, the others would only be there in several hours, but an unseen force urged him on.

He caught sight of his reflection in a darkened shop window. He was more of a ghost than a human being. He looked down at his feet and legs, what was left of them. Since the destruction of his body in the blast, he could see only a faint echo. Maybe he was a ghost, he just hadn't realised it.

Reaching the far side of the bridge he headed for the ring. In the moonlight the stones appeared much smaller than those Sally had conjured up at the Arena. He wondered why the people of Avan had replaced one ring by this smaller version. He dismissed the question immediately without even trying to consider it. He didn't care. What difference did it make?

He'd spent much of his existence gathering knowledge with which he'd often been able to surprise or help Sally. She'd never wondered what he did during those long hours of silence when he didn't speak to her. Libraries wherever he went were always a haven of peace during the night, what better time and place to study for someone who had no need of sleep. During the daytime, he sat in unnoticed on lectures at the university, his favourite subjects being religion, history, philosophy, sociology, anthropology, psychology and astronomy. Despite his dour mood, he couldn't help laughing at the idea of his being a well-educated ghost.

For all his wanderings, he always returned to her. Sally was his anchorage, his safe haven, his home port in the material world. Becoming a part of her albeit momentarily couldn't make up for his forfeit body, but it was some small consolation. He smiled at the comparison that sprang to mind: she was like a luxurious canapé on which he could recline in delicious comfort and wellbeing. Not one of those uncomfortable canapés that served as an instrument of torture in psychoanalysis, rather, a place to dream freely in complete security, in her arms as it were.

He circled the ring, weaving in and out of the ancient stones, trailing his frail fingers over the weather-worn surface. To think they had stood there several thousand years. If he could merge with them as he did with Sally, what memories would they reveal?

Something stirred nearby. It wasn't a person, that much he could sense, but its presence was strong. Whatever it was made him uneasy. Yet somehow he knew that the uneasiness he felt was not his own, but that of the presence itself, as if there were a guardian spirit watching over the ring and it was extremely wary. As he moved on, the wariness diminished and finally seeped away till he dismissed the fears it had evoked as a figment of his imagination.

He'd read books about the Celts and their rituals and about the energy of their sacred places, but his readings had left him unsatisfied. So many questions remained unanswered: the exact role of these rings in maintaining the balance of the Earth's energies, for example. He might have got part of the answer from Keira or Jenny but he had no way of questioning them directly and he'd never mentioned his thirst for knowledge to Sally, the only person he could talk to. He sighed. What good would it do? His wistful knowledge curled like wisps of smoke inside his head. It might easily be blown away by the next gust of wind.

"Mind what yer doin' yer clumsy oaf!" a nearby voice whispered, startling him.

He'd thought himself alone, caught up as he was in his musings.

"Yer almost knocked the bloody stuff out of me 'ands!"

Two dark figures were planted at the foot of one of the largest standing stones. Armed with a shovel and a pick, one of them was hacking away at the hardened ground while the other cleared the earth that had been freed.

"Enough! We ain't diggin' to Australia!" the shadowy figure said, chuckling at its own joke.

Vee moved closer, trying to understand what they were up to.

"Gimme that box," one of the men ordered. "And be bloody careful. I still got things I wanna do."

It's a bomb, Vee deduced. He swore. As he did he felt the presence of the guardian once again, furious this time. Rage boiled in Vee's almost non-existent stomach making him want to spit fire. He'd stumbled on the Starless Square. Everything fit. Having failed to disrupt the weekend's events and discredit the Department, they'd shifted to a higher level in the escalade of violence. Hundreds of people would be gathered around these stones in a few hours.

He had to do something. But what? As a close adviser to Sally he'd always had good ideas. But for once he was at a loss. The two men had already buried the device and were busy covering the traces.

Scare them, Vee thought. He gathered his strength and seized the pick, sending it flying across the middle of the ring. Simultaneously he felt the rage of the guardian spirit reach out and crackle around the intruders.

One of the men stood bolt upright, frozen in place, as the tool clattered to a halt against a smaller stone. The other was bent over double holding his stomach groaning in pain.

Vee got hold of the abandoned shovel, dragged in noisily across the ring and brought it crashing down on a nearby stone causing the two men to scream.

"Let's get the 'ell outa 'ere!"

"But I haven't set the detonator."

A cloud of red-hot rage whirled around the stone enveloping the two men in its tight embrace. Vee made the most of the distraction and used the shovel in a desperate attempt to unearth the bomb, hoping his efforts wouldn't set off the damn thing. He didn't get far. One of the men grabbed the shovel from his hands and flung it away.

"It's the Devil!" the other man whined, still clutching his stomach. "This place is 'aunted. To 'ell with the bomb. Let's get out of 'ere."

From the corner of his eye, Vee saw that the first man had run to the centre of the circle and was kneeling as he attempted to force an object into the ground. The detonator! Vee ran across the ring and flung himself at the man, knocking him off balance. The detonator fell to the ground. The man tried to push Vee away, but he couldn't get a grip on him. Vee crawled away searching for the detonator.

The moon had gone behind a cloud forcing them to feel their way with their fingers. The other man must have had the same idea, because he too was on all fours rummaging around in the dark. Suddenly he heard the man call out

"Got it!"

Vee flung himself in the direction of the voice, using the last of his remaining strength. The man crumbled in a heap.

"Blast!" the man swore as he struggled with Vee, trying to get to his feet and run.

A brilliant light seared through him, blanching the colour from everything. The bomb!

"Not again!" Vee screamed, though his voice went unheard.

A thunderous roar followed fast after the light, blasting everything in its passage.

"Oh no! Not again!" Vee thought and his thoughts were carried up and away by the shock only to fall as pale ashes on the red-hot anger that smouldered in the dark corners of the Park.

Hard awakenings

"What the hell …!" Jock couldn't make sense of the world.

He'd been riding a horse through a forest, the smell of pines surrounding him. The path was full of wild young people who kept changing into different animals. That much he remembered. Something had dragged him from his dream. He groaned when he realised it was the phone. Switching on the bedside lamp, he reached for the receiver, his eyes still half closed.

"Jock," he muttered.

It was the Chief Constable. "Sorry to get you out of bed, Jock. There's been an explosion in Hoyt Park. Several people are dead. As a crowd is expected there at sunrise, we need everybody we can get. Can you come as quickly as possible?"

Jock straightened up and glanced around the room. Discarded clothes littered the floor. How did they get there? They weren't even all his.

"And if you know where Mandy is, ask her to come. I haven't been able to reach her," the Chief said and hung up.

Jock lay back on his bed, trying to figure out what was happening when someone yawned next to him in the bed. Startled he spun round. Good Lord. Mandy was sleeping in his bed! Of course: it came flooding back.

After a quick shower and a coffee black as the night, the two of them looked approximately human. They donned their uniforms and made their way to Hoyt Park. They went on foot, it was not far, especially if they cut across the footbridge. The cool night air helped wake them.

The moment they reached the river, a cloud of smoke and dust greeted them. It stank of burning and explosives. The cloud was so thick they had to feel their way across the river using the rails on either side of the bridge. They could hear sirens and headed in that direction once they hit the Park. It was there they found two ambulances and several police cars not to mention three fire engines and an army truck.

"We've gone over the whole crater," a sergeant in an army uniform was saying.

Must have been the explosives expert, Jock guessed.

"We've found no trace of other explosives."

The Chief greeted Jock and Mandy with a nod and turned back to the sergeant.

"Our guess is that there was just one bomb placed over there under the largest of the stones. The explosion smashed the stone, catapulting the debris over a large area. Some of the greenhouses in the botanical gardens have been completely destroyed. The blast itself dug out a massive crater and flattened almost all the remaining stones, projecting several of them over a considerable distance. One of the stones ended up embedded in that mound over there."

One of Jock's colleagues from the nightshift then made his report. "We found the remains of two bodies. We suspect they were men. We can't be sure there weren't more victims. It was a complete mess. Judging from the state of the bodies the two must have been quite close to the bomb when it went off. They were ripped apart. We've sent the bits off for identification."

The Chief turned to Jock who gathered he was expected to say something.

"One of the two young women who sang at the Arena last night is to sing for the rising sun here this morning. There were nearly two thousand five hundred people at that concert, so we can expect a large crowd."

"We should cancel that," the Chief commented. "Can we contact the organisers?"

"I'm not sure we should do that," Mandy ventured.

"You can't surely suggest that we let her sing on the very site were two people have just been blasted to bits, even if they were terrorists," the Chief retorted, incensed by her suggestion.

"There have been a series of strange happenings these last two days. All are connected with the events organised by the Theosophy Department and all of them sought to hinder them happening," Mandy said, surprising herself with the clarity of her vision.

Jock tried to interrupt her, but she ignored him and continued talking.

"Whoever these terrorists are, they clearly want to stop this greeting of the sun from taking place. My guess is that they planned to have the bomb explode later, probably during the performance but they were killed in planting it. We know that others are working with them because two of them are in the clinic right now. There may be others, we can't be sure, but I am certain that if we cancel the event this morning we will be going in the sense the terrorists want. So if the organisers agree to pursue in the circumstances, I would let them do so. That would make it easier to deal with the crowd too."

The Chief looked at her surprised. "Are you alright, Mandy? I've never known you so eloquent." His hand flew to his mouth as his tongue tripped over the last word. He coughed to cover his confusion. "I suppose you're right. See that a security cordon is set up around the crater." He turned to the army sergeant. "Can you folks give us a hand to check the crowd to make sure there is no more trouble." Turning back to Mandy, he added: "I'll let you liaise with the people from the Theosophy Department. If they don't want this, we'll call everything off."

When the Chief moved away accompanied by the bloke from the army, Jock pulled Mandy to one side and congratulated her. "Looks like you just got promoted." He bowed to her with mock obsequiousness. "What went wrong?"

She stuck out her tongue but quickly pulled it back in, hoping no one had seen. "I have no idea. The words just flowed into my head and made such obvious sense that I had to say them. The truth is," and she lowered her voice, "I think my night with you gave me wings."

He gave her a playful push on her shoulder. "Well I hope you don't use those wings to fly away because I'm counting on having many more nights like that one."

A slight problem

Keira wanted to arrive at the standing stones before the crowd did. She had visions of people wandering about the sacred ground within the ring, their chatter disturbing the peace. Of course the folk of Avan did that the rest of the year, but this was special. The moment she intended to greet the sunrise, the ring took on another dimension.

Leaving Irina on the far side of an improvised wall of covers that had stopped the girl shocking her during the night, she crossed the hall to the bathroom, not bothering to get dressed. She figured everyone would still be asleep. To her surprise and embarrassment she bumped into Brent.

"You make a very interesting sight, in the middle of the night," Brent noted, grinning.

She hesitated between wrapping a towel around herself or giving him a wet kiss. In the end, she did neither. "I want to get a shower before I head for the ring," she told him, stepping into the shower cubicle. "You want to join me?"

To her disappointment, he ignored her offer.

"I'll wake the others. Everyone wants to come. But I'll let Sally sleep on. She was exhausted and didn't sleep well. She can keep an eye on the Professor if necessary."

"You should let Irina sleep on as well. She was very tired too."

By the time she was dressed the house was alive with activity. Fran had got up to make them tea and coffee. Breakfast would be later. Fran had donned one of Rafter's dressing gowns that must have come from Japan or China. Embroidered on its back it had a splendid gold dragon with bright red teeth spewing fire from its jaws. Despite their short night everyone was bubbling with excitement and anticipation.

"I love the period before dawn," Jenny was saying. "When the first birdcalls break the silence of the night."

When their cavalcade came to a halt at the gates of Hoyt Park, it wasn't a scene of peace that greeted them, but rather one of desolation and destruction. Several fire engines stood idle in the car park, the firemen rolling up hoses and chatting quietly together, and a police cordon blocked the gate. There was even a truckload of soldiers.

Beyond, in the Park, Keira could not see the standing stones. A thick cloud of smoke masked the ring. Keira felt nauseous. Unaccountably reluctant, she moved towards the gate where a policewoman stopped her.

"You are the person who sang at the Arena last night," the policewoman said recognising her and held out her hand to shake Keira's. "My name is Mandy. You're Keira, aren't you? My colleague Jock and I want to have a word with you."

Brent had joined them and all three went into the Park in search of Jock.

"We have a big problem," Jock began, once the introductions had been made. "About a hour ago, two men planted a bomb in the circle of stones. It went off, killing both of them and destroying the ring and a large area around."

Keira staggered back as if struck by the blast. That bomb had been intended for her. Her, and all the people attending. Brent caught hold of her arm to stop her falling.

"This is terrible," she said in a strangled voice. "To what lengths will they go?"

"We need to have a serious talk," Mandy said, "but right now only one thing is important: in a short while hundreds, maybe thousands of people will begin arriving to hear you sing. I convinced my Chief that the concert should go ahead, provided that is, that you agree."

Trying to shake off the nausea that welled up in her, she freed herself from Brent and sent him to fetch Jenny. Then turning to Mandy she asked: "Why did you decide to let us continue? It wasn't the most obvious choice."

"You're right. And if I had the time, my answer would probably be quite complex. Let's just say I had an intuition and I followed it."

Keira was impressed. She hadn't had many dealings with the Avan police, so she couldn't judge, but this woman seemed somehow out of the ordinary. Keira also noticed the looks of complicity, almost tenderness, between her and the policeman. She's in love, she thought, startled at the direction her thoughts had taken.

When Jenny hurried to join them, Brent had already broken the news.

"I knew something was seriously amiss," Jenny said. "There's a frank hostility in the air as if an unseen force were trying to repel anyone who gets too near."

"That must be why I feel so sick," Keira said.

Mandy raised her eyebrows at their words.

"Not all of us can perceive things like Jenny," Keira explained. "Can you take us to see the damage?"

Without a further word, Mandy turned and headed off into the cloud that hung heavy over a large part of the darkened park. "Careful! Keep close behind me."

As they moved forward Keira felt not only increasingly sickened, but also oppressed. She felt weak and dizzy, fearing she might fall.

After a while Mandy halted, calling for them to stop. "The crater is only feet away."

What with the night and the cloud, everything lay obscured.

"What we need is a wind," Jenny said. "To blow the cloud out to sea."

Keira cast an anxious glance at the policewoman whose features she could just make out in the gloom. Rather than a look of disbelief, she looked intrigued. What an extraordinary woman.

Indeed, a voice echoed in her head.

She cast nervously around trying to figure out who had spoken, but everyone was silent.

"So you hear voices too?" the policewoman observed, speaking just loud enough for Keira to hear.

"It would seem so."

Jenny's premonition was clearly correct as a wind began to rise driving the smoke cloud further away over Hoyt Park in the direction of the sea. As it did, it uncovered a gaping hole were the stones had once stood. Smoke continued to hang in corners of the crater that must have measured more than twenty yards across. A number of the stones had been flattened by the blast, but many had been projected tens of yards away from their original place.

Keira clasped the pendant that hung around her neck, the one that Grace had given her indicating that she was a member of the Sisterhood of the Stones, and she burst into tears. She couldn't help it, she let out an ear-shattering wail that tore through the silence. Her grief resonated with the grief of the place shaking her to her core. Both Brent and Jenny took Keira in their arms to console her. The two police officers looked on, an expression of discomfort on their faces.

"How could they?" Keira gasped through her sobs. "Are their ideas so important that they would kill us and destroy the Earth?"

Unfettered ideas are always destructive, the voice said to her.

Keira turned to Mandy, and wiping the tears from her eyes she spoke with conviction. "Yes. I will greet the rising sun but above all I will sing for forgiveness for this dreadful deed. It will be like a requiem for lost opportunities and broken hearts."

Jenny stepped forward and took Keira's hand. "But first we need to appease the guardians of this place before the people arrive," Jenny explained. "The atmosphere is so hostile it will drive many of them away or make them feel very uncomfortable."

"How can we do that?" Brent asked.

"I will pray to the guardians," she replied, "and Keira you must use your voice to help dissipate their anger."

Looking around the crater Keira could see a small grassy area on which one of the smaller stones remained standing. "I will sing from that place over there," she said pointing to it.

"That's good," Jenny commented. "You'll be right next to the most important of the guardians."

"If you can keep the crowd away from me," Keira continued, "and from the crater that will be fine." Then she turned away from them saying: "I will help you appease the guardians, Jenny, but first I need to be alone."

The policewoman stopped her. "We can't let you wander off on your own. It might be dangerous. The people who did this are not alone. This is not their first attempt to wreck your plans. What if they try again? I will accompany you, but I will stay at a distance to leave you some peace."

Keira didn't bother to reply, but strode off towards the sea with Mandy trailing in her wake.

Communication

The girl sat unmoving on a bench, her back straight, her head held high, looking out over the sea. Mandy followed her gaze. The sun wouldn't rise for over an hour and the smoke clouds obscured the moon. She turned her attention back to the girl who was deep in thought. All was quiet and nothing moved but the gentle wash of the sea on the rocks that protected the coast road along that side of the Bree estuary.

"It's a disaster," the girl exclaimed, startling Mandy.

She thought she was being addressed and was about to reply when she noticed Keira was staring fixedly in front of her.

"You felt it too!" the girl continued.

The hairs on Mandy's head stood on end. As a child she'd once heard people speaking in voices at the evangelical church her parents attended. Standing there in the lamplight witnessing this one-sided conversation had her feeling like a terrified little girl again.

A vague form shimmered some feet in front of Keira.

"Can the sisters help?" Keira pleaded. "I hope you can get through," Keira sounded worried. "Yes. Healing and appeasement. I understand. Thank you, Grace."

The shimmering form faded. Keira sighed and turned back to Mandy. "We must go. I need to talk to my friends before the ceremony begins."

Mandy was moving away from the lamppost she'd been leaning against when a distant explosion caused them to look across the estuary towards the Arena. Flames were shooting up from the building that had crumbled in ruins.

Mandy pulled out her phone and dialled the station. "The Arena is on fire. No. I'm still at Hoyt Park. I can't leave, I have things to do." She snapped the phone closed and looked at Keira.

"Let's talk on the way," Keira suggested, crossing the road and entering the park.

"So?" Mandy asked, hoping to jog the girl into replying as they trotted along the path.

Keira slowed her pace. "The Arena was built on the site of an ancient ring like the one destroyed in the park. The two rings were strongly bound together and, even now, powerful energy currents flow between the two. That sort of thing doesn't diminish with time although mostly it remains dormant. Maybe our concert reawakened the link. The explosion here must have set off a chain reaction in its sister ring across the Bree. I just hope the effect doesn't extend to other rings. We must find Jenny. She will know." Keira accelerated her pace.

Mandy pulled out her phone and called Jock. "Can you find Jenny? We urgently need to talk to her. Meet you at the entrance to the park."

Jock suggested another meeting place because the crowds were already beginning to arrive.

"People have begun arriving," she informed Keira. "There are already several hundred gathered around the crater. And apparently the national television has turned up."

When they arrived Jenny was in hushed discussion with Jock and Brent in front of the ruins of the main glasshouse of the botanical gardens, one of the closest buildings to the ruined ring. Jenny looked worried.

"Jock told us the Arena had collapsed," she said anxiously, before Keira had the time to speak.

"Yes," Keira confirmed. "I spoke to Grace. She told me there are disturbances across all the rings of the Sisterhood. Can you check the state of the damage here, Jenny?"

The worried look had not left Jenny's face, if anything it had got worse. "I've looked here. The damage to the Earth's networks is relatively small. It would take a much bigger explosion to upset those fields. But there are other very strong currents that link this place to elsewhere. I will check further afield."

The young woman moved a few steps away and closed her eyes. Mandy shifted to Jock's side and lightly touched his hand. He looked worried. She wondered what the others had told him before she arrived. She wanted to ask, but Jenny had returned.

"The shock wave has spread to the Arena. The two rings are directly linked by a strong current, what we call a vortex." Seeing people's confused looks, she added. "It's actually two vortexes with a large energy channel running between them. One site feeds the other."

"So is that why the Arena collapsed?" Jock asked.

"I doubt it. At worst, the ruins of the Arena might become a very unpleasant place to be. You'll have to look elsewhere for an explanation. There is however a disturbance on a different level, but that is currently beyond my grasp. I suspect it has something to do with the evil intentions of the people who destroyed the site here."

Mandy looked confused. "You mean people's intentions can be so destructive that they alone cause physical damage?"

Jenny looked at Mandy for a long moment. "Yes."

The idea that people's thoughts could be so devastating alarmed Mandy.

You need to appease the guardians before the celebration, a man's voice reminded them, startling them all.

The voice seemed to be in Mandy's head, but clearly each member of their little group could hear it.

Jenny was right, you should use both prayer and song, the voice explained.

Ignoring the early arrivals, Jenny, Sally and Brent moved to the place from which Sally was to sing. Mandy and Jock exchanged one or two sharp words and Jock hurried away unwilling to get involved. Mandy trailed after them intrigued.

"There are a number of guardians," Jenny explained in a whisper.

Mandy could hardly hear, so she moved closer.

"They are organised in a hierarchy. We need to appease all of them, but above all the most important of them. He's standing next to the Theosophy Department building that is at the mid point between the two parts of the vortex. There is also a Ley line that runs perpendicular to the vortex at that point."

She paused to take a deep breath. "I suggest we proceed as follows. I will say a quiet prayer that you can echo in your minds or reinforce, as you think fit, pointing your thoughts in the direction of the Department. You can join in if you wish. You don't need to speak out loud," she told Mandy. "Once we have finished I suggest you sing for the guardians, Keira."

"But what?"

"Let yourself be guided by your feelings. That is how the guardians communicate with us. OK?"

Keira and the others nodded.

Mandy worried she might do something wrong. Jenny must have read the concern on her face because she added: "Don't worry. Just think positive!"

Once Jenny had invoked the guardians and expressed her sadness at the damage done to the two rings she promised that they would do everything in their power to restore the rings to their former glory. She asked permission to hold the celebration for the rising sun as in days of old and thanked them for welcoming them and all the others who had convened for the celebration.

Then Sally sang a wordless song the music of which expressed a deep longing for the harmony of other times and of times to come. As she sang the chatter amongst the gathering audience silenced and a palpable tension filled the air. When the song ended, the hostility that had surrounded the crater had lifted and Mandy felt much lighter and less tired. She regretted Jock hadn't been there to witness what had happened.

Greeting the dawn

According to the police, nearly a thousand people had gathered in the dark around the smouldering ruins. Those at the back could see nothing of the damage done, but word seemed to be passing quietly from person to person till the front-line eyewitness accounts were known to all. A small wooden platform had been hurriedly erected at the place where Keira was to sing. It had a couple of steps leading up to it.

Keira took a deep breath and climbed up till she was in full view of everybody. Thanks to the spotlights of the TV cameras she could be seen despite the darkness. Brent, Anju and Dieter had explained to the television crew that they would have to turn off the lights and stop filming when the ceremony began.

"Welcome," Keira said, projecting her voice out over the crowd. "I am so sorry that you have to be the unsuspecting witnesses to a catastrophe of proportions that are difficult to imagine. Misguided people have destroyed the Avan standing stones and in so doing have set off a chain reaction that has contributed in some small way to the collapse of the Arena concert hall. The two places are tightly connected because there used to be a giant ring where the Arena stood and their energies are linked."

The crowd stood absolutely quiet, listening to her every word.

Jenny climbed the steps to join Keira and spoke to the crowd. "This place is a sacred site and is watched over by a number of powerful guardians. You probably won't be able to see them, but they make their presence strongly felt. We have spoken to them and they have kindly accepted us here despite their anger at the destruction of the site. We have promised to do our best to restore this ring and the one that used to stand where the Arena was built. Keira's singing for the rising sun will be a first step in that direction."

She paused a moment as if in silent prayer. "Later this morning," she continued, "I will examine the energy fields around the ring and take stock of any damage that may have been done. Luckily the Earth's energy field is quite resistant to such things. I plan to map out the energy lines and will need all the help I can get to do that, so if you would like to learn something of the Earth's energy field, do join me here at ten o'clock."

Jenny stepped down and Keira spoke again. "I wish we had time to answer the many questions you must have, but the sun will rise in a short moment and it is time to begin the greeting." Suddenly remembering something, she addressed the crowd again. "One last thing: as Jenny said, this was and still is a sacred place. The guardians will not tolerate any bad behaviour so I ask you for complete silence during the whole ceremony, not just out of respect for the place but also so as not to disturb my concentration. Thank you."

As if her thanks were a sign, the television spotlights flicked out one after another and the cameras were switched off plunging the whole park in almost complete darkness. Keira turned to face the East, raised her outstretched arms and called out the ancient words of welcome. Three times she called out, startling some of the birds that were patiently awaiting the rising sun. They burst prematurely into song and with that Keira sang the Gaelic song that Grace had taught her, letting its tender melodies work their way into the hearts of the crowd, softening them up, making them more receptive and bringing tears to the eyes of many. It was her answer to the sadness of death and destruction that had marred their experience of the ring.

She let a poignant silence hang in the air at the end of the song and then, as the very first hints of colour tinged the sky in the East, Keira called out to the Sisterhood, and let her own voice ring out over the ruins and in so doing she broke through the heavy sadness that hung over the site. Hers was a cry of joy and an affirmation of life. Digging deep inside herself she sought the original location of the stones, and using those, she let her voice slowly circle the ring. Grace's voice and those of the other sisters joined her and their fluid female voices proceeded around the ring, blessing each stone in turn, even those that were long gone and forgotten.

As the first rays of the rising sun crept up bright red over the hills that circled Avan, the voices of the sisterhood soared in the air and joined the joyful chorus of birds greeting the new day: flamboyant, cheerful, rich in colour, outspoken, sensual, powerful, transcendent. And little by little the voices quietened, the sisters withdrew and Keira finally ceased her singing, leaving only the birds like the orphans of a celestial chorus. Keira slowly lowered her outstretched hands and closed her eyes in thanks.

People stood waiting quietly, suspended in the first rays of the rising sun. The relative silence seemed to last for ages and then the crowd began applauding, timidly at first and then ever stronger. Keira climbed slowly down the steps from her makeshift stage and embraced Jenny and Brent who were waiting for her. All three of them walked through the crowd that opened up to make way for them and, as they moved forward, people turned to follow them, forming a long procession behind them.

Many people reached out to touch Keira lightly as she passed as if she were a saint or a holy woman. She was both touched and embarrassed by their display of appreciation and affection. She didn't feel that she deserved such veneration. All of a sudden in that moment of triumph and recognition she was reminded of her nightmare at the hands of a band of men in the Reaches. She felt soiled and unwholesome once again.

The pain of that violence and abuse which had receded with time, suddenly surged up again, joined by the profound sadness and the feeling of loss that sprung from the desecration of the ring. She broke down in sobs, seeking refuge in Brent's and Jenny's arms. People around became still as they witnessed her suffering and although they could not imagine its cause, they could feel its depth and many tried to find a way to console her whether it be with words of encouragement or a light touch.

The only way Keira could overcome the dark shadows that threatened to suffocate her was to sing, so climbing up on a rough stone, supported by Brent and Jenny one on each side, she sang a lullaby in the Gran dialect. Her friend and mentor Ma'gina, the very person who had coaxed her back from the horrors she'd suffered, had taught her it. She remembered having sung it for a young girl in the Reaches that had been a victim of rape.

Unaware of the history behind the song, people seemed very willing to join in and accompany her, so, as it was not so difficult to learn, she taught them the song and they all sang together. And when she'd finished and the applause had died down she spoke out. "Now let's go home and have some breakfast. I'm starving."

Waylaid

Throughout the celebration Mae had remained in the car park with Tom who had been unable to get any closer to the ring because of the crowd. When Kean and several other watchers joined them, Mae left Tom in their company and wandered off across the car park to talk to the television crew.

"I wanted to thank you for respecting our wishes," she told the producer.

"It was a most amazing performance. I wish we could have filmed more," he replied. "But you were right, all our lights and equipment would have spoilt the effect and disturbed people."

Mae hadn't had many dealings with national television, but she guessed his attitude must be unusual. From what Tom had told her, TV people didn't always pay too much attention to the impact their presence had on the things they filmed.

"We did manage to film the lullaby," he admitted. "There was enough light to film without flooding the place with our spotlights."

He looked like she ought to be pleased, but the news made her wary. "What do you intend to do with the material? You understand of course, that you cannot use it without Keira's written permission." Mae regretted that she knew little about performing rights, but made a mental note to find out more.

All of a sudden the man was extremely busy and wanted to rush off. Mae placed a restraining hand on his arm. "I trust your reaction does not indicate that there is a misunderstanding between us."

"We will show a small extract on the national news. That will probably be all." He sounded impatient.

"Good. So long as you understand that the performer retains all the rights to her performance."

The man turned and hurried off. Mae watched his retreating back for a moment trying to judge whether her demand would be respected. She was about to return to Tom when a voice surprised her.

"Well done. If you don't show them, they'll walk all over you."

She glanced at the person who'd spoken and was prepared to ignore him. She didn't like being accosted by people she didn't know.

"You're with Sally, aren't you?" he asked.

His question had her surprised and puzzled. How did this smooth-looking thirty-year-old guy know Sally? He didn't seem her type at all.

As if hearing her unspoken question, he answered. "I met her during the guided tour."

She was anxious to return to Rafter, she didn't like being away too long, and she had no time for chattering.

"My name is Collin."

"Pleased to meet you Collin." She held out her hand stiffly to shake hands. "I have to go now. Goodbye."

"Are you all so evasive?" His chuckle surprised her.

"Maybe that depends on whether or not we feel we are being harpooned by a person we don't know." She hoped he would take her irritation for humour.

"Sure," he said, clearly disappointed. "But if ever you need help with television or film rights, I might be able to help." With which he walked away, leaving her standing alone, wondering why she had been so rude, and regretting it.

She had taken only a few steps when a couple of police officers stopped her. A weird idea flitted across her mind that they were going to arrest her for being so impolite to Collin.

"My name's Mandy," the policewoman introduced herself, "and this is Jock, my colleague."

The woman grinned at some personal joke that Mae couldn't understand. Was she getting jumpy and irritable with lack of sleep, she wondered?

"You work with Keira, don't you?" the policewoman began.

Mae nodded, hoping that the less she said, the sooner she could get away.

"There are too many people around her for us to reach her, so we'd like to leave her a message. Would you mind?"

Mae nodded again. Where was her usual polite, convivial self?

"I'd like to personally thank her for going ahead with the celebration. I imagine it wasn't an easy choice in the circumstances."

"I will tell her at breakfast," Mae said, won over by Mandy's evident sincerity.

"There is one more thing you should tell her and Jenny," Mandy added. "They were wondering if the explosion here had set off the explosion in the Arena. It would seem that something quite different was the cause. Our experts have found an unused smoke canister wedged in the air conditioning unit. It seems likely that that triggered the fire later."

This news was important indeed. Jenny would be relieved to know the danger was less than she thought. Jock's telephone rang at that moment and he stepped away to answer it.

"Whatever," Mandy pursued, "it is possible that the same people who blew up the ring were at work at the Arena. There seems to be an organised group trying to stop your events. We will make every effort to avoid that happening again, but if you have any information about these people, it would help us greatly."

Mae really liked Mandy. She seemed so relaxed and happy. Happy?

She puzzled over her choice of word for the policewoman, but it really fit. She appeared trustworthy, so Mae decided she could tell her some of what she knew about the Starless Square, glossing over the interrogation Frick had undergone at the hands of Brent.

She had just finished when Jock returned, a worried look on his face. "They've discovered a body at the Arena: a young man," Jock informed them. "He was found near one of the main fuse boxes."

"Did that have anything to do with the place exploding?" she asked.

"It might well have been him who planted the smoke canister," Jock guessed. "As the electricity had been turned off, whatever he wanted to do with the air conditioning wouldn't have worked. He would have had to turn the electricity back on."

"Did the explosion kill him?" Mae asked.

"No. He was already dead. His body had been completely crushed by something extremely heavy. We have no idea what."

Mae must have turned pale because the policewoman asked her if she felt OK.

"It's all these deaths," she pretended. "I will give Keira your news," she added hurriedly and, taking her leave, headed unsteadily in the direction of Tom and the others.

Keira had finally managed to break free of her fans and Brent and Jenny were accompanying her to a car. Mae decided not to mention the body till later. She did however relate the policeman's thanks to Keira.

"I see you met Collin," Brent said laughing. "He's charming isn't he?"

Mae couldn't understand why, but the mention of his name made her furious.

"Did he tell you about his plans to make a film with us?" Brent continued.

The idea of him prying into their affairs to make a film irritated her even more.

"No," she snapped, giving him no chance to utter a word. "I'm sorry, he gets on my nerves."

"You should let Irina give you a massage," Keira joked. "That would surely help you relax."

Mae ignored the probable sexual innuendo, which made her feel even more alone and miserable, and climbed into the car.

A world of knowledge

Extraordinary! There was no other word to describe it. For someone who loved gathering knowledge, who relished the thought of spending all night in a library or attending lecture after lecture or studying the intricate ways of the world and the behaviour of people around him, his new state was extra ordinary.

He wasn't sure how to describe it to himself or even who the 'himself' was that he was doing the describing to. He didn't even know if 'he' was the right pronoun. He could just as easily be 'she', but he stuck with the 'he' out of habit. It was like being pure knowledge, whatever that meant, with awareness of self as an added perk. It was all there, all the knowledge that existed. All he had to do was stretch out his mind and he had access to any knowledge he wanted. In those conditions, 'mind' was probably not a suitable concept. It was too limited to embrace the unfathomable experience he was having.

Such a vast store of knowledge was accessible, but he couldn't know it till he'd looked at it. Attention was the key word, not only in terms of knowing, but also in terms of survival. He'd had to learn that the hard way. Just after the explosion, he became aware of so many fascinating titbits of information assailing him that he felt like he was exploding a second time. His attention was being ripped apart and he didn't know where to look or how to protect himself. He felt so confused and lost. It had given him a splitting headache, except that he had no head to ache.

He'd finally closed his eyes, metaphorically at least, shutting out all the knowledge and cutting off its constant demands for attention. It was a frightening experience. He was terrified that he might wink out completely if he shut himself off from knowledge, but to his relief that hadn't happened. And then, very cautiously, he had squinted at the world, trying not to open the floodgates too wide. To his great pleasure it worked. He found he could focus his attention on a very narrow area of knowledge and even think about it without being pestered by the infinitely great rest of it all.

What made his situation all the stranger was the feeling that he had a self and that self was no less substantial than it had been when he had been named Vee, although now he floated free of all attachments and was entirely without a physical form. He wondered about the concept of self and, setting aside the shelves and shelves of reference books about the subject that jostled for his attention, he could see that his experience of it lay in a point of view, an anchorage without material form from which he looked at the world and the knowledge about it. It was that anchorage or point of view which had substance and that he called 'self'. He was constantly aware of it and recognised it as being him. That made him think about the name Sally had given him: 'Vee'. The more he thought about it, the more he thought he ought rather to be called Mee. He savoured the name, repeating it several times. Yes, he would adopt it; it fit him well.

Mee could re-work the infinite knowledge available to him provided he didn't try to take it all on in one go. Unlike a library, or a network of computers, he was able to think about and assess what he 'knew' thus creating new knowledge that added to the stock available. He was able to decide and act. He liked to think that the way he approached knowledge gave him a sort of 'personality' that others, if they got to know him, would be able to recognise. Oh! And he liked to laugh! He'd already discovered some absolutely hilarious contradictions in the knowledge available to him.

To make things more complicated, not that complexity bothered him, he revelled in it, he was not necessarily at one given point at any given time. Normally when a human being thought of a point of view, it was linked to a specific time or place. During the preparation for and the celebration of the rising sun, he had found he could be in several places at once. The point of view was more a question of orientation with respect to knowledge. He'd been able to speak into several heads at once.

That was the other facet of his new self that gave it solidity: he could influence what people thought. Not that everybody necessarily did what he said. But at least he could be heard and that gave him the impression he had a hold on the world, at least to some extent. At the same time, he seemed to have lost the ability to move objects. He'd tried, but his 'hand' just went right through the stone he'd tried to pick up.

A strange but pleasing idea struck Mee: perhaps he had been promoted from a half-ghost to an angel. But something told him he hadn't quite reached that level. Why? Because the world around him remained unpredictable. He had no access to knowledge about what was going to happen. He had heard of the Akashic records that the Theosophists described as a secret account of all knowledge about the universe and human existence, past, present and future, but he had no access to future knowledge. It must be on a different plane to which he didn't, as yet, have access. The thought that one day he might gain access to that repertory pleased him immensely although he didn't relish the thought that he might have to be blown to smithereens to do so.

Mee was about to take stock of the scene around him when a thought struck him. That was another thing that hadn't changed, he could still see the world although he saw it from one place at a time while he could now be 'present' in several places simultaneously, at least sufficiently to be able to make his voice heard. He'd not tried out the ability much, but he suspected he could only speak to those places that were within reach of the place he was seeing at any one time. He revised his theory and felt much happier and more convinced about its new form. He was present in one place at any one time, but he could project his voice from there, like a ventriloquist, to many other places nearby.

Mee glanced around and realised that the ruins of the ring lay deserted in the early morning sunlight. His friends had driven off to Rafter's place much earlier. Even the stragglers who'd hoped to spend a moment with Keira and who had lingered on in the car park were gone. The police and the army had set up a barrier around the crater with a prominent sign saying: "Police! Keep Out!" and then they too had left.

He wondered if they were aware of the ambiguity of their sign, probably not. It pleased him, and would have made him chuckle if he'd been able to. He floated over to the barrier and stared into the gaping hole the bomb had left. To think that he had survived an explosion that had projected giant stones through the air, making them land yards away.

Mee examined one of the largest stones that lay on its side near the crater. He did so against the backdrop of the entire history of the place: where the stone had been mined; how it had been transported to the site; the mechanisms used to raise it and fix it in a vertical position; the rituals that had taken place there; the later civilisation that had tried unsuccessfully to destroy it; ...

Something was odd, though. The stone had developed a considerable 'lump' on one side that disfigured it. He could find no record of such an occurrence. Circling round the flattened stone he realised it must be a body rolled up in a ball in a small cavity between the stone and the earth. The body was in a filthy state, it's clothes tattered, its shoes in ruin. But something about the lines of its face and the high forehead was familiar. He consulted the multiple records he had access to and ascertained that it was in fact Dr. Frick.

The only way he could determine rapidly whether the body was alive or dead was to talk to it. Mee wondered briefly what you said to a potentially dead body. The question had such a ludicrous side to it that he could imagine Shakespeare rejoicing at the thought of it. He doubted that a direct approach: "Are you dead?" would be a good idea. In the end he opted for the ridiculously mundane.

"Would you like a cup of tea?" Mee asked, making his surrealistic request sound both caring and discreet.

"I'm dead," the body told him categorically, not without vigour.

Mee felt momentarily out-manoeuvred till he realised that Frick was probably caught up in his own thoughts. Now there was a problem. How could a dead body talk or think even? Unless of course it was a ghost. But he had the impression that a ghost would not talk with such conviction.

"You can't be dead," Mee reasoned with Frick. A futile exercise, of course, the last thing you could do with unreason was try to bring it to reason.

"How would you know?" Frick retorted. "You're hardly alive yourself."

Ah! He thought, the man is aware of me. And he chuckled at his unintentional play on words. That's a good start.

"Why are you in this distressing state, Dr. Frick?" Mee asked, trying a more fatherly tone.

"I've been picked on," Frick replied without the slightest hesitation.

"Who, may I be so bold as to ask, has been picking on you?" Mee pursued, adopting a somewhat anachronous approach hoping to set himself outside time and, above all, beyond blame.

"You should know," Frick spat, rolling over and sitting up, leaning against the stone.

The conversation was taking a rather sterile turn, Mee thought. "What makes you think you're dead?" Mee asked, trying to get back to essentials.

"Because I was bitten by a poisonous snake."

"Yes I know," Mee replied, having read the story up to that point. "You were trying to torture that young girl to get her to confess like her mother."

Frick staggered to his feet and lunged in what he must have imagined was Mee's direction and collapsed face first in a heap dust stirred up by the explosion. A rather futile exercise, Mee thought, as he wasn't to be found in any particular direction.

Spitting the dust from his mouth, Frick protested. "I didn't do it!"

"No technically you didn't, Dr. Frick. But a man called Jon Adams did, in 1723 to be precise. What you do not know, Dr. Frick is that you are a reincarnation of Adams."

Frick rolled his eyes in disbelief. "What nonsense!" He cackled like a lunatic. "You won't get me like that." So saying, he sank on his backside on the pile of dust setting up his own personal dust cloud that rose majestically around him and set off a fit of coughing.

"I don't need to 'get you' as you put it," Mee pointed out. "You have already been cursed. There's no more to say." What Mee meant was that as talking was all he could do, there was no way he could undo the curse. But Frick must have understood his words as a further condemnation.

"I can't be held responsible. It wasn't me."

"Is that not what your victims pleaded?"

Frick got to his feet somewhat unsteadily and started to stagger around the upturned stone. "I refuse!" Frick said, stamping his feet.

"That's not the right answer," Mee pointed out. "Maybe if you said: I accept, you might have a chance."

Frick was getting increasingly agitated. He waved his arms wildly as he stomped around the stone and screamed "No way!"

Mee considered leaving the miserable Frick to his fate, but he still thought he might be able to save the man. Of course, he had read the curse but he had no idea what the 'atrocious suffering' would be that would end Frick's life.

Frick must have come to some decision because he rushed across the grass towards the crater and pushing over the police barrier he flung himself into the heaps of dust and debris. He rolled over several times, carried forward by the impetus of his mad flight, sending up a cloud of dust that obscured most of the ruin.

Frick was wracked by violent coughs as dust filled his mouth and nose. He tore at his mouth, desperately trying to breath, but he was drowning in the dust. The more he struggled, the more dust rose up. His arms flayed as if he were trying to fight off a band of assailants.

Mee could have sworn he heard women and men cheering with glee. Frick was on his back now, his hands clawing at his throat, his spine arched unnaturally upwards, his form almost rigid with fear and shock. Then almost as abruptly, Frick's back sank into the dust, his arms fell to the ground and he was still.

"Goodbye, Dr, Frick," Mee said quietly, sadness in his voice and he floated off to visit other horizons.

Chapter 10 ~ Family Breakfast

Uneasy futures

"Can you check the bread? I reckon it's ready," Martin said as he pressed oranges.

Fran peered through the glass door of the oven. "You're right. It's ready." She lifted the loaves out of the oven and placed them on a grid to cool. Two loaves were sprinkled with sesame seeds that had gone a golden brown and the two others, made of darker rye flour, were covered with tiny black poppy seeds.

When Keira and the others had left to celebrate the sunrise, instead of returning to bed they had set about preparing breakfast. They were also to watch over the Professor, but he slept peacefully for the first time in some days, so they had spent their time between the kitchen and the dining room. They had planned a buffet, thinking that people could choose their food and then join Rafter in the living room.

"Have you ever wondered if we have discovered our vocation in cooking or if we are meant to move on to other things?" Martin mused. He wouldn't normally bother with such a question but something Jenny had said that morning about exploring new vistas had put the idea into his head.

Fran was tasting some jam they'd made with several sorts of wild fruit and spices and wine. She licked her fingers, clearly appreciating the taste, in no hurry to reply to Martin's question.

"It seems a waste not to use the other things we have learnt, like your university studies and research," he pursued. Not that the question had been bothering him, but now it had cropped up he wanted to mention it.

"If it is acquiring gifts you are talking about," Fran responded, "I'm quite happy with cooking. When I think of the responsibility involved in having gifts like those of Sally or Keira or Jenny, it makes me shuddered. As a group, we haven't given it much thought, but I have thought about it a lot."

Martin was surprised and even a little uneasy. Fran had never said it bothered her. But that might be quite normal as they had a very easy-going, loving relationship that went well with the pleasure of delighting others with good food. The relaxed, uncomplicated way they were with each other suited him perfectly. Unlike his sister, Jenny, he was not much of an intellectual. He liked to get things done, preferably with his hands. If his sister had not been such a promising artist, he often thought he might have enjoyed doing sculpture, but he didn't fancy living in the constant shadow of his sister.

Fran had aligned herself with him, he suddenly realised, apparently setting aside her scientific activities and her passion for thinking things out. Suddenly he worried that she might suffer from that loss.

"What do you mean by responsibility?"

Fran was tasting a new preserve they'd made with wild flowers. "Mmmm!" she said by way of reply.

He chuckled and washed the berries they'd collected the day before.

"If I could transform the world around me, like Sally does, I would constantly be concerned that I might misuse or even abuse my powers."

Martin had never thought of it that way.

"One thing worries me though. Do you feel frustrated because I am not an intellectual, you who love books and passionate debate?"

She looked at him for a moment, cocking her head to one side as if deep in thought and then burst out laughing. Her reaction had Jim perplexed. She must have seen his confusion because she hurried to his side and flung her arms around his neck, planting a wet kiss of his lips.

"I love you as you are," she whispered in his ear. "As long as you don't burn the scones!"

Blast! He'd forgotten them. He whisked them out of the oven. Luckily only one or two were a darker colour.

"You are mistaken, though if you think I have given up my scientific pursuits. In fact I have been reading a lot about the medicinal role of food. I have been trying to explore the impact of nutrition on genes and DNA. That way I can combine my knowledge about molecular biology and my experience with cooking." She burst out laughing again.

He wasn't sure if she was kidding him. He felt uncomfortable, something that happened rarely. She noticed, of course. He couldn't hide anything from her.

"I'm serious," she reassured him, brushing flour from the tip of his nose. "Some people working at the extreme limits between science and transcendence, like the Theosophists, had postulated that the DNA contains much more information than we originally thought. What was hitherto discarded as noise might contain vast stores of knowledge that could add up to what mystics called the Akashic Records."

"What's that?"

"A sort of compendium of all human knowledge along with the record of all that happens in the universe whether past, present or future."

Martin struggled to get his head around the idea but it was too big. "How can such an impossibly large source of information fit into such a tiny thing as a cell?" he asked as he mixed oat flakes, crushed millet, chestnut flakes, nuts and dried fruit to make Muesli.

"It might not be so impossible. Just think how much information is needed to build a human body from next to nothing. It's all contained in the DNA."

Martin hadn't thought of it like that. Well, maybe it could be possible.

"Those people who believe the Akashic records are to be found on a cellular level also maintain that they can be accessed by a special sort of meditation. If we could explore that, it might provide the answer to Tom's problem about foreseeing the future."

She took the yoghurt they'd made the day before out of the fridge so that it wouldn't be too cold and poured out the fresh milk they'd collected from a nearby farm at the end of Rafter's Road.

"But what about you?" she asked. "What do you dream of doing, in addition to cooking that is?"

The question gave him a feeling akin to vertigo. Not that he'd ever suffered from such an affliction: he climbed the most perilous mountains and went down into the deepest potholes without the slightest qualms. But Fran's question left him giddy. He'd never told anybody what it was he really wanted to do. And he hesitated to tell even Fran. He blushed with embarrassment.

She raised her eyebrows in the most theatrical way as she waited for his answer.

"I have always wanted to do sculpture," he admitted, half expecting her to laugh.

"What a wonderful idea! I could easily imagine you doing that." She clapped her hands as if she were a little girl discovering a treasure. "Oh yes! You should."

Shocking

Sally was grateful Brent had let her sleep, although she regretted not having seen Keira greet the rising sun. In fact, she had awoken soon after the others had left, but had continued to lie in bed, examining the numbness she felt at the loss of Vee. Downstairs she could hear Fran and Martin busy in the kitchen. She could have joined them, but preferred to remain alone.

She had to admit that she felt less empty than the evening before. Maybe it was Keira's medicine or Jenny's magic, or was it possible that the wound had already begun to heal? She had stretched out her mind in search of Vee. Maybe he had discovered how to conceal himself. Several times she thought she felt traces of him, but they were very faint and drifted away every time she got close. She'd finally got dressed and went down to see if the Professor was awake. He wasn't. So she sat for a while, plunged in her thoughts, by his bedside until she heard the others and went outside to greet them.

"Did you sleep well?" Jenny asked. Sally nodded.

"It's a shame you didn't come," Brent said with a wicked smile, "you missed Collin. He was asking for you. Now he's developed an interest in Mae."

Mae groaned and threw something at Brent but missed. "Maybe I should dump him in another world and leave him there," Mae commented.

"But you hardly spoke more that a few words to him, according to the Watchers," Tom added.

Sally jumped down the steps, ran to Mae's side and put her arms around her. "Stop teasing my friend," she told them, although she couldn't help grinning at the playful atmosphere. She walked arm in arm with Mae in the direction of the house.

"How was the celebration?" she asked Keira as she paused at the foot of the steps.

"Strange and extremely emotional."

Sally figured there was more to tell but that Keira was in no mood to do so.

It was Irina that filled her in. "The people from the Starless Square had blown up the ring. All that was left was a giant crater full of dust."

Keira confirmed Irina's words with a nod.

"That's terrible! So you had to cancel the celebration? I bet people were disappointed."

"No we didn't," Brent put in. "The police suggested Keira go ahead and, having talked to Grace, she agreed."

"It was most wonderful," Irina enthused. "The audience were delighted. There were over a thousand people according to the police and there was even a TV crew present. It's to go out on the national news."

Mae freed herself from Sally's arm and climbed the steps without looking back and disappeared inside, presumably going to see Rafter. Sally followed and the others traipsed after. Inside they were greeted by a delicious smell of newly baked bread.

"Mmm!" Irina said, "Fran and Martin have been at work."

The girl had come back from the celebration more electric than usual, as if the ceremony had further charged her batteries. Sally didn't feel so oppressed by Irina's presence as she had in the beginning but she felt there was something worrying about the charge the girl carried. Unaware exactly why she did it, she laid her hand on Irina's shoulder. Maybe she'd thought she'd be able to feel that energy and possibly guide some of it away like a lightening rod. Instead a shock shot through her. Her hair stood on end, her legs trembled and she felt like she was on the verge of having an orgasm.

Jenny chuckled. "Sorry. We should have warned you not to touch her. She's like what we call in French an 'allumeuse'. She sets people on fire sexually."

"Wow!" Sally said, distracted by the idea. "That's a powerful weapon!"

Jenny laughed and Irina giggled.

"No touching the Professor," Sally ordered, "that would kill him for sure."

The others went through into the dining room were Fran and Martin had laid out a mouth-watering breakfast for them, but Sally hung back in the hall to kiss Brent. Pulling him tight in her arms she led him to the door and they slipped out onto the porch.

"I've missed you," she said.

He kissed her, by way of reply.

"I bet you didn't have much time to miss me."

"You are right. You haven't heard a fraction of the story yet."

She was torn between staying alone with him and having him tell her the story or joining the others and seeing if the Professor was awake. Brent told her the essential. The two terrorists had been killed in the bomb explosion. The place was in ruins. The police had cooperated remarkably. And the Arena had collapsed, although probably not because of the explosion at the ring. She had hundreds of questions, but they couldn't stay there any longer, they had to join the others. She kissed him one last time and they went inside.

"I hope you've left us something," Brent called out, joking, as he entered the dinning room.

Fran and Martin hadn't skimped on quantities. There was plenty left. There would even be enough for seconds. Next door, Sally could hear the Professor's voice. He was talking to Mae and the others. He called her over the moment she entered and suggested she sit by his bed, next to Mae.

"My favourite women," he whispered.

All the dream class were assembled. Only An was absent. She was having breakfast with Tricia, Maria and Beth at Tricia's place.

"You have some unfinished business Professor," Keira reminded him. "You left us hanging there with Tess about to come and tell you everything after twelve months absence."

Sally turned to look at the Professor. He had slept and was rested, but the lines on his face seemed to have deepened and the unmistakable signs of suffering had not been removed by sleep. Rafter handed Mae the tray on which he'd had his breakfast, cleared his throat and began to talk.

Story's end

My time of waiting was nearly over. I must admit I was really nervous. I suppose I had become a little wild, living as I did alone in the middle of a forest with no one to talk to. I hadn't seen Tess for twelve months: who knew what might have happened during that time. When I got up after a sleepless night, I washed and shaved. I'd grown a long beard over the months but I needed to shed it for her. Tess's note had said she would come in the morning but I had no idea when. I tried to read a book, an effort that proved impossible, so great was my anxiety.

I paced the clearing, mulling over what might have prevented her from coming all that time. Had she been ill? Or was her husband forcing her to stay in the house? Or had there been a war that I was unaware of? My head spun with ideas, each more far fetched than the one before. It was not just the ideas that made my head spin. I had eaten no breakfast and that, combined with lack of sleep and intense worry, was making me giddy. I staggered to an armchair on the terrace, slumped in it and promptly fell asleep.

When I awoke I could hear noises inside the house. Several people were talking but I couldn't make out what they were saying. It sounded like women and children. I was about to stand when I realised that someone had spread a blanket over me and slid a soft cushion under my head. It was then that Tess appeared, stepping out of the front door and turning to greet me.

I had long imagined that moment. I had seen us rushing into each other's arms and kissing passionately. Instead we just looked at each. She had changed, her face and figure had filled out. She hadn't become fat but she had put on weight. She seemed more feminine almost motherly. I stood and moved towards her, hesitant, wondering what I was expected to do. I imagine she felt something similar. I might have shaved but I probably hadn't been able to divest myself of the wildness that had become mine.

It was Tess that made the first move. She stepped forward and ran her hand across my cheek and through my hair. Then she leant forward and, pulling my face closer, kissed me, cautiously, as if she were afraid I'd run away. I put my arms around her and we were lost in a passionate embrace that lasted forever.

It was a little voice that said: "Is this Daddy?" that broke us apart and had me startled and alarmed.

I couldn't possibly have heard right. The child must be talking of someone else. But Tess took the little girl by the hand – she must have been about four years old – and said. "Yes. This is your Dad."

I couldn't take my eyes off the child. Mine? How could that be? The sound of crying from within interrupted me as I was about to ask a question. Tess hurried back into the house, leaving me alone with the girl. I had no idea what to do or say.

The girl was less embarrassed. She chattered happily. "Mummy told us a lot about you," she explained. "She said you worked with many people in a big place for learning."

"A university, it's called."

"I didn't imagine you so tall?" the little girl confessed. "And I thought you'd have a beard," she continued.

"I did have one till this morning."

"Why did you not come and see us?" she asked.

"I … I …" I was at a loss for words. How could I explain that I had no idea she existed, that I had a daughter, living probably only a short distance from where I was studying? "I didn't know."

"Surely Mummy told you she was having your baby," the girl said, trying to come to terms with something that went beyond her understanding.

"Tess left suddenly. I never knew why. When we met again, she didn't tell me about you."

The girl looked perplexed and hurt. I could feel myself getting angry. I'm not sure if it was because this child had been kept a secret from me or because suddenly I had a child that would surely change my life in ways I might not want.

We were standing there looking at each other with a mixture of disbelief, confusion, anger and hurt when Tess returned. In her arms she was carrying a tiny baby that couldn't have been more than a couple of weeks old. I shook my head. I didn't want to believe what was happening. This must be a nightmare. I could think of only one thing to do: run.

"Tess?" I said, unable to articulate my distress and panic.

"Yes," she replied. "This is also your daughter."

She came forward and placed the baby in my arms. The girl, whose eyes were wide open looking at me, had curly ginger hair, freckled skin and bright green eyes. Her eyes were so intense that I could hardly look away. There was clearly something about her mother in the baby's face. If I tried hard, I could even make out some of my own traits in hers. I glanced at the other girl and saw what I had not been prepared to see before: she also looked like both her mother and father. What I felt then was akin to an earthquake. As if two parts of me were shifting with relationship to each other causing me to shudder right into the depths of my being. It was only afterwards that I was able to put a word to my feelings: It was love, the love I felt for my two daughters.

Tess led us inside. She had prepared a meal while I slept. She offered to take the baby, but I insisted on keeping it in my arms and invited the other girl to sit on the chair next to me. As we ate, Tess explained what had happened.

"I had to leave Avan suddenly when I discovered I was pregnant. I had no idea what would happen to a child from my world if it were born in yours. Maybe it would get ill like people sometimes do when they pass between the worlds. I was in a panic but I planned to come back once I'd figured things out. My parents forced me to marry a man from the Patriciat. Luckily he was very understanding, he knows all about you, but there was no question of my returning to join you."

It had never crossed my mind that she might get pregnant. I have to confess to being an ignorant, self-centred male. I still had a lot to learn.

She went on to explain that she'd fallen pregnant a second time when I had turned up in her world. "No it wasn't my new husband," she protested, seeing my dubitative look. "Ours was an arranged marriage. He makes a good companion, I enjoy talking to him and attending Patriciat events with him, but we were never intimate like that."

Seeing that she was pregnant yet again, her husband had suggested she get rid of the child, but she had refused. When he learnt that I was staying in the house in the woods, he refused to let her come and see me. He said he would accept her having the child on one condition: that I then take both children back to my world and look after them without her. He even took the matter before the Patriciat Council that sanctioned his solution.

"We have three days together," she told me, "then you must leave with my daughters." And she burst into tears and both the girl and the baby cried with her.

I was at a loss what to do. I couldn't console them all. So I cradled the baby in my arm, rocking it gently backwards and forwards while I put my other arm around the girl, cuddling her up close to my shoulder. Tess sat across the table watching the three of us together, tears streaming down her face.

When the children were finally asleep and laid to bed, Tess and I talked for hours. I wasn't competent to look after two little children, I told her. I didn't even have a job. And if I had to look after the children I wouldn't be able to do the kind of job I was destined for. Both of us were miserable.

Not only would we loose each other, probably forever, but also our children would be separated from her and perhaps even from me. As we debated what to do, we came to the conclusion that I would leave the girls with foster parents till they were adult and then I would tell them their story and send them to visit their mother. In reality, I was unable to find a foster mother to take both girls so they had to be separated. That caused even more pain as I felt they would have been better off together...

Rafter broke down and stopped telling his story at that moment, unable to continue as tears streamed down his cheeks. "I did it all wrong."

He was unable to continue talking because he was interrupted by a bout of coughing that shook his whole body. Mae handed him some medicine. When he finally calmed, Sally handed him a handkerchief with which he wiped his face and blew his nose.

"You didn't tell us the names of the girls?" Keira pointed out.

Rafter did not answer immediately, as if he were gathering the strength to speak. "The eldest girl was called Mayeva, but we called her Mae for short."

Everyone looked at Mae. She looked astounded but also delighted. She starred at Rafter who nodded in confirmation. "I've always dreamed that could be so," she said between her tears. "That I could legitimately call you Father, that was my secret wish." And she cautiously put her arms around him and kissed him on his wet cheeks. "Dad," she said and both of them laughed and cried together.

"But who was the other girl, the little one?" Keira asked.

"Can't you guess?" Rafter asked.

All of a sudden, Sally felt extremely uncomfortable, so much so she thought she was going to be sick. Ok. The thought had playfully crossed her mind, given that she hadn't known her real parents. Then Teresa had told her she was Sally's mother and that her father was someone from her own world. Teresa. Tess. Sally gasped. A little, green-eyed baby with freckles and ginger hair: it was her.

"Yes, Sally you are my daughter," Rafter confirmed.

Inexplicable, uncontrollable anger boiled up inside her. "We spent so much time together. Why didn't you tell me?"

Rafter looked sad and tired. "I ... I was afraid. Several times I decided to tell you both, but I couldn't bring myself to do it."

Sally got to her feet, trembling all over, quite unable to contain the contradictory emotions she felt. "How could you? I've been hoping to find my true father all my life and you wait till the very last minute to tell me."

The Professor's face was wracked with guilt and misery. "I'm sorry," he whispered, "I'm so sorry."

Sally couldn't take it any more. She thought she was going to burst.

She took one last look at Rafter and ran for the door. Father, she thought. How easy it had been for Mae. Why not her? She loved him with all her heart but she couldn't accept the way he'd treated her. It wasn't fair. The years of unspoken suffering crashed over her making her want to scream.

As she opened the front door she heard Rafter say: "Let her go. She's very angry. She'll be back. I'll wait for her."

It was then that she slammed the main door behind her and ran across the car park to the road beyond and set out as fast as she could for no particular destination.

Dad

The others must have sensed that she wanted to spend time alone with Rafter as they started to drift away, saying they needed to get a nap before Jenny's seminar or had to prepare for the buffet at midday. Mae remained by the bedside, Rafter's hand firmly clasped in hers.

"I don't think I could ever get used to calling you 'Dad' even if it is the nicest sound I've ever heard," Mae confided, her face almost cracking, so wide was her grin. "I don't even know your first name."

"It's John," he said. "John Llewellyn, in fact. But nobody has ever called me that. Not even Tess."

He coughed violently and had considerable difficulties breathing. Mae had to wait till he was calmer before she could give him some of Keira's medicine.

"It's a beautiful name."

"You're biased. My father was Welsh. And my grandfather was called Llewellyn. It is said to mean 'like a lion'." He chuckled causing him to cough again.

"My Lion Professor."

"I hardly roar any more."

"Have you ever seen Tess since those days?"

Rafter was silent a long moment. "No. We never met again."

Mae hesitated. She had an idea but was afraid it might upset him. She knew so little about the man despite having worked with him for quite a while. Deciding to go ahead, she asked, "Would you like me to fetch Teresa?"

Rafter looked at her shocked and worried. Clearly the idea had not crossed his mind. She could see he wanted it, he wanted it badly, but something was warring inside him.

"I'm not sure that would be a good idea. We didn't leave each other on very good terms. In those last few days together, surrounded by our two girls, I tried to convince her to abandon her husband and the Reaches and travel with me and you two back to Avan. She refused. It was a question of honour. Something to do with the Patriciat that I couldn't understand." He looked stricken at the memory, regret written in giant letters across his face.

"We argued often, sometimes quite violently. On one epic occasion our shouting woke you two. You were both frightened and crying. It was late in the evening. In the end all four of us cried together and finally fell asleep cuddled together on the double bed. That's where we all awoke on the last morning. Tess couldn't bear the idea of leaving you both. She had wanted to slip away before you woke, but fate had it otherwise. When it was time for her to return to her husband as agreed and for us to travel back to Avan, she broke down. A wild fit took her and she started shouting at me that it was all my fault."

"That was very unfair."

"Not really. I was largely responsible for our predicament." He lapsed into silence.

"She can't still be angry with you," Mae said, not heeding her natural penchant for caution. She had so little time left with her newfound father and she knew she would be tortured by many unanswered question once he was gone.

"When she finally left she forbad me to return to see her. 'It would better like that' she said."

Mae resolved to fetch Teresa in the Reaches, but for that she would need the help of An. She had never met her mother so An, who had suddenly become her half-sister, could guide her to their house. The only trouble was that An was away at Tricia's house trying to convince her parents to let their daughter go on a trip to An's house without being able to say where she lived.

"Were you never tempted to return to the Reaches?"

"Often."

"But you never did?"

"No."

All of a sudden she saw how tired he was. She had been so engrossed in questioning him she'd forgotten his illness.

"You should rest."

He put his hand over his mouth in an attempt to conceal a yawn. "You are right, Mae. In the mean time, I would like you to do one thing for me. In the cupboard next to my desk in the Department are a whole series of papers that you and the Dream Class might find useful later. You should go and fetch them now before something happens to me and you no longer have access to them. You never know how the university might react. You'll also find a wooden box with the papers. Bring that with you too, but don't open it. Not now at least. You needn't worry about the books. If ever you should need them I have copies here or elsewhere."

Mae couldn't help pulling a face. She was loathed to leave him for however short a time.

He must have understood because he added: "I'm not going right now. You have time. And anyway I promised to wait for Sally to return."

She couldn't help tears overflowing and running down her cheeks.

"Don't cry, my love. All is as it should be."

"Yes, Dad," she said, although she wished things were not at all as they were.

At the Playe's

"This is delicious," An exclaimed as she served herself a second helping of toast and beans.

She was sitting in the dinning room in Tricia's house. Maria and Beth were with her and Tricia. All four had made their way there on foot, crossing a sleepy Avan after the ceremony at the ruins of the standing stones. The Playe family lived in a large house not far from Professor Rafter's. Mr and Mrs Playe had been surprised to receive a visit from the girls so early on a Sunday morning. Apparently they had a reputation for being late risers on Sunday.

"Do you not have beans where you live, An?" Tricia's mother asked.

"No we mainly eat bread and jam and dried fruit."

"Why don't you eat cooked foods for breakfast?" Tricia's father commented from the kitchen where he was frying eggs and grilling bacon and sausages.

"Habit, I suppose," An replied.

"You should have been at the ceremony," Tricia told her mother.

"I am amazed you all got up at the crack of dawn to attend a religious ceremony," her mother retorted.

"It wasn't religious," Beth pointed out. "It was the celebration of the rising sun, like they used to do thousands of years ago in such places."

"Sounds pagan to me," her father said, carrying in a dish piled high with eggs and bacon and sausages and beans and toast.

An was unsure what Tricia's family thought was normal and acceptable in terms of religion, so she kept quiet.

"And you say the ring had been blown up. Wasn't it dangerous to go there?" her mother asked.

"No," Tricia insisted. "The police and the army were there and they said it was safe. If it hadn't been safe they would never have let a thousand people get so close."

"A thousand!" Tricia's father exclaimed. "We never even get a fraction of that in the cathedral, not even at Christmas or Easter."

"Keira's singing was so beautiful, Dad," Tricia said. "She sang a wonderful lullaby in an ancient language called Gran."

Her father looked perplexed at the name. An hoped he wasn't one of those people who rushed to find the dictionary or the encyclopaedia whenever there was a word they didn't know. She doubted that the Reaches would be mentioned in any book from this world.

"Isn't that the young woman who sang at the Arena yesterday evening?" Tricia's mother asked.

"Yes," Tricia told her. "She's a friend of An's and she gave us free tickets. I've never seen anything like it," Tricia continued, going on to explain all she'd seen.

An was afraid that the description might frighten Tricia's parents. But they couldn't be immune to their daughter's enthusiasm.

"It sounds delightful, love," her mother commented.

To An's astonishment, these people had the television switched on throughout the meal. She wondered if they were waiting for a programme they wanted to see, but nobody was paying the thing much attention other than the occasional glance and the sound was turned down too low to hear what was happening.

"Hey look!" exclaimed Tricia suddenly. "That's Keira!"

All turned to look. Tricia pressed the remote control that lay on the table next to the slices of toast, causing Keira's voice to fill the room. An would never have known what a remote control was if Sally hadn't shown her how to use it. It was the lullaby Keira had sung at the end of the ceremony, perched on a stone. Despite the poor quality of the recording, it was still extremely moving. Unfortunately the news presenter interrupted the song, saying they could hear it later in their programmes. An was not surprised to see Tricia's mother had tears in her eyes.

"That was truly wonderful," the woman said.

"Oh look! That's us!" Maria exclaimed, excited to see herself on TV.

It was indeed. The television was showing an extract of Anju's demonstration. They all sat in silence absorbed by Anju's pyrotechnics.

"She's an extraordinary athlete," Tricia's mother said. "How did you three get involved?"

"Anju is a friend of An's too," Tricia explained. "She was showing us some self defence moves when the TV turned up."

"And that's a girl called Sarah," Beth added. "She's much younger than us, but she tells the most wonderful stories. She performed at the Arena with Keira."

Tricia's parents looked astonished. "So many celebrities," her mum said. Then Tricia's father asked one of those questions that An had been hoping to avoid. "And what do you do An?"

She could see Maria was about to reply but Beth kicked her under the table.

"Lot's of things," An said, hoping she had diverted attention from Maria who was furious at Beth. "I've learnt a lot about healing." It might be a less risky gift to admit. "I have a very good friend who runs a sort of dispensary where they work with plants and natural medicine. She taught me a lot."

"Tricia was telling me you have no schools where you live," Tricia's mother ventured. "How do you learn?"

This is getting no easier, An thought. "Well, yes. We learn a lot from our parents and from our friends and from people around us. My stepbrother was the first to teach me self-defence, for example. Ma'gina, the old woman I mentioned, taught me healing. Another friend called Grace taught me singing. She taught Keira too."

Beth was bouncing up and down with excitement in her seat. "Is that why you want to create a new sort of school?" she asked, completely forgetting Tricia's parents.

An had to smile at the girl's enthusiasm, even if it didn't make the conversation any easier. Of all the three, Beth was the one who loved learning most.

"A new school?" Tricia's father queried.

"School is maybe not the right word," An explained. "We call it the Dream Class. Our idea is that within our group we share what we know. Keira can sing and is very good at healing. Sarah and Brent tell stories. Jenny works with energy of the earth to help things grow. She's also a very talented artist. Anju and Dieter do self-defence. And so on. So in sharing what we know we all learn a lot from each other. Then later we can teach other people and learn from them." She left out Sally and Mae's skills thinking that would alarm the poor people.

"An has promised to teach us things too," Tricia said.

"Yes," An hastened to add, fearing that Tricia might forget herself and tell them about transformations or travelling between the worlds. "The girls had some problems with a bully from a nearby school and I promised to get Anju to teach them self-defence."

It seemed like the most propitious moment to suggest the girls visit her. "I wanted to ask them to join us for a short while so they can take part in some of our 'classes'," An explained.

"And where is this 'dream class' as you call it?" Tricia's father asked.

"It is wherever we are together," An said, chuckling inwardly to herself. "But mostly it's in some quiet place where we can concentrate and we won't be disturbed."

"Well, I don't see why not," Tricia's father said, to An's surprise. She hadn't imagined he would give in so easily. "As long as it doesn't interfere with your studies. You could go for a weekend, from time to time."

Tricia got up and flung her arms around her father's neck. "Oh thanks, Dad. You're a real sport!" She turned questioningly to her mother.

"Well if your father says yes, I agree, but only if your studies are not affected. You need good grades to get into university."

"Now we have to talk to my parents," Beth said.

"And mine too," Maria added.

"Hold on a moment, you three Misses, before you go rushing off, there's a little matter of the washing up to be done."

"Don't worry Mrs. Playe," An said with the authority that came from all her unsaid years. "We'll tidy up. Why don't you leave this to us. It's a beautiful morning for a walk." An could feel she'd set off a slight shock wave as her other personality surprised Mr and Mrs Playe, but the idea appealed to them and they must have felt reassured leaving their daughter in the hands of a wise woman, even if they didn't know it.

They had hardly started tidying up when the phone Sally had loaned An rang. It was Mae. She was at the university and wanted An to meet her urgently.

"Is there a problem?" An asked, worried by the tone of Mae's voice, not daring to ask if the Professor's health had suddenly deteriorated.

"No. I just need to do something and I can only do it with you."

An glanced at Tricia and the others who were watching TV instead of cleaning up. "Is it ok if Tricia, Maria and Beth come along?" she asked, realising she had hardly done anything without them these last few days. When Mae agreed, An asked: "Tell me briefly what it is you want to do." She listened to Mae as she watched the three girls jostling for a place in the one armchair in front of the TV. "Let's meet in about fifteen minutes in Sally's flat near the station. I have a key," An said and she flipped the phone closed.

"Right girls," she said, trying to keep a serious face. "I'm glad you've finished the washing up because I have to leave immediately and only those who have finished can come with me."

Tricia threw a cushion at her, closely missing upsetting a crystal glass water jug on the table. "You sound like my Mum," she protested, sticking out her tongue.

"That would be confusing," An said, trying to imagine the situation and failing to do so. "Turn off that machine and help me get this finished. We've got to get to the station in fifteen minutes," she said, setting about washing the pile of soiled dishes.

"Where are we going exactly?" Beth asked.

"On a journey," An replied unable to keep herself from making a mysterious face.

Beth must have understood immediately, because she flung her arms around An in her enthusiasm, almost smashing the pile of dishes waiting to be dried on the draining board.

"Already?" Tricia asked delighted, having also grasped what An meant.

Only Maria hadn't understood. The girl looked perplexed. "Where are we going?" she asked looking somewhat shamefaced.

"To An's home, Silly," Beth told her.

"But I have to tell my Mum," Maria cried out, alarmed. "She'll be worried."

"Don't fret," An told her. "We are only going for a very short time. We'll be back later today. We just have to fetch something."

Or rather somebody, she corrected in her head. She wasn't at all sure Teresa would accept. According to Mae, Teresa had been Rafter's lover a long time ago. An's mother had never mentioned the man. And she could be very stubborn but then so could Mae who was as persuasive as she was stubborn.

Flight

At the end of Rafter's road, where it met the main avenue to the station, a footpath set off at right-angles in the direction of the sea, doubling behind the hospital and then running parallel to the railway sidings till it reached the sandy scrubland that bordered the beach on the far side of the port from Avan.

Sally stomped along the path not bothering that the occasional gorse bush snagged her ankles and made them bleed. The gulls must have sensed her filthy mood because several of them dived squawking at her, pulling up at the last minute.

"You'd be angry too!" she harangued them. "He could have told us ages ago. Why did he wait?" She aimed a kick at a bush that had clearly been mistreated by other passers-by. She cursed when her shoe flew off and landed in bushes several yards away. She hopped to fetch it, then, ill-balanced on one foot, she tried to put it on and almost fell over doing so. "Are you mocking me!" she shouted to nobody in particular.

I wouldn't dream of it, a voice said close by.

She spun round trying to see who had spoken and, loosing her balance, fell headlong into a bush. Luckily it wasn't gorse. She expected to hear a roar of laughter and was furious in anticipation, but only silence greeted her. Crawling on to her knees and forcing herself to get up, she glanced around trying to catch a sight of the person who had spoken.

Who ever it was had had plenty of time to hide while she struggled in the bush, so she decided to ignore him and head for the narrow footbridge attached to the railway line that spanned the mouth of the port. It was the only direct way across to the seafront and the area close to the Arena. Judging from its state, the way was rarely used. Wind had heaped sand over the steps to the bridge which itself was rusty, although it still looked sturdy.

Someone had sprayed a giant inscription in multi-coloured gothic script on the side of the railway bridge: My Father, thou art in Heaven.

She froze where she was. The words shocked her. What was she doing wandering around all on her own, shouting abuse at the elements when her newfound father was lying at home, dying in his bed? Every second she spent there was time lost. What did it matter if he'd made her so angry? What did it matter if he was the silliest man alive for not telling her earlier? He was still her father. She turned round abruptly and clattered down the obstructed steps sending up a cloud of sand

and began to run back along the way she'd come.

A wise decision, the voice said, startling her.

She almost tripped over the exposed roots of a bush as she halted her headlong pace and began searching for the source of the voice.

For someone who has had a voice in her head for so long, you astonish me. Can't you imagine where my voice is coming from?

Sally had several emotions simultaneously: disbelief, relief, anger and intense love. Not surprising, she thought, that she felt confused. Her heart was beating wildly as she struggled between all four emotions. Vee? she asked, tentatively, hardly daring to raise the question. It didn't feel like him. Vee had had a distinctive character that was akin to a private corner of her head where he resided. This voice didn't quite fit. It wasn't a part of her. Yet it was somehow familiar.

No. I am not Vee. Although a part of me may have been him at some time in the past. My name is Mee.

Sally slump to her knees and collapsed sideways till she was reclining on the sand. She couldn't help herself; she burst into tears. I thought I'd lost you forever, she said, reliving the anguish she'd felt when she could no longer feel him.

Well, strictly speaking, you have.

He was no longer the playful voice that wouldn't hesitate to tease her. His voice had adopted a much graver and wiser tone. And he was right; there was no privileged link between them. She could not feel him as she once had as a part of herself.

I suppose you'd say that I've become emancipated.

Suddenly she remembered Rafter and got to her feet. I must go back to the Professor, she told Mee. What a strange name she thought. Why don't you come with me and tell me what happened. There was a moment's silence during which she wondered if he had left again. Then he spoke.

I will join you later. Give my regards to John Llewellyn.

Who could that be, she wondered.

It's Rafter's name. And he was gone.

John Llewellyn! What a beautiful name, she thought, wondering why he'd never used it. She couldn't possibly be ashamed of such a powerful name. So the professor had Welsh origins. The return journey was much shorter, partly because she jogged most of the way. In no time she was entering Rafter's house.

In her head she'd rehearsed what she'd say: Dad, father, John,

Professor, … in the circumstances they all seemed quite odd. She thought of excusing herself. She'd been so rude and inconsiderate. And what if he'd passed away in the mean time. She just couldn't let herself think such a thing.

Calm down. Everything will be all right, Mee said soothingly and then he flitted away again.

She found the professor alone. Mae had apparently left and the others were busy elsewhere or already underway. The house was quiet. Creeping into the room, she sat as quietly as possible in the chair Mae had vacated. She studied his face, having the impression she had never seen it before. Who was this man she now had the right to call 'father'? Not just her Professor or her tutor or her employer.

Her musing was interrupted by Rafter saying, "Surely you don't think I couldn't sense my favourite daughter when she arrived?" He smiled, his eyes still closed.

"Father," she tried. "Dad… I'm so sorry for how I behaved. Please forgive me."

He opened his eyes and looked at her silently for a long moment. "I believe it is I that should be asking for forgiveness."

She shook her head, tears welling up in her eyes making the world blur.

"I certainly can't forgive myself for being such a coward. Day after day I saw how you progressed and developed. I was so proud of you, both of you. I couldn't have asked for a better gift than to see you both blossom out into womanhood but also power."

"Tell me, Dad, would you like me to fetch Teresa for you?" she asked, wondering if she dared broach the subject.

He smiled. "Mae asked me the same question. As I explained to her I don't think Tess would like to see me. We parted on difficult terms. But I would like you to do one thing for me: tell Tess how much I have always loved her. And thank her for giving me such beautiful and wonderful children."

He closed his eyes for a while as Sally took hold of his hand.

"I have sent Mae to fetch some papers in my office. They are very important. You will need to study them. I have been working on the question of travelling between the worlds for many years and my work is quite advanced. There may be information in there that might be useful to you and the Dream Class."

He rested again. Sally thought he must be asleep but he began talking again without opening his eyes.

"You must pursue the idea of the Dream Class. It's the most inspiring project I've ever heard. You probably won't be able to do so within the university. It was never the right place. But you'll figure out how to do it."

"You should rest, Dad," she told him. "I think some of the members of the Department are planning to pay you a visit this afternoon. We want you in good shape for that."

He smiled and shook his head slightly. "If ever I don't get another chance to say it, Sally, you should know that I love you and your sister more than anything."

"And we both love you, Dad. I think we felt you were very special for us. Now it has been confirmed." A sob caught in her throat and hung there, as if her heart was trying to reach up and out to him.

Good friends

How many times had she entered Rafter's office, Mae wondered: hundreds, maybe many more. Yet this time it was like the first and possibly the last. She'd vowed she wouldn't spend ages reminiscing but it was hard not to. She could picture the Professor sitting in the bay window reading a book with the morning sunlight warming his back; so calm, so confident, so ... she cut short her memories and crossed the room, weaving between the armchairs where the students generally sat, till she reached the wooden filing cabinet next to his desk. The key didn't fit well, presumably Rafter hadn't used it very often, but she finally managed to open the door.

Inside, true to form, the papers were impeccably organised in folders and files. She'd brought two carrier bags. One was enough for the papers. The other she used for the wooden box. She didn't need to fight the temptation to peek inside because the box was locked. Concealed under the box she found a photo turned face down. On the back was written a date and a place she didn't recognise. Flipping it over she discovered Rafter with his arm around the shoulders of a young woman that Mae guessed must be her mother, Tess. The two were laughing and looking lovingly at each other.

Hearing the distant cathedral clock strike the hour, she inserted the photo inside her pocketbook. She locked the cabinet and picked up her carrier bags ready to go when a knock came at the door.

"Come in!" she called out, fleetingly feeling guilty about making off with Rafter's affairs, even if it was the Professor who'd told her to do so. It was Lyra. "Good morning, Professor Enquist," Mae said, grinning. She didn't usually greet Lyra so formally as the professor was one of her best friends. "You doing overtime?"

"I could say the same to you, my friend," Lyra replied, grinning too.

"Rafter ..." but try as she may, Mae couldn't help tripping over his name. Tears sprang to her eyes. Lyra looked alarmed.

"He's not ....?"

Mae shook her head. "No. He's OK, but weak."

"Then what is it?" Lyra pursued.

"He's my father," she blurted out.

"Who?"

"Rafter."

"I didn't know he even had a wife let alone a child," Lyra said, clearly astonished at the news.

Mae stood planted in the middle of the room, tears streaming down her cheeks, a carrier bag heavy in each hand. Lyra came forward, relieved her of the bags, took her in her arms and hugged her. Mae felt embarrassed, not so much because she was crying but because she was helpless. All her life she'd been steadfast and loyal: the person people could count on, the one who was the lifeline for everybody else when they floundered. Suddenly that edifice came crashing down and she crumbled with it. Something in her was giving up.

The thought of renouncing left her feeling lost and terrified. Who was she? She'd always battled her way forward. She'd always lived for the others. Maybe the fight was no longer necessary. Maybe she could lower her guard now that she was no longer alone. She desperately tried to shrug off her emotions and regain her self-composure, but they clung desperately to her.

Ushering her into one of the armchairs, Lyra produced a small bottle from her pocket. "You remember my magic potion?" she said, shaking a couple of drops onto Mae's outstretched tongue. "Better?"

Mae nodded.

"When did you hear this?"

"Just now. He told Sally and me. Sally is also his daughter... my sister."

"But surely this is good news?"

"I couldn't have asked for better."

"They why are you crying, silly girl?" Lyra ran her fingers through Mae's hair.

Mae laughed, despite herself. "Maybe because I am so happy. Or maybe because my father, now that I have finally found him, is about to die."

They both fell silent. Mae shook herself. She had to get underway if she was to meet An.

"Would you like to accompany me?"

"Why not," Lyra replied, helping Mae get to her feet.

"Where are you going?"

"To the Reaches."

Lyra halted in her tracks. "Where?"

"I have to convince my mother to come back and see my father before he dies. It's the least I can do."

Lyra looked worried. "But I have no ability to travel between the worlds."

"You won't need it. I can transport people between the worlds without the slightest problem."

Lyra didn't seem any happier that the obstacle was removed. "Do we leave from here?"

"No. We have to go to Sally's place. I want to leave these papers for the Professor there. And I am to meet An and her friends. An is my half sister. I need her to guide us, because I have never met my mother."

They found An and the three girls waiting in Sally's flat. An presented Tricia, Maria and Beth to Lyra. They raided Sally's larder, packing food and drink into a backpack they found in Sally's cupboard, just in case.

"I'm nervous," Maria admitted, blushing.

"You're not the only one," Lyra said looking dubitative. "I may be a university professor, but I have never done this kind of thing either." She grinned at Maria.

"Well if a grown-up is nervous, them maybe I shouldn't be ashamed of being nervous either."

Lyra laughed. "Let's be courageous, both of us," she whispered.

Mae pulled out her phone and dialled Sally.

"Where are you?" she asked. "And is he OK?" There was a pause and she added. "I'm going to the Reaches to fetch Teresa. I'm taking An with me and her three friends. Oh and Lyra Enquist."

There was another pause.

"Yes. We'll be back as soon as possible. Bye sis!"

Beth had sat down on Sally's bed and begun reading one of her books.

"Bring it with you," Mae said, "you can read it if we get a free moment."

Pulling out the gold pendant the little people had given her, Mae called everybody together. "Come on girls, it's time to go."

"Hold on a moment," An said. "How are you going to find Teresa? She's travelling with my father in the south of the Reaches and you've never met her."

Mae knew she had only half the answer to the question but she was in a hurry. That could be dangerous, she realised. She took a deep breath and calmed herself.

"I thought we'd go to your house in the forest, the one where my father lived for so long. I have already been there. Then we try to find some way from there to your mother."

"We'll never be able to find her quick enough if we have to travel over land," An pointed out. "I have no idea where she is."

Try the photo, a voice said in her head.

Of course! She hadn't thought of that. Thanks, she thought back to the unknown voice.

You're welcome. My name's Mee, by the way.

Mae pulled out her pocketbook and extracted the photo. "I'll use this."

"Wow!" An said. "Where did you get that? It must be very old. I've never seen my mother look so young."

"I'll explain when we arrive."

"What's all the hurry?" Beth asked, still plunged in the book.

"I don't want to arrive too late," Mae said. She didn't need to say anymore, everyone understood. Mae grasped Lyra's hand on one side and An's on the other.

"All hold hands tight," she instructed, checking that Tricia, Maria and Beth were also holding hands in the circle. Then looking at the photo as she clutched the pendant in her other hand she said a silent prayer that it would work and the familiar wrenching feeling told her they were on their way.

Chapter 11 ~ Land Art

Angels

Clyde sat cross-legged on the tabletop, hands folded in his lap, eyes closed, back straight, his pitch-black hair standing on end. He gave off a deep feeling of serenity. Somebody had loaned him a pale blue t-shirt that was much too large for his thin frame and grey tracksuit trousers but his feet were bare. He'd been completely naked when they'd found him, Mandy remembered. Much of his body had been tattooed with weird hieroglyphs that were now gone, judging from his face.

"Morning, Clyde," she said cheerily as she entered his room in the clinic.

He didn't respond. He might well not have heard.

"How are you feeling this morning?" she asked.

He raised his hand to silence her, his eyes still closed, but said nothing. They hadn't had time to question him earlier, too many other things had happened. The head of the ward told her that Clyde had been no trouble, so much so that they had foregone any medication pending a full examination by the doctor. He'd slept most of the time and when he wasn't asleep he seemed to meditate, like he was doing now. He hadn't wanted to eat but they had managed to convince him that he ought to. He particularly liked warm milk, she'd been told.

"Thank you for waiting," he said softly, opening his eyes and looking at her in surprise. He blinked several times before continuing to talk. "The angels were talking. I didn't want to interrupt them or miss anything they said."

She wondered if she should humour him and ask about the angels.

She didn't want to get dragged into his craziness. She was a policewoman, not a therapist.

"They told me to help you."

"What were you doing in the chapel, Clyde?"

"Fighting off the black spirits." His face twisted with fear. "They came because of the drugs, I believe. I used to take a lot, but I've stopped now. The angels told me to."

"That's good," Mandy said, trying to be encouraging but feeling extremely self-conscious. She was relieved that no one was with her to witness what she said.

"Why did you take your clothes off?" she asked, trying another avenue.

"An angel told me to."

"Why?"

"To find the way, I think."

"Did the angel draw all those hieroglyphs on your body?"

"No. I did that."

"Why did you do that?"

"As a reminder."

"A reminder?"

"That I was on the wrong side."

She couldn't see where that line of thought was going. Better to start anew. "Where did this happen?"

"At the Arena."

"Why were you there?"

"To do something bad." He hid his eyes with his hands, moaning like a naughty child fearing punishment.

"What was that?"

"To hurt an angel."

"And did you?"

"No. I couldn't. She was too strong."

"Why did you want to hurt her?"

"It was a mistake."

"A mistake?"

"I thought she was a witch."

"A witch?"

"Yes those that were burnt under the starless sky in the square."

She had the distinct impression she was missing something important.

"Starless?"

"Because of the smoke."

It didn't make sense. "Which square?"

"The Starless Square."

She finally realised he was referring to the square that bordered the cathedral. "What happened there?"

"They burnt witches."

"And did you burn witches, Clyde?" The thought made her shudder.

"We wanted to. We tried. But the angels said it was not good."

"We?"

"The Starless Square."

She sighed. This was getting her nowhere. Drained and exhausted by their conversation, she decided to try one last time. "The Starless Square?"

"It's a group."

"You belonged to it?"

"Yes. We met in the Starless Square."

That seemed highly unlikely. Why would a group of people bent on evil meet in a square in full view of everybody?

"You met in the Square?"

"No. In the pub?"

"Ah!" she couldn't help saying. She'd forgotten the pub of the same name next to the cathedral.

"We met there from time to time."

"Were there many of you?"

"Seven."

"Did the angels tell you to meet?"

"No. Frick did?"

"Frick?"

"Dr. Frick, from the university. I don't think he knew about the angels."

She tried to recall the name of the man they'd found wading through the mudflats near the university. Peter Glat. "Was Peter Glat with you?"

Clyde nodded.

"Who else was in that group?"

He gave her several names that she didn't know. She noted them down. "Tell me, Clyde, what made you think that angel was a witch?"

Clyde bunched up his knees and wrapped his arms around his legs. "Frick told us there was a group of witches in the university."

Mandy paused as the pieces of the puzzle fell into place. "Were these witches in the Theosophy Department?"

Clyde nodded.

On a hunch Mandy decided to try using Clyde's angels to help her. "What do the angels say about these people?"

"That we were wrong."

"Why were you wrong?" She wasn't sure where this was leading but she felt caught up in something that had its own momentum.

"It was complicated. I couldn't completely grasp what the angels said." He straightened up and closed his eyes again. "Something about good and evil, about the dividing line between the two, and things being out of tune," he whispered and fell silent.

Enough, she thought. "Thank you, Clyde."

But he did not respond.

"And thank your angels for me," she added as an after-thought and stood, heading for the door. How could she possibly write a report on that interrogation? Her chief would just laugh at her.

Barking up the wrong tree

The Watchers had been present at the greeting of the rising sun, mingling with the crowd, shadowing the police and army and circling the perimeter of the site. Luckily, Tom thought, they had not been there when the bomb went off. Now Kean and the others were ranging across Hoyt Park and around the university in preparation for Jenny's seminar. Apart, that is, from a small group keeping an eye of Rafter's house.

Tom rolled his wheelchair around the car park heading in the direction of the entrance to the park. Sex with Jenny had left him feeling more alive and more invigorated than he'd felt since before his accident. He took a deep breath, sensing the fragrances of the many flowers wafting over from the gardens and the flowering borders in the park. It felt good to be alive. Only one thing marred his morning joy: the Watchers. Their work had not been a success. They had been unable to foil any of gambits of the Starless Square. Luckily Frick's group had been their own worst enemies.

Maybe he was barking up the wrong tree, he told himself, smiling at the strange English idiom that likened the wise seeker to an enraged dog. All the others had found their gifts, even Irina who was new to the group. He had thought he would find his own calling through the activities he'd learnt in the Reaches as a watcher. But his efforts to predict the future, even on a short-term, had proved unsuccessful.

"Woof! Woof!" he called out, mocking himself, as he wheeled under a tree.

He had to chuckle. It was so silly.

Why silly? a voice asked.

He spun his chair round thinking someone had addressed him but he realised that the voice had been answering his thoughts so it must be in his head.

Telling the future has always been a challenge that attracted humans, the voice said.

I had been referring to the barking, Tom thought.

I can't tell the future, either, the voice mused not paying attention to his clarification.

Tom wondered what the voice could mean. It sounded preoccupied.

I have access to all available knowledge but not to knowledge about the future. The fact seemed to trouble the voice.

Have you ever heard of the Akashic records? the voice asked.

Odd you should say that, Tom thought. Fran mentioned them at breakfast. She didn't have time to go into details.

Tom rolled his chair through the entrance to the park and headed off down one of the avenues that led in the direction of the former ring of standing stones.

I've been going through all I can find about them, the voice pursued. But what I've learnt is no use to me personally.

Tom wondered why that should be.

Because it requires a body and that's the one thing I don't have.

Tom had the impression he could hear regret. Who are you?

Sorry, the voice replied. I keep forgetting to introduce myself. I spend so much time flitting from one person to another that I forget the basic rules of politeness.

Tom couldn't help smiling at the idea of a disembodied voice worried about being polite.

It's important, the voice chided.

My turn to say sorry, Tom thought.

My name is Mee, the voice said. You might say that the explosion here created me.

Tom had arrived at the verge of the crater. It was all the more spectacular in the light of day.

How could this have created you? Tom asked waving his hand over the crater.

It's a long story, Mee said. But to put it briefly, my former self was trying to stop the two terrorists from planting their bomb when the thing went off. I was convinced that was the end, but I lived on, enhanced in some ways, handicapped in others. That was when I discovered I could tap into the vast store of knowledge available throughout the world. Mee became silent.

Tom had no way of knowing if Mee was still with him or had gone off somewhere else. The Akashic Records. Yes, he'd like to know more.

Good, the voice continued.

I think Fran would be interested too, Tom put in.

OK. I'll find an occasion to tell you both some of what I know, Mee said, maybe later today. Now I have to help Jenny.

Tom offered his thanks.

By the way, Mee said, there's a body buried in the middle of the crater. It's Dr. Frick. I tried to dissuade him, but he insisted on drowning himself in the dust. Maybe someone should get it moved before Jenny arrives and all those people turn up.

Tom was shocked at the news. He had disliked Frick for all he'd tried to do, but he didn't wish him dead. Tom pulled out his phone. The policewoman who'd been there during Keira's ceremony had given them her number if ever there was any further trouble. As he dialled, he tried to remember the policewoman's name. Mandy. But you couldn't just phone a policewoman and address her by his first name, Tom thought.

Her name is Mandy Delaney, Mee told him.

Thanks, Tom replied. "Constable Delaney?" Tom asked.

"No," a male voice replied. "This is Jock Glas, her colleague. Who's calling?"

"Tom Dedardel. We met at the celebration for the rising sun, I believe."

"Ah yes. I remember. The young man in the wheel chair. So what can I do for you?"

Tom took a deep breath. "I think we've got another body on our hands."

"What do you mean?"

"I have reason to believe there's a body buried in the crater left by the explosion"

"But we combed that whole area and found no other bodies."

"This body got there afterwards according to the information I have received."

"OK," Jock said, sounding a bit peeved. "I'll get there as soon as I can."

The body

Jock wasn't sure if the deep distrust he felt for these people was due to the way catastrophes occurred whenever they were around or the alarming knack they had of knowing things that couldn't be known or of doing things that were impossible. He hopped onto his bicycle and pedalled along the almost deserted High Street, waving to the newsagent as he went by. When he reached the footbridge over the Bree, a couple of swans were paddling up river against the tide, a regal couple. He thought of Mandy and wondered when he'd next get a chance to sleep with her. He set his desires aside and rode through the park to the edge of the crater where he found the young man in the wheel chair. Leaning his bicycle against one of the fallen stones, he approached Tom.

"So where is this body you've found?" he asked not bothering with greetings.

"I didn't find it constable," the young man clarified. "I was told it was here."

"So where is it?" Jock asked.

"I believe it is in the middle of the crater."

There were no signs of footsteps on the dust.

"Could I ask you a direct question, Tom, isn't it?" Jock asked, irritated at the need to be polite.

Tom nodded. "Fire away constable."

"Who informed you about the body?" Jock asked, pretty sure he wouldn't get anywhere with such a direct question.

"Do you ever hear voices?"

There was not the slightest hint of irony or sarcasm in Tom's voice. All the same, Jock couldn't help wondering if he was being taken for a ride. "I've been hearing them more often since I've met you people." Jock chuckled.

Tom laughed too.

"But seriously though. Yes I did hear a voice in my head talking to your friend Jenny. Mandy, my colleague heard it too. Otherwise I might have thought I was going crazy." He shuddered. Could they get into his head so easily? Was there no limit to what these people could do?

"Well that voice has a name. It's called Mee," Tom said.

"Quit pulling my leg," Jock said, annoyed at not being taken seriously. There was no respect amongst young people any more.

Tom looked perplexed at Jock's forceful reaction. Then he must have realised what the problem was because he said "Ah! I see" and, chuckling, he added. "Not M-E but rather M-E-E," he said spelling out the words.

"I'm sorry for the misunderstanding," Jock said. This whole thing was making him touchy.

"Mee told me that Dr. Frick killed himself by suffocating in the dust in crater. Apparently Mee tried to dissuade him. But Frick didn't want to listen."

Jock could understand Frick's hesitation. If he himself had been driven to distraction and a voice started speaking to him, he'd probably refuse to listen to it too. "Did this the voice tell you anything else?"

Tom paused to think. "Yes. He said he tried to stop the two terrorists from blowing up the ring but he got blown up in the process along with them."

"So he's a ghost," Jock said, thinking out loud. The idea of a ghost was marginally more reassuring, if only because it was more familiar from popular culture than a disembodied voice that went around trying to stop people doing harm to themselves and others.

"I don't think so," Tom mused. "In our experience there was such a voice before, but it was bound to a single person. Maybe it's the same one and the explosion freed him from that attachment."

It might be useful to have help from such a voice, Jock thought. Then he envisaged his work as a policeman aided by voices talking in his head and he immediately dismissed the idea with loathing.

"Well thanks for being so frank, Tom," Jock said and he stepped down into the crater, not without misgivings. He had fantasies of being swallowed up by the dust or some alien beast that would surge unbidden from a hole in the earth. He tried unsuccessfully to reason with himself. Being with people to whom the impossible happened regularly opened the door on a frightening world in which the unimaginable suddenly became terrifyingly feasible. He shivered despite the warm sun on his back.

As he neared the middle of the crater, his feet sank deep into the dust making his progress even slower. He glanced around trying to see if there were any bumps in the otherwise even surface that curved from lip to lip of the crater. If he lowered his head slightly he could just make out a slight bulge not far from him. He waded over in its direction, then, sticking out his hand tentatively, he plunged it into the dust and hit an object. Clearing away the dust gently for fear that he too might suffocate in a self-made dust cloud, he uncovered the shoulder and arm of a body.

Standing there in the crater middle, his feet buried to his knees in dust, an arm and a shoulder protruding in front of him, he pulled out his phone and called the station. He couldn't help sighing. This weekend was beginning to take its toll. He felt weary of his job for the first time ever. I need a holiday, he thought. No! I need to be free of these people, he corrected.

"Yes Chief. There's a dead body down here in Hoyt Park." He paused to listen to his Chief swearing at the other end, then proceeded. "I have reason to believe it is Dr. Frick from the university. He killed himself by suffocation in a bath of dust in the middle of the crater left by the explosion."

His Chief swore again, which was uncharacteristic. "What list?" Jock asked in reply to something his Chief had said. "The Starless Square? What a weird name." Jock listened to his Chief's explanation. "Yeah! Send an ambulance … and someone with a couple of shovels."

Having retraced his steps back to Tom who sat watching him from his wheel chair, Jock clambered out of the crater. There was a strange, almost peaceful air about the young man, as if he were quite detached from the world around him. Jock found it unnerving.

"What do you know about the Starless Square?"

Tom hesitated a moment before replying. "It's a group of people that have given themselves the mission of ridding the world of what they believe to be witches."

Jock had a hard time stopping his mouth from falling open. This was worse than a nightmare. He just wished he would wake up, but he knew it was a vain wish.

"Witches?" he managed to say.

"Led by Dr. Frick here," Tom said pointing at the body protruding from the dust, "they were convinced the people in Theosophy Department were witches and warlocks. That's why they have been waging war on the Department all this weekend. We have been keeping an eye on those we knew about but luckily for us, most of their plans backfired."

Jock stood there speechless. He was already aware that they knew about the threat from the Starless Square. Mae had told him. But what flabbergasted him was that they were being repeatedly victimised, according to them, but not once did they turn to the police. He couldn't understand it, unless of course they were trying to hide something.

"Why did you not tell us?" he finally managed to ask.

"It would have been a little hard to explain. And we had no idea how serious they were in their intentions." Tom paused a moment and starred at Frick's body. "Would you have believed us yesterday if we had told you that they tried to immolate a young girl in the Starless Square next to the Cathedral in front of a crowd of unsuspecting spectators on a guided tour?"

Jock felt sick and bewildered. Mae had not told him about that. How much had she concealed? He wanted to run away. Only his training held him in place.

"I need to deal with this body," he said, sounding more of a policeman than he felt. "But when I have done that I want to come and have a serious talk with this group of yours."

"Sure constable," Tom replied. "Later this afternoon would be a better time." He suggested Jock join them at the watchers meeting place in the disused warehouse. "You might like to bring your friend Mandy with you."

The mention of Mandy took Jock by surprise. He shuddered. What did they know about him and Mandy? Had they been spying on the two of them? Maybe they'd even taken pictures. It wouldn't do to be exposed for having a torrid affair with his colleague. His imagination was running away with him and the speed of it was frightening.

He began to reconsider Frick's death and why the man would have killed himself. Jock had read about black magic and voodoo. The connection was not reassuring. Were he and Mandy under such a threat too? Despite the calm appearance and the apparent innocence of this young man in a wheel chair, Jock was not sure he could trust these people. Tom must have noticed his discomfort because he added: "I suggested she come because she has also had a lot of contact with us."

A brainwave

Jenny sat on the same patch of grass at the crater's edge that Keira had sung from earlier in the day. She sighed, resting her head on her upturned hands that in turn rested on her knees. How was she to teach a large group about the earth's energy fields? She had so little time to prepare.

It was only eight-thirty, but the sun was already warm. Any dew there might have been had long since evaporated. Several people must have entered the crater because traces of footsteps crisscrossed the cavity. In the middle someone had even dug up the earth. There were no limit to people's morbid curiosity. To think that two people had been blown to smithereens amid that dust. The thought was depressing. The depression seemed too strong to be hers alone.

She cast about seeking the presence of the guardians. Sure enough, one was standing nearby. She greeted it with reassuring thoughts. She turned her attention to the sun, instinctively drawing on its energy to chase away the blues that were settling over her and the ruins like a thick winter mantle trying to cut her off from warmth and comfort.

She had never taught before and felt quite incompetent to do so. She'd read parts of one or two books on the subject, but most of what she had learnt came from personal experience and most of that had been in another world. Not a very solid basis to teach from. It was as if she lacked the legitimacy; no one would take her seriously. Mee had promised to help, but she had no way of calling him. He might be anywhere. Who knew if he could hear her thoughts from a distance?

She got to her feet and made her way around the massive hole, stepping round giant stones that had partly resisted the blast. She splayed out her fingers at her sides and let the morning air course through her hands like water. She could feel the rise and fall of the earth's energy as she crossed the lines of force that led to the crater or skirted it. Balling her hands into fists, she pushed them into her pockets, not wishing to begin her search for solutions quite yet. More than anything else, she wanted to be alone.

In the distance she could see Tom in his wheel chair talking to one of the watchers. Their lovemaking had both pleased and upset her. It had awakened desires that she had kept locked away since his accident. It must have been the performance at the Arena and the extremely high level of energy that had aroused them so. Not imaging he'd ever be capable of sex again since that fateful day in the Reaches, she had given up on her own sexuality.

Despite her extreme sensitivity to the earth's energies, she herself felt somehow lifeless, as if she had dried up within. How ironic. She had given herself to nurturing the earth and making things grow while, all the time, a vital shoot inside her had shrivelled up. Now something had begun to stir and that worried her. She was no longer used to the shifting of her own vital energies. She greeted them more as an additional complication that a welcome arrival. What's more, she had no idea if Tom would be able to continue responding to her awakened desire.

She was worried about him. Something was not right. They had had little time to talk since last night, but she had the impression he was depressed. He seemed preoccupied and she wondered if it was due to his own feeling of inadequacy when it came to sex. That must be hard for a man to bear. Could his inability to have sex be more of a loss for him than his mobility?

She had always avoided the subject for fear of hurting him. Now she vowed to talk about it at the first occasion, but with the full life they led, who knew when that might be. She glanced in his direction and he saw her and waved. She skirted the remainder of the crater and headed towards him. Now might not be the best occasion, but she wanted to bring the subject up as soon as possible, preferably before her exploits later that morning.

"Jenny," he said, smiling by way of greeting. He held out his hand to her taking hold of hers and pulling her closer. She felt his arms close around her waist and his hands serpent down the small of her back to her backside.

"Mmmm!" he said laying his head against her belly.

Oh yes! She thought. He really has awakened me. She must have groaned unknowingly because he chuckled.

"That was good last night," he confided.

Tears sprang to her eyes. "Yes," she replied. Pulling back, she squatted in front of him, leaning on the armrests of his chair. "I was worried,..." she began.

He raised his eyebrows.

"...that making love would upset you..." and she faltered.

At first he looked at her uncomprehending then his face relaxed. "You mean you were afraid I would feel insufficient?"

She nodded. "You seemed so preoccupied these last days."

"Oh that! That has nothing to do with sex or making love to you. I have been feeling insufficient, but not because of my sexual capabilities. Rather because I could not find my gift, unlike all the rest of you."

A wave of relief washed over her. She was almost tempted to laugh, but then she noticed the seriousness of his expression and checked herself. "I had no idea that worried you. It's not because Irina suddenly discovers a startling talent that you should feel inadequate."

"I thought I might be able to crack the problem of predicting the future, but that hasn't worked."

She was deeply touched by the sadness in his face. He'd always been such a joyful person. She cursed for having taken him to the Reaches. "Most of us had no idea what our gift would be. Who knows, maybe the answer lies elsewhere for you."

"Well I do keep my eyes open. Maybe my way does lie in the future." He laughed at his unwitting joke. "Mee has promised to teach me about the Akashic Records. Fran mentioned them too. Maybe an answer can be found there."

She got to her feet. In the distance she could she could see a small group of people arriving near the crater possibly for her so-called seminar. She kissed him and as she turned to go she said: "Patience. I'm sure the answer will come soon now."

"Good luck with your land art," he called out.

She stopped in her tracks. Brilliant, she thought. She couldn't help grinning. What an excellent idea. She could think of several ways in which her work in general and what she was about to do could be inspired by land art. She spun round and ran back to him. "You're a genius," she said. And she reeled off a list of things she'd need to make his new idea work.

"I'll talk to Kean," Tom said. "I'm sure he'll have a solution."

A recording

"Blast!" Keira swore under her breath.

So much for catching up on some lost sleep after their early rise for the celebration. Why would anyone phone her at such a time on a Sunday morning? She rolled out of bed, making sure she didn't touch Irina. She didn't want another orgasmic shock right now. They really needed to find a way for the girl to shield herself when in contact with others. She was a walking liability. Keira had to search for her phone which was buried under Irina's clothes strewn across the floor. Sharing a room with Irina was a chaotic experience.

"Keira," she announced, sliding her finger across the touch screen of her phone to accept the call.

"Amanda Stock, BBC records," a female voice said. "Sorry to phone so early on a Sunday," the woman apologised. "But we have an emergency."

Keira was puzzled. What could an emergency at the BBC have to do with her?

"We broadcasted an extract of your song this morning on the national news. Since then we have been inundated by thousands of requests to hear the whole song. People want to know where they can buy a copy. Our recording is not so good. So we'd like to ask if you'd agree to come into our Avan studio to re-record it. And if you have any others like it we might make a record. We work with a major record label that would be able to distribute it."

There was a time, ages ago, when Keira would have dreamed of such a thing. Now the request was a nuisance.

"I'm leaving on an extended tour tomorrow. I have no time now," Keira replied. "What's more, I don't think my songs would be so good sung in a studio."

Ms. Stock tried every tactic she could to persuade her to record her song but Keira continued to refuse. Finally, in desperation, the woman suggested recording the song in the ruins of the Avan ring. "Some of the money from sales of the record could be contributed to repairing the ring."

The idea of repairing the ring appealed to Keira; to undo some of damage done by Frick's henchmen. "OK," she agreed after further discussion.

"Excellent. You've made the right decision. You won't regret it."

"Where are your studios? I'll drop by to talk about practical arrangements."

They were not far from the library where Keira used to work. "I'll be there in thirty minutes," Keira said.

Brent was seated in the kitchen talking to Sally when Keira entered.

"Are you going to Jenny's seminar?" Sally asked.

"No. I have to go to the BBC studios. They want to record my songs."

"Great," Brent said, enthusiastic. "Shame Mae is not here. It would be good to have someone to negotiate the question of rights."

"Where is she?" Keira asked unaware that Mae had left.

"She's gone to fetch Teresa in the Reaches," he informed her, lowering his voice to a whisper. "She hopes to be back this afternoon."

"No use to me then," Keira said pouring a cup of tea. "I'm going now."

"Want me to come?" Brent asked glancing at Sally.

Keira couldn't help noticing the quizzical look on Sally's face. The relationship between the three of them had become somewhat complicated with Brent's public declaration of his love for Sally. They hadn't yet found how best to be with each other in the new circumstances.

"Sure," Keira said. "As long as Sally's OK with that."

Sally burst out laughing. "You silly girl," she said standing and moving to Keira's side. "Have you forgotten that I still love you?" She put her arms around Keira's neck and planted a passionate kiss on her lips.

Keira was embarrassed and didn't respond.

"I do believe she's a little bit put out," Sally said to Brent who came to join them taking Keira in his arms too.

"Maybe we should take her to bed immediately and show her how strong our love for her is," Brent suggested. "Provided that is that she isn't disappointed with us after being spoilt by Irina's magical hands."

Keira gave him a shove in the ribs and all three laughed. She liked what she heard even if she knew it was probably only playful banter. She pulled away from their ostentatious embraces and said: "I'll hold you two to that the moment I get back." Grabbing Brent by the hand she asked: "Are you coming then lover boy?"

The studios were in a converted building not far from the back entrance to the cathedral and across the road from the site of the former apothecary that Sally had revealed during the guided tour the day before. Despite it being Sunday a receptionist greeted them at the main entrance and led them to Ms. Stock's office. Deep leather armchairs and a thick carpet were the first impressions that greeted them when Amanda Stock opened her door along with a strong smell of cigars.

"I'm sorry about the cigar smoke. It's one of my few vices," she said grinning as she opened a window. "Take a seat."

"This is my friend Brent," Keira said introducing him.

"Do you sing too Brent?" Amanda asked.

"No I tell stories," he replied.

"Well if you are half as good as the young girl at the Arena yesterday evening, you must be really good."

Keira found the situation hilarious but managed to keep a straight face. "So you were at the Arena?"

Like many others, the woman was full of praise for the event although she could say very little about what actually happened.

"I have put together a portfolio of six or seven songs that I could sing if you want to make a record," Keira said, changing the subject. "If I am to sing in the ruins of the Avan ring, I suggest we call the record just that: The Avan Ring. If it were possible I would prefer that my singing be a public performance. If we were to record this evening just before sunset it might be possible to let people know so they can attend. We are holding a large buffet at midday in the Starless Square and are expecting a lot of people to attend. We could announce it then. Maybe you could also announce it on the radio and the TV as some sort of coproduction."

Amanda whistled tunelessly as she let her breath out, forcing it between her pinched lips. "You don't go in for half measures."

"What do you think?" Keira asked.

"It's a bit short notice," Ms Stock said, hedging.

"Are you afraid about attendance?" Brent asked. "Or about getting a team ready for recording in time?"

"The former," she replied.

"I wouldn't worry about that," Brent said in a convincing tone.

Keira could see he was using his magic on the woman and was intrigued to see how she literally melted at his words. A broad smile spread across her face and she seemed delighted.

"What a wonderful idea," she enthused.

Keira asked about royalties from the record and Ms. Stock mentioned the usual conditions. The conditions didn't seem unreasonable to her but she had no experience of such things.

"Might I suggested that a percentage of the royalties be put in a fund for the reconstruction of the ring and that the BBC match that sum from their earnings from the recording," Brent suggested.

He looked almost angelic, Keira thought. The woman had no chance against him.

"Maybe you could have a contract prepared to that effect before we leave this morning," Brent casually suggested. "By the way," he added, "you might like to send a team down to film at the ring now. I believe Jenny's demonstration of the energy lines around the damaged ring might be quite spectacular, visually speaking. It might be a good way to illustrate our joint venture to re-build the rings."

Hardly had he finished speaking than she was on the phone to a colleague trying to organise a camera crew to rush to the scene.

Leave me alone!

A distant keening broke the silence.

Sally sat up, alarmed. It couldn't be Rafter. He was fast asleep. She had just checked. She stilled her breathing and listened again. There was no mistaking it: someone was suffering. The sound was unnerving. It called her. Moving into the entrance hall, the muffled wailing increased. It was coming from upstairs. She climbed the stairs, uncertain what to do. To her knowledge, she and Rafter were alone in the house. The higher she went the louder the keening became. Someone was crying in the attic. She felt the hairs on her neck stand on end and her arms broke into goose bumps.

Narrow wooden stairs wound upwards to rooms that none of them used. The members of the Dream Class were lodged on the first and second floors. The attic had been uninhabited for years. Sally pushed open the door that stood at the top of the stairs, tensed to spring back if ever anything went wrong. The attic was one giant room bordered on opposite side by sloping walls that ran parallel to the roof. The place was cluttered with all manner of objects: old fashioned armchairs, an upright piano, rickety piles of cases and trunks some overflowing with clothes, lines and lines of bookshelves bulging with file after file. There was even a bed protected by a grey dustcover.

It was from the far side of the bed that the unearthly keening continued.

Sally rounded a large dresser that blocked her view and caught sight of Irina curled up on the floor. All around her sat a host of shimmering forms, some tiny, dwarf-like, others absurdly large, towering over the girl's prostrate form.

"I can't," the girl wailed. "I can't."

Some of the forms rose and floated away, others drifted closer, swirling about the unhappy girl.

"Leave me alone. I can't help you."

"Irina!" Sally said, causing the forms to scatter and disappear. "What's the matter?"

Irina moaned. "They won't leave me alone."

Sally took a few steps closer checking to make sure the shimmering forms had not reappeared. "I saw them. Who are they?"

Irina shrugged. "I have no idea. They seem to cling to me. I can't get rid of them."

Sally's normal reaction would have been to take Irina in her arms, but given the girl's ability to shock people into an orgasm, she kept her distance.

"Why did you come up here?"

Irina opened her eyes and looked through her tears at Sally. "People hate me."

"No they don't."

"No one wants to come near me."

Sally shook her head. "It is just that you shock people if they touch you. That doesn't mean they don't like you."

Irina rolled over and leaned against the bed. "What can I do? I will never live a normal life again. And now these creepy things have latched onto me. It's disgusting. They crawl all over. It's as if they feed off my energy."

Sally wished Mee had been there. He might have had an answer. "Are you sure they are draining your energy?"

Irina scratched her head. "Well, no, actually. It's more like they enjoy being near me. They seem to get a kick out of it. Maybe my shocking nature makes them feel more alive." Her face twisted in a disgusted grimace.

Sally knew little about elementals, which was what she guessed they were. Most people were oblivious to those sentient beings that shared the world with us. She'd skipped the option about elementals and other entities in her undergraduate course. It hadn't appealed to her, and in all her travels between the worlds, this was the first time she'd come across them.

To be honest, she couldn't help finding them sinister. She had vague memories of having read somewhere that elementals could neither talk nor hear but they could feel intentions and could think messages into your mind. Maybe they'd felt Irina's despair and had come to help her.

"Have you tried asking them to help you? Maybe that is why they are here."

Irina sat bolt upright, a startled look on her face. "What?" Her surprise turned to disgust as the idea sank in.

"Why don't you try?"

The revulsion on Irina's face became more pronounced.

"You certainly won't manage if you make that face. They can sense your feelings. You're going to have to believe they can help."

This wasn't going to work. The girl had got it into her skull that these 'beasties' were repugnant and no amount of persuasion would change that. Sally needed an approach that would catch the girl off guard. Then she had a brainwave. "Have you ever prayed?"

Irina shot a look at Sally, her eyes full of suspicion, as if she sensed a trap.

"I'm serious."

"Well ... er ... yes." She sounded embarrassed. "Why?"

"I think what you need is a prayer."

Irina scoffed. "You are making fun of me!"

"No! This is far too important to make jokes about it. What do you do when you pray?"

Irina seemed disinclined to reply.

"Trust me."

"Er ... I close my eyes..." She shut her eyes to illustrate her words.

"And then?"

"I put my hands together, like this." Irina placed her two hands together, fingers outstretched and pointed upwards.

Doing so, Sally knew, helped the energy circulate in the body, bringing together the key energy points in the palms.

"Then I concentrate my thoughts and speak directly to God."

"How do you do that?"

Irina hesitated a long moment. While she did, Sally concentrated on calming her thoughts and centring herself, but she kept her eyes open. Glancing around she saw that the elementals had started to congregate around them again. The sight sent tingles through Sally's fingers and toes.

"I begin by addressing God, saying something like: 'Please God...' and then I express my wish. I end up by thanking him."

The attic was now thick with elementals but there were also several other entities Sally hadn't noticed before. They were like bright white lights. She couldn't help feeling awed at their presence and bowed her head in acknowledgement.

"Now you are going to say a prayer for help with handling your new gift. Keep it simple and direct. Don't try to dictate what should be done. Leave the solutions to God. And don't forget the please and thank you. You don't need to speak out loud, but you can if it helps." Sally spoke in a whisper, awed by the hush that filled the room. She had never felt anything like it. It was as if they had been elevated and the air or something like air had become more rarefied.

"Dear God," Irina began. "Please guide me that I can use my new gift to do good and not harm." A very long pause followed during which the girl looked as if she were listening intently. Then she whispered: "Thank you."

Sally realised that she too had closed her eyes. When she opened them all the elementals and the entities had gone but a bright white light persisted around Irina.

The girl sat there cross-legged for quite a while, a smile on her face. Little by little the white light dissipated until, when it was all gone, Irina opened her eyes and looked at Sally. That look sent a shiver through Sally leaving her feeling unsettled.

"Thank you for helping," Irina said, and she unclasped her hands and held out her right hand to Sally. The gesture was clear enough, but Sally hesitated.

"It won't hurt."

Sally gingerly advanced her right hand and laid it in Irina's. Despite her fears, no terrible shock shot through her, just a pleasant feeling of wellbeing. Sally chuckled in relief.

"Wow! It worked,"

"All you have to do is believe," Irina told her.

Coloured lines of force

An ancient, open-back lorry rattled its way down the narrow path through the gardens till it reached the crater's edge. Coming to a halt, Kean jumped out along with several of the watchers. Jenny left the small group of spectator/helpers who had already arrived and moved to join Kean.

"Did you manage to find everything?" she asked.

Kean broke into a broad grin. "We found even more. Wait till you see." He walked round to the side of the lorry and pointed to what looked like a heap of netting. "It's extremely strong and very large but light weight. I thought we could use it to span the crater so nobody has to go down into it when we run lines over the top." He went on to explain the mechanisms they'd found to anchor it to the ground so it would hold the weight of several people walking across it.

"How long will it take to install it?"

"About half an hour, I reckon, if we have some help."

"Good," she said, impatient to get on. "Show me what else you've got."

They had found various different coloured ropes and similarly coloured curved spikes to fix the ropes to the ground. There were hammers and a sort of pincer that could be used to remove stakes and spikes. There were also tools to cut the ropes. There were pulleys and other tackle to stretch and fix the netting.

Jenny called over the group of spectators that had grown considerably since she left. There must have been nearly thirty people.

"Welcome," she said and beckoned to even more newcomers who were arriving from the car park. "To begin with we are going to form two groups. One will work with Kean here," and she pointed to Kean who raised his hand by way of salute. "They will stretch a fine netting over the crater so we can work more easily without having to go down into all that dust. The other group will work with me and we will plant the first markers to indicate where the energy lines come from as they approach the ring."

She paused to glance over the crowd that continued to swell. There must have been nearly fifty people. "If you choose to work with Kean, you won't miss anything because I will recapitulate my explanations as soon as the netting is strung and then all of us can work on the energy fields. So those of you who want to help Kean, if you would join him over there, we can begin."

Some twenty people, mostly men, went to help Kean. The others crowded closely around her. Amongst the people present she spotted Moira and John from the Blavatsky Foundation. She waved to them. There were also several professors from the Department: Gavin Trundle, Chris Dryman and Martin Aschlyman. She called them over and shook hands. Then she presented them to the group around her. It was at that moment that she saw the TV crew arriving.

"It would seem like we have a visit from the TV," she announced and, excusing herself, she pulled out her walkie-talkie and called Tom. "Could you deal with the TV people? Make sure they don't get in our way. If they come too close with all that electrical stuff it will muddle things and distract our attention from the energy currents. If they want an interview I will do one at the end."

"There are a number of networks of energy that girdle the Earth forming a uniform grid like that netting over there," she began. "I am going to deal with two of the major ones. In their natural form, an explosion like the one that shook this place shouldn't affect them because they emanate from deep within the Earth. The builders of sacred sites such as this one had such a mastery of energy fields that they could modified the position of the lines to enhance the energy and the experience of the place. As intention is one of the major forces used to displace lines, the violent intention driving the terrorists might have had an impact. It is unlikely though. Making changes to the work of the original builders would have been beyond the scope of the thugs here, no matter how hateful their intentions."

A young man raised his hand to speak, a perplexed look on his face. "You mean thought can displace energy lines where explosions can't?" he asked.

"Yes. Although not so much thought as strong intention."

He shook his head in disbelief. She paused to see if there were any other comments and when there weren't she pulled her telephone out of her pocket and turned it off. "You'd all do well to turn off your mobile phones for the duration of our work."

She moved around the ring, followed by the large group till she reached its north side.

"One of the networks is called Hartmann. Its lines generally run north-south and east-west. The lines which are equally spaced go in sets of seven and each seventh line is double. Lines alternate, one negative, the next positive. As a result there is a positive double line after seven lines and then a double negative line after seven more. Every seven double lines there is a triple line, alternating negative and then positive."

Jenny closed her eyes and stretched out for her awareness of the earth's energy fields. "There's a triple positive line flowing into the ring from the north at the middle of the ring," she said. "Let's mark it with a red cord," she said, thinking out loud. Turning to Ben, one of Lyra's assistants, she said: "The thickest red cord, would be the best and a few stakes to hold it in place."

He nodded and hurried off to the lorry, returning with ropes and stakes but also a mallet. Jenny indicated a point on the lip of crater and one of the group helped Ben plant a metal stake. Another person threaded the red cord through the ring that topped the short stake and doubled it back through the hole, securing it in place.

"Make sure the ring is at ground level, so no one trips over it," Jenny warned. Then she took some twenty strides northwards and halted, checking that she still was on the line and then indicated a second point on the ground in which a stake was driven.

"Now it's your turn to feel the energy. Use your outstretched hand. If you like you can imagine you have an eye in the palm of your hand. You might feel a prickling, or a slight barrier in the air or warmth. Get acquainted with what it feels like. Use the red cord as a reference and know that a triple line could be as much as a yard wide."

She drew back and watched as people ranged out along the line and tentatively felt the air in front of them. As she watched, she pulled down energy from the cosmos and fed it into the group. Heightening their energies would make them more aware of the energy around them. Several people laughed as they felt the line. She walked around and encouraged those who were hesitant and helped those who didn't understand what they had to do.

"Good. Now I want you to look for the next line. It should be parallel to this one about two yards away. It might be more difficult to sense because it is only a single line, but you should be able to feel it. When you think you have found it, hold up you hand and I will come and check."

As the group scattered further afield looking for the next lines, she continued to feed energy into them. Then she signalled to Ben and asked him to find narrower red and blue cords to mark the positive and negative lines. People progressively became more and more confident in their ability to find the lines and little by little a series of parallel lines took shape. By the time Kean's helpers had finished fixing the netting over the crater, all the north-south lines to the north of the crater were mapped out.

Jenny sent her group to the south side to complete the lines on that side of the crater while she began the same work with Kean's group, tracing out the lines on the east side of the crater. Kean's group had more difficulties. It would seem that their choice of group had been dictated as much by their reluctance or inability to feel these energies as by any manly choice of pursuit. Those who persistently felt nothing she paired off with someone who was more sensitive. While one person sought the line, the other prepared the ropes.

Her round was interrupted by one of the women waving wildly at her. Jenny hurried to join her.

"There's something odd here. The energy seems to be flowing upwards. It's quite different from the lines," the young woman said. "And I feel all strange. I'm full of a mixture of sadness and anger."

Jenny chuckled. "That's because you are standing in the same place as one of the guardians."

The woman scuttled sideways. "I'm sorry," she said, looking at the empty space where she'd been standing. "Is he angry?" she asked Jenny.

"No! He is just communicating his feelings to you. He's not angry at you, but at those who desecrated this place."

The young woman stretched out her hand in the direction of the guardian. "Oh!" she exclaimed when she felt the presence again.

"It might not be a good idea to do that too often. Many guardians do not take kindly to people continually waving their hands through them."

"Should we put a marker here?" the woman enquired. Jenny shook her head. It would like putting a pointer that said: I'm here, come and annoy me. "I think we'll leave him in peace."

Three sides of the crater were complete, only the west remained to be mapped out. Jenny called everybody together. "Before we cover the west side of the ring, we first need to look at the ring itself." She looked to Kean. "Can we stand up on your netting?"

He grinned. "Sure. We tested it. It wobbles ever so slightly but you should be able to keep your balance." To prove his point he climbed up onto the net and held out his hand to her. She took it and stepped onto the netting.

"This is where things get a little more complex," she said holding out her arms to keep her balance. "We have to see what the Hartmann lines do inside the ring. We also have to see what else is going on there."

She knew the answers of course because she could see the whole area mapped out in her head, that was why she had left the west side till last, but she decided some suspense would be better.

"Let's begin with the positive level three line coming in from the north."

She made her way gingerly across the net till she reached the point mapped out on the edge of the crater. Using her hands, she followed the line that simply crossed the space and joined the same line on the other side. Kean wove a red rope through the netting to mark the passage of the line.

"I would ask some of you up here to feel the line but several other things are present here and that might confuse you."

"Is it another of those guardians?" a woman asked. It was the same one who'd been standing in the place of a guardian.

Jenny chuckled. "Well, yes! There are several guardians within this space but that wasn't what I was thinking about. But we are getting ahead of ourselves."

She moved to the next line above the triple line and followed it as it curved eastwards around the outside of the ring till it met its counterpart on the other side.

"In fact all the other Hartmann lines curve around the ring like the one I have just traced out."

"You mean the makers of this place did that?" one of the teenage girls in the audience asked.

"Yes."

"But why did they do that?"

"I can only partly answer your question," Jenny began as she explained how the lack of lines affected people who entered the ring. "We are so used to feeling them in our everyday life, we don't even realise they are there. But with them gone we immediately feel the difference. The 'sacred' feeling we associate with some churches is due to that."

While she talked, Kean and Ben had added a series of lines curving around the exterior of the ring joining the lines on each side, alternating red and blue for positive and negative. Jenny indicated that they could do the same for the lines that circled the south side of the ring.

"You may remember, at the beginning of our work I said we would look at two types of lines. Well now is the moment to look for the other ones. They are called the Curry grid. Unlike the Hartmann lines they run diagonally at forty-five degrees to the direction of the Hartmann lines. The same system of double and triple lines applies but they occur not every seven lines but every five. We don't have time to map them all out today, but I will trace in the main ones: two triple positive lines that cut diagonally across the ring forming a cross with its centre in the middle of the ring."

She walked to the northeast edge of the ring and traced the passage across to the southwest. And once Kean and Ben marked its route using green cords, while she traced out a second line perpendicular to it for them to mark too.

"Just to let you get a feel for the Curry lines, I'd like you to complete these four lines out beyond the ring."

She let the group spread out and move towards the four corners and begin searching in the air in front of them. She closed her eyes and glanced rapidly at the energy of the group and found that it was still very high so she didn't raise it any more. If she pushed them too far, they'd start to get tired and might even fall asleep or fall unconscious.

She sent Ben and Kean to fetch a special white rope they'd found that had been made such that strips of white cloth were bound into the rope at intervals making it look like a wild fringe. As she waited, she noticed that the TV crew had been filming unobtrusively with portable cameras. From her vantage point on the netting, the patterns they had traced out on the land were quite beautiful and she was reminded of her decision so long go as they were fleeing through France. She had wanted to become an artist of the land. She hadn't meant doing land art, but that was how things had turned out and the TV crew were busy documenting her work for her.

The four main Curry lines traced out, people wandered back and grouped around Jenny.

"We have one more thing to do before lunch," she told them. She moved away to the middle of the ring. "The energy level here is already very high because both the positive triple Hartmann and the positive triple Curry lines cross here."

The girl who'd spoken earlier interrupted her. "I don't understand what you mean by positive and negative. Is it like electricity?"

"You do well to ask. We are all made of energy and that field of energy extends out beyond our physical bodies. When we are in contact with such positive energy, our field expands making us more receptive and open to experiencing higher things. We feel better too. With negative energy, that field contracts and with prolonged exposure we become ill. That's why it is not good to sleep where two negative lines cross."

The girl seemed satisfied with the explanation, so Jenny continued.

"Here in the middle of the ring there is another phenomenon. It's called a vortex. Like the name suggests, it swirls around the centre spreading progressively outwards. This one rises to a height of about a hundred yards above the Earth and descends about sixty yards below. The spiral does not go on for ever, after a number of turns it then shots off to join a second spiral situated elsewhere. They can be miles apart. The two spirals and the link between them make up the whole vortex."

"So where is the second spiral?" someone asked.

"Can't you guess?"

"The Arena," another person suggested.

"Exactly. The Arena used to be the site of a similar ring and the two are connected by a vortex." She traced out the spiral on the netting and Ben and Kean fixed the white rope in place. It covered nearly half the ring and then ran off westwards following the Hartmann line in the direction of the Theosophy Department and the Arena across the River Bree.

"One of the functions of a vortex is to link the Earth to the cosmos," Jenny explained. "This vortex is dormant at the moment, but on special occasions it would have been woken up, as it were, and then its dimension and its energy would have been much, much greater."

"Can you turn it on?" a man asked, clearly excited at the idea.

"That would not be wise." Jenny frowned. "An active vortex attracts all manner of beings, not all of them friendly."

"Wow!" the man said, letting the air rush out between his teeth in a breathy whistle.

"The final thing we will do this morning is to give you a feel of the vortex. It might be inactive but you will be able to feel its energy quite clearly. I suggest you file carefully across the netting so you can feel what it is like."

One by one the group made its way across the netting to pass through the vortex and then cross to the other side of the ring where they gathered around Jenny, quietly asking questions. Once everybody was across Jenny spoke one last time, taking on a serious tone.

"These are powerful phenomenon and need to be treated with caution and respect. You have been able to catch a glimpse of them this morning. Should you wish to venture further you should seek expert help before you do." Then smiling she added. "Now let's go and taste Fran and Martin's delicious cooking. I don't know about you but the sea air and this work with energy has given me an appetite."

Chapter 12 ~ Food of the Gods

Hold your nose

"We've got a problem," Tom's tense voice hissed over the phone.

Sally shifted to the door so as not to disturb the Professor who slept on. "What's the matter?"

"The Starless Square has struck again. They've squirted liquid pig's manure across the square by the Cathedral. It stinks so much we can't possibly hold a meal there."

Sally glanced at her watch. They had an hour before people would start arriving. She hesitated about leaving the Professor alone, but this was an emergency. Maybe Mae would get back in the mean time.

"I'll join you as fast as I can," she told him and hung up.

Well at least this time nobody had got killed. She chuckled despite herself; they were quite creative in their steadfast opposition. Then a sobering thought crossed her mind: there couldn't be many of them left. One had died in the collapse of the Arena, two in the explosion at the ring and one more, the despicable Frick, had suffocated to death in the dust amongst the ruins of the ring. The police had told them that two more were in a mental hospital.

Tom had been right: it really stank. She parked her car not far from the square, but could already smell the stuff. Covering her mouth with a thick scarf she made her way around the back of the Cathedral heading for the Community Centre. The cobblestones were wet and slippery with the stuff. She wondered how the person had managed to get away with it without being spotted. She was glad she'd donned a pair of wellingtons from Rafter's place. Anyone who walked over that surface would probably have to throw away their shoes.

Her mind raced trying to find a solution. It was a shame Jenny wasn't there, she might have been able to make it rain. That would have helped a bit. She ran through the things she could do herself. Maybe she could transform the manure into flowers. It seemed a tricky thing to do. The stuff must have found its way into all the nooks and crannies between the cobblestones. What a disaster! She couldn't see how to save the event, unless they moved all the food elsewhere. If they changed venue, how could they possibly let people know at the last moment?

Then she had an idea. She pulled out her phone and called Tom. "How long ago did this happen?"

"Fifteen minutes."

"Is all the square covered?"

She heard him ask someone a question then he was back with her. "The whole square is affected."

"How many watchers are available?"

There was a pause as he counted. "Fifteen I think."

Good, that ought to be enough. "Can you post someone at each of the three entrances to the square. They are to let no one enter till I tell them. We also need to stop people coming out of the Cathedral or the pub. Do you think they can manage that?"

Tom hesitated. "I'm sure they'll figure something out. The biggest problem is the Cathedral, there are so many exits."

"Try to get someone on each entrance. Nobody must enter the square while I do my work."

"Ok. Anything else?"

"Yeah. Have them use the walkie-talkies to let you know when they are in place. Once all is ready, tell me and I will do my work."

"Transformation?"

"Yes. I need one more thing: three of your strongest men to catch the person who did it. Have them ready to help me when I whistle."

She heard Tom chuckle. "Great. I'm looking forward to this. I'll let you know when all is set up," and he hung up.

Hurry, she thought.

She wasn't at all sure she could manage what she planned. Thrusting aside her doubts, she hurried across the square to the steps in front of the Community Centre. The square was a giant L shape and from the steps she could see almost all of it. She was surprised to see that all the watchers were equipped with boots as they sped away to take up their places. Seeing Kean nearby she asked about the boots.

"There was a whole army of them in my father's warehouse," he explained, his voice muffled by the handkerchief he held over his mouth and nose.

"I am going to wind back time till the person crosses the square, if I can. I will then block him so we can overpower him. Then I will roll time back till just before the damage was done and fix it there. Well not time but the state of the square."

The door of the Community centre opened and she saw Tom rolling his wheelchair to join them. "Everyone is ready."

"Ok. Here we good."

She turned her attention back to the square and the large expanse of cobble stones. The sun was bright and it glittered off the disgusting mixture. She slowly explored backwards in time till she saw the glitter recede across the square. She halted briefly, but she saw no signs of the muck spreader or whatever they'd used. Maybe things didn't work like that. She continued to roll time back until she could no longer see any signs of the liquid manure on the stones and continuing even further back for safety she fixed the place at that point. Then she took a deep breath and turned to face Tom, Kean and the others.

"I've cleaned the place, but I can't make the people who made this mess materialise. We'll have to find some other way to get them."

Tom pushed forward slightly. "Kean, Ben and the rest of you, check the square is now completely clean, then come back here and report."

They ran across the square to its furthest reaches.

"The smell hasn't completely gone," Sally noted. "It may be our boots."

"We'll have to change our shoes. But what we really need is a wind or some perfume," Tom jested.

"I can't do the wind, but I can do the perfume," Sally said smiling.

When Kean and the others reported back that the square was now completely clean, Sally got to work again. She coaxed climbing plants to grow up all the walls around the square. As they did, they burst into flower and it was soon possible to smell the heady scents that the flowers gave off. The whole square was ablaze with bright colours. The watchers might have seen Sally transform the surface of the square but very little had been visible. The sudden spurt of flowers was much more spectacular. Several watchers stood staring, their mouths fallen open.

"Extraordinary!" Ben exclaimed in a forced whisper.

"Let's get rid of these boots," Sally said, ignoring their awe. "Then we can put out the tables for the food."

"What are we going to do about the remaining members of the Starless Square?" Kean asked.

He had a point. They might try something else.

"We'll leave people posted at the entrances to the square to check those who come in. Ben can you do that?" Tom asked. Ben nodded.

"And a couple of people should try to locate that pig farmer. What was his name?" Tom wondered.

"Gerald Twine," Kean reminded them.

"Could you look after him, Kean? Take a couple of people with you." Tom said.

"What do you want us to do to him, turn him into a piglet?"

Everyone laughed, some glancing still awestruck at Sally.

"Just keep an eye on him for the moment. We'll figure out what to do with him later."

"I'll come with you," Irina said smiling at Kean.

She must have been listening to their conversation from just within the Centre. Something about the sparkle in her eye made Sally wonder if the girl wasn't making a play for Kean. Well, good luck with that, she thought. Kean looked far from happy about having her along.

"Be careful," Sally warned. If Kean gave her the cold shoulder, it might send her spiralling back into depression. Sally was also worried the girl might be tempted to show off her new gift.

"I will," Irina said.

Excuse me Miss!

If she had thought she would get away quickly and eat with her friends near the Cathedral, Jenny hadn't reckoned with the insistence of the TV people.

"Excuse me Miss," the young girl said, blocking Jenny's path.

Jenny was tired both from the effort of maintaining the energy of such a large group and from improvising her seminar. She hadn't been sure she could do it, but she'd managed. If she needed proof of her success, it was all around her. An animated group of people of all ages accompanied her praising her work and asking questions.

"Excuse me," the girl repeated, taking hold of her arm.

Jenny would have ignored her, but the girl was not ready to be ignored. Resigned, she told the group she'd join them later and turned to the girl.

"You don't take no for an answer!"

The girl grinned. "I was told not to let you get away. The director said you might try to slip off so I was forewarned."

Jenny wondered why the director had thought she would attempt to escape. The moment she saw him, she understood. It was Collin, the man who'd pestered Sally and then Mae. Was it to be her turn?

"Collin. What can I do for you?"

"It's more what I can do for you."

"And what is that?"

"I want to show you some of the things we've filmed."

Now that interested her, although she feared the worst. Surely this clumsy man for all his suave appearance could not possibly have made a good job of filming her performance. What a disappointment! She'd been so pleased that her work had been documented. She hadn't counted on it being in the hands of a bungling idiot.

"How did you get to do this job? I didn't know you worked for the BBC."

"I don't but they urgently needed a director and I was available and on site. Apparently they have plans to make a record with Keira and would like to illustrate it with material filmed here."

This was news to Jenny. She knew Keira had been to the studio but she'd been too busy to find out what had happened.

"Take a seat," he invited as they entered a TV van.

She found herself in front of a number of monitors, one of which was much larger than the others.

"This is all raw material, but I thought you'd like to see."

He typed in a code on the keyboard causing a video to play back on the screen. The cameraman filmed along the energy line as people searched the air for traces of the energy. It was filmed close enough that only the searching hands were visible. The composition of the picture was beautiful and the choice of frame was excellent.

Collin typed in another code and the video raced forward only to stop at a sequence filmed close to the ground as one of the coloured ropes was laid. It was excellent. Jenny could feel herself getting excited. Collin fast-forwarded once more to a scene in which she was explaining the vortex. The cameraman had managed to film from sufficiently high up that Jenny was framed by the red and blue lines of the Hartmann grid that circled the ring.

"This is wonderful!" She glanced at Collin, who looked almost shy. "The images are visually interesting. It's good material."

"Would you like to help me edit the material?"

"I'd love to, but I'm not sure I'll have the time."

"I know, you are all leaving tomorrow."

"Let's see what we can do. I can't promise anything."

"I know you must be exhausted, but would you mind doing an interview out by the ring? It would take about fifteen to twenty minutes."

Jenny finally agreed.

He called together the crew and led her back across the grassy area around the ring now criss-crossed with many coloured ropes and cords. He had her explain the different things she'd explained during the seminar, but this time for the camera. She liked the way he was careful about the setting and that he made every effort to have her explanations seem natural and not filmed for television.

"I have one last question," he told her once they'd filmed most of her presentation. "Maybe it would be good if you stood in the middle of the vortex to answer."

She complied.

"Tell me, why do you work like this with the Earth's energies?"

Jenny hesitated. She'd never asked herself the question.

"I have always had a feeling for such things, but only recently did I begin working seriously with these energies. I know some people believe we are here to raise our energy and that of the world. They see it as our road to a better world. It's an interesting idea but I'm not advocating a particular worldview. For the moment I am just getting to know the world around me. I enjoy teaching like I did here, but otherwise I have no particular far reaching ambitions for the moment."

It wasn't quite true. She thought of the idea of the Dream Class but decided it was neither the time nor the place to mention it. He thanked her and handed her his card should she find time to help with the editing.

"Are you coming to eat with us?" she asked as she turned to leave.

He immediately took her words as an invitation and, waving the crew to go on, joined her as she walked towards the footbridge over the Bree. It wasn't what she had in mind, but then he wasn't at all as bad as the others had made out.

Kean still had the lorry he'd used to transport the material to the ring for Jenny, so they went with it in search of Twine. It was hardly an inconspicuous way of travelling, but he had no time to fetch a more appropriate vehicle.

"We'll ditch the lorry when we get closer and go on foot," Kean suggested as he drove them out of town.

He glanced at Irina from the corner of his eye. She was sitting next to him on the bench seat and on the other side of her sat two other watchers, Tim and Steven, the latter who had already investigated Twine's pig farm.

"It's just round that bend," Steven warned them. "We could park the lorry over there amongst those trees."

The farm was concealed not only by the curve but also by a small outcrop of wooded ground that nestled in the bend and overhung the road. Kean pulled the lorry in amongst the trees just short of the bend and turned off the motor.

As they all climbed out, Kean wondered why Irina had been so enthusiastic about joining them. She couldn't have been more that seventeen and struck him more as a liability than an asset. She'd chattered all the way: something about ghosts and spirits in the attic. He hadn't been able to make much sense of it. One of his friends had a sister that age and she was a real pest, the sort of person that seemed to systematically do the wrong thing at the wrong time.

What's more, he'd caught Irina staring at him several times, only to look away blushing when he caught her eye. Don't tell me she's got a crush on me. Aren't I lucky! He let his breath out in a whistle between his teeth and turned his attention to what they were doing. He quizzed Steven about Twine's pig farm and decided they'd do well to make their way to the top of the outcrop to get a better view.

The climb was steep, the narrow path winding its way between the rocks and trees. They'd had to stop several times for Irina who quickly got out of breath. When they finally reached the top a stench of pigs greeted them.

"Smells like we're in the right place," Irina whispered.

Kean looked out from between the bushes and trees to see the farm laid out below. The living quarters were quite small, wedged between two bigger farm buildings. On one side a low, squat building housed the pigs that could be heard squealing. On the other side was a large barn, presumably to park vehicles and farm equipment. In front of the barn stood a battered ice cream van with the remains of a painting of a curly-haired girl on its side, waving an ice cream. A man was hunched over a pulley system, offloading a large cistern from the van via its back door.

"That's Twine," Steven whispered.

At that moment the pulley gave way and the cistern crashed to the ground amid curses from Twine. Liquid manure seeped out its side and formed a viscous pool at Twine's feet.

"And that's how he managed to sneak into the square unnoticed: the liquid was concealed in an ice cream van," Kean said.

Steven pulled out a camera and took a few shots of Twine at work.

They withdrew from the edge, relieved that the stink decreased the more they moved into the trees. Sitting uncomfortably on some rocks, they discussed what to do next. Steven wanted to get more photos for what he called 'their evidence', but Irina pointed out that Sally had erased any trace of the stinking liquid in the square making his evidence useless. Steven huffed at her remark, but didn't otherwise respond. Everyone admitted begrudgingly she was right. Irina wanted to go down and confront the man, but the others overruled her, saying that might be dangerous.

"Either we stay here and continue to keep an eye on him or we return to the Centre," Kean concluded. He could see little point in remaining. If Twine were to leave, they would never be able to get down to the lorry fast enough to follow him. So they made there way back down.

As they arrived near the lorry they were horrified to find Twine leaning nonchalantly against their vehicle, a rifle gripped in his hand.

"Well, look what we've got here!" he said with a flourish of the rifle. "Now what would you young people be doing climbing on my land? If it was to get a better view of my farm, I will willingly take you on a guided tour." He brandished his gun, pointing it at the road in the direction of his farm. "After you."

As they made their way under the overhang towards Twine's farm, Kean berated himself for not putting a lookout near the lorry. How was he to know? Twine must have heard them and come looking.

"Keep your eyes open," he whispered to the others, echoing Tom's advice to them as watchers. "Every detail counts."

Irina looked at him. This was not the place for explanations. He just hoped she'd keep her mouth shut.

Several dogs began barking as they rounded the bend and

approached the farm. The animals leapt up, pulling with all their force at the chains that held them in place.

"What a warm welcome," Twine commented. "I thought I'd give you a souvenir of your visit, something to remind you of a pleasant stay on a pig farm."

Kean shuddered at the thought of what the man might have in mind.

"But first I have some questions for you."

He herded them in a corner by the barn and seated himself in a wooden chair opposite them. Irina made the most of a moment's distraction to whisper: "Whatever you do, don't touch me until I tell you it is OK."

Kean glanced at her uncomprehending.

"And don't try to stop what I am about to do."

The tension must have gone to her head, Kean thought. She took a step forward and he stretched out to stop her but she managed to avoid him. "Heed my warning or you'll get hurt."

Kean took another step after her, but Steven put a hand on his shoulder and held him back.

"Let her go," Steven said.

"I have some answers for you, Mr. Twine," she said as she moved closer. "Did you know that four of the Starless Square are already dead, including your leader, and two others are in a mental hospital."

Twine looked shaken, but he made an effort to control himself.

"Are you threatening me miss?"

"I would never do that, Mr. Twine. I don't need to."

"Keep your mouth shut, little witch! I know what you are. You're a witch."

All the time Irina was inching closer. Kean was terrified she would get shot. He felt responsible. What would he say to the others if she got hurt. He wanted to reason with her, but Steven still held him back.

"I think she knows what she is doing," Steven whispered.

"If I am witch, as you say, then what are you, Mr. Twine?"

"The voice of justice and all that is good."

At each word, Irina advanced almost imperceptibly. "How do you know what is good?"

The dogs that had lain down in front of Twine now got to their feet and were growling deep in their throats. He held them back by their chains as they strained forward to get their teeth into Irina. The chains, which were made of metal and looked new and shiny, ran across the yard to where they were both fixed to the wall near the farmhouse.

"I don't need to justify that. You are a witch. That's all that counts."

Slowly, ever so slowly, Irina squatted down as if she were about to tie up her shoelaces. "Did no one ever tell you never to trust a witch?" she said to him, a radiant smile on her face.

You'd have said an angel, Kean thought.

Suddenly lunging forward, she grasped the two chains with both hands. What happened then took Kean and the others completely by surprise. The two dogs howled and arched over backwards, writhing on the ground, whimpering in pain. In shock, Twine let go of his gun that clattered to the ground and he clutched his sex. Then he screamed a long piercing scream. Kean instinctively stuck his fingers in his ears but it was not enough to shut out Twine's agony. The man squirmed in his chair and collapsed to his knees, crying.

Irina let go of the chains, stood up and started to move towards Twine who slumped to the ground moaning, his hands still clutched to his sex.

"No more! No more!" he groaned.

The horror of what he'd seen had frozen Kean. Now he shook himself and cried out "Enough! Enough Irina!"

She stopped in mid-step and turned to look at him, her two deadly hands outstretched in his direction. Her eyes were wild and her lips bore a cruel grin. Her face barely recognisable. Terror gripped him as he realised that he was to be her next victim.

"No Irina. Snap out of it!" he shouted unable to run away as she advanced on him. "No Irina."

"She's possessed," he heard Steven say, his voice miles away.

Kean slumped to his knees as Irina came to a halt a couple of yards from him. He was not a religious person, but Kean prayed, he prayed with all his force, that he would be protected, that his friends would be protected, that whatever it was that had possessed Irina would leave her, that this nightmare would stop. He willed it with all his force, with all his heart.

When he finally looked up, Irina was still standing a short distance away. His eyes must be playing up because she shimmered like a mirage. He glanced back at the others, but they didn't shimmer. Instead, the shimmering encircled them all.

"You've created some sort of barrier," Steven exclaimed.

Whatever it was that was holding Irina off, it swirled round and round. He took a tentative step towards Irina and the swirling cloud moved with him and engulfed her. The wild look drained from her face and she sank slowly to the ground, unconscious.

"Go get the lorry, Steven. We need to get her back to the others," he said.

How were they going to carry her? If her touch knocked them out they'd need a stretcher. He turned to Tim saying: "I'm going to try to touch her. If that puts me out you'll need to find some way to carry her."

Tim nodded, a frightened look on his face.

Kean steeled himself and stretched forward one finger to touch Irina's cheek. He had visions of being flung across the yard, but nothing happened. Her skin was remarkably soft. Relief gushed through him. He ran his hand through her tousled hair and lifted her head gently. Then he took her in his arms and struggled to his feet with the help of Tim. When Steven arrived with the lorry, Kean laid Irina on some covers in the back and sat down next to her holding her hand.

The Akâsha

The trestle table, one of many laid out in the Community Centre, was covered with a wild diversity of cakes. Martin was spooning a small pile of crushed, roasted almonds on some of the cakes, Tom was draining the brandy from raisins that had soaked overnight and Fran was placing them delicately on top of other cakes.

"These are sweet almonds," Martin explained to several spectators nearby. "They come from the same family as bitter almonds that are used to make cyanide."

Fran wondered if he realised that what he said was not reassuring. "There's no risk from these almonds," she hastened to add, smiling at him.

He chuckled. When they'd finished, a group of Lyra's students who'd been working with them on the feast for several days, carried out some of the trays and placed them on tables in the square. The weather was beautiful Fran had been told, although she had not been out for a long time. Martin went with the students to make sure the arrangement was to his liking.

Fran caught hold of Tom's wheelchair and wheeled him to one of the quieter corners of the Community Centre. The place was one spacious hall now filled with table after table of food and drink prepared for the buffet. There was also a large kitchen and a small meeting room for committees. Fran unfolded a chair and placed it next to Tom.

"Have you heard from Mee?" she asked as she grabbed two of the nearby cakes and sat down.

Tom shook his head.

She offered him a cake. "I made them."

"Maybe he's busy," Tom speculated, taking one.

I was indeed, Mee said, to their surprise. I have been studying all I could about the Akashic Records.

"So what have you found?" Tom asked.

Mee chuckled. How many years have you got?

Tom made a face and Fran couldn't help laughing.

Apparently our friend Mme Blavatsky wrote a lot about the subject. In fact, I got sidetracked reading what she wrote about the Akâsa.

"What's that?" Fran asked, fetching a couple more cakes. "I'd offer you one Mee, but I suppose that would be a bit mean."

It would indeed! I'm pure spirit.

Did she detect bitterness in his voice?

In a way, I suppose I am part of the Akâsa.

"I don't understand," Tom complained.

The Akâsa is a Sanskrit word used to mean various things, Mee explained. It is the all-pervading ether, the wind that moves the world, the life-fluid, the spirit and soul of man. Each time you breathe in you are filled with Akâsa. It is an ever-present potential that only becomes manifest when you exert will or spirit on it. Left to itself it blindly follows the laws of nature, as Mme Blavatsky puts it, but influenced by the will of an adept it is the driving force of many apparently miraculous things.

"Will?" Tom asked. "You mean like in prayer?"

Exactly. Mee sounded excited at his discovery. I believe all your gifts as you call them use the Akâsa and they work when you exert your will on it, rather like when you say a prayer. Each of you has learnt different ways of manifesting the force of the Akâsa.

"But what is the connection with the Akashic Records?" Fran asked, wondering if Mee had got lost in the sheer mass of information available since the beginning of history and beyond.

I have to go, he suddenly said.

And that was that. Fran looked at Tom and he looked back, their faces echoing their confusion and disappointment.

"What was that about?" she asked, wondering if she had offended him.

Tom just shook his head.

Fran sat silent for a long moment staring at her shoes thinking over what Mee had told them. The more she thought about it, the more extraordinary she found it.

"Wow!" she said, startling Tom who must have been caught up in his own thoughts. "A universal principle!"

Tom looked perplexed. Not surprising, she thought, he wasn't a scientist. She had to smile, wondering if she was still one herself.

"Mee pointed to a force or a substance, I'm not sure which, that underlies all that the members of the Dream Class are able to do. It probably contains the key to your desire to tell the future, too."

"But why 'universal'?"

"Well science is constantly searching for underlying principles or forces or fields that explain a wide range of phenomena, the wider the better. Scientists are fascinated by coherence: the way a whole load of diverging building blocks fit together to make complex entities and then how those complex entities work so well with other entities. With the Akâsa, Mee has given us both a principle and a force that might explain all the magic we do."

Tom groaned. "Only I don't do any magic!" He pouted.

"Maybe you're better off without it," Sally said soberly, joining them. "Kean's just returned with Irina. She's in a comma. Apparently her magic got out of control."

Tom looked worried. "Are the others all right?"

"I think so. Kean is putting Irina in the little meeting room."

Asleep

Kean pushed his way into the meeting room through the growing crowd and laid Irina carefully on the large wooden table, freeing her arms from around his neck. His feelings were in utter confusion. He was furious at her for letting her magic get out of control. He was profoundly upset by what she'd done to Twine, however horrible the guy had been. He was frightened of her, remembering how she'd marched on him, her deadly hands outstretched. He felt very protective, having held her unconscious body close to him throughout the journey back to town. And now that he'd let go of her hand and no longer felt her warmth, he felt at a loss.

Not that he had much time to think. Sally was pushing her way through the crowd, closely followed by Moira and John. Several members of staff were there. Spotting Prof. Dryman, Kean asked him to clear the room so they could have some peace.

Moira flung her arms around Irina and began sobbing. "My baby, my baby,..."

"It's all right..." Kean began. He was about to say she was just unconscious, but saw Sally shake her head.

"It's a shame neither Keira nor Jenny is here," Sally said.

"What about Lyra?" Chris Dryman asked. "I though I'd find her here with her students."

"She's on a mission with Mae," Sally replied. The two women were good friends so the news was plausible, but all the same Chris shot her a questioning look. Sally didn't respond.

"What happened?" John asked, laying a calming hand on Moira's shoulder.

Once again Sally shot Kean a meaningful look.

"Irina insisted on coming when we went to check on a pig farmer. We suspected him of trying to mar our festivities." Kean's mind galloped forward trying to figure out an acceptable way to describe what Irina had done. "The man must have heard us because he came with a shot gun."

Moira whimpered.

"He took us prisoner at gun point, but Irina spoke to him. It was really weird: the man had a fit and collapsed to the floor." Kean cast a warning glance at Steven and Tim. "Then she collapsed, and she's been unconscious ever since."

"I think she's just asleep," Steven said. "Listen, she's snoring."

He was right. Well that was a relief.

"I'll take her back to our hotel," Moira announced, wiping the tears from her eyes.

The suggestion was logical enough, but what if she had another attack. Moira wouldn't understand and somebody else might get hurt.

"That might not be a good idea," Kean ventured.

"Why ever not?" Moira asked, raising her voice.

This was all too much for Kean . He looked desperately at Sally, but she couldn't help. He took a deep breath and spoke.

"When she attacked Twine, the pig farmer, she lost control and turned to attack us too."

Several people gasped. Moira stared at him in disbelief. His shoulders slumped and he felt helpless. The memory of it shook him completely. He wiped his hand across his face to conceal his emotion.

"It might happen again when she wakes up. That's why I think she should stay here for a while."

Moira spluttered. "What nonsense! How dare you imply that I don't know what is best for my daughter!"

Kean stood in front of her, his arms dangling dejected at his sides, his head hung in resignation.

"Stop!" Steven said, moving between Moira and Kean. "You are very unfair. Kean is just trying to spare you the worst. His kindness and consideration deserve better. He almost died this morning at the hands of your daughter. He saved all our lives. I don't know how, but he did. And in the end, he had the compassion to take your daughter in his arms, despite the potential dangers to himself, and bring her all the way here."

It was all too much. Tears streamed down his face. He turned to run from the room, but Sally blocked his way and wouldn't let him go. She took him in her arms hugging him tight, causing him to break down, shuddering violently and sobbing as he relived the worst moments.

When he finally calmed, Sally handed him a handkerchief and Fran offered him a tiny elf-like cake on an elf-sized plate.

"The Littl' Peopl' say they're very good after strong emotions," she said smiling.

He took it and ate it in one bite. It was delicious and really did make him feel better.

Fran gave him a second cake grinning. "They were made for people much smaller than you."

He took more time with the second cake, savouring its strange but delicious taste. As he chewed, he glanced around the room, noticing that everybody was watching him. Several of his professors were there. He felt so stupid and blushed.

"Don't be ashamed of your emotions," Professor Aschlyman told him. "They open the door to many things."

Steven and Tim grinned at him.

As for Moira, she looked contrite. "I'm so sorry. I didn't realise."

He nodded and continued looking at the people gathered around him. Next to her, held tight in her arms was Irina, awake now and staring at him like all the others. She freed herself from Moira's arms and took several unsteady steps in his direction. It was all he could do not to flinch when she touched his cheek.

"Thank you. I'm so, so sorry."

Kean pulled her into his arms and she laid her head on his shoulder. "Everything is OK," he whispered. Over her head he noticed the same shimmering white he'd seen earlier. It was now drifting around the people in the room.

"So how did you manage to resist the attack, Kean?" Martina Aschlyman asked when the two pulled apart and Irina went back to stand next to Moira.

"Prayer," Kean replied.

That shouldn't surprise anyone, least of all Prof. Aschlyman, they were after all in the Theosophy Department and the force of prayer was a phenomenon they talked about in several of their courses. But the staff looked surprised. There seemed to be a gap between what was taught and people's experience.

"And what happened?" Martina asked intrigued.

Not really surprising that the subject should interest her, she was professor of occult sciences.

"A swirling white cloud surrounded us and when Irina entered the cloud all the anger and hatred drained from her."

Irina looked at him wide-eyed. "I don't recall."

Martina whistled through her teeth. "Well I'll be blowed! I've never been able to get such results from my students."

"Maybe those are not the kind of experiences you are aiming for Martina," Chris put in. "Personally I try to avoid life-threatening situations."

Typical of Chris to make light of the drama they'd just been through. Although Kean didn't miss the serious look Chris gave Sally. When Rafter was gone it would probably be Chris who became head of Department.

"You've got a more theoretical approach, Martina, compared to mine," Liam pointed out.

Kean remembered the hours of practical dreamwork they'd done with Prof. Lettrot. It had been so tedious that sleep was almost invariably the end result. He would not admit it in front of his professors, but he'd learnt far more during that weekend than he had done in the five years of his undergraduate studies.

"Well you can discuss the relative merits of your teaching styles," Chris said grinning, "but I'm here to taste the delicious food that Fran and Martin have made."

Everyone laughed.

Chris took hold of Fran's arm and walked with her out of the room.

All the others trouped after them in ones and twos.

"Well done," Sally whispered, pulling him gently to one side. "You were great."

Demonstration

The gym was small but sufficient for the ten police officers that needed to use it. Built in the basement of the police station, next to a number of prison cells, it could well have been a sinister place were it not for the laughter of those officers present at an improvised demonstration by Anju and Dieter. Mandy had organised it.

"Keeping up good neighbourly relations" Anju remembered Dieter saying when Mandy had suggested the idea.

She'd replied something like: "Do you miss the police?"

He'd tried to tickle her, but had ended up on the floor breathless with her sitting on top of him. Oups! She needed to concentrate if she were to parry Dieter's attacks. Her ability to sense what the attacker was about to do had developed considerably. It required a lot less effort, but she still had to pay attention. She sidestepped and ducked, using one hand and an outstretched foot to floor Dieter, much to the amusement of the watching policewomen. She hadn't yet managed to teach Dieter the kind of anticipation she'd developed. Maybe it couldn't be taught.

"How do you do that?" one of the policewomen asked.

"I'm not sure. I know what he is going to do before he does it."

"Could you teach us?" the woman asked.

"I don't know. I haven't managed to teach it to Dieter yet."

She grinned at him and he made a display of pouting. He certainly didn't seem bothered by being surrounded by all the police officers and finding himself in the weaker position. He'd changed a lot. She remembered the battles of words and minds they'd had in the beginning. He no longer related to her that way. It wasn't that the fight had gone out of him; he just didn't need to fight her, at least not that way. You're getting distracted again, she told herself.

"Let's try," Anju suggested, grabbing the young woman by the hand and pulling her to her feet. "Attack me."

The young policewoman was quick and her style was unfamiliar, but Anju saw what was coming and merely avoided the attack. The woman grunted as she stopped in mid-move and narrowly avoid falling.

"Again," Anju said.

The woman tried something quite different. This time Anju paid particular attention to how she knew what would happen. "It's like lines and forces drawn in air," she explained as the woman picked herself up off the floor.

"I'd be quite happy enough if I just had your combat skills," one of the men said.

"We taught them to a group of women who had a problem with the men in town."

Someone laughed.

"Typical," one of the policewomen said.

Anju wasn't sure if the woman's comment was directed at the laughter or the problem.

"We used dance to help them learn."

"Could you teach us?" one of the women asked.

"We leave tomorrow on a long journey and we have no idea when we will be back," Dieter explained.

"It's going to be quiet around here without your group around," Mandy said wistfully, glancing at Jock.

"So you were also in the police?" one of the men asked.

"Yes."

Anju knew he didn't want to talk about it.

"Why did you leave?" the man pursued, clearly not noticing Dieter's reticence.

"I met a very good combat teacher." Dieter stared at his shoes.

"Who was that?" the man asked.

The others laughed at him.

"If you haven't figured that one out," Mandy told him, "you need to go back and take some extra courses in detective work."

"Or maybe have your eyes tested," someone else added still laughing.

"Don't pull his leg," Anju said in his defence. "He was so engrossed in the combat he didn't notice anything else."

Everybody laughed again.

Their bantering was interrupted by the Chief sticking his head around the door of the gym. "Got some work from you, Mandy and Jock. Looks like more of the same."

Jock glanced at Dieter and Anju. "Would you like to come with us?"

Anju glanced at Dieter who nodded almost imperceptibly. "Sure. As long as we're back in an hour to go to the festivities in the square by the cathedral."

"It shouldn't take long," Jock said.

The police officers applauded them by way of thanks. Some also shook hands or gave them a pat on the back.

"Let us know when you're back in town," one man said.

"You want to call for reinforcements?" Anju asked smiling, catching the possible ambiguity in what he'd said.

The man was embarrassed. It was the same one who'd quizzed Dieter about being a policeman.

"Sorry about that?" Mandy apologised when they were in the police car with Anju and Dieter sitting at the back. "He's a bit clumsy and doesn't catch on very quickly."

Anju had forgotten the man already. She was more concerned about why they had been invited to go on a mission with Mandy and Jock. It didn't make sense.

"I thought you were apologising for setting us up like that," Anju said on a hunch.

An uncomfortable look flitted across Mandy's face. Anju couldn't see Jock's. He was driving.

"What do you mean?" Mandy asked clearly making an effort to keep her voice level.

"… so we could come along to the crime scene…" Anju clarified.

Mandy blushed.

Dieter must have been thinking along the same lines. "Is it not normal procedure to take people along for an investigation? … unless of course you hope to get a confession…."

Mandy was embarrassed and sat silent.

"I like you people, …" she finally said with a sigh, turning her head so she could look Anju in the eyes.

"The trouble is," Jock interrupted her, "we've had four, maybe five deaths this weekend and two people are in a mental institution and each one of them seems to have something to do with you lot."

"I personally doubt you are to blame, but you have to admit it is more than a coincidence," Mandy hastened to add.

"What do you imagine we are going to be able to tell you?" Dieter asked.

"I have no idea," Mandy replied, ill at ease.

"Our boss thought it would be a good idea," Jock informed them.

From the tone of his voice, Anju suspected it had actually been his own idea. She glanced at Dieter. "Ok. Let's see what comes of this."

Anju placed a hand lightly on Mandy's uniformed shoulder.

She felt Dieter tense as she did so. He would never do such a thing. A person in a uniform was not to be touched. Anju felt she could look beyond the uniform and see the person and Mandy was clearly torn by what was happening. She felt Mandy's fingers gently touch hers then Anju pulled her hand away.

The police car pulled into the entrance of a small, run-down farm. The moment they opened the car a dreadful stink of pigs overwhelmed them.

"How did you find out about this?" Dieter asked, slipping into his older role as a detective inspector.

"Someone phoned to say they'd seen something strange." Jock told him.

"Strange indeed!" Anju said.

Several things caught her eye. First there was a dilapidated ice cream van. Its back door was wide open and propped up against it at a weird angle was a large cistern some of the contents of which had overflowed forming a murky puddle. Judging from the smell it must by liquid manure.

The second thing that caught her attention was a bizarre tableau. A man sat slumped forward on a chair, his hands clutched between his legs. On either side of the chair two large dogs lay on their backs their legs pointed rigidly in the air. They were unmoving. Anju supposed they were dead. Maybe the man was too. Nearby a rifle lay abandoned on the ground.

She looked at Dieter, but all he had for answer to her unspoken question was a shrug. She turned to Mandy and Jock. Mandy stood frozen on the spot, looking aghast at the scene. This weekend must have driven her to distraction. Jock, more business like, had moved forward and was checking the man for signs of life.

"His body is completely rigid, but he's still breathing, although it is very shallow," Jock informed them. "Call an ambulance, could you Mandy?"

While she phoned, Dieter went to examine the dogs. "They're also alive, but they are stiff as boards."

Jock glanced at Dieter. "Drugs?"

Dieter shook his head. "Look at their hair. It's standing on end. More like an electric shock."

Anju went over to the shiny metal chains by which the dogs were attached and followed it to the house wall. The chains were simply fixed by a large nail in the wood. There was no sign of burning around the nail.

"I don't think it was electricity," she mused. "That amount would have left burn marks in the wood."

Dieter looked up to see what she was pointing at then returned to examining the gun. From what he could judge without touching it, the weapon appeared to be loaded but hadn't been fired.

"An ambulance is on its way. It'll be here in about ten minutes," Mandy informed them.

Anju pulled out a walkie-talkie from her small backpack intending to call Tom when Jock looked at her suspiciously. "I'm trying to see if our healers have a solution," she explained.

"I don't think that's a good idea," Jock said.

"It might save his life."

"If you people are involved here I don't want you warning them. They might run away."

Anju couldn't help laughing at the stupidity of it. All the same, she was inclined to call but a voice in her head cautioned her.

Don't bother. I'll tell them. It was Mee.

She'd heard about him although this was the first time he had spoken to her. Anju slipped the walkie-talkie back into her bag. What should we do? She asked him in her head.

He's in no danger. The effects will wear off soon enough. If you crush up an aspirin in water and get him to drink some that should help ease the muscles.

When she came back to the world around her she noticed Joke and Mandy looking at her strangely.

"Voices in your head?" Jock asked.

Anju nodded.

"Mee, is that what he's called?"

Anju nodded again.

"Well, tell us what he said," Jock asked.

So Anju told them.

They had an aspirin in the first-aid kit in the car and there was water in the barn. It wasn't easy getting the mixture down his throat as his jaw was clenched tight, but they managed to trickle the liquid, a small amount at a time, through the corner of his mouth where two teeth were missing. Mandy had the disgusting task of holding his lips apart.

After a few minutes his breathing came easier and he began snoring. The ambulance should be there any minute. The four of them stood at some distance from the unconscious man their backs to him as they speculated on how such a thing could have happened. An ominous click had them spinning round to discover the man staring at them, his gun in his hands pointed straight at them.

"So now you dress up as the police," he raged. "Do you think you can fool me like that! I know you for the witches that you are! You're not getting me. Not like you got the others."

Jock took a step towards the man who swung the gun so it was pointing directly at him.

"One more step and I'll blast you to smithereens."

Anju didn't like the look of the situation. The man had such a wild expression in his eyes. It was hard to predict what he might do next.

"I really am a policeman," Jock tried to explain.

Anju could see that no amount of reason would get the better of this man.

"We came to investigate a report that you were not well," Jock pursued.

Good, Anju thought, just keep him talking. Tell him that Mee if you are around.

Jock didn't look away from the man as he continued to speak. "It looks like you are feeling somewhat better now. We called an ambulance as you were unconscious when we arrived. It should be here at any minute."

Anju struggled with the forms of attack and defence she saw traced out in the air around her. She could see no way that would avoid someone getting hurt.

"Would you like to lodge a complaint against these witches you are talking about?" Jock asked.

"The bastards did away with my friends." The man shook his gun.

Anju was afraid the thing would go off by accident.

"Which friends are those?" Jock asked calmly.

"Those of us against witches."

"And what do you plan to do to those witches."

Anju glanced at Mandy. The policewoman was staring at Jock, terrified.

"Burn 'em of course!" the man said without hesitating.

"And how many have you burnt already?"

Anju had to hand it to Jock; he was both clever and courageous.

"Three already. But it didn't work out right."

"That's a shame. What went wrong?"

The man glanced at his dogs, alerted to their presence by the fact they'd started snoring. He gave each of them a kick in the ribs. A shocking muffled crunch was followed by a sickening whelp. He must have broken some of their ribs. He ignored them.

"The first two tried to cast a spell on us when we set fire to their house."

Mandy let out a gasp, but the man paid her attention.

"The other one was saved by her fellow witches only yesterday. It would have made a nice bonfire, right there in the Starless Square, just like they did of old." He laughed.

He was completely insane. For the first time he got to his feet, staggering slightly. It was then that the lines in the air congealed, falling snugly into place and Anju knew she could finally act without anyone getting hurt.

She flung herself sideways knocking Jock to the ground, rolled over and tugged at the dogs' chains causing the dogs to jostle the man knocking him off his feet. It was then that the gun went off. The trajectory, Anju knew would lodge the bullet in the barn door. The man struggled back to his feet as she swung round and cart-wheeled close to him causing him to loose his grip on the gun as he stepped back, off balance. Before he was out of reach her outstretched hand pushed him gently making him fall over backwards and hit his head on the chair leaving him unconscious on the floor.

"Good Lord!" Jock swore as he struggled to his feet, dusting off his uniform. "Mandy are you all right?"

She clung to him, trembling. "I was so afraid for you. I've never felt that frightened before. I don't think I'm cut out for this job."

"Nobody's hurt," Anju tried to reassure her.

Jock seemed to remember they were not alone and he pulled away from Mandy.

"Don't be embarrassed Jock. Love is a beautiful thing," Anju said and hugged Dieter and gave him a kiss.

It was a complicated moment. She could see it well enough. Her with Dieter, the illicit couple and Mandy and Jock, well not illicit, but unconventional. She laughed and Mandy laughed too. It was then that the ambulance siren could be heard in the distance.

"Once you deal with him," Anju said, "you should come with us to the festivities."

Jock cast a glance at Mandy. "I don't think that would be a very good idea, we have other things to do."

Mandy shook her head. "But I want to go, Jock. I really do," she said clasping Jock's hands tightly in hers.

Crowded places

As Brent and Keira entered the square down the narrow alley that led from the High Street, laughter and the sound of voices greeted them. The square was almost unrecognisable. Climbing plants grew in a riot of colours up every wall. A large number of tables were scattered here and there and around each a crowd had gathered. Who would have thought this place had once been the sinister square where no stars ever shone.

"Extraordinary," Brent said.

Keira was looking wide-eyed at the scene. "I wonder where the flowers came from?"

"Sally, no doubt," Brent guessed.

One of Lyra's students greeted them, offering each a glass of a fruit juice, the prominent taste of which Brent recognised as one of the spices from the Reaches. It suddenly made him nostalgic for Lucie. He let go of Keira's hand that he'd been loosely holding. He'd left Lucie only a few days earlier on her way to the Lost Meadows, but it seemed like years. A familiar yearning tugged at him making him feel restless. He wasn't in the right place, yet again.

Brent spotted Anju and Dieter accompanied by the two police officers who'd been at the ring.

"You know Mandy and Jock," Anju said.

Brent was surprised to see that Anju had her arm around Mandy's shoulder. The policewoman had taken off her uniform jacket almost as if she wanted to hide what she was.

"We've been giving Mandy a hard time," Anju told them.

When Brent looked confused, the girl explained. "With all that has happened this weekend she's beginning to wonder if she really made to be a policewoman."

Mandy looked embarrassed. So his intuition had been right. "I thought you were very good at the job," Brent said. "I wish there were more police officers like you."

Mandy smiled at the compliment but said nothing.

"Don't let us stop you from tasting the delicious food Fran and Martin have prepared," Keira said. "I'm sure we'll have a chance to talk more later."

"Yes," Jock said. "A meeting is planned in a warehouse with all of you later this afternoon."

Tom had warned them about it. Brent was apprehensive. "See you then," he said as he turned to go.

As they wove their way through the crowd, they met Naniu and Alo. Naniu stood out, dressed as she was in a brightly coloured Asian costume. Keira explained her recording project to Naniu while Alo asked Brent for news of Rafter. In the excitement at the recording studios, Brent had forgotten about the Professor.

He was tempted to tell Alo the news about Sally and Mae, but suspected Sally would prefer to tell Alo herself. He suddenly wondered if he was jealous. How good to discover you too had an illustrious father.

"He's in considerable pain, but doesn't show it that much. He sleeps a lot. And when he's not asleep he talks to us." Brent couldn't help smiling at the fond memories of their discussions. "You should come and see him this afternoon," Brent suggested, wiping a solitary tear from his eye.

Alo looked sad. "Yes, I'll come with Naniu."

Keira and Brent moved on, heading for the steps in front of the Community Centre were he could see Sally. One of Lyra's students offered then various tasty titbits from large platters covered with a great diversity of small savouries.

"That one is particularly good," the student advised. "I helped Fran make them. We collected a whole load of local herbs and plants to make them."

Brent tried. It was delicious. "Mmm! You're right," he mumbled as he took a second one. It was then that they met Jenny who, surprisingly was accompanied by Collin. The two were in animated conversation.

"Looks like Collin has finally found one of us that has the patience to talk to him," Keira whispered.

"You know Collin," Jenny said when she noticed them. "He's just made the most wonderful film of the work we did at the ring."

Brent shook Collin's hand. "You work for the BBC?" Could this be the person Amanda Stock had sent to film Jenny's work?

"Contract work," Collin explained. "In connection with the recoding you are to do this evening," Collin added turning to Keira. "You should sing here. It would be a good way to announce your performance this evening."

Keira looked appraisingly at him. "It would indeed."

"You should look at some of the material his team filmed at the ring," Jenny added. "It is really excellent."

Brent could see Sally waving to him from the steps, so he excused himself and headed for the entrance to the Centre. Keira followed. On the way they saw Fran and Martin who were busy explaining how they'd made some of the cakes that were being handed out.

"How'd it go?" Sally asked when they finally reached her.

"I'm to record the music in public at the ring this evening. Part of the profits from the record will go to rebuilding the ring. The BBC has agreed," Keira told her.

"Great," Sally said, giving her friend a big hug. "They filmed Jenny's work to promote the record."

"We just met Jenny. She's with Collin, who apparently did a great job of filming her work," Brent put in.

Sally laced her arm in his and pulled him closer. With her other arm she did the same with Keira. "You should sing a song," Sally suggested. "To announce the concert."

Their conversation was interrupted by a platter of multicoloured deserts made with wild berries. Each tiny tartlet was different. Brent tried several. They were delicious. Their size made him think of the Littl' People who'd taught Fran and Martin to cook. The cakes were just the right size if you took your time to savour them.

Sally beckoned to Fran and Martin to join her on the steps. It was not easy for them to get away from the many people who wanted to congratulate them or to ask questions about recipes. When they finally made it to Sally's side, she raised her voice, projecting it out over the crowd that filled the square.

"I think perhaps we should thank Fran and Martin for their work in preparing this feast for us all," she said.

The crowd responded with thunderous applause.

When they quietened, Fran said a few words. "Thank you. I'd particularly like to thank all those students and assistants of Professor Lyra Enquist who have so generously helped us make the food and drinks you've tasted today."

"They have worked very hard indeed," Martin added.

The crowd applauded again.

"And if you want recipes they should all be able to help. They've been excellent students," Martin added causing people to laugh.

Sally spoke. "I have some news for you. Those of you who attended the concert yesterday at the Arena or who were present at dawn this morning at the Avan Ring will have heard Keira sing. She is going to give an additional concert this evening at nine o'clock at the Ring. It's free and you are all invited. The concert will be recorded by the BBC and part of the profits from the record will go to rebuilding the ring."

The crowd burst into applause and a great many cheered, some even whistled.

"So as an appetiser, Keira's going to sing a song for you now."

Cheers and applause greeted the news. Keira stepped forward.

"I'm going to sing two songs," she said. "I wouldn't want to keep you from such delicious food for too long."

Several people laughed.

"The first song is a lullaby. I sang this the first time for a young girl who had been abused by her uncle. I sing it now in memory of her courage and her vitality. I sing it also for all those girls and women who have suffered a similar fate."

A hush fell over the crowd. The atmosphere had become suddenly serious at Keira's words. As Keira sang, people couldn't fail to be moved by her voice. It wound its way around their hearts. Many had tears in their eyes.

When the applause had died down, Keira presented her second song. "This song, which is in Gaelic, was taught to me by a dear friend called Grace. She is the head of the women guardians of the rings like the one here in Avan. Their job and mine is to carry out the sacred rituals in the rings in this world and in others."

Brent wondered what the crowd would make of this reference to other worlds. It was not such an uncommon idea although few people talked as if they had really visited other worlds. No one seemed to react at Keira's words. Once the song was over the crowd pressed her for an encore. Keira refused.

"These are not my festivities, but those of Fran and Martin and their food of the gods," she said. "They are the people you should celebrate," she insisted and she turned to Fran and Martin to applaud them.

People joined her and applauded the two cooks as Keira stepped down leaving the place to Fran and Martin.

Chapter 13 ~ A Story's End

Reunited

"Mae? Is that you?" Rafter called out.

The house had been so quiet and peaceful, he guessed he was alone. Everyone must have gone to the celebrations near the cathedral. He drifted in and out of sleep, half dreaming, half recalling broken fragments of his past. But now he was fully awake and he could hear scuffling of feet in the entrance and the sound of whispers. He turned, not without difficulty in his makeshift bed to look towards the door hoping to see who had come to visit him.

There, standing in the entrance was the last person he ever expected to see again. His heart took a bound and almost faltered. Teresa. He closed his eyes and opened them again, wondering if he might be hallucinating. His chest had hurt so much he'd had to take a strong painkiller an hour earlier. Maybe that was playing havoc with his eyes. But when he looked again she was still there.

"Tess," he said, his voice a whisper, tears flowing down his cheeks. "Tess is that you?"

She took several hesitant steps towards him.

"Yes, my love," she said, whispering like him. "It is me, come at last." She burst into tears. He held out his shaking hand to her. She hesitated just out of reach.

"Take the last step, my love."

She stretched out her hand and took his in hers. She felt so soft and warm and welcoming. He curled his fingers around hers and pulled her towards him. She knelt at his bedside and laid her head on his shoulder, sobbing as he wrapped his arms around her.

"Oh John!" her muffled voice said.

In that moment he realised he had been waiting for her all his life. He ran his fingers through her hair. It was as beautiful as ever although she had some grey hairs here and there.

"I'm so sorry," she sobbed.

"Shhh," he whispered. "You are here now. That's all that matters."

A sharp pain shot through his chest causing him to gasp. She pulled away and looked at his face.

"I am no longer the John you knew," he said, realising that she could probably hardly recognise the suffering old man he'd become.

"John Llewellyn Rafter, you are the only man I really loved." She looked him in the eyes.

"And you are the only woman in my life," he replied squeezing her hand.

They stayed in each other's arms a long time without talking. The house was quiet again. Had the others left, he wondered?

"How did you get here from the Reaches?"

"Your daughter came to fetch me."

"Your daughter too."

"Our daughter."

"But which one, we have two?"

"Mayeva."

"Mae." Of course she would." Trusty Mae, the one who had looked after him so well.

"She's become a very beautiful young woman," Tess said. "Where is the other girl? She was only a baby when she left."

"Sally is with friends at a big celebration. She should be back soon. But you already met her in the Reaches recently."

At that moment another sharp pain stabbed through his chest. There was no way he could conceal it. His body tensed and his hands flew to his heart. She pulled away and looked at him.

"I have brought you some medicine. It will not stop the inevitable," she said, tears streaming down her cheeks, "but it will ease the pain without clouding your mind." She pulled a small flask from her pocket. He opened his mouth and she shook a few drops on his tongue.

Maybe it was his imagination but some of the tension went out of his chest, he was able to breath a little easier and he could almost relax for the first time in days. He thanked her, patting the bed next to him for her to sit down. She couldn't be very comfortable kneeling there on the hard floor.

She got to her feet, not without difficulty, her knees seemed to be troubling her, but instead of sitting next to him as he expected, she lay down beside him and wound her arms around his shoulders cuddling close to his feverish body.

"My little Welsh magician," she whispered in his ear.

It was one of the terms of endearment she'd used when they'd first met. "Oh Tess! You come right at the end. I have so little time left. I'm no longer a little Welsh magician. I'm a university professor at the end of his career about to leave his place to younger and more gifted people."

"Shhh. You were one of the most gifted men I ever met."

Rafter sighed. "These young people are such a joy. They learn so quickly. And they have so many natural gifts. I am very happy to hand over to them. Sally, Mae, Brent, Keira, Jenny, Anju,… there are so many of them. They will do great things. That is why, now you are here with me, I can leave in peace."

"Not yet my love. Mae was worried she'd arrive too late. You must wait till she and Sally can say goodbye."

He nodded. "Then if you agree, I will sleep one last time in your welcoming arms."

Suspended

"Hey Mae!" Sally exclaimed flinging her arms around her sister's neck almost knocking her off her feet in her enthusiasm. "Great to see you back."

Although they had been friends for a long time, Mae wasn't used to such demonstrations of affection. She put it down to high spirits due to the weekend's festivities. She glanced at Lyra and winked at her as Sally hugged her half sister An. She'd spent some very good moments with Lyra during the trip when An went off with the girls to explore the town.

One by one the whole Dream Class filed into the kitchen amidst kisses and hugs and squeals: Brent, Keira, Tom, Jenny, Anju, Dieter, Martin and Fran.

"Shhhh!" Mae warned. "I think Rafter's fallen asleep in Teresa's arms."

"Teresa?" Brent asked in a hushed voice. "You managed to get her to come?"

Mae grinned.

"It wasn't easy," Beth told them. "Mae was really great!"

Everyone turned to look at the three girls who were huddled together in one corner of the kitchen intimidated by all these people.

"So, how were the Reaches?" Brent asked.

"Wonderful," all three said in unison, their faces beaming.

"You realise, of course, that we will not be able to let you out of here now you know our secret," Brent said, keeping a straight face.

The girls' faces fell and Maria gasped.

"Don't pay any attention to him," An laughed. "He's pulling your leg."

They all looked relieved.

"Mae told us we would have to be careful," Tricia said.

"When can we go back?" Maria asked.

"So you found some nice boys there," Fran teased.

Maria blushed.

Everyone laughed.

Fran tousled Beth's hair causing Beth to blush as well. Mae had already noticed that Fran had a fond spot for the intelligent girl. They had a lot in common.

"So how did you manage to persuade our mother?" Sally asked as one by one people sat around the table.

Fran and Martin laid several trays of assorted leftovers on the table. "If anyone can stand anymore," Fran said, grinning.

Several people groaned theatrically and Fran made a show of being upset. The new arrivals from the Reaches had no such problem. They helped themselves without restraint. They'd had little time to eat during their journey. Congratulations fused from every side for the food. Lyra was particularly lyrical about Fran and Martin's culinary skills.

"It was mostly the work of your students," Martin assured her.

"Now you're trying to pull my leg," Lyra joked.

Mae didn't feel hungry though. She'd managed to bring back her mother, whom she'd met for the first time in difficult circumstances, and she was happy she'd managed. But Rafter's health had further deteriorated. She could see it in his face. He was in terrible pain. He wouldn't last much longer. She shrugged off the thought, not very successfully, and replied to Sally.

"Well first of all," she began, "it wasn't easy to find her."

"It was lucky you found that photo," An interjected.

"Photo?" Sally queried.

"Our parents before we were born," she replied laconically.

"Show me," Sally ordered, abrupt in her eagerness.

Mae was reluctant. The photo had become her talisman. She didn't want to share it in public. "I left it in my bag," she lied.

Lyra gave Mae a strange look and then came to her rescue. "It was the photo that enabled Mae to find Teresa."

"We just 'popped out' right in the middle of a small town. Lucky it wasn't as busy as here. Someone might have noticed us appear from nowhere," Beth mused.

"What was Teresa doing there?" Keira asked.

So much for telling her story, Mae groaned to herself. This was more like an interrogation.

No its not, a voice said in her head, startling her. They're just interested and happy to see you all.

Vee? She thought.

No Mee. Vee is gone.

She had never spoken to Vee so the experience of having a voice in her head for the first time was disturbing.

"She must be tired," she heard Jenny saying and she realised everyone was looking at her with concern in their eyes.

"Sorry," she apologised. "I was talking to Mee. I'm not used to having voices in my head. It's a little disturbing."

Sally chuckled. "So now you know how it was for me."

"Teresa and her husband were busy trying to get support against Horst's mercenaries," Mae continued.

"When my parents left our home to travel south for help, "An explained, "there were loads of wild men roaming the countryside killing and plundering, especially to the north around Granwich."

"I saw one," Maria said, disgust in her voice. "He was filthy and violent and he had a deep bloody gash across his face."

"Any news of Horst?" Keira asked.

"And Lucie?" Brent asked, his voice shaking.

Mae and An shook their heads.

"Nothing," An said.

"Teresa was not having much luck getting support. People didn't want to bother about trouble elsewhere," Mae pursued

"Typical," Tom put in.

"Teresa didn't recognise me when I found her. Not surprising really. She'd seen me only as a baby. She was disinclined to believe me."

"She was afraid to believe," Beth mentioned.

"And worried about what you'd demand of her," Tricia added.

An's young friends were too perspicacious, Mae noted.

"How did you convince her to come?" Sally asked.

"When she wouldn't come for Rafter or for us, her daughters, I threatened her."

Everyone looked astonished.

It was true, her behaviour had been out of character. "I told her she would be cursed for the rest of her life if she didn't take this last opportunity to see Rafter."

Beth chuckled. "Mae was magnificent. I thought she really was going to curse the woman. She was furious."

"You're exaggerating," Mae said, embarrassed.

"No I'm not," Beth protested.

"No she's not," An added, "you were, how should I put it, ... majestically terrifying."

Everyone laughed at the description. Mae was even more embarrassed.

"It was exactly what was needed," Lyra said in her defence. "Teresa finally accepted. It was then that she started to ask so many questions about Rafter and you Sally and Mae. We would have come back earlier, but she wouldn't stop and insisted on getting answers."

"She was so caught up in her questions she didn't even think to offer us food," Maria said, taking a further handful of cakes from an almost empty tray.

Everyone laughed causing her to blush.

An winked at her. "Don't mind them."

"Mae was sick with worry," Beth added. "I think if Teresa had continued firing questions at us any longer, Mae would have gagged her and put her mother over her shoulder to carry her back."

Mae had to smile. Thanks heavens An's little friends had been with them. Their company had helped a lot.

"Something like that," Mae admitted making a face. "But what about the festivities?"

Everyone wanted to talk at once. Mae made herself comfortable, leaning back in her chair, and listened to all they had to say.

Confusion

Early afternoon on Sunday was traditionally a time when the people of Avan went for a walk in Hoyt Park, wandering along the broad alleyways between the flowerbeds admiring the roses or sauntering across the large expanses of lawn where children played freely. If you wanted to meet someone and have it appear to be by accident that was the time and place to do it. But Kean was not seeking a chance encounter. His encounter had already taken place. He'd agreed to accompany Irina back to the hotel where John and Moira had been staying down by the sea. She'd seemed distressed at the idea of returning to London with John and Moira. She had controlled herself for her goodbyes at the Community Centre, but now she was agitated. He didn't like to see her so worked up. He was afraid she'd have another attack.

A number of yards separated them as they sauntered towards the sea in silence. She walked, her hands clasped in front of her, her eyes cast down, each step heavy and hesitant. The ambiguity of his feelings towards her persisted and he suspected she felt his ambivalence. That might explain why she kept such a distance. It made him feel more like a chaperon or a nurse than a friend out for a walk.

"What exactly happened when I turned on you?" she asked, startling him.

He glanced at her but she was looking steadfastly at the ground just in front of her. "I prayed for help and protection both for us and for you. And a white swirling cloud appeared around us..."

"What do you think it was?"

He wasn't sure. He had a hunch, but he didn't want to believe it. Although he'd studied elementals in one course at the university, he had had no first hand experience of them, let alone angels. She stopped walking and looked up at him. Tears welled in her eyes.

"I don't want to leave you all. I will feel so alone. And I'm afraid."

He didn't like to see her suffer, but he had no idea how to console her.

"I'm sure you'll be back soon." He didn't sound convinced, even to his own ears.

"But everyone will be gone," she wailed.

He moved closer despite his unwillingness and put an arm around her shoulder, thinking that might comfort her, but she shook it off.

"You don't like me either. Nobody does. You're just sorry for me." She pouted, her face streaked with tears. "Everybody is sorry for the little girl who has fits and almost kills people with her hands." She sat down on a large boulder. "Go away! Leave me alone!"

Kean was taken aback by the sudden violence of her rejection. He

315

didn't want to go away. But if that was what she wanted.

"I'm sorry you see it like that. I didn't mean any harm but I'll leave you if you want."

She shot him a troubled look. "What? I don't understand."

"You told me to go, so I will."

"Oh! I didn't mean you."

It was his turn to be confused.

"I meant them." She waved her hands in the air about her.

"I don't understand."

"I mean all those forms swirling around me. They seem to come every time I get upset."

He looked where she was pointing but could see nothing.

"Surely you can see them. There are so many. I feel like I'm going to suffocate."

Her expression was resigned as she closed her eyes and lapsed into silence. Kean paced back and forth, trying to remember how he'd managed to call up the angels at Twine's place. He had to laugh at the idea: imagine finding angels in a pig's sty! Seriously though, if he could remember he might be able to see whatever it was that was pestering Irina.

He'd told everybody he'd prayed, but what had he done? He'd been terrified at the time. His life had depended on a desperate and useless gesture that had miraculously worked. He gave up on his analysis. It wasn't getting him any closer to a solution.

Stop thinking about it and do it!

The thought came unbidden, almost as if someone had spoken it. How could he possibly have thoughts that were not his own? It didn't make sense.

Stop dithering!

This new thought was more imperative than the first. Kean was beginning to get alarmed. Drops of sweat formed on his brow and coursed down his face. Was he going mad?

Would it reassure you to know I am a voice speaking in your head?

He'd heard that Sally had a voice in her head called Vee. Could it be something like that?

Stop calling me 'it', the voice said. To the best of my knowledge I am as much alive and conscious as you are. More so maybe!

Kean apologised silently and set about praying. He wanted to see what it was that was bothering Irina and he wanted to know if he could help her. His mind immediately started spinning out solutions.

Forget that! This time the voice was almost rude.

Kean dropped the ideas as if they were red-hot and spoke his request once more. Then he waited, expectant. To his disappointment nothing happened. Maybe it only worked in life threatening situations he speculated. He glanced at Irina, hoping she was looking less dejected.

He gasped.

To his surprise he saw a cloud of forms jostling around Irina vying for her attention. Afraid that if he examined them too closely they'd flit away, he scrutinised them out of the corner of his eye. Some hung majestically in the air or turned slowly around the girl. Others seemed riveted to the ground, as if they had roots. Irina worked like a magnet attracting them. Then he felt it, a force emanating from her that tugged everything in her direction. It tugged at him too.

"You're attracting them," he burst out in surprise.

"I know. Sally told me that." She remained unmoving, her eyes closed.

"It's like a magnet field. I can feel it."

She glanced up at him questioningly then looked back at the ground in front of her. "I think I attract them because I hate being alone."

"That can't be true."

She looked up, irritated at being countered. "Why not?"

"Because I'm here with you."

"Are you sure?"

"I might not have been here before, but I certainly am now." As he spoke he noticed the forms were slipping away, being replaced by the white shimmering he'd seen before. "Extraordinary!"

"What?"

"My angels chased away your demons."

"They're not demons!" She pouted. "When they are not pestering me, I like having them around. They whisper ideas to me."

He chuckled.

"What?"

"A voice spoke to me too. I was trying to pray and he told me to stop thinking about it and get on and do it."

She looked at him as if he were a weird phenomenon. "That must be different. Mine don't speak. Rather they show me pictures and make me feel things. I think that is their way of communicating."

He glanced at his watch. They would be late and John and Moira would miss their train. "We should go."

She didn't move.

"You're going to be late."

She still didn't move. "Kean?" she asked, not looking at him.

He didn't answer, anxious about what was coming next.

"Kean? Do you love me?"

Well there it was, out loud. He should have been relieved, but he felt a rush of panic. It was much worse that confronting a pig farmer with a loaded gun. He looked away, seeking inspiration. The white cloud around him seemed to have got much denser. He wondered if he could drown in it. Part of him screamed 'no!' and he could feel his muscles locking into flight mode. He glanced at her just as she glanced at him.

"You don't have to answer." She looked embarrassed.

He had such confusing and conflicting feelings about her he didn't know what he felt. "I ..." he began. "I think I do."

She nodded, a gesture that left him perplexed. "And do I love you?" she asked.

If she hadn't been so serious, he might have suspected she was making fun of him. What a question. How was he to know? He hardly knew her.

"Look at me," she suggested.

He did as she said. Wasn't it enough to say he loved her?

You're not really looking! The voice was back in his head bringing a headache with it.

He looked again. Something fell away, like he'd shed a skin, if that were possible. As it did, he felt a sharp pang in his chest. "I believe you do."

She stood and took a hesitant step towards him but got no further. Her movement was frozen in mid-step by the sound of a female voice crying out in the distance.

"Irina! Irina! Hurry. We'll miss the train."

Halted a few paces from each other, Irina and Kean exchanged a momentary glance of exasperation and then turned as one to face Moira who was running across the lawns of Hoyt Park towards them.

"We've been waiting for you," Moira said, clearly annoyed. "What on earth have you been doing?"

Moira made a move to grab Irina's hand but Irina pulled away. Instead she held out her hand to Kean who took it. Moira looked from one to the other and back again. Then she shrugged, turned abruptly in the direction of their hotel that overlooked the sea and set off at a brisk pace.

"Hurry. The taxi is waiting."

Adieu

When Rafter awoke, the Dream Class came to greet Teresa and be with the couple, possibly for the last time.

Mae preferred not to follow them. Instead she went outside and sat on the steps of the porch, her head rested on her hands. She wanted to steel herself for what was to come. The end was close. Knowing he would wait for her, she selfishly kept out of the way hoping that would stall the moment. She knew it wasn't fair, but she couldn't help herself. Tears crept into her eyes and lingered there despite her efforts to stop them.

At the noise of several cars coming down the drive, she looked up. It was the five remaining professors from the department. Lyra was already with Rafter. Martina, Chris and Greenacre were in the first car. Gavin and Liam in the second. The five of them were chattering amiably as they got out of the cars and crossed the car park towards her. Seeing the tears in her eyes, Chris stopped, and looked questioningly at her, not wanting to ask the question out loud. The others were silent now too. She shook her head causing more tears to flow.

"He's awake and receiving visits," she told them her voice shaky as she wiped the tears from her eyes. "He's very tired and in a lot of pain, so maybe you should keep your visit short." Chris nodded and the others agreed. Mae stood and opened the front door for them.

"Ah! A deputation from the Theosophy Department," Rafter said, his voice weak, but his humour as always present. "Have you come to ask for a raise?" He attempted a smile.

"No. We've just come to visit an old friend," Chris said, wending his way amongst the young ones seated on the floor. He shook Rafter's hand and placed a friendly hand on the old man's shoulder. "It's a shame you missed the weekend."

The Dream Class moved back to make way for the staff who each shook hands with Rafter, exchanging a few quiet words.

"So are you pleased with the weekend Mae organised?" Rafter asked.

Mae wondered why Rafter did not present Teresa who was sitting next to him on his bed. No doubt he had his reasons.

"It's not finished, I heard," Martina told him. "There's to be an extra concert this evening and a record and possibly even a film."

Rafter knew nothing of that and Mae could see that he had gone beyond such considerations. But as always, he put his concern for the others first.

"The weekend has been a wonderful success," Gavin said.

"And we didn't have any of the trouble we anticipated," Greenacre added.

Tom shook his head, but nobody contradicted the professor.

"Mae and you others did a wonderful job," Liam added.

Rafter beckoned Mae over from the doorway where she was standing, trying to be inconspicuous. Rafter patted the bed next to him lightly and Mae sat down. Rafter called Sally to his side as well.

"Colleagues," he began.

So this was it, Mae thought, the official announcement. But he didn't get any further because Naniu and Alo arrived at that moment. They too greeted Rafter with gentle hugs and kisses and then found a place to sit.

"As I was about to say, I have a secret to reveal from the dark past and the bright future of Professor John Llewellyn Rafter."

He paused a moment to catch his breath. The pain was sapping the little energy he had left.

"I'd like to present my wife."

Everyone without exception, Mae included, gasped.

"Teresa and I were married a long time ago in a small village in Wales near my home town."

Right to the end he'd kept that fact a secret, even from his new found daughters. Teresa looked shyly around the room at all these people she didn't know but said nothing. Mae put her arm around her mother to reassure her.

"To cut a long story short, we had two children, two girls but were unable to look after then."

He had to pause again grasping his chest because of the pain.

"Those girls are here now: Mae Rafter and Sally Rafter."

"Good Lord!" Greenacre gasped. "I had no idea."

"Neither did we," Sally informed him.

There was an embarrassed silence while Rafter caught his breath again. Then he added: "All the official papers have been signed and are filed away with the notary along with my will and testament."

Nobody knew what to say or do. Mae could see it in people's faces.

"I always thought you were keeping something from us, but I never imagined anything like this," Lyra said. She had had more time that the others to get used to the idea.

"You knew," Liam said almost accusingly.

"Only since I went to fetch Teresa with Mae."

Mae could see that several people wanted to question Lyra, but Sally stopped them.

"Our mother comes from the Reaches. Mae went to fetch her there. That we were born in the Reaches might explain why we find it easier than others to travel there."

More questions, more explanations, Mae thought. She turned to look at Rafter. He was almost green with pain. "I know you've only just arrived but I think our father needs some rest," she told everybody. "If you'd like to have a drink, I'm sure Martin and Fran can rustle up something for you next door."

"I think it would be better if we left," Chris said.

Such a sensitive man, Mae thought. People began to stand and the staff members took it in turns to say goodbye to Rafter. Several of them had tears in their eyes. Naniu and Alo also said their farewells, Rafter whispering a last quiet message to each of them.

The members of the Dream Class were also standing to leave, but Rafter asked them to stay. So they all sat again, turning to look at the Professor. He spoke first to Sally and Mae. "I love you both more than you know," he said looking at each in turn. Then he added. "Take care of Teresa for me. She deserves much better than she got." And he leant forward with great difficulty and kissed Teresa. "You are the love of my life."

"I love you, John," she said through her tears.

Then addressing them all he said: "I want you to take good care of Sally and Mae for me." He paused a moment to fight off the pain. "I hope that you manage to make your Dream Class become a reality." Pain cut into him again. "Hold on to that dream. It is a treasure worth fighting for."

He closed his eyes making Mae fear the worst but then he opened them again. "In my will I have tried to help you in my own modest way. The Dream Class is the future. You are the future." Pain interrupted him once more. "I am really happy I was able to get to know you all a little." He coughed violently. "Now it is your turn."

Each of them moved forward to say goodbye. Then he closed his eyes saying "Thank you" almost inaudibly. Mae took one of his hands, Sally the other and they helped him lie back on his bed next to Teresa.

"I love you," Sally said.

Mae too whispered "I love you" in his ear and then he was gone. Mae could feel it. She knew Sally could too. They both burst into sobs. John Llewellyn Rafter was no more.

Out for the count

Mandy took hold of Jock's hand. It was cold and clammy. She wound her fingers around his, hoping to bring warmth and life back to them. She didn't give a damn if the Chief Constable was there, surveying her every move. They'd exchanged some hard words on the way to the hospital. She couldn't agree with him. It was not Jock's fault that Twine had got away. There was no proof. Until Jock woke up, they couldn't know what had happened.

She kept her eyes fixed on Jock, who lay unconscious in bed, a thick bandage around his head. After a protracted silence the Chief rose and left asking her to call him the moment Jock revived. She would do no such thing. Jock needed peace and quiet to recover, not an inquisition. How could she have worked so long in such an atmosphere? She took a deep breath and relaxed, a little.

"Oh Jock!" she said softly, finally alone with him. "What have they done to us?" Although she was unsure who 'they' were. His eyelids fluttered and he groaned, but he didn't wake.

It was a hand resting on her shoulder that awoke her. It could only be Jock. She must have fallen asleep with her head on the covers of his hospital bed. She kept her eyes closed and stayed as still as possible, savouring his touch. She wanted it to go on forever, but the hand withdrew.

"I know you're awake," he said.

She didn't reply, but reached out for his hand and pulled it gently to her lips, kissing it.

"I love you," she said between kisses.

He pulled his hand free and used it to raise her chin so he could see her. She opened her eyes to find him scrutinising her face, and when he leaned forward she thought he would kiss her, but instead he groaned.

"Your head?"

"Yes."

"Are you hurt anywhere else?"

"No. He hit me over the head with something hard and heavy."

"The nurses found one of those steel chamber pots covered in blood next to you on the floor."

He groaned again.

"Do you want me to ask them to give you a pain-killer?"

"No it doesn't hurt much. It's the thought that hurts me. How could I have been caught out like that?" He lapsed into silence.

"The Chief was angry," she told him. "Said it was your fault."

Jock groaned again. "He would."

"But I told him he was wrong and when he insisted, I told him to go to hell."

Jock laughed, his laughter rapidly cut off by a groan as he put a hand to his head. "I'd like to have seen that."

"I felt guilty, ... but I also felt very proud!" She laughed. She leant forward and kissed him gently on his forehead. "I'm going to hand in my resignation on Monday."

He gasped. "What am I going to do without you?"

"Resign like me," she suggested, knowing full well that it probably wasn't the same for him. "We'll find something interesting to do." A glance at his face showed he was unhappy. "You enjoy being a policeman?"

"I do," he replied. "The job makes me feel useful and competent. I have no idea what else I could do. I'm not even sure I could do anything else, except perhaps odd job man."

Another long silence followed. She had thought a lot about her work during the weekend. Her encounters with the people from the Theosophy Department had accelerated a process that she realised had already been underway for quite a while. It was the sudden flowering of her relationship with Jock that had clinched things. She couldn't bear to have his life at risk.

"I was terrified when I saw you lying there, motionless in a hospital bed. You could have been killed." Tears overflowed and ran down her cheeks. "I am so frightened something will happen to you."

He made tiny shushing noises, like one would with a child that had hurt itself. "There, there." He patted her gently on the head.

She closed her eyes and let herself be comforted. Was she becoming a weakling? One who gives up when the going gets tough? "You have to be hard skinned to be a policewoman. This weekend has changed me. You have changed me, my love for you."

He shook his head and groaned. So much for saying it didn't hurt! "It's those people from the Theosophy Department," he said, his tone accusatory.

She nodded. "They are different." She paused searching for the words. "They have a different way of approaching life and that approach appeals to me. I couldn't live like them, but I enjoy being with them. And I believe it is thanks to them that we finally got together."

He looked at her, perplexed.

"They created something that night at the Arena, something magic, and that broke down the barriers we'd thrown up between us."

He looked thoughtful and did not reply immediately. "I don't know." He shook his head. "Don't you think you are idealising them?"

Was she? Maybe. But she did feel attracted to them and would be delighted to find a way to remain in contact, other than locking them up in prison. She laughed at her own thoughts. He looked troubled. "I was thinking I'd like to spend more time with them, but not by throwing them in jail."

"Why not lock them up. At least that way you would have to stay in the police."

She glanced at her watch. It was time. They had fixed a meeting with the university people in a warehouse. She stood. "I'll tell you what happens."

He looked perplexed. Maybe the blow to his head had caused some loss of memory. "The meeting with the people from the Theosophy Department," she reminded him.

He shifted in his bed as if he were about to get up. "I can't let them abduct you in my absence." From the seriousness of his face, his words were not meant as a joke.

"They are not going to abduct me!" She laughed. "You are staying in bed. You are suffering from severe concussion."

"Nonsense. My head is as hard as a rock."

"That's true, my love. It's called stubbornness."

"Hand me my clothes." He pushed back the covers and swung his feet to the ground.

She refused. "I'll call the doctors and have them give you a sedative."

To her surprise, he agreed. "Call a doctor. We'll ask him what he thinks."

"The doctor is a woman," she corrected as she stepped out in search of her. It took a while to find the person but she managed to persuade the woman to come, saying it was urgent.

"So Mr. Glas, you want to run away from us already?" She pushed him gently back onto the bed and took his pulse. She examined his eyes with a narrow torch and listened to his breathing with a stethoscope. Then she pressed in several places around his neck and shoulders.

"Does that hurt?"

It didn't.

Turning to Mandy, she said: "You might like to step outside while I examine the wound."

Mandy hesitated, but then did as she was asked. Outside, she paced the corridor, wondering what she would do if he remained in the police and she left. That sort of mixed relationship was not easy. She knew so much about police work she'd always be worried about him. It was a dangerous job, even in Avan.

The doctor called her back. "I think he can leave, if he wants. The scan revealed no permanent damage. There don't seem to be any problems of balance. You've been very lucky, Mr. Glas." Then she turned to Mandy. "You'll have to keep a very close eye on him and make sure he doesn't do anything rash." She winked at Mandy.

Mandy had to laugh, despite herself. "I'll keep him under very close surveillance," she promised, waving a finger at Jock.

"You do that," the doctor said.

The wake

Mae laid cushions around her father then removed the gold ring and its chain that hung around her neck. The ring had been made by the Littl' People and originally belonged to Teresa. She gently slipped it over John Llewellyn's neck.

"You asked me to keep it safe for you and now I give it back."

Keira and Jenny had helped Mae and Sally prepare Rafter. Washed and dressed in his favourite suit, they had transported him to the conservatory where he now lay on a temporary bed improvised using a large table. Jenny told them the house was situated on a key energy line that ran through the Cathedral and the Theosophy Department. According to her, the conservatory had the highest energy in the house. She had worked to raise that energy even higher, calling on all the forces nearby.

"I have never known such a collection of positive beings to help me," she said, tears in her eyes.

Sally transformed the glass roof of the conservatory as she had once done in the Reaches giving the impression that the Professor lay under a brilliant starlit sky. She also made Evening Glory clamber up the walls and across parts of the roof, its bright yellow flowers shining in the late afternoon sun.

"For you, John Llewellyn," Sally whispered.

Teresa had been unwilling or possibly unable to help them. She sat now, her head bowed, on a chair next to her husband's bed, her hand placed on his. She refused to talk. Instead, she fixed Rafter with her tear-filled eyes and pined.

When all was ready, the four young women, Mae, Keira, Jenny and Sally, stood in front of the bed facing the Professor with Teresa seated at their side and Keira began to sing.

"Oh my love," she sang, her voice more melodic than Sally had ever heard it.

"Come my love." Keira's soprano voice rose and fell lifting the word 'love' high into the sky. Cascades of shooting stars fell in the starlit sky.

"Come with me my love." And one by one the voices of the Sisterhood joined Keira as she sang, singing across the expanses between the worlds, unworldly yet profoundly down to earth. The place rippled with music causing the form of things to blur and tremble.

"Come feast on love." Through her tears Sally stared at her father. He was swathed in bright white light that turned slowly and rose and fell about him, pulsing with the rhythm of the music. It was almost as if the light and the music were lifting him up. She could have sworn there was a smile on his lips. Gone were the signs of pain that had plagued his last days. Only happiness remained. Teresa's mouth had fallen open in surprise and joy.

"My love, take me with you," Teresa pleaded.

Out of the corner of her eye, Sally could see other nebulous white forms joining them. They brought with them a feeling so bright that it was pure beauty.

"Oh my heart, come feast on love." The chorus seemed to swell even further. Could those angelic forms also be singing with Keira and the Sisterhood?

"Come feast on love."

Glancing over her shoulder, Sally saw that all the Dream Class had silently joined them, their faces transfixed by what was happening.

"Oh my beloved." Several of the angelic forms had woven their way between Sally and her friends to come and stand next to Teresa.

With the help of Mae, Teresa climbed up onto the table and lay down next to Rafter. Mae pulled the pendant she'd received from the Littl' People from around her neck and placed it carefully in Teresa's outstretched hand. Whispering quiet words to her mother, she then withdrew.

An must have understood what was happening because she came forward and kissed her mother on her forehead. "Till next time, Teresa," Sally heard her say, despite the singing. Then she stepped back to stand next to Sally and the others, tears in her eyes.

As the choir sang "Come feast on love" for the last time, the white forms that surrounded both John Llewellyn and Teresa rose slowly into the air followed by a host of angels. A profound silence fell over the conservatory, a silence so dense and pregnant that it was almost unbearable.

They've gone, Sally realised. And in so thinking she turned to An who was next to her and broke into sobs. She could hear Mae sobbing too.

"Grieve not, my love," An told her. "They couldn't possibly have had a more beautiful end."

"Did Teresa get her wish? Did she go to join him?" Sally asked.

"Yes. They've both gone. But they'll be back. Of that I am absolutely certain," An said.

Sally turned to look at her fellow members of the Dream Class. They all bore the marks of profound sadness mingled with intense joy and even elation.

"I think we need to drink a toast," Brent said, his voice surprisingly deep and calm. "Martin, have you and Fran got something special for us to drink in honour of John and Teresa?"

The request seemed to shake Martin out of a dream and he smiled. "Of course, my friend. We've been saving a couple of bottles for a special occasion."

Fran went to fetch glasses and Martin returned with a pair of dust-covered bottles.

"D'rick gave us these. We brought them all the way from the Reaches. He said we would know when the moment had come to drink them. Now is the time I think." He uncorked the first bottle releasing an exquisite odour of wild flowers in the conservatory. He poured and Fran handed round the glasses.

"To John Llewellyn Rafter and his wife Teresa Rafter," Brent said solemnly and every one raised their glasses saying "To John and Teresa."

Fran hurried away and returned with a tray of tiny salty cakes. "D'rick told us this fruit wine should always be drunk with these cakes, so Martin and I baked them specially this morning, just in case."

"A toast to D'rick and the Littl' People and their excellent pupils, Fran and Martin," Jenny called out.

"Here, here," several people replied.

And the round of toasts continued till the two bottles were completely empty and everyone, even Tricia, Maria and Beth, had been celebrated and praised. Everyone was in pretty high spirits. The wine was strong and the emotions too. Sally felt light-headed. She hugged An and then Keira. It was then she noticed the sadness on Mae's face. Taking her by the hand she pulled Mae closer and hugged her.

"We'll see them again. I am convinced of it," she told Mae.

But Mae shook her head and cried softly on Sally's shoulder. "I loved him so much. If I had one unspoken dream it was that he be my father. He was my idol, my model, my secret love. What will I do without him? I feel completely lost."

Sally hugged her sister tighter. "You will do great things, Mae Rafter. You will help us all make the Dream Class a reality and much, much more, no doubt."

Unexpected turnings

"Extraordinary!" Brent exclaimed as Tom and Kean led him through the large open spaces of the warehouse on their way to the meeting room above. "This place has so much potential!"

He loved the way the girders arched upwards and then curved over to meet each other and the immense glass windows that flooded the space with late afternoon sun. He could imagine all manner of things happening in such a space: exhibitions, concerts, performances, theatre, poetry readings, … even as a habitat for artists it had its own magic.

"What does your father plan to do with it, Kean?"

"He doesn't want it. He said I could have it if I could find a good use for it." Kean showed them the remaining stock of brightly coloured ropes and cords they'd used for Jenny's work on the ring. At the end of an immense corridor between two large halls, Kean held the lift door open so Tom could wheel his chair in.

"Let's talk more about this place between now and the funeral,"

Brent suggested.

Tom knew the way, but Kean insisted on accompanying them to the meeting room.

"Leaving for London this afternoon was very hard on Irina," Kean told them.

Brent had had little to do with the girl, so he'd hardly noticed she'd gone.

"I think she has a crush on you," Tom commented, trying to keep a straight face.

Brent laughed. "She's pretty."

The fact that she was considerably younger than Kean was not so important. Most of the younger girls they hung around with like An or Anju or Tricia and her friends were quite mature and interesting to talk to. Brent noticed that Kean blushed. A long silence followed that neither Tom nor Brent chose to break.

"Ok," Kean admitted. "I seem to have got 'involved'. I feel..." He hesitated about the word. "...drawn to her."

Tom chuckled, he was clearly having fun teasing Kean. "You mean she bewitched you?"

Kean seemed uncomfortable with the idea, possibly because Tom's joke was too close to the mark.

Brent decided to come to his rescue. "Why was she upset?"

"She wants to stay with the Dream Class. I guess she's afraid of her powers."

Brent had heard several accounts of what she could do with her hands. There was reason to be alarmed.

"And she's constantly pestered by elementals," Kean added.

"She should talk to Jenny about that," Tom put in, becoming more serious. "Sharing their experience might prove useful."

Maybe it hadn't been wise to let her go with Moira and John to London, but so many other things were happening, it was difficult to keep track of everything. They'd hardly had a moment to talk freely amongst themselves all weekend. "Perhaps we should have insisted she stay," Brent mused.

"I'm not sure Moira would allow it," Kean replied. "She puts so much faith in her ability to mother the girl."

"Well I suppose they'll be back for the funeral," Brent pointed out. "We can sort things out then."

Kean went back down to the entrance to indicate the way to the others and to guide the police to the meeting room when they arrived.

Brent had the impression that Irina's imminent return had relieved Kean. "You shouldn't tease him too much," he told Tom. "He's finding this very difficult. He's discovering a sensitiveness he was unaware he had."

Tom grunted and was about to make a comment when the door opened and Jenny, Anju and Dieter arrived.

"Sally and Mae decided to stay at Rafter's house," Jenny informed them.

With their mother gone to join Rafter, it would do the two sisters good to be alone together for a while, Brent thought.

Shortly afterwards Keira arrived with Fran and Martin. Brent decided to seize the opportunity before the police got there to talk about Irina. Everyone was seated around the large table on which the Watchers' map still lay sprawled.

"Kean said Irina was upset about leaving. He's concerned about her gifts getting out of control. I think maybe we should insist she stay with us for a while."

Keira made a face. "I for one am relieved she's gone. She latched on to me like glue."

"Well you are such a loveable person," Brent teased. "I can imagine people getting hung up on you."

Keira bunched up a stray piece of paper that was lying on the table and threw it at Brent.

"Seriously though," Brent continued, ducking the projectile, "I don't think she will bother you so much in the future. She may have found her support elsewhere."

The noise of voices down the corridor warned them that people were approaching so they interrupted their conversation. The door opened and Mandy and Jock entered followed by Kean.

"Whatever happened to you", Jenny asked Jock, standing and coming to greet the two.

"It's nothing," Jock said shaking his head and clearly wishing he hadn't.

"Have a seat," Brent suggested, greeting them too.

Once everyone was seated, Brent went quickly round the table introducing all those present. "Neither Sally nor Mae could be with us. Their father, Professor Rafter, has just passed away and they are in mourning."

"That's sad news indeed," Mandy said. "Please convey our condolences to them both."

"I didn't know the Professor had any children," Jock said, surprised and intrigued.

"Neither did anybody else till quite recently," Keira told them. "Not even Sally or Mae."

"Do tell us what happened to your head," Keira continued, clearly concerned.

The enormous bandage around his head was quite alarming.

"I hope it had nothing to do with us. You don't seem to have had much peace and quiet this weekend because of us," Keira added.

Mandy was unable to conceal a look of discomfort.

Leaning his elbows on the table, Jock put one hand to his head. "I was hit over the head by a friend of yours."

"A friend?" Anju asked.

"A man called Twine. You'd know him a mile off, he stinks of pigs."

"Ah!" Anju said. "Him."

"I was keeping watch over him in the hospital. I thought he was unconscious, but apparently he wasn't. He hit me over the head with a steel bedpan."

Several people winced.

"So Twine is at liberty?" Dieter asked.

"Yes. I suppose he is," Jock said glancing at Mandy who shook her head.

"We were waiting for you to come round," Mandy explained, "to find out what had happened."

Tom pulled out his walkie-talkie. "I need to warn Ben and the others and ask them to keep an eye on Sally and Mae. They might be in danger."

"I see you are well equipped and just as well organised, but that probably won't be necessary," Jock said.

"Why not?" Tom asked.

Jock shrugged. "He wasn't in very good shape."

Tom called all the same.

"Let's get straight to the point," Brent said, adopting a business-like tone. "You asked to see us. Despite it being a very bad moment, most of us have come. What do you want?"

He wondered if they were foolishly opening Pandora's box by accepting to answer questions. It was too late to have doubts, though. Jock cleared his throat as he placed one hand on the side of his head. Despite his denial, he was clearly in pain from the wound he'd received.

Brent glanced at Keira and Jenny. Both were looking at the policeman with concern.

"We have four bodies in the morgue, two madmen in a clinic and another one out in the wild, apparently because they were bent on putting a stop to your activities. Several of you have told us things about what is happening. We've heard the story of a group of people called the Starless Square. You accuse them of hounding the Theosophy department, believing it infiltrated by witches. But too many things don't add up. How did the respected Dr. Frick end up dressed as a tramp, drowned in dust in the middle of a crater? How did a small-time drug dealer turn up on the altar of a chapel by the sea, naked except for a number of strange hieroglyphs scrawled across his body? How did an amateur photographer get stranded knee-deep in the low-tide mud of the Bree, stark raving mad? Nothing in your story explains these things."

Dieter burst out laughing.

Jock looked at him, apparently irritated at his behaviour. Mandy looked alarmed.

"Let me tell you a part of my story," Dieter began, adopting a more sober expression. "Like you I was in the police. I was a chief inspector in the German special force. I was investigating a complex, incomprehensible series of events. Almost all the paths led me here to Avan, to the Theosophy Department. When I met the late Professor Rafter ..."

Dieter paused, his face torn with emotion. Brent hadn't realised how much Dieter was attached to Rafter.

Dieter wiped tears from his eyes and continued. "... and several of the people gathered here, I told them, just like you: it doesn't make sense. Do you know what they said?"

He paused to blow his nose. Anju touched his arm lightly and he glanced at her tenderly.

"They said I didn't really want to know and if I were to know, it would be no use to me. I think we can say the same to you. You will probably sleep better if we tell you nothing."

As Jock seemed to ruminate on what Dieter had said, Mandy spoke for the first time. "Friday midday I was an ordinary policewoman, bent on doing my job as well as possible. Now, two days later, I am about to hand in my resignation."

Brent couldn't help notice the look of irritation that crossed Jock's face. Was he so upset at her leaving?

"With everything that has happened this weekend, I can no longer do that job correctly. You have all been instrumental in making that change take place. But above all it is because I have finally found the love of my life," she glanced tenderly at Jock, leaving no doubt about whom she was referring to.

Several people smiled. Jock seemed less happy. Had they had a row over her decision?

"I suspect your magic, if I can call it that, hastened the process. I'm not sure if I should thank you or curse you. Monday I shall be out of work. And my love, who insists on continuing his dangerous job, may well be lost to me."

"Wow," Martin said, "we really have muddled up your life."

"I'm not so sorry," Mandy replied. "As I said, I think it might have been coming anyway." She paused a moment, looking at Jock who looked away. "I for one would like to know your secret," she decided. "I am fascinated by your group. You strike me as more alive than any other people I know. Apart from Jock, that is."

All eyes turned to Jock, who was scowling. Mandy's declaration had left him on his own. He looked uncomfortable.

"I am sorry that our way of doing things has forced you to make such a difficult decision," Keira said to him. "If you like I can help you in a way that will not change what you finally decide. I can give you some medicine that will ease the pain in your head. I am a trained healer and I have treated several people in your condition. The question is: do you trust me?"

Brent approved Keira's strategy. She was giving Jock a chance to break down one insurmountable decision into a number of smaller ones.

Jock looked Keira in the eyes for a long moment then glanced at Mandy who nodded almost imperceptibly, before he turned back to Keira. "It's not that I don't trust you, but it really isn't necessary. I had almost forgotten I hurt my head."

"So you have to chose between two frustrating options," Brent summarised.

"Thanks!" Jock said, his voice heavy with irony.

"Would you like time to decide?" Brent asked.

"No I have made up my mind," Jock said firmly, all hesitation gone. "I too want to hear your story."

Brent couldn't have guessed which choice the policeman would make. It could have gone either way. Despite his general affability, Jock was a bit of a mystery, almost as if he were holding something back.

He is, a voice said in his head.

Mee?

The voice nodded.

Brent briefly wondered how he knew that a disincarnate voice could nod, but Mee left him no time for such distractions.

He's got a miniature recorder. He plans to record all you say.

Brent had difficulties believing Mee. Why would someone like Jock do such a thing? It didn't make sense.

Let's just say he's a fan of the Starless Square.

Brent gasped causing everyone to look at him. "Sorry. I forgot to do something."

It was a lousy explanation, but it would have to do.

Can you tell Anju and Dieter to block the door? he asked Mee.

Mee didn't reply but Brent saw the Dieter moving casually towards the doorway and at the same time Anju moved closer to Mandy. Was the policewoman in danger, he wondered? Maybe Anju was anticipating one of Jock's moves. When the two were in place, Dieter nodded to Brent.

Mee, could you tell the others what is happening?

Mee must have done so because all the faces on the Dream Class suddenly snapped in his direction. So much for being discreet!

Brent got to his feet slowly and turned to Jock. "Are you sure you are OK?" He could have used his power on the man but he didn't want to resort to that, yet. "Maybe Keira should have a look at your wound." He had a hunch that the wound was a fake. Why would one member of the Starless Square hit another?

Jock shrugged off the idea. "You were going to tell us what really happened." The man's nonchalance was unconvincing.

"That may no longer be possible, Jock," Brent replied calmly.

The policeman was startled by the unexpected response. He quickly glanced around the room and must have realised something was amiss. Brent saw Jock slide his hand into his hip pocket.

"I wouldn't do that, if I were you, Jock. People get hurt when guns are drawn."

Not heeding Brent's warning, Jock pulled a revolver from his pocket and pointed it at Brent.

"What's going on, Jock?" Mandy asked, alarmed. She made a move towards Jock, but Anju held her back. "You shouldn't be carrying a firearm," Mandy said, trying to shake Anju off.

"These people can't be trusted. That's why I'm carrying a gun. They'll wrap you round their little finger. Don't your realise, you're already largely under their influence. You'd even give up the police for them." Judging from his tone, he was clearly disgusted she should do so.

"That's not true Jock," Mandy pleaded, still trying to get free of Anju. "It's because I love you."

"Well if you want me to love you, you'll have to stop running around after them." His tone was harsh.

She stopped struggling with Anju. The abrupt change in him had shocked her.

"It would seem we can't trust you either Jock," Keira said.

"We have all been misled," Brent said unable to keep the disappointment from his voice. He'd had hopes for Jock. "You too have been misled Mandy. Jock is not just the regular policeman you thought he was. He is also a supporter of a secret society called the Starless Square."

Her hand flew to her mouth to stifle a scream. "That can't be."

Jenny took her from Anju and put her arms around the sobbing woman. Anju shifted closer to Jock, who still had his gun pointed menacingly at Brent. With his free hand, Jock ripped the bandage from his head and flung it to the floor. He did have a bloody wound, but it was clearly superficial. He'd lied about that too.

"So are you going to kill me like the others or are you going to drive me crazy?"

"We don't need to drive you crazy, Jock. You're doing that to your self."

Careful, Mee warned. Don't push him too far. He's terrified and unpredictable.

"What did you plan to do with the recording?" Brent asked, keeping his voice calm.

"Unmask you filthy witches and warlocks for what you are."

"And how would you do that?"

Jock waved his gun at them. "You have admitted you do magic and have been responsible for several deaths."

While Brent continued to converse with Jock about the man's plans, he sent out his voice and whispered into Jock's head.

"Get out of my head," Jock suddenly screamed, firing a warning shot at the ceiling, smashing one of the neon lights sending a show of sparks and glass cross the table.

Brent was afraid. He was by no means invincible. One bullet would be enough.

He lowered his inner voice till it whispered so softly in Jock's head that it was barely audible. He had to disarm Jock. Afterwards Anju and Dieter could overpower him. Sleep was his first idea, but it wouldn't work. There might be a mishap. Blindness wouldn't help either. He opted for progressive paralysis, causing the muscles in Jock's hand to seize up little by little. The change had to be almost imperceptible. Brent had the immobility spread slowly to his wrist and forearm. He glanced behind himself to make sure nobody else was in the line of fire and extended the paralysis all the way to the man's shoulder.

Everything happened so quickly it was hard to know what occurred in the resulting confusion. Jock must have noticed his arm was paralysed. His eyes suddenly spread wide in alarm. He tried desperately to pull the trigger and fire at Brent, but he couldn't move. He went to shift the gun to his left hand. It was then that Brent dived out of the way and Anju swung into action, knocking the gun out of Jock's hands. The gun hit the floor with a jolt and went off sending a bullet through one of the windows that exploded in a multitude of tiny glass fragments. Several people screamed.

Brent rolled over. When he looked up, Jock was unconscious at Anju's feet. Dieter was still standing unperturbed in the doorway. Brent wished he had such confidence in Anju's abilities. Mandy was crying in Jenny's arms, muttering, "He tried to kill you."

Brent struggled to his feet, asking: "Is anybody hurt?"

Several voices confirmed that everyone was OK. Fran had already seized a brush and was pushing the glass out of harm's way.

"I'm sorry you had to witness that," Brent apologised to Mandy. "I had no idea what was going to happen till Mee tipped me off."

Mandy looked at him, tears streaming down her face. "To think I loved him," she muttered, shaking her head.

"I don't think his love for you was all a lie," Jenny said, handing Mandy a handkerchief.

"What are we going to do with him?" Anju asked prodding Jock with her foot.

"How long will he be out?" Keira asked.

"As long as we need," was Anju's reply.

Fran had finished cleaning the glass from the table and chairs and was placing several thermoses on the table along with a box of cakes. Brent had to chuckle. "We'll get fat with you two looking after us."

"Not likely," Martin put in. "It's all carefully calculated!"

So, having tied up Jock, just in case, they sat down to eat, drink and debate what to do. Mandy wanted to call the station and tell her chief. She was prepared to give evidence against Jock.

"I don't think that will work," Anju commented.

"Why not?" Mandy wanted to know.

"Imagine what will happen. When you tell your story, Jock will counter, saying you have been brainwashed by us," Anju pointed out.

"But what about the gun shots?"

"They were caused when one of us drew a gun on him and Jock had to wrestle the arm from us."

"But surely the finger prints will show you didn't touch it."

"He could say we manipulated it while he was unconscious," Dieter pointed out.

"What about the recording?" Tom asked. "Couldn't that be used as evidence against him?"

"It might just as easily be evidence against us," Fran pointed out.

Dieter fished the recorder out of Jock's pocket, but, to their surprise, nothing had been recorded.

"Could your voice have got it wrong?" Mandy said hopefully.

Dieter turned the tiny machine over in his hands and examined it closely. "Look!" he said, pointing to one end of the thing. "The erase button has been forced in. When he fell the blow must have erased everything."

"Is there any way the recording could be recuperated?" Martin asked. "Like you can get information back from damaged hard disks."

"Maybe," Dieter said.

"Better not leave it on him, just in case," Anju added.

"What about amnesia?" Keira asked.

"What do you mean?" Mandy asked, looking uncomfortable.

"Well, the blow on his head could have caused him to forget what happened recently. And if he can't remember this weekend, he couldn't accuse us."

"I don't like it," Mandy said. "It's not honest."

They were testing her allegiances, Brent realised. With Jock's recent memory erased, he might not remember his love for Mandy.

"I'm sorry," Brent said. "It is probably the only way to keep both us and you out of serious trouble."

"Me!" she exclaimed unbelieving.

"I imagine that if he was prepared to shoot us, he would also be willing to sacrifice you as our accomplice, especially if you spoke out in our favour."

Mandy groaned, putting her head in her hands.

"Could you bring on his amnesia, Brent?" Keira asked.

Brent wasn't sure. If he could invent a story that talked of memory loss, he would manage. "I should be able to."

"I have to leave soon," Keira said. "I need to be in the park to prepare the concert."

Normally everybody was to go with her.

"We have to move him somewhere else," Dieter pointed out. "He can't be here with us when he awakes."

"Ideally we should take him back to the hospital, but they mustn't see us," Anju mused.

"The police have probably noticed he left the hospital. Our boss was eager to know what happened. Maybe I should take him back to the hospital." Mandy looked unhappy at the prospect. "I will say he was agitated and I tried to calm him, but he collapsed. That would explain why I brought him back to the hospital."

She was right, Brent realised, although he didn't like putting such a burden on her. He was afraid she might break under the strain. "Good. Now leave me alone with him for a moment while you organise how you are going to get him and Mandy back to the hospital."

Jock lay in front of him in a crumpled heap. Brent rolled his deadweight over till the policeman was on his back and began whispering softly in his ear.

Chapter 14 ~ The Pyre

Sound and fury

Twine heaved the bicycle into the air above his head, flung it with all his force and collapsed to the ground. The bike sailed over the ditch and smashed against a rock making a satisfying shattering sound as the lamps and mudguards broke into smithereens. Twine picked himself up and staggered the last hundred yards to his farm. His legs ached from pedalling and his backside was raw with the effort. Why did people always padlock the most comfortable bikes?

"Nobody's gonna put me down," he shouted, aiming a vicious kick at one his dogs that slunk up to him. It yelped and cowered away. The pigs were squealing like on slaughter day. Nobody had let them out and nobody had fed them either, but he had no time for that.

Revenge was the only thing that mattered. That bloody girl had made him look so damned stupid. Every muscle in his body hurt because of her and her magic. He'd get his own back. He'd see all the witches burn at the stake. He'd do it. He. The last remaining member of the Starless Square.

The drum of shit lay at a precarious angle, propped up at the back of his broken-down ice-cream van. He fixed the winch to the drum and hauled it up till it was level with the floor of the van. Then shoving and grunting, he managed to force the dead weight back inside the van. He wouldn't be able to close the doors. Who cared? He'd lash them tight with a bit of rope.

The petrol was in the barn, but when he tried the door it was locked. The police must have locked it. Sod 'em! He had no keys.

They'd confiscated every bloody thing at the hospital. The hospital pyjamas were all he had left.

Why did that policeman let him escape? It made no sense. The guy could have stopped him. He'd been all lost and fuzzy. No match for a thickly-built bobby. Yet he'd been able to overpower the bloke with hardly a fight. The bedpan had been a great idea. Not that he'd had much force left to swing it with. He'd completely misjudged the blow, almost missing his target. The thing glanced off the blighter's head. It shouldn't have knocked him out. But the bloke fell like a stone. Twine had up and scarpered.

Yeah! The door. He looked around for a crowbar or something heavy to smash the door. Nothing suitable was at hand. He climbed into the van and found the keys where he'd hidden them under the dashboard. The police hadn't thought to look there. At the third attempt the ruin spluttered into life. He revved up the engine and crashing the gears he drove the van full tilt at the barn door. The shock flung him forward, hitting his head against the windscreen. He swore.

The door shuddered, but did not give. The front fender fell off and the glass of the headlights fell in tiny tinkling bits and pieces. He slammed the vehicle into reverse and backed wildly across the yard, narrowly missing one of the dogs that howled and jumped out of the way.

He rammed the van into gear and gaining more speed, smashed a hole in the barn door, causing the remains of the door to rise up on its hinges and keel over onto the van, denting the roof. Paying it no heed, he drove deeper into the barn, the ruins of the door ripping a large hole in the roof of the van. He weaved left and right till the bits of the door fell away, taking much of the van roof with them.

The tank full of petrol was buried in the far corner of the barn, topped by an old-fashioned hand pump. A workbench blocked the way. Using the vehicle as a battering ram, he shoved the workbench to one side and drove as close as he could to the pump, riding rough shod over tools and boxes scattered on the floor.

Propping a ladder against the side of the van, he threaded the tube in through the gash in the roof, stuck the nozzle into drum and began pumping. How could those women have managed to knock out all the other members of the Starless Square? Was that not what the police had said? Dead or mad! Only fire could get the better of witches.

He was busy imagining how he'd do it when a strong smell of petrol reached him. The tank must have been full and petrol was flooding over the floor. He pulled the tube out and threw piles of rags on the petrol to mop it up. So much had overflowed, that he had to stuff the van with rags to soak up the inflammable liquid. Sod it! What did it matter? It was all going to burn anyway.

He gingerly turned the ignition, ready to jump from the van if ever it caught fire, but nothing happened. Phew! He was a lucky bastard, he told himself. A survivor! No wonder he was the only one left. He edged the vehicle back out of the barn and parked it in front of his house. He needed matches. There were some in the pigsty.

Again the door was bolted. Damn police! He smashed it open with his foot causing the pigs to squeal even louder. The uproar was unbearable. Stopped him thinking straight. He roared as loud as the pigs and ran amok in the pens, ripping the doors open and chasing the pigs this way and that. Several times he was knocked over by terrified beasts. They trampled him in the muck in their panic till they finally found the open door and ran squealing out into the yard, dispersing in every direction.

Twine heaved himself to his feet, one of his arms useless and numb, smashed by the hooves of the crazed pigs. When he put his weight on his left leg, pain shot through it and up his back. Using a pitchfork as a crutch, he hobbled to the door. Blast! He'd forgotten the matches. Sod it! He wasn't going back. He struggled to the vehicle. Despite being covered in pig shit, the smell the petrol was still strong.

Tossing aside the pitchfork, he heaved himself up into the driver's seat, and wiping the muck from his face, he turned the key in the ignition and pulled out onto the road. Then he jammed on the brakes causing the drum to shift ominously in the back of the van. Where was he going? He hadn't figured that out. Filthy and stinking as he was, he could never ask the way. He'd get arrested. He slumped over the steering wheel and closed his eyes. You aren't going to give in so easily! he berated himself. Pull yourself together.

He tried to recall what the police had told him, but he'd been in such a state he couldn't remember anything. Not really knowing what he was doing, he rummaged in the glove pocket of the van. There he found a crumpled copy of the programme of the weekend's festivities organised by the Theosophy Department. He'd needed it to know when their meal was to take place. The first name he saw was Professor Rafter. The guy was head of the Department and had given a talk. He plunged back into the glove pocket and pulled out a battered telephone. Dialling directory enquiries, he asked for the address of

Professor Rafter.

Easy as pie!

He started up the engine and drove off down the road towards Avan, singing at the top of his voice.

Future and formalities

The candles spluttered in the late afternoon silence. Mae shifted in her chair causing it to creak.

Sally sighed. "What will you do once this is all over?"

"Will it ever be over?"

Sally grunted. It was probably the closest she could get to laughing in the circumstances.

In a way, Mae wished their adventures would never end. She couldn't face returning to work as secretary of the department. Much as she loved working with other people and enjoyed organising things, it seemed so mundane compared to all they'd done this last week.

"I can hardly see myself back at the university with a new head of department. It was working for Professor Rafter that appealed to me most."

She glanced at where her father lay, a faint smile on his face, next to Teresa. Mae looked away unable to contemplate the Professor's face any length of time. Absentmindedly she peered out the window where she could see Ben leaning against one of the trees on the far side of the car park.

"I think I'd like to see how I can get the idea of the Dream Class on a more solid footing. Maybe we can get some money from the Blavatsky foundation." Rafter had expressly said he wanted them to go ahead with the Dream Class and she wanted to respect her father's last wish. "I'll miss Lyra though. She's become a very dear friend."

It was Mae's turn to sigh. "How about you?" she asked, trying to cast off the blues that numbed her.

Sally didn't respond immediately. When she did, she shook her head as if trying to shrug off a thought she didn't want to have. "I haven't given it a thought, apart from our talk about the Dream Class. I too think I will leave the university. I no longer want to pursue these studies, not like that. Doing a thesis in my field seems like an absurdity and it wouldn't be with John Llewellyn."

She ran her fingers through her hair as she turned to face her father. "I think I'd like to continue teaching, though. In some form or another. Teaching the others when we were on the run in France was a real pleasure." She looked away from their parents, resting her head on her hands. "Money is going to be a problem. Maybe I can find some way to make use of my gifts." She lapsed into silence.

When the doorbell chimed through the corridors of the deserted house, Mae got up wearily and left Sally alone with their parents.

"Good evening Doctor. I'm glad you were able to come at such short notice."

The only doctor she'd been able to contact on a Sunday was the specialist at the hospital who had treated Rafter. He'd been sad to learn about the death of the professor although not surprised. He'd willingly accepted to examine the body and sign the death certificate.

As the man took off his coat and handed it to Mae, he expressed his condolences, adding. "You were his secretary, I believe. How good of you to go to such lengths to look after your employer."

Mae sighed. "Professor John Llewellyn Rafter was my father," she informed him, her voice drained of emotion.

He halted mid step and apologised in embarrassment. "I didn't know."

"Neither did I ... till today."

He looked perplexed, but said nothing as he followed her out into the conservatory. The sun was setting making the flower-bedecked room seem all the warmer and more welcoming.

The doctor glanced at the two bodies side by side on the table and gasped. "Two?"

Maybe she should have told him over the phone, but it would have been difficult to explain.

Sally stood and shook hands with the doctor. "Yes. This is my mother and John Llewellyn's wife, Teresa. She was with him at the end and chose to follow him when he passed away. She simply lay down next to him and died."

The doctor looked a little worried. "Excuse me for asking, but did she use any substances to help her die?"

"No," Mae replied, upset at the suggestion. The possibility had never crossed her mind. "Once she'd found him after so many years apart, she just couldn't bear to be separated."

"I will have to examine them both before I sign the certificate. I suggest you leave me alone with your parents while I do so. I'll call you as soon as I have finished," he said, placing a small leather bag on the table next to the bodies and opening it.

Mae followed Sally out of the room and they walked slowly along the hall, their footfalls resounding in the emptiness, till they reached the front door. Sally heaved it open and they sat down next to each other on the steps under the porch. Across the car park, Mae could see Ben half concealed amongst the trees watching. She raised her hand to indicate she'd noticed him and beckoned him over.

Ben was one of Lyra's assistants, so it wasn't surprising that he was particularly interested in healing. When he'd had a moment free from being an apprentice Watcher, he'd spent considerable time talking to Jenny and Keira. He was quite short and round both in face and figure. He was a likeable sort of fellow. Mae always saw him as good humoured and attentive to others. He came now and sat next to her on the steps but remained silent respecting their silence.

A thrush had settled in the massive oak that sprawled amongst lesser trees by the side of the drive. Mae marvelled at the intricacies of its song with the many different sequences of notes and sounds. What could possibly drive the bird to put such untiring effort into what, after all, was a senseless pursuit? Could it know that people delighted in listening to it?

Ben must have read her thoughts, or maybe it was the way she had cocked her head to one side to listen, because he commented, "Beautiful, isn't it?"

"Yes, but somehow pointless."

"Who knows what the reasons for its singing are?" Ben responded philosophically, placing his hand lightly on her arm. "Maybe in the larger order of things it's supposed to play a key role." He shifted his hand as if he were about to remove it, but she placed her other hand on his and held it in place. She found his touch comforting.

Sally must have sensed something was happening between them. Or maybe she was just restless. She rose and walked off around the house leaving the two alone. Mae leaned closer and laid her head on his shoulder and he put his arm around her. Neither said a word. It was comforting to be able to let herself go, not so much to cry as to allow herself to feel the warmth and comfort of the person seated next to her.

They were still sitting together in silence when Sally reappeared after her tour of the gardens. The sun was beginning to set and the shadows were lengthening. A light breeze had got up and it was no longer so warm on the steps. Sally and Mae rose to enter the house and Ben took his leave and returned to his vigil at the foot of the tree in which the thrush had been singing.

By a coincidence they met the doctor in the corridor as he came in search of them. "I've finished," he said and handed Mae a sheath of papers. "You'll need these for the authorities when you announce the death. Keep them in a safe place."

She set them inside her bag that lay on the table in the hall. "I'll take them tomorrow morning," she said and thanked him again for coming out on a Sunday.

He donned his coat and turned to the two young women. "Your father was a great man," he said, clearly moved. "We didn't always see eye to eye about his treatment. But he bore his illness with great courage and dignity. I am proud to have known him." He shook hands with each of them and left.

Sally and Mae turned and headed for the conservatory to the sound of the doctor's car fading in the distance. The sun had almost set and the light was sinking. Mae lit a number of additional candles and closed the windows to shelter the tiny flames from the breeze blowing outside.

"I hope that breeze doesn't hinder Keira's recording," Sally said as they resumed their places next to their parents.

Mae didn't reply.

"Tell me, why did you put your pendant in Teresa's hand like that?" Sally asked, pointing at the gold glistening between Teresa's clasped fingers.

"It's silly really," Mae said after some thought. "As I gave Teresa's ring back to John, I thought she might like to have something from the Reaches too. Maybe, who knows, perhaps they'll be able to cross back there to be together in the after life."

A shattered peace

Ben settled in to wait, glancing all around, taking stock of the situation. All was quiet, the thrush had stopped singing and even the distant traffic on the road had ceased. From his vantage point he could see down the curving drive to the entrance of the property in one direction and in the other he could see most of the front of the house. Mae had placed a number of larger candles along the windowsills of the conservatory where they flickered gently. They were the only light in the house.

He thought over the few minutes he'd held Mae in his arms and hoped it had been of some comfort to her. How terrible, he thought, to discover you have parents and then to loose them both almost immediately. He strained his eyes to look closer at the conservatory. He saw both Mae and Sally stand and leave the room. A light came on in the entrance and then the stairwell was also lit up. They must be going to their rooms on the first floor. Sure enough, lights came on in two rooms on the first floor. He even saw Mae walk in front of one of the windows.

The peace was suddenly shattered by a distant roar coming from somewhere behind him. Ben spun round, but could see nothing. The noise got louder and louder but it didn't make any sense. Then he caught sight of a dark form turning into the drive and heading fast in his direction. It must be a vehicle, but its lights were turned off. As it swung past the oak behind which he was hiding several things happened. A dreadful stench of pig manure and petrol enveloped him at just the same time he saw the markings on the side of the vehicle. It was an ice-cream van the top of which had been ripped away. In a split second a horrifying picture surged into his head.

"Stop!" he screamed. Jumping out onto the road, he ran full tilt after the van. "Mae! Sally!" he screamed. "Mae! Sally!"

The van had almost reached the house and seemed to be accelerating when a first floor window opened and Sally peered out.

"Look out!" he shouted as best he could despite his fast breathing.

Sally saw the van at the moment it hit the wall of the conservatory. Made only of wood, it buckled under the onslaught of the vehicle and gave way. The van continued its course till most of it was inside the room. The impact had sent candles flying in every direction. The van exploded in flames letting off an intense heat. In seconds, the conflagration had spread to a large part of the front of the house.

In the short space of time it took Ben to get to the house the flames had already reached the roof and the heat given off was so intense that he couldn't get anywhere near. He tore round the back. The fire had not yet reached there, but it would only be seconds before it spread to the whole house. From a first floor window he heard Sally and Mae calling for help.

It was too high to jump. There was no ladder. There was no tree nearby they could scale down. The only thing he saw was the garden hose. Praying that it was not rotten, he unravelled it as fast as he could. Behind him smoke was beginning to pour out of some of the windows.

"Catch this!" he screamed as he threw up the hose, using the nozzle to gain momentum. "Tie it securely to a radiator. And climb down."

Mae disappeared from the window. When she came back flames

had reached nearby rooms.

"Hurry!" he shouted, not sure they could hear him over the roar of the fire.

Sally clambered out and let herself down the hose. It stretched but held her weight. The moment she reached the ground Mae climbed out of the window and began to make her way down. An ominous cracking sound was followed by a gust of flames that surged out of the window. Mae was only half way down when the hose snapped under the heat and she plunged to the ground. Ben, who had anticipated such a thing, was standing right beneath her. He caught her, trying to soften her fall. A dreadful cracking sound was followed by a scream, his own, and the two of them fell to the floor. The pain was so terrible he blacked out.

When he came to, he found himself lying on a grassy bed under the oak at a safe distance from the smoking ruins of the house. Mae was stroking his forehead gently with her fingers.

"Don't you go too!" she repeated, sobs in her voice.

"It's OK," he tried to reassure her. "I think I must have broken my arm or my collar bone. Look in my jacket pocket. I have a small box of medicines. There should be something to calm the pain."

As she searched through his pockets she asked: "Does it hurt anywhere else?"

He didn't think so.

"But what about you?" he asked, trying to move but thinking better of it.

"I'm fine, thanks to you. We are both fine."

"Where's Sally?"

"She's gone to the neighbour's to call the fire brigade."

She finally found the box and Ben indicated the painkiller which she gave him. "Rest," she said, lowering his head gently back into her lap.

The mixture worked rapidly. Keira had given it to him. "Just in case," she'd said. They heard a number of people coming noisily through the wood.

"It's Sally," Mae told him. "And the neighbour."

"What a terrible thing to happen," a man was saying. "What is the world coming to?" He was carrying a large torch as it would have been dark were it not for the glow from the ruins.

"How are you, Ben?" Sally asked.

"Ok," he replied not wanting to bemoan his condition.

"He's broken his arm," Mae told them.

"The ambulance and the fire brigade should be here soon."

A look of concern crossed the man's face when he saw Ben. "Would you like us to transport you to a more comfortable place?"

"I couldn't possibly be more comfortable than I am here." He chuckled despite the pain.

Mae, who'd been stroking his hair, stopped and pinched his ear lobe but way of rebuke. "No taking advantage of a damsel in distress."

"I think you've got the wrong story," Ben joked.

The wailing of sirens as the fire engine entered the drive interrupted their discussion. An ambulance followed it closely. The firemen drove past and stopped near the house. Not that there was anything left to save; the house was gutted. But at least they could make sure that the wood around the house didn't catch fire. The ambulance stopped right next to them and two ambulance men climbed out. They examined Ben's arm and shoulder and helped him walk to the back of the ambulance where he lay down on a stretcher.

Mae joined him. She insisted on accompany him to the hospital. Sally was to stay and talk to the fire brigade and then call the police. The ambulance man was about to close the door when Mae stopped him.

"I nearly forgot my bag," she told him and clambered out and returned almost immediately with her bag. "It's got the papers from the doctor in it," she explained to Ben as the ambulance turned and drove back down the drive. "I went upstairs to put them in a safe place. It was that that saved my life."

One more case ...

The Chief Constable sat behind his desk, staring at the doodle he was drawing on a piece of paper. From where Mandy stood, it looked like a forest of arrows shooting off in all directions punctuated here and there by black squares. She stood next to Jock across from the Chief waiting for his response. Mandy knew it would be unwise to press him. He wasn't always the quickest of people, but his temper was quick enough if you tried to hurry him.

"I don't understand," the Chief said, his words muffled by the hand in front of his mouth. "You maintain," he added, jerking his head at Mandy, "that Jock rushed out of the hospital and you followed him till he collapsed unconscious near his flat."

Mandy nodded.

The Chief looked at Jock. "And you can't remember anything of the last week."

Jock groaned and shook his head. Then he groaned again, presumably from the headache that shaking his head produced. "Nothing."

"Must've been the impact of that bedpan Twine hit you with," Mandy added.

This shouldn't have been new to Jock as he'd heard her tell the story once, but he still looked uncomprehending at her. "Bedpan," he repeated groaning, as if the word hurt.

The Chief was shaking his head in disbelief. "You two have really overdone it this time."

The ringing tone of his telephone interrupted him. "Yes," he replied wearily as he picked up the receiver. He turned in his swivel chair so Mandy could see little of his face, but she could have sworn he grimaced at whatever he was being told. "Ok," he said even more wearily. "I'll send someone over." He hung up.

"Jock," he snapped, getting to his feet. "Go and have a rest. For a couple of days. And get an appointment with your doctor for that head of yours." Jock began to protest, but the Chief silenced him. "If you don't do as I say, I'll have you escorted home by an armed guard."

Jock turned and left, not looking happy.

When they were alone, the Chief sat back down. "Do you think he's cracked?"

"No," Mandy said, thinking it wiser to support Jock. "I'm sure he'll feel better once he gets over the shock."

The Chief grunted. "I have work for you. There's been a fire in the suburbs. Looks like arson. I want you to investigate."

"What the address?" she asked. When he gave it, she immediately recognised the address of Professor Rafter. She had to turn away to conceal her emotions. "Was anybody hurt?"

"How do I know? Go and find out."

She took her leave, hurried through the offices, jumped into one of the available police cars and set out for the hospital and beyond to the Professor's house. What could have happened? She prayed that the house had been empty. Although she knew the Professor had just died so it was unlikely the place had been deserted. Worry gnawed at her as she drove far too fast. Being in the police had its advantages.

The house was not that far. In minutes she had turned the car into the drive and slowed as she saw a fire engine in the distance pulled up in front of a smoking ruin. She parked the car next to a giant oak and as she got out she spotted a young woman almost hidden where she leaned against the trunk of the tree.

"I'm Sally, one of the Professor's daughters. Can I help you?" the girl said. Mandy presented herself.

She'd seen the girl the other night at the Arena but Sally hadn't attended the meeting at the warehouse.

"What happened here?" Mandy asked. "Was anyone killed?" Only one question at a time! They'd hammered it into her during her training. But she was so worried, she couldn't help it.

"One person died but there are three bodies in the ruins."

The reply exasperated her. She wanted straight answers, not guessing games. "This is no time for riddles," she responded, unable to conceal her irritation.

Sally sighed. "I'm sorry. This has been a trying day."

"I could say the same," Mandy retorted, feeling her shoulders sag. "Excuse me," she added, straightening up. "I know a number of people from your group and I like them a lot. I just want to be sure they are all OK."

"None of my friends died in the fire," Sally reassured her. She told Mandy about the death of her father and then her mother, and how an ice cream van had driven straight into the conservatory setting fire to the whole place. "It stank of petrol. There must have been a lot of petrol in the van. The driver was the only person who died." She went on to explain how Ben had saved their lives. "My sister Mae has gone with him to the hospital."

Mandy was about to walk to the ruins, leaving Sally beside the tree when a small, bright blue car turned into the drive and halted behind the police car. A tall, middle-aged man in a grey suit and a colourful tie stepped out and greeted Mandy.

"Good evening, Constable," he said politely with a slight bow. Then turning to Sally he went on: "My condolences, Miss Rafter," sadness written all over his face. "My name is David Peters. I've been looking after your father's affairs."

Sally looked surprised. How could the man possibly know the girl's father was dead, Mandy wondered?

"The specialist from the hospital phoned. The Professor asked him to inform me if the worst should happen," he said by way of explanation to unasked questions. The man glanced down the drive in the direction of the smoking ruins. "Oh dear! What happened here?"

"A mad man set fire to the house," Mandy informed him.

"Was anybody hurt? Is your sister OK?" he asked, clearly worried by what he saw and he muttered something about 'increasing the security'.

"The only person who was hurt was the young man who saved the life of Sally's sister," Mandy said, taking control of the situation. "But from what I've heard, his life is not in danger."

"I didn't know anyone was looking after the Professor's affairs for him. What sort of affairs did my father have?"

Mr. Peters glanced at the policewoman and replied. "This is maybe not the place to talk shop. We can go into details early next week." Then he changed subject. "I gather you and your friends were staying here with Professor Rafter."

Sally nodded. "The whole Dream Class was staying here."

Mandy had never heard the expression before but Mr. Peters seemed well aware of it.

"Yes. Your father told me about your group. He was delighted with the idea. Most promising, most promising indeed! But now you need somewhere else to stay in the interim."

Sally nodded again, looking quizzically at the man. "Do you have a solution?"

"Actually you have a solution yourself although you don't know it yet."

Sally looked at the man with what Mandy guessed was irritation although the young woman was trying hard to conceal it. "As the police constable said to me earlier: This is not the time for riddles. Please explain."

"You and your sister own a house down by the sea called the Lodge."

Mandy knew the place. It was an enormous property that was sometimes used as a five star hotel and a luxurious conference centre. In fact she'd heard that several speculators had tired to buy it, unsuccessfully.

"Own?" Sally spluttered.

"I realise this must be confusing for you. The Professor liked his secrets," he said with a smile quickly replaced by sadness. "When you were very young, your father gave you and your sister a number of properties that have been held in trust for you two ever since. The Lodge is one of those properties."

Sally stood with her mouth open staring at him.

"So you needn't worry about having a place to say. There's no shortage of rooms. They are maintained like a private hotel and the staff are ready and waiting for you," he added grinning. "I would offer to have the cook prepare an evening meal for you all, but I know you have your own culinary experts so I leave the choice up to you."

Sally did not reply. She still seemed in shock.

"What happened to the body of the Professor?" Mr. Peters asked, turning to Mandy.

"I presume it went up in the flames. Apparently the van that sparked off the fire drove straight into the conservatory where the Professor and his wife lay in rest," she told him.

The man looked troubled. "I know the doctor came," he said to Sally. "Did he sign the death certificate?"

"Yes," Sally confirmed. "Mae has it in her bag."

Mr. Peters gave a sigh of relief. "Good. That will avoid a lot of paper work and delays. Without the certificate there'd have to be a full enquiry before the estate could be wound up and the succession clarified. With the death certificate things will be a little easier. I will contact the insurance to recuperate the money due for the house…" Then he suddenly stopped in mid sentence. "I apologise. I promised we would not talk of affairs today."

He placed a reassuring hand on Sally's shoulder. "I have helped your father for years and will willingly continue to help you and Mae if you will accept my services. But we can talk about that later." He paused again, removing his hand. "Would you like me to drive you to the Lodge?"

Sally shook her head. "That's kind of you, Mr. Peters, but I prefer to wait here to greet my friends and give them all the news. We will come to the Lodge later. Don't worry about the food. We'll figure that out when we arrive."

Mr. Peters handed Sally his card and took his leave.

Mandy left too and headed off to talk to the firemen. As she walked away she glanced back over her shoulder. She had complained that the weekend had completely muddled up her life, but looking at Sally leaning against the oak with her eyes closed, she realised that her own experience was nothing compared to the upheaval Sally's life had undergone.

Filming

With Amanda Stock's energetic support, the BBC was really putting its weight behind Keira and her music. Collin was well placed to appreciate that. A newcomer rarely got such enthusiastic backing. Not only had they consented to record her first disc live at extremely short notice during an improvised concert in the open air, but they had also allotted him a crew of five mobile cameras and a special mobile van to coordinate the recording.

Not that he would stay cooped up. He needed to get out and see what was happening. His company had developed a portable electronic palette that enabled him to move around freely and yet still see what each camera was filming. He was using many of the same people who'd filmed for him earlier at Jenny's seminar. He knew them well and knew they had a flair for racy images and daring camera angles as well as having an unswerving sense of what was beautiful, but could also be trusted to follow his instructions. The combination rarely went together.

He wanted to weave in some of the material filmed earlier. His idea was to play on the title of the record that was to be called The Avan Ring. He also hoped to do an interview of Keira after her performance. He should be able to get enough material to make both a short promotion for the record as well as a longer documentary about Keira and possibly Jenny as well.

Jenny greeted him warmly when she arrived. Keira was more circumspect.

"So you are to film the concert?" Keira asked.

He explained what the BBC wanted and went on to talk of his own plans. "So if you would agree to an interview at the end, that would be very helpful."

He preferred to do the interview after the event because you could still feel the buzz of the performance in the person's enthusiasm and excitement.

Keira was reticent.

He could have kicked himself for being so clumsy in his first contacts with the group.

Jenny came to his rescue. "The interview he did with me was excellent. And the filming of that and my work was very good too."

He could see that Keira was hesitating.

Finally she agreed. "But we'll do the interview before the performance, not afterwards. Afterwards is never a good time.

Everyone will want to talk to me and I will be tired."

"How much time do you need before the interview?"

"Half an hour."

"Down by the ring?"

"OK."

He didn't leave her though because he wanted to see what was planned for the performance.

They met Amanda Stock who presented the chief sound engineer.

"Where exactly will you stand when you are singing?" the engineer asked.

"Over there on that patch of grass," she said striding towards the place. "We had a small improvised stage this morning for the greeting of the rising sun. Kean?" she said turning to one of the young men following her. "Have we still got that?"

"Sure it's in the lorry in the car park. I'll have it brought over." He flicked open a walkie-talkie and moved away to call someone.

Impressive organisation, Collin thought, for such an apparently informal group.

"I have to be able to sing in every direction because the spectators are all around. How are you going to handle that?" she asked the engineer.

"Don't worry. We'll use clip-on radio mikes with a backup set if anything goes wrong. We'll also have a number of other mikes to get a feel for the atmosphere of the place and the audience." Then he turned to Collin. "Are you filming the whole thing?"

Collin nodded.

"I can feed you the sound from our recording if you like so you can pair it with your cameras."

"Great," he said, knowing that doing so would save him a great deal of work now and during the editing.

Keira wanted to be alone for a while to meditate, so everyone left her and Collin went to talk to his camera crew. Jenny joined him.

"You people look rather subdued," he commented. "Is something wrong?"

Jenny explained about the death of the Professor and the discovery that he was the father of both Sally and Mae.

He expressed his condolences and then thought it best to remain silent for a while. "Is that why they are not here?" he asked some time later.

"Yes. They are keeping a vigil for their parents."

"You realise the death of the Professor means that your two friends have just become very rich ladies."

Jenny looked surprised and disbelieving.

"Rumour has it that he had a quite a fortune."

"I doubt it. He always lived without the slightest unnecessary extras."

He changed the subject. "I have to talk to my cameramen," he informed her and she left him to his work. He would have liked her to join him to discuss questions of camera angles and lighting and get her artistic opinion, but he realised her mind was elsewhere.

Before he carried out the interview he went in search of Kean. When he found the young man in the car park he explained his plan. "I'd like to have a way for my cameramen to move around close to the ring. Do you think you could manage to set up ropes so as to keep a circle of about a yard and a half wide free around the outside of the ring?"

"No problem," Kean said and he pulled out his walkie-talkie again.

The interview with Keira went quickly. He'd have preferred to have more time. That was one of the problems doing it before the performance. Never mind. He'd had Keira stand next to several of the fallen stones. He questioned her about her music and her relationship to the stones. He was fascinated by her answers and would willingly have asked a lot more, especially about the link between music and the stones, but time was short and he couldn't let his curiosity get the better of him. Any more material and he wouldn't be able to use it anyway.

After thanking the BBC for helping her make her first record and explaining the project to rebuild the ring, the concert began with Keira soberly announcing the death of Professor Rafter. The news sent a shockwave through the audience, many of whom seemed to know or had heard of the Professor.

He noticed that quite a lot of people had tears in their eyes. As Keira stood with great dignity through the minute of silence she'd called for, his cameramen were able to get some very interesting shots of her face. Her calm demeanour, her exquisitely chiselled features, her sparkling eyes and the obvious intelligence of her face allied to her powerful presence contributed to making her a most endearing, if not revered personality. He could understand why members of the audience had wanted to touch her, a bit like a saint, after the ceremony for the rising sun. There was something about her that drew you and enchanted you.

When Keira began her first song he shifted his cameramen to give him wider shots of her that also included either the spectators or the colourful ropes Jenny had set up. He needed a visual link to Jenny's work if he was to use the material he'd filmed with Jenny. It was also an opportunity to get a glimpse of the anticipation and excitement of the audience right at the beginning of the concert.

It was startling how quickly the young woman had become a star without the help of a record label or a PR agency. Maybe that was part of her charm, that she didn't force herself on you like so many other would-be stars did.

Keira introduced her second song that was to be in Gaelic, explaining that it was a tragedy about the love of a man for a woman who dies in his arms, shot by a hunter who mistook her for a deer.

As he watched the song unfolded, the beauty of Keira singing, the almost effortless way with which she sang fascinated him. It was as if she offered herself up as a willing channel through which the music could express itself. He coaxed his cameramen to seek out that 'silent work' of singing in the shots they filmed.

As the concert progressed, the sun moved closer to the horizon causing the warm evening light to play on her face and her body as she stood there alone singing amongst several fallen stones far bigger than her.

In the material his cameramen filmed they were able to capture the unworldly nature of her singing as she called to the stones and the way those stones mysteriously responded to her voice sending sounds swirling around the ring. He had some of his team shoot close-ups of the standing stones that the blast had left suspended at weird angles. The evening light cast long dramatic shadows and sculptured the textures of the stones accentuating all the tiny asperities of the weather-worn megaliths. The resulting images were painfully beautiful.

The reactions of the audience caught his eye as Keira sang a song that was both funny and tragic about a man who fell in love with a bird. He had several cameramen film people in the audience, their close-ups revealing the sudden bursts of spontaneous laughter, the tears of sorrow that welled up unbidden, and the deep-seated compassion as it lit up their faces in response to her voice and the words of her song. She was not just a singer, he realised, but a sculptress of emotions.

Keira ended her concert with the same lullaby she had sung after her celebration of the rising sun early that morning, the very song that had had so much success on the radio all day. She explained the conditions in which she'd first sung the song, talking of the misery of a young girl abused by a much older man.

He hoped that her explanations would be kept on the record; the mixture of songs and explanations was extremely powerful, knitting the whole work as one rather than stringing together individual, unconnected songs.

The memory caused tears to spring to her eyes as her face clouded with suffering. Such was the depth of the emotion that she could not immediately sing. The scene was so poignant, he was sure the entire audience wanted to console her. The images his cameramen filmed made him think of a Pietà, as if she were cast in marble, her head hung ever so slightly to one side, the imaginary little girl cradled in her arms.

When she finally began to sing the music was so moving it sent shivers running down his spine. He wasn't sure if it was joy or sadness he felt. He had the cameramen concentrate on rendering the dense emotions that underlay the song in the vision of this young girl singing unaccompanied, all alone on stage, her head held high, her voice rich and enticing.

When the song came to an end the audience were in raptures and noisily insisted on an encore. She proposed to sing the lullaby again, but as they no longer had to worry about the recording this time she suggested the audience participate. Many of the people already knew the song and willingly joined in. She took time to explain and illustrate what she was singing till the whole crowd sang with her on the choruses.

It was an ideal occasion for him to mingle shots of Keira encouraging the people to sing with other shots of her surrounded by an ecstatic audience singing along. He wished he could have filmed scenes like those from the morning celebration when people, in their reverence for her, had briefly tried to touch Keira as she passed, but they seemed more intimidated this time and most kept a respectful distance once the concert was over.

Reception committee

The fire brigade was long gone. Barely an ember glowed in the ruins although it still radiated considerable heat even at that distance. Sally sat on a folding, canvas-covered camping chair next to a similarly flimsy table under the spreading branches of the ancient oak, the deserted drive at her side. Around her shoulders a tartan blanket lay slung.

Constable Mandy, who sat next to her on a second camp chair, also had a blanket across her shoulders. On the grass next to her chair lay her abandoned uniform jacket topped with her hat and tie. In front of them on the Formica tabletop stood a storm lamp throwing a pale light over the whole scene, penetrating only a short way between the trees. A thermos and two sturdy paper cups stood on the table along with a portable telephone.

Sally took a welcome sip of warm tea and sighed. Mr. Peters had sent one of his staff to ensure they were comfortable as they awaited the return of their friends. The two women formed an incongruous welcoming committee.

Draining her cup, Mandy launched into a description of the scene with her chief when she and Jock reported what had happened.

The position of the young policewoman was extremely uncomfortable if not dangerous. "What if he gets his memory back?" Sally asked, half to herself.

"Seeing his reaction to your group, I imagine he would be murderous."

Even in the pale lamplight, Sally could see fear etched on Mandy's face. Changing the subject, she said, "Well it's good you plan to quit the police. What would you like to do?"

Mandy stared into the dark between the trees a long moment before answering. "I haven't had much time to think about it. I like working with people and helping them. I suppose I could be a clerk or even a secretary if I went to night school."

Sally was reminded of something her father had told Mae a while ago, 'You're much more than a secretary'. Echoing that memory she said: "I believe you could be much more than a secretary. Not that secretaries are worth nothing. On the contrary. They often play a key role that most times goes unrecognised, especially by their bosses."

Further conversation was interrupted by the sound of several cars arriving. Headlights swung into the drive and drove closer till they came to a halt next to their table. Several people burst out, bubbling with laughter.

"What are you doing?" Keira asked clearly amused at what she saw.

To Sally these laughing people were like aliens. She'd waited all this time for them to arrive, but now they had, she couldn't fit them into her world. In the mean time, everyone had joined them, milling around the camping table laughing and making jokes. Jerking her thumb over her shoulder, Sally indicated they should look in the direction of the house. The laughter ceased abruptly.

"God!" Keira swore. "What the hell happened?"

"Hell is the right word," Sally said wearily. She'd managed to put what had happened out of her mind, now it came flooding back.

"The pig farmer got it into his head to ram the house with a van full of petrol," Mandy explained. "The fire spread extremely rapidly. In minutes the whole house was in ruins."

"What about Mae?" Lyra demanded, her voice trembling with fear.

"She's OK," Sally told her. "Ben saved our lives. Thanks to him we used the hosepipe to escape from a first floor window."

"Where are they now?" Lyra pursued.

"Ben caught Mae when she fell. She was unhurt but it broke his arm. They're at the hospital and should be back soon."

Brent pushed his way through the crowd and put his arms around Sally, pulling her close to him. She clung to him. If she had any more tears left, she might have cried again, but she felt shrivelled up and dehydrated. She pulled away and took a sip of her tea.

"Where did all this come from?" Brent asked pointing to the table and chairs.

"Mr. Peters had it brought so we'd be comfortable waiting for you."

"Whose Mr. Peters?" Tom asked as Jenny pushed him closer. "The neighbour?"

"No. He was administrator of the Professor's estate."

"Where are we all going to sleep?" Martin asked as he stood holding Fran's hand.

She guessed his mind was also on food. They must all be starving after the concert. "That's no problem," she said, finding unexpected and welcome pleasure in being mysterious.

"You got tents hidden back there?" Jenny asked.

Sally had to chuckle, despite the grimness of the circumstances. "No. I'm inviting you to stay in my house," she said maintaining the suspense. Out of the corner of her eye she saw Mandy looking at her reprovingly. "Ok, my ex-police friend here disapproves of me playing with your nerves. Mr. Peters, when he came earlier, explained that Mae and I own a little house down by the sea. Apparently our father gave it to us many years ago without us knowing."

Sally could see Mandy was grinning and Tom must have noticed because he said: "You're keeping something from us, aren't you?"

"Well yes. It's not quite so little." Sally said still maintaining the suspense.

"The two daughters own the Lodge," Mandy told them.

"But that's enormous," gasped Keira.

"Apparently it's fitted out like a private hotel with staff and everything. We're expected there tonight," Sally revealed.

"What are we waiting for?" Martin asked, seeming impatient.

"He's hungry!" Fran told them and everybody laughed.

"We have to wait for Mae and Ben," Sally pointed out.

As if mentioning their names had been a summons, two cars turned into the drive and parked behind the others. Out stepped Mae, arm in arm with Ben whose other arm was bound up in a sling. They were followed at a distance by Mr. Peters. The group opened up to let Mae and Ben come through and stand next to the table. Everybody was full of praise for Ben and his bravery and wanted to know exactly what had happened. Sally noticed that he was shyer that usual. She also noticed that her sister had not let go of Ben's arm.

Love strikes again, a familiar voice said in her head.

Mee, she exclaimed silently. Where have you been?

Busy.

Seeing Mr. Peters standing in the shadows, his hat held in his hands, Sally got up from her seat and walked through the group to join him.

"Let me introduce Mr. Peters," she said and went round the group, introducing him to each of them in turn. The last person to be introduced was Mae. "I don't need to tell me who this is."

"Indeed not," Mr. Peters said. "I've been following you and Miss Mae ever since you were babies." He held out his hand to shake Mae's but instead she stepped forward and hugged him. It clearly wasn't behaviour he was used to, but he didn't seem flustered by it.

"Let's all go to the Lodge," Mr. Peters suggested when Mae let go of him. And turning to Martin and Fran he added. "We can also see about food."

Everyone laughed and was heading for the cars when Sally turned to Mandy. "Why don't you join us for a meal, Constable Mandy?"

Mandy made a face. "The Constable must decline," Mandy said sternly, disappointing Sally. "But Mandy willingly accepts," she added with a grin. Everyone laughed.

Black holes

Jock paced from his bedroom to the kitchen holding his head

between his hands trying to alleviate the throbbing, took a swig of lukewarm beer that he must have forgotten to put in the fridge and then, holding his head in his hands, paced to the living room where he switched on the TV, cut the sound when it blared in his ears and turned about, retracing his steps back to the bedroom.

He was puzzled. There was an unfamiliar smell in the air. He sniffed, following his nose till he ended up leaning close to his pillows: perfume, a woman's perfume. How could there be perfume in his bedroom? What had he done during that gash in his memory?

Leaning over his bed, his head throbbed even more, so he straightened up and returned to the kitchen where he slumped in a chair and took another swig of beer. Warm beer was disgusting. Who was the woman who'd left her perfume in his flat? He got to his feet and went to inspect the bathroom. If a woman had been there, surely there'd be signs in the bathroom.

Two towels lay crumbled in a heap on the floor. Sure enough, one of them smelt of the same perfume. He chucked the towels in the dirty washing basket and returned to the kitchen, where he glanced in the fridge and found it alarmingly empty. Whatever he'd done, he hadn't gone shopping.

Grabbing another bottle of beer in the kitchen, he yanked the cap off with a bottle opener and went through into the living room where he stood looking dissolutely at the television balancing from one foot to another, unable to find a comfortable position. He was ill at ease in his own body. Estranged, as it were. He didn't belong to himself.

The news was on. He turned up the volume. The newsman was talking about a concert in Hoyt Park. The music sounded familiar. Haunting. A close-up shot of a young girl singing unaccompanied gave him a queasy feeling. He knew her face, he was sure of it. The queasiness continued to increase till it became unbearable and he had to make a dash for the bathroom where he threw up the beer he'd drunk.

When he returned, his head hammering worse than ever, the news had shifted to a spectacular fire in a large house on the outskirts of town. The photo of the professor who had lived in house had his head swimming again. He flicked the remote, killing the TV. The nausea had to be due to the TV rather than anything on it.

Once again in the kitchen in search of another beer to rid his mouth of the filthy taste, he leaned against the sink and looked at his reflection in the darkened window. He looked awful. Not just the wound on the side of his head. He had dark patches under his eyes like he hadn't slept in weeks. God was he tired. Exhaustion hit him like a wave. He could hardly stay upright.

He downed part of the bottle and left the rest on the draining board. Then he staggered back to his bedroom where he lay down cautiously on his bed, expecting a riot of protest from his head. To his surprise the headache had calmed. Instead he was enveloped in sickly perfume. "Mandy!" he exclaimed. And sprung to his feet.

The effect was disastrous. His head spun wildly and he took a nosedive, finding himself back on the bed face down, suffocating in the perfume. He elbowed himself up and eased himself off the bed and into a standing position. Why hadn't he thought of it before? During the last week he must have spent a lot of time with Mandy. They often worked together. If she were to tell him all that had happened, he'd be able to fill in the blanks.

He searched for his phone. It was nowhere to be found. Rifling through his jacket pocket a second time, he found several unused cartridges that had slipped through a hole in the lining. How weird. He never carried a firearm. He recognised the calibre. It was the same as the guns they used for practice down at the station. But why would he have them in his pocket?

He went back to the kitchen for another beer. Realising he hadn't finished the last one, he took both bottles, one in each hand, back into the living room. He turned on the TV mechanically then turned it off immediately. He didn't want the queasiness to begin again. He sank into the sofa and glared at the blank screen. To his annoyance, it answered none of his questions.

He had to phone Mandy. He cursed himself for cancelling his fixed phone line. So much for saving money! He'd have to ask the neighbours. The prospect didn't appeal to him. He hardly knew them. The man was in business, he thought, but he had no idea what the woman did. With the hours he kept, he rarely saw them.

He went to the bathroom and dabbed his wound with a moistened cloth. It looked spectacular, but once he'd cleaned it, the hole was quite small. He dried his face and stuck a plaster over the remaining gash. Better to cover the damage. He cleaned his teeth and ran a brush through his hair. That would have to do, he thought as he glanced at his reflection in the mirror.

He rang the doorbell. Nothing happened. Maybe it didn't work. Maybe they were out. He rang a second time, just in case. It was then that he heard a rustling within. Someone was fumbling with the lock. Finally the door opened just enough for him to see the face of a small beady-eyed man peering up at him. So this was his neighbour. He'd never seen him before.

"Good evening," he began. "I'm your neighbour."

"Good evening, Constable," the man responded, opening the door a little wider.

"I seem to have misplaced my phone. I urgently need to phone a colleague. Would you mind if I use your phone?"

The man did not invite him in, but instead he shuffled away and came back carrying an old-fashioned phone. Jock thanked him and dialled Mandy's number. No answer. He let the phone ring a long time. Nothing.

"She doesn't seem to be answering. Would you mind if I phone the station to see if she is there?"

"Go ahead."

Jock dialled the station and got through to his chief which was the last thing he wanted. "Have you seen Mandy?" he asked. He didn't wish to divulge the reason for his call but he had no better pretext for phoning.

"I told you to rest."

"I need to ask her a question. Have you seen here?"

"I have no idea where Constable Delaney is. She was out on a case and we haven't seen her since. She's probably gone home. She was exhausted."

Jock wanted to ask what the case was but his chief put an end to the conversation, telling him to go to bed. Jock handed the phone back to its owner, bid him goodnight and retreated to his flat.

In the kitchen once again, he realised he'd finished the beers. And there was nothing to eat. He didn't feel up to fetching food from the nearby deli. He took off his jacket, hung it on the balcony to air and lay down on his bed planning to think things over. Within seconds he was fast asleep.

Chapter 15 ~ The Lodge

The visit

An abrupt halt! There were no other words for it.

The cheerful group pulled up short of the entrance to the mansion, their chattering ceased, their laughter suspended in mid air, all eyes fixed on the shining brass plaque next to the door. On it they could read: The Dream Class, and on the line below: A Private Trust.

Mae was shocked to see their dream materialise in such an official form. It couldn't possibly be the same thing. A sinking feeling of dispossession gripped her. Could someone have waylaid their idea? Better to opt for a more benevolent explanation: the over enthusiasm of Mr. Peters or the Professor himself. She tried to understand what such a public pronouncement of their desires could mean.

"It is hardly our style," Keira muttered.

Mr Peters shifted to stand in front of the plaque. He must have noticed their reactions. "When the Professor spoke of your plans for a 'Dream Class' he was enthusiastic. He wanted to do everything in his power to make that a reality. We had already set up a trust to manage your properties. The Professor suggested we modify the name. If the new name is a problem, we can always change it."

"That's not the problem. The name is excellent," Sally said, placing a hand on the man's shoulder. "But seeing it sets off a very odd feeling. Like it has nothing to do with us."

Many nodded.

"It must be a shock to see your idea engraved in brass at the entrance to a place you do not know. But once you get acquainted with the Lodge, I hope it will seem natural to you."

Mae didn't have the heart to tell him that most of them would be leaving in the very near future.

The Lodge stood in a large park between the coast road and the sea, the drive to the main entrance being not far from the tiny railway halt for the university. The only other building nearby was a small hotel about half a mile down the road. Judging from the little Mae could see by the lights dotted close to the ground, the building was in two parts: the original mansion and a more modern building, the two linked by a long glass walkway flanked by offices on the seaward side.

Mr. Peters had not used the main drive to enter the property. Instead he had opened a gate onto a narrow lane that led through rolling hills to a small carpark concealed in a dip in the ground. Surrounded by trees, it was a short walk from the older building.

The mansion was impressive. Mae could picture life there in its heyday, the opulent Avan society received by the master and mistress of the Lodge. Built of the same green stone as many of the buildings in Avan, it had four floors and there were probably rooms under the rafters.

The building appeared old, but the window frames looked new. The place must have been renovated recently. It had been tastefully done, avoiding modifications to the original spirit and outward form of the building. Shroud in darkness, the Lodge seemed deserted.

"Shall we go in?" Martin suggested, moving towards the door.

"You wouldn't be hungry, would you?" Tom asked feigning innocence.

Everybody burst out laughing and Mr Peters stepped forward and unlocked the door onto an empty hallway. "This is your private entrance. It hasn't been manned because we use the main entrance to the new Lodge. This place is reserved for you."

Rather than continue into the house, he turned right down a short corridor to a door. There were no steps, so Tom could get around easily. Beyond the door Mr Peters led them along a long corridor walled in glass, on the sea-side of which there were a series of offices and small meeting rooms. The architect had used a mixture of transparent and frosted glass affording a glimpse into the rooms and beyond to the sea.

At the far end they stepped through a door into the main reception area. It was spacious and comfortable, almost homely, not like a hotel at all. In the immediate area around the entrance there were armchairs dotted here and there and thick carpets and low tables and potted plants and oil paintings on walls. The most astonishing feature was the glass roof that spanned the entire entrance area. In daytime, Mae imagined, it must be a pool of light. No wonder the plants thrived.

The receptionist, who was probably in her early twenties, greeted them warmly, stepping out from behind a small table made of teak. "It's good to meet you all, at last. My name's Pauline."

"How long have you been waiting for us, Pauline?" Brent asked.

"Since late this afternoon," Pauline said, laughing. "Seriously though, most of the staff began working here a year after the renovations, but a skeleton staff has been working here ever since the Professor bought the place. I was one of the first people here. It was my very first job."

"How do you manage to finance such a place?" Mae asked, turning to Mr. Peters.

"Mainly by hosting high-level congresses from time to time. The Lodge has an excellent reputation in the right circles."

Mae glanced around the reception area. It was plush without being extravagant. She noted that the oil paintings which were painted with vigorous brush stokes of bright expressive colours were clearly originals. They had caught Jenny's eye, because she walked over to examine them more closely. The shiny golden brown of the reception table was echoed here and there about the whole area by a judicious use of teak, in the furniture, in the bookshelves and in some of the fittings.

"Where's the kitchen?" Martin asked. "We've got some work to do." He rubbed his hands together like an eager child.

"It's down stairs. I'll show you," Mr Peters offered.

"In the basement," Martin said, pretending to be shocked.

"Not at all," Mr Peters responded. "It might seem confusing at first, but the Lodge is built on different levels so, even if it is downstairs, the kitchen is on the ground floor with direct access to the herb garden."

The man was less serious than Mae had at first thought. She was beginning to like him. Before leaving with Martin and Fran, he asked Mandy if she'd mind accompanying him "I'd like to talk to you in the quiet of my office?"

Mandy looked surprised, if not a little anxious. The man must have noticed because he added: "I want to talk about the security of our friends here." He waved his arm in a circular movement encompassing the whole group. Mandy looked a little less anxious.

"Pauline," Mr. Peters said as he turned to go, "could you take our other guests on a tour of the building? We'll show them the original lodge after dinner."

"With pleasure," she said, then glancing at Ben and his arm in a sling she asked: "Are you all right?"

"I'm fine," he insisted. Ever since they'd left the hospital Mae had been worried about him. He was clearly in pain despite the pills the hospital had given him. She tried to convince him to rest while they went on their visit, but he refused. So she took his good arm in hers and let him lean on her.

Pauline was tall, much taller than Mae, and quite slim. She looked like a gymnast or a basketball player.

"This building is not really public. Only participants at organised events get access," Pauline explained. Walking away from the reception, she led them to an area which seemed much more studious. The roof was considerably lower and no longer made of glass. Chairs replaced armchairs, the tables were higher and whiteboards were fixed to the walls.

Mae was surprised not to see computers. She said so.

"We provide people staying here with iPads if they wish and we've developed our own Apps for such things as paying the bill, choosing from the menu and perusing and annotating congress documents. This area has wireless connection, but we've limited access to specific areas so some places are quieter and more meditative." She opened a door into one of several large rooms next to each other in which there were seats and tables as well as the latest electronic equipment for complex meetings.

Returning to the reception area, they turned right and moved into yet another area with a different atmosphere. The roof there was higher than in front of the meeting rooms, higher than the glass roof of the reception area. The effect was surprising: it drew you up to your full height and left you feeling inspired. Along one side was a bar. Apart from a number of bar stools people were expected to stand. Opposite the bar, Pauline opened one of a number of doors into a much larger meeting room that could seat one hundred and fifty people.

"We call this the Grand Hall. It can be used for large meetings but it can also be used as a cinema or a small concert hall."

Keira wove her way forward between the chairs and climbed onto the stage where she sang a few lines of one of her songs. "Good acoustics."

"I love that song," Pauline told Keira. "I heard it several times on the radio today."

Keira grinned. "I'll sing it for you after we've eaten."

Pauline was clearly delighted.

"I've got something special for you," Pauline said, linking arms with Keira in an easy-going way and led her out into the area near the bar. Curious, the whole group followed as they took the lift to the floor below. "There are stairs, but with the wheelchair it is easier this way." She unlocked double doors and pushed them open dramatically. Inside was a long, relatively low room at the end of which a wall of windows gave onto the gardens and the sea beyond. In one corner near the windows stood a grand piano.

"This is the music room cum dance studio," Pauline announced. She pressed a button by the door and a curtain along the far wall pulled back revealing a mirrored surface reaching from floor to ceiling and stretching most of the length of the wall. She threw open doors in the wall next to the door, revealing cupboards you could walk into. Inside was a wide variety of musical instruments.

"What do you use this room for?" Keira asked.

"Very little up to now. But the Professor insisted the architect include a space for music and dance. I'm sure you'll find a good use for it."

"Sure will!" both Sally and Keira exclaimed in unison.

Returning to the reception area, Pauline took them through a series of glass doors into the restaurant. It was a clever system that probably stopped odours of food spreading to the rest of the building.

"When the weather is good we can seat eighty people in the restaurant and thirty on the terrace overlooking the sea."

Mae particularly liked the restaurant with its wide expanse of windows on two sides, one looking out onto Erin Sea and the other down over a garden lit by low lights along the paths that crisscrossed it. The garden was boarded on the far side by the old Lodge. At sunset it must be particularly beautiful, she thought. The form of the garden caught her attention. It was walled. Along all four sides, ran a covered walkway backing onto a wall. "It's like a cloister."

"Exactly," Pauline responded. "The Professor insisted on having several meditative spaces in the building. Many places where people meet for congresses or conferences are highly charged. That might be stimulating but it is also exhausting. The architect came up with the cloister idea which includes a garden for herbs and medicinal plants."

Jenny was clearly interested, as was Keira. The mention of food sparked off other thoughts.

"Will we eat here?" Jenny asked.

"This evening, yes," Pauline answered. "But the rest of the time you might prefer to eat in the dining room in the old Lodge, especially if there is a congress or an event here. We have a simple way to transport food there from the kitchens. Let's not talk too much about eating," Pauline joked, as she turned to leave the restaurant. "You must be starving and I still have two things to show you."

She led them to a set of lifts near the entrance to the restaurant. "I want to show you one of the rooms our seminar guests use." They filed into a number of lifts headed for the first floor. "As we deal in high quality meetings, the rooms are equipped accordingly." When they reached the first floor landing, she took out an electronic key and unlocked one of the doors.

They took it in turns to peek inside. The view over the sea in daytime must be marvellous. The room was surprisingly spacious. Mae wondered if that impression wasn't due to the sparing use of furniture. She liked the lack of clutter and hoped her room would be similar. She tried the bed. It was extremely comfortable. She could do without the flat screen TV and the DVD player, though.

The group milled around in the hallway talking quietly in small groups while the others visited the room. Ben was still holding on to her arm, looking very tired. She used the welcome pause to brush his hair from his eyes.

"How do you handle security?" Dieter asked.

"That's a complex question. You'd have to ask Mr. Peters. I'm sure he'd love to talk to you about it. I do know that security arrangements are under revision because of what happened to you during the weekend."

It would be good if Dieter and possibly Tom could add their expertise on the question, Mae thought. They really didn't want a madman like Twine driving into the Lodge with bombs stuffed under the bonnet. The thought made her shudder.

"I have one final thing to show you before we go for the aperitif. We'll take the lift to the top floor and then go on from there."

The top floor appeared to be made up of rooms similar to the one they'd visited. Mae wondered what Pauline could possibly want to show them.

"Over here," Pauline called out as she opened a door to stairs going on up. Either they weren't on the top floor, or they were to go out onto the roof. The stairs culminated in a small hallway in front of double wooden doors. A small lift took Tom's chair up till it was flush with the next level. Pauline waited till everybody had arrived before she opened the doors and they climbed a short ramp.

"Spectacular!" Anju exclaimed.

"It's paradise," Dieter added. Everyone agreed.

The ramp came out in the corner of a very large room with windows running the full length of the walls on all four sides. Below you could see the tiny lights of the walled garden in the shadow of the old Lodge. Mae could have sworn she saw Martin gathering herbs. The lights of Avan lit up the sky to the south where the spire of the Cathedral stood out above all the other buildings. Mae could even see the lighthouse flashing next to the Port. Turning seawards, looking due north across Erin Sea she could see the legendary Hoyt Islands shining faintly in the first light of the Moon.

"We call this the dojo in the sky," Pauline said, clearly delighted at the impact of her surprise. She threw a switch and concealed lighting came on. Now Mae could see that a tatami covered the whole floor to within a yard of the windows.

Anju did several cartwheels on the mat, testing it. "Excellent!" she said coming back towards the group. Dieter made a playful go for her, but Anju, with her usual foresight, sidestepped and gracefully sent him flying onto the mat.

"I can see some of you will find good use for this place. I hope you'll let me continue using it," she added, doing her own cartwheel across the surface.

"With pleasure," Dieter said and Anju feinted an attack, but for once he got the better of her and she ended up on the floor.

"Looks like you're in for competition," An joked.

Anju stuck out her tongue at An then rolled over and got to her feet.

"Anyone for an aperitif?" Pauline asked to cover her embarrassment.

Anju ignored her and seemed intent on using the dojo immediately. Mae, who had visions of Anju and Pauline in a ferocious cat-fight, was relieved when Anju accepted to go back down with them.

An's telephone rang at that moment. "It's Maria. The three girls went to the Professor's house and found it in ruin. They are in a state of shock. Anybody got a car so I can go and fetch them?"

"I'll ask our chauffeur to take you," Pauline said pulling out her phone. "The car will be waiting for you in front of the main building."

"Can you open these windows?" An asked.

Pauline answered by sliding aside one of the windows, although An's question had her looking confused.

An didn't bother with explanations. She ran and jumped through the open window, transforming immediately into a large owl that glided down to the main entrance.

Pauline screamed, staggering backwards, and would have fallen had Dieter not caught her, much to Anju's annoyance. The receptionist was deadly pale.

Keira put a hand on Pauline's shoulder. "Some of us can do things that most people would not believe in."

"Are you all right?" Jenny asked.

"I thought she was ..." Pauline's voice trailed.

"... being impetuous," Brent said laughing. "Let's go have that aperitif before someone else does something rash."

Mae had to admit that An's action had shocked her too. She felt a little unsteady. As they walked down the short ramp she wasn't sure if she was supporting Ben or the contrary.

A golden opportunity

Mr. Peter's office was in the middle of the long glass-lined corridor they had used earlier.

"Take a seat, Constable," he told Mandy, indicating one of several armchairs grouped around a low table.

Although the walls were made of glass, the architect had cunningly used lightly frosted glass in many places to provide light and warmth but conceal those within from the sight of people outside.

"Is it not rather hot in here when the sun is out?" she asked.

"Not at all. Thanks to a natural ventilation system, the circulation of air keeps the temperature comfortable all year round and renews and refreshes the air continually."

Now he mentioned it, she could feel that the air was not like that half-dead air you found in most enclosed spaces. It was fresh and alive, stimulating even.

"We use this system throughout the buildings. One of the principal vocations of the Lodge is to provide a place that is propitious for thought and exchange. Such a place requires a constant supply of living air, the sort you find walking along the beach when a breeze is blowing in off the sea and not the stuffy half-baked sort you find in air-conditioned conference centres."

Mandy laughed. "Marvellous." She liked him for the mixture of seriousness and passion with which he went about his work. "You wanted to talk to me about security, Mr. Peters?"

"Well, yes. Indeed. Our young friends awaken all sorts of passions in people, not all of them healthy. This weekend has made that plain. One of my tasks is to keep them safe and I suspect our current arrangements are not sufficient."

Mandy had to admit that the police's efforts to investigate the Starless Square had not been very successful either. "What do you plan to do?"

He ignored her question. "What do you know about security, Constable?"

She laughed. "Very little." There had been courses about the subject during her training and afterwards, but she hadn't had the time or the inclination to take part. "It's not such a preoccupation for people doing my sort of job." She hesitated, but decided that being forthright was probably the best bet. "To be honest, this weekend has made me realise that I am not the right material for a policewoman."

Mr. Peters didn't seem in the slightest put out by her admission. "Why did you come to that conclusion?"

Mandy would have liked more time to sort her ideas on the subject. "I have never been so afraid. I felt completely vulnerable. What's more, the people around me, those that I have come to appreciate a lot, this Dream Class as you call them, seemed vulnerable too and I couldn't do much to protect them. The police were at a loss. They're not very efficient in such circumstances."

Mr. Peters looked at her for a long moment, thoughtfully. "So what would you advise?"

Mandy had no idea. That was why she felt helpless and wanted to quit the police. But then again, nobody had ever bothered to ask her what should be done and she had never taken the time to ask herself either. "Give me a moment." Mr Peters nodded and sat quietly, his hands folded in his lap.

"There's something about the complexity," she mused. "People whose job is to maintain law and order in a small town probably aren't the best equipped to understand things when they get so complex. We are bound to a set of rules that don't always fit. My boss was always looking for simple answers. The 'quick fix' he called it. I'm not sure that works. It certainly didn't this weekend."

She was surprised at the ideas that flowed into her head when she put her mind to it. "And then there are the unpredictable things that happen. Rules are useless then. How can we possibly handle the unpredictable: the madman with his van full of petrol; the streaker who saw angels?"

Mr Peters raised his eyebrows, but didn't interrupt her.

"You're right about the Dream Class being exceptional people. I caught a glimpse of some of the things they are able to do. They defy our normal understanding. That too makes protecting them both easier and more difficult. Maybe if we knew more about their abilities it would help. We might even learn from them. Anju's skills in combat are extraordinary, for example. They would no doubt help us protect them...." Her voice trailed off as the ideas that jostled in her mind defied coherent expression.

When she looked up, Mr Peters was smiling. At other times she might have felt embarrassed or self-conscious, but for once she stood her ground and cocked her head to one side.

"Would you like to work for us?"

"Me?" His question surprised her. "Why me?"

He laughed again. "I like the way you state that you have no idea of security but when I ask you what you would do, you concisely describe many of the major challenges we are confronted with."

Mandy had to admit she had been surprised at her own eloquence. But did she really want to continue working in the same field? When she'd thought of leaving the police it had been to do something quite different, although she had no idea what.

"What would the work entail?" She had visions of playing bodyguard and that didn't please her at all or worse still, of being stuck in some far-flung hut making sure that ill-intentioned people were kept out.

"I'm not sure exactly. To begin with, I imagine you will have to get to know the members of the Dream Class better and in particular talk to those who have something to say about the security of the place and themselves. You'll need to know the lay of this property very well and also the other properties that belong to the Trust. If you think you need training, I can organise that and I can also organise meetings with experts if that will help. But first of all be with the Dream Class as much as possible and the two of us can have a short meeting once a week to discuss any ideas that may have arisen."

The picture that formed in her mind of the work was so appealing she had to stomp on the brakes to stop herself accepting then and there. "I have one problem that I must explain before we go any further." She wondered how she could tell him about Jock. The fact that he was a serious liability might ruin her chances of getting the job.

"Over the last year I have worked with another constable called Jock. As you said, the Dream Class can spark off unexpected emotions. Jock was no exception. What happened to him I can only describe as madness. He threatened the members of the Dream Class at gunpoint. A head wound might partly excuse his behaviour. But it can't explain everything. The Dream Class dealt with him with both courage and efficiency. That is not the problem. The problem is that in doing so they made Jock forget all that happened during the weekend. Now, he is a stubborn man and, even if he doesn't manage to regain his memory, he will still spend hours piecing things together. There is a serious risk that he will try to attack the Dream Class again or he might even try to get at me."

Mr Peter's face was serious. "Do you tell me this because you think it might discourage me from hiring you?"

"I thought you ought to know. And yes, I imagine it might influence your decision."

"Well I appreciate your honesty and it does influence my decision, but not in the way you think. In fact, I believe it makes you all the more apt for the job I have in mind. You have a better insight into the difficulties we are facing. Having said that, it might be better if you 'disappear' for a while, so you keep out of this Jock's way."

They went on to discuss practical details like pay and gratuities. "When can you begin?" he asked, winding up the discussion. "The sooner you can start, the better for us but also for you."

"I have accumulated so much overtime and a backlog of holidays that I could start immediately."

"Excellent," he said standing and holding out his hand to seal their agreement. "I'll have a contract drawn up and we'll send the driver to collect your things immediately."

"It will be as if I had disappeared," Mandy said, not without apprehension, her thoughts flitting to Jock.

The kitchen gardens

"What an extraordinary sound!" Martin exclaimed spinning round to see what was causing it. He was reminded of a couple of notes, faint but distinct, of an alpine horn, an instrument he'd often heard played at home. He loved the way those horns could speak to the mountains, bouncing back off the uneven rock surfaces creating a surprising counterpoint. It made him nostalgic for the Jura for the first time since they'd left. The short outbursts of music were offset by the rise and fall of a faint rustling like that of distant waves or the wind in the trees.

He and Fran were admiring the herb garden planted just outside the westerly windows of the kitchens. It was part of a much larger walled garden, each wall of which was different, but all of them providing a covered walkway like a cloister. The pair had escaped the kitchens, or rather the chef, on the pretext of visiting the gardens to fetch herbs.

"He must have carrots growing in his ears," Martin said, causing Fran to burst out laughing. "I've never met anyone so closed to new ideas." Martin was still flabbergasted at chef's complete lack of interest in what they knew or could do.

"We've been spoilt by the enthusiasm and the openness of Lyra's students," Fran replied.

The wall behind them was that of the kitchens and the entrance to the underground car park. The restaurant above stretched out a number of yards over the walkway providing shelter should it rain. The kitchen wall was a work of art in itself. Made of small pieces of glass set at varying angles, it had been treated so that large parts of the glass were one-way mirrors reflecting multiple images of the gardens with here and there a pane of transparent glass affording glances into the kitchens beyond.

Martin was pleased they couldn't see the chef striding about his kitchen. He could see them though as the wall was entirely transparent from within, affording an uninterrupted view of the walled garden.

As they wound their way though the gardens to the northern wall that backed onto the sea, Martin was fascinated by the multiple fragments of himself and Fran reflected in the kitchen wall and the way they constantly changed as he moved. It gave him a sinking feeling in his stomach.

From a distance, the north wall looked like a rough stone construction some ten feet high with small climbing plants and moss dotted here and there. Close up Martin could see that under the layer of plants it was made of multiple irregular vertical folds, some much thicker than others. He thought it must be concrete but when he touched it, some folds were too thin to be concrete.

"It's glass, I think," Fran said.

The surface must have been specially treated, because it was pitted with many tiny holes making it rough like weather worn stone. In fact, many of the tiny stones that must have been used to make it remained embedded in the glass adding tints of brighter colours in places. From where they stood it was clear that it was the wall that was making the sounds they heard. Small openings between the vertical folds allowed the wind to squeeze though causing the glass to vibrate.

"Like organ pipes," Fran remarked. "Different lengths make different notes."

He wondered if the sun could also ease through causing a play of narrow shafts of light across the gardens during the daytime. At the foot of the wall was a boarder of shingle that went well with the varying greys and greens of the wall. The walkway itself was paved with flagstones and was covered with an irregularly corrugated glass roof that served as a shallow reservoir for water.

"It's from a nearby spring," Mee told them as he flitted by.

Tiny holes above the wall let a thin stream of water filter through, causing droplets to form on the moss and fall a drip at a time, cascading from one plant to another till they finally reached the shingle below. Fascinated, Martin and Fran stood for a long moment watching the drops form and fall.

They crossed through the gardens towards the south wall that was nearly fifteen feet high and was entirely made of glass. Large areas, especially in the lower part, were translucent and crisscrossed with pastel patterns that reminded him of colourful waves.

"It's silkscreen printing," Fran informed him as she ran her fingers across the surface. "In an art school near my university in Germany they were experimenting with such techniques. It's amazing what you can do with glass."

It took Martin a moment to realise that the upper part of the wall was composed of the row of offices they had seen earlier. As he looked he spotted Mandy talking to Mr Peters.

This wall was the only one of the four where the walkway was not only covered but closed in. There were a number of doors in the glass wall between the walkway and the gardens. Peeking inside, Martin realised that it was much wider than the other walkways. It was big enough for a small vehicle. And sure enough, as he glanced down the walkway in the direction of the new building he caught sight of an electronic cart rather like those used in airport terminals. He guessed that must be how goods and food were delivered to the old lodge.

A final wall completed the fourth side of the square, extending beyond the old lodge. It was made of the same green stone employed for the house. Nooks and crannies had been left between the stones in which a wide variety of hanging plants grew. A narrow overhang covered with tiles akin to those used on the Lodge roof protected a walkway.

"We'd better get back, just in case he fiddles with our meal," Fran said.

Martin sighed. Conflicts were not good for cooking.

As they turned to make their way back to the kitchens, they both breathed in deeply, savouring the rich scents of herbs and flowers. Doing so had a welcome calming effect. It was the best time of the day to smell flowers.

"We'll have to bring plants here from the Reaches," Martin said, "if we are to make many of the recipes the Littl' People taught us."

Fran touched the leaves of the herbs then cut and collected a number for the evening meal.

Back in the kitchens Fran gave the herbs to one of the assistant cooks to be washed while Martin examined a selection of vegetables and helped prepare them. The chef hovered behind him as if seeking to find fault. They had planned to serve roasted vegetables with slices of roast lamb. Fran had already given instructions on how to cook the lamb joints. The chef had scoffed at her ideas but the assistants, after looking nervously at the chef, had obeyed. They didn't often cook meat as most of the Dream Class preferred vegetarian food, but occasionally they made an exception.

When the roast and the vegetables were almost ready, it was time to sprinkle them with herbs before returning them to the oven for a short period. Fran explained her choices of herbs to Keith James, the head cook.

"You wouldn't get our regular customers eating that," Mr James commented, disgust written all over his face.

He was a tall thin man with greying hair, steely blue eyes and a pock-marked face, no doubt from some childhood illness. Mr Peters had told them that Mr James had owned a restaurant in town before he came to work at The Lodge.

Martin had wondered how the chef would react to them, especially as they were much younger and less experienced than him. In fact the chef had remained aloof until he happened to mention that he'd helped design the kitchens. When Martin and Fran said how much they liked his ideas he'd relaxed slightly. The kitchen reminded them of the cooking area in the Littl' People's community building. The burners and ovens had been placed in the middle, grouped together in small units each with its own extractor hood. All around were surfaces on which food could be washed and prepared. Above and below these, cupboards had been built for kitchen utensils as well as sauces, herbs and condiments. The layout made it possible for a considerable number of people to work together to produced a large variety of meals.

In the restaurant above the tables had been laid and the Dream Class would soon be sitting down to eat. Everything was almost ready. A series of small plates of mixed salads garnished with flowers gathered from the gardens lay in orderly rows on one of the work surfaces. Nearby small bowls of chocolate mousse toped with mint leaves for the dessert had been prepared. The vegetables were ready and the meat sliced, all of it placed in a special oven to keep it hot but not dry it out.

The chef seemed relieved that the ordeal was over. "You don't need to bother with cleaning up," he said, dismissing them.

Martin glanced around the kitchen. They had in fact tidied up after themselves and only plates, glasses and cutlery would need washing. The man's attitude annoyed Martin so much, he followed Mr James through into his office and indicated Fran should join him. He closed the door after them and turned to the chef.

"We have enjoyed cooking in your kitchen," he began. "It's a shame that our presence is so disagreeable to you."

The chef interrupted him. "I hardly need anyone like you telling me what to do."

"You might like to remember, Mr James" Fran said calmly, "that our friends are the new owners of the Lodge."

The man scowled.

Returning to the kitchens to thank the staff, they left the chef to digest the news.

Reserved meets carefree

The chauffeur gasped when An stepped out from behind him. "I'm sorry Miss. I didn't hear you," he stammered, making every effort to mask his astonishment. He introduced himself as Trevor and opened the back door to the limousine for her.

"If you don't mind, I'd prefer to sit up front, Trevor."

He opened the forward door without batting an eyelid.

"You know where to go?"

"Yes, Miss. The late Professor's house." Trevor lapsed into silence concentrating on the road and An looked out the window as they drove away from the Lodge.

She didn't know this world very well, but wondered at the riches of the Professor. It didn't seem that easy to accumulate wealth in a place like Avan. Had he inherited the Lodge? That was often how people got rich in the Reaches. Her mother had inherited the house they lived in. Presumably it would now be hers. She shuddered at her mother's death. Typically spectacular, she thought, a smile on her lips. An resolved to tell her so next time their paths crossed.

"Mr Peters told us that the Professor had several properties," she mentioned, hoping to draw the chauffeur out.

"Yes. In Wales but also in the Lake District and Scotland."

By the time they turned into the drive to the Professor's house, An still knew very little about the Professor's fortune.

Tricia, Maria and Beth were huddled at the foot of the giant oak, across from the charred ruins of the house. They looked pale and frightened in the headlights of the limousine.

The moment Trevor pulled on the brake, An sprang from the car only to be enveloped in a pall of smoke. Running to her friends, she flung her arms around them and pulled the girls close.

"Oh An!" Tricia said with a sob. "We were afraid that ..." and her voice trailed off.

"Shhh," An said. "Everything is OK. Nobody was hurt."

Trevor cut the engine and dipped the headlights. They stood a long moment in the half-light, wordless, the three girls struggling to shift from what had been a tragedy to a happier ending.

"Where is everybody?" Beth finally asked shaking off the misery that continued to oppress them all.

"I'll show you," she replied, pulling the three reluctant girls towards the car.

Trevor stood by the rear door, holding it open for them. Maria eyed him, licking her lips. An had paid little attention to the chauffeur, but looking at him now with what she imagined to be Maria's eyes she realised he was quite handsome. He was several inches taller than Tricia and had a neatly trimmed moustache that made him look older than he probably was. The dark suit should have had the same maturing effect, but something out of place made her think of a boy dressed in men's clothes.

"Are you not going to introduce us?" Maria demanded, eying Trevor unashamedly. Trevor, in comparison, held himself stiffly aloof.

"This is Trevor, our chauffeur," An informed them.

He bowed.

"And this," she said pointing at Maria, "is Maria. You need to be wary of her, she's a man-eater."

Maria smiled alluringly at Trevor then aimed a friendly punch in An's direction.

"And these are Tricia and Beth, my best friends."

He nodded a stiff greeting, but said nothing. Maria wanted to sit up front, but An insisted she join the other two girls on the back seat where she sat pouting for about thirty seconds.

As they pulled out onto the road that led to town, Beth sighed causing An to swivel her head to get a better look at her friends.

"Beth?" An questioned.

"I can't get used to it," the girl said sighing again.

"What?"

"Not more than ten minutes ago we were mourning you, having been dealt parts in a horror movie. Now you're telling us everything is OK. The change is so brutal my body can't keep up. I'm still shuddering from the nightmare and I have to be happy." She promptly burst into tears. An leaned back and held her hand. Tricia and Maria cuddled up close.

"Where are we going?" Tricia asked.

"To the Lodge," An told them.

"Why are we going there? Isn't it some sort of private club?" Maria asked.

"It's a conference centre," An corrected. "It's also our new home."

She caught a glance from Trevor who showed interest for the first time. "Sally and Mae have inherited it from their father, the Professor."

Beth moaned. "The trouble with you lot is that things change far too quickly. A couple of hours away and we are already out of touch."

"Come off it, Beth," Tricia reprimanded her. "You know you revel in the excitement. Admit it!"

Maria nuzzled Beth's ear. "Be honest. It's only because you want to be with An all the time!" Maria whispered loudly in her ear. "There's no way we'll let you have her all for your own in bed," she warned.

An glanced at Trevor who had blushed. Apparently he wasn't so indifferent.

Interesting game you're playing there, a voice said in her head making her jump.

Mee, of course, she thought, calming her thumping heart.

She had no time to reply for he had already gone. Game? Was she playing a game? She'd taken Mee's comment as a criticism, but it didn't necessarily imply judgement. The way she reacted in the company of her friends was quite different from the wise young girl who went by the name of An and who came from the Reaches. Although her appearance had not changed, it was almost as if she were a different person. She ought to be used to transformations. This was a different kind of transformation though and she hadn't even realised she'd done it. Odd.

She enjoyed being with Tricia, Maria and Beth. Something about them rub off on her: they were so often joyful and carefree. In a way she encouraged them. But was she being irresponsible? Was she leading them on? She was as much the insouciant schoolgirl as the serious young lady who'd seen so much of life.

She glanced back at her friends. Tricia smiled. To hell with it! She was going to make the most of it while it lasted. Her reverie was interrupted by Trevor who brought the limousine to a halt and announced that they'd arrived. Tricia whistled between her teeth.

"Wow! Is this where you all live now?" she asked, admiration in her voice.

"Thanks Trevor," An said as she reached to open the door. "Come on, girls. Let's go eat!"

Dinner and after

Raucous laughter rang from the reception and muscled its way into the restaurant as the door flew open and several youngsters burst in, jostling each other playfully. All heads turned to see who was riding rough shod over the sophisticated hush of the Centre. How quickly the Dream Class had adjusted, Sally thought, even though they had the place to themselves. All the same, they'd need a place to let off steam and be more playful if they were to stay any time.

"Trust you, An!" Sally said, standing to greet her half sister and her friends.

"Pauline is still recovering from your dashing departure, An!" Brent added.

"I see you girls are fully recovered from your shock," Sally added, addressing the three teenagers who accompanied An.

Tricia and Beth both calmed the moment they sensed the atmosphere and looked around the plush restaurant, intimidated. Maria continued to laugh, her eyes bright with excitement.

"Wow!" she said glancing around the room for the first time. "Are you going to throw us out for causing a disturbance?"

"No!" Fran said as she accompanied the waitresses who carried in the salads. "But there's an awful lot of washing up to do. Seriously though, you'd do well to sit down. You're in the way."

A long table had been laid in front of the window looking out over the deserted veranda. Sally recognised the handwork of Fran and Martin in the flowers dotted here and there. There were also a number of pebbles that looked like they came from the seashore. Sally couldn't resist adding her own little touch. She let her mind wander to the roof, transforming it into a starlit sky.

Several waitresses gasped, as did Pauline who'd just come in from the reception. A stern remark from Mr Peters had all of them continuing their business as if nothing had happened. Mr Peters who had been deep in conversation with Mandy, leaned across the table and spoke quietly to Sally. "It might be wise to avoid such ... er ... demonstrations ... at least until we've got the staff primed."

Sally let the transformation fade.

"There's a phone call for a Miss Delaney," Pauline announced. Mandy turned pale, but made no move to go.

"Who is it?" Mr Peters asked, taking control.

"A certain Jock Glas. I told him I didn't know who Mandy was and would check if the person was here."

Sally saw Mandy shudder.

"Tell him no one of that name is here," Mr Peters instructed.

Pauline hurried off.

"What's that about?" Mae asked.

Mr Peter looked around the room, his glance settling on Maria and company. "Can everybody here be trusted?" he asked Mae quietly.

"Every member of our group, including An's young friends, are trustworthy."

He nodded as if confirming something to himself. "I have asked Mandy to work for us," he said raising his voice. The announcement was met with general approval and several people even clapped. "As you know her position has become somewhat difficult following the events of the weekend. It would be better if she remained incognito for a while. I plan to send her on a tour of the properties that belong to the Foundation so she can get to know our work better."

Sally was about to ask a question when the waitresses arrived with the main dish. Once everybody had been served, Sally asked Keira to sing grace. Mr Peters seemed to approve, but then no one could resist Keira's singing.

"Mr Peters," she asked as everyone set about the roast vegetables and thin slivers of lamb. "How many properties did our father own?"

The man wiped his mouth with his napkin before replying. "Very few in fact."

The news relieved her.

"Most of them belong to you two, through the foundation."

Sally's knife and fork fell from her fingers, hitting the plate with a clatter. "How many?" she managed to ask.

"Around twenty," Mr Peters told her. "Although not all of them are as big as this one." Then he added, grinning: "Except the disused factory in Wales and the castle in Scotland, that is."

"You're pulling our leg," Mae put in.

"Not at all."

Sally sat back in her seat trying to come to terms with the immensity of it.

"I told the Professor to inform you earlier. I was concerned it might be a shock. But he had his reasons."

The waitresses were clearing away the plates and Fran and Martin appeared as the desert was being laid on the table. Brent stood and raised his glass. "I propose a toast to our resident cooks who do magic with food." Glasses were raised and a cheer went up. Fran and Martin bowed and the latter wished them "Bon appétit!"

It was Mae's turn to get to her feet. "I'd like to offer a toast to Mr Peters, to Pauline and to all the staff at the Lodge for their welcome tonight and for the good work they have done in running this place … quite unbeknown to us." Several people laughed as others called out "Here! Here!" and the glasses were raised again. Mr Peters thanked them.

They couldn't leave it there, Sally thought as she pushed back her chair and rose. "I would like to offer a toast to a man who has changed all our lives, by his example, by his teaching, by his fatherly advice, by his good sense and canny judgement, our father, John Llewellyn Rafter." A hush fell over the room and everybody got to their feet and raised their glasses. "To John Llewellyn," they said in chorus. Sally hastily wiped her eyes, noticing that many others shed tears.

"You should plan a memorial ceremony in the next few days," Mr Peters suggested once they were reseated. "It doesn't need to be religious. On the contrary. I don't think that would be appropriate. The Professor was well loved in town and we owe it to him and to the town's people to mark his going with respect and dignity."

"I'm glad you mention it, Mr Peters," Mae said. "I was mulling over the idea."

"Not something sad," Keira mused. "Stories about him, music and dance, …"

"Where?" Sally asked.

"Maybe in the cathedral," Mr Peters said.

"I thought you said it was not to be religious," Sally questioned.

"It can be in the Cathedral without being religious. The place has a great atmosphere," Mr Peters said.

"The Cathedral is on the same Ley line that goes from the Hoyt Islands, through this building, through the Theosophy department and even the Professor's house,…" Jenny informed them.

"Then we must hold it in the Cathedral," Brent concluded.

Mr Peters offered to organise the use of the building, leaving the programme of the event to them.

The old building

Mr Peters bid them good night and they thanked him again for his hospitality. He still had paperwork to see to, he explained. Mae really liked the man and was looking forward to working with him. It was Pauline who led them down to the walled garden and along the covered walkway to the entrance of the old building.

"That song was so beautiful," Pauline said to Keira as she pulled out the key to open the door. "I wish I could sing like you."

Keira chuckled. "Maybe I'll teach you to sing, if you're good."

The door opened and they were on the verge of stepping into what was to be their temporary home when police sirens blared in the distant night.

"Blast!" Mandy swore.

Frozen by the sound, they listened horrified, as the sirens drew closer. Pauline pulled out her phone and flicked her fingers across the screen. Putting the device to her ear she listened intently for a long moment then turned to them. "Mr Peters said it would be better to get you out of the way. Follow me!"

They entered the older building and followed her down a narrow corridor in the basement. The sight of a dead end had Mae alarmed.

"Where now?" Mandy asked, fear in her voice.

Pauline studied the wall then tapped on it with her fist. The wall swung inwards revealing stairs going steeply downwards. "Be careful the steps may be wet and slippery. When you reach the bottom, wait for me."

"What about Tom?" Mae asked.

"There's no other way down. Can you carry him?"

Martin and Dieter heaved Tom from his seat and made their way down the stairs. Brent followed carrying the wheelchair with Jenny.

At the foot of the stairs they stood assembled waiting for Pauline to join them.

"Does anyone know why we are running?" Anju whispered.

They looked at each other perplexed.

"Maybe Jock got his memory back," Dieter speculated.

"I doubt it," Brent commented.

"He's a stubborn man," Mandy pointed out. "He'll dig till he finds something, memory or no memory."

Pauline finally arrived.

"What are we running from, Pauline?" Mae asked on behalf of them all.

"The police," Pauline replied.

"But why should we be afraid of the police?" Sally asked.

"Mr Peters said you were expecting trouble ..." Pauline replied, her voice trailing off.

"Look where hasty thinking gets you," Anju said with an undertone of scorn that Mae had never heard from the girl before. The skirmish with Pauline must have touched her more than Mae had realised.

"It's not her fault," Dieter said coming to Pauline's rescue.

Silly man. Couldn't he see he was making things worse? Pauline was near to tears. Mae let go of Ben's arm and stepped between Pauline and Dieter much to the latter's annoyance. Putting her arm around the young woman's shoulder, she moved her away from Dieter, saying, "The situation is complicated. You were just doing what you were told to do."

"Where does this corridor go?" An asked, pushing her way through the group with the three girls trailing after her.

"To a private landing stage where several boats are moored."

Pauline said, freeing herself from Mae's arm. "We thought you could escape that way."

An turned to face the group. "I suggest Brent and I go and check what is going on. But we need to get outside so we can fly nearer and see what is happening."

Finally understanding what An was getting at, Pauline turned pale. "Follow me. I'll take you outside, down by the sea."

An and Brent accompanied Pauline who strode off down the corridor while the rest of the group followed at a more leisurely pace.

Mae fell back and linked arms with Ben, encouraging him to lean on her. "How do you feel?"

"Looking forward to a bed to sleep in."

She wondered briefly if that would be the same bed as hers. He was in no fit state for adventures in corridors, she thought. He was in no fit state for adventures in bed either. Their pace was so slow that the others were soon far ahead.

"I hadn't realised Anju could be so jealous," she mused.

"Shame really," Ben replied. "Dieter was only joking, but now things have become so serious. The longer it goes on, the harder it will be to set right."

They continued to shuffle down the corridor that went on forever.

"Are you the jealous type?" he asked.

She'd had so little to do with love, she wasn't sure. "I don't think so. I've not had much experience."

"How odd. I knew you didn't show much of your own feelings, but I always imagined you as having a steady boyfriend for years."

"Hey! I'm not that old. But no, there is no boy friend."

"Do you prefer girls?" he asked matter-of-factly.

"Not that I am aware of." She chuckled. "I have some good friends, like Lyra, but I have no girlfriend in that sense." It felt strange talking to him about such things but not because it made her uneasy. On the contrary, she felt so at ease with him. "How about you? Do have a girl friend or a boy friend?"

It was his turn to chuckle. "Neither. I'm not interested in men … in that way." He blushed. "And I've been too busy working on my thesis to have time for women."

She had a whole series of questions she wanted to ask, but they had caught up with the others and the intimacy was lost. The mooring place was just ahead and they could hear the remainder of their group talking quietly somewhere nearby.

The 'mooring place' was actually a low building housing several boats. They followed the sound of voices along a raised walkway on one side of the building and exited by a small door that led to a large terrace jutting out over the sea. Partly sheltered by an artificial overhang that hid them from sight, the group sat in canvas chairs, clustered about several round tables. The murmur of conversations was lost in the backwash of the waves. In the distance, the Hoyt Islands stood out in the moonlight.

It was in that light that they caught sight of the two owls plunging towards the terrace. Landing lightly they hopped from one foot to another and transformed into An and Brent.

"Wow!" Tricia said, eyeing An as she pulled on her trousers. "I wish I could do that."

It took the pair a moment to adjust to their human form, but once they were dressed and steady on their feet they came forward and sat at one of the tables.

"So?" Sally asked.

"The police are looking for Tricia, Maria and Beth," Brent told them. "Not at all for the rest of us."

"Your parents phoned the police," An explained addressing the three girls. "They'd heard of the fire at the Professor's house on the news and were worried."

"Apparently the Professor's neighbour told the police that our group had gone to the Lodge," Brent added.

"So much for being incognito," Mandy muttered.

"Mr Peters stalled the police," Brent continued. "He said he would send one of his staff to look for the girls. You should take them back An and it might be better if Sally went with you so somebody older is accompanying you. There's a path that leads from here to the new building. It's not far. The police are waiting in the reception."

Chapter 16 ~ Partings

Rude awakenings

The heat was bitterly intense, forcing him to shield his face as the fury of the fire seared into his skin and singed his hair. The angry flames licked at the woman and wound their way up her legs, tied as they were to the stake in the centre of the pyre. He fought to look away, but his eyes were riveted on the terrible tableau. Fascinated, his gaze roved up the young woman's body keeping pace with the rising flames. Her head hung to one side, strangely still, her hair concealing her features. Suddenly her head snapped upright revealing the tortured lines of pain etched on her face. Her eyes locked onto his and pierced him. "Mandy!" he screamed and flung himself with all his force beyond the grips of the inferno.

Heaving himself up from the floor, Jock staggered into the bathroom and splashed cold water on his face and down the nape of his neck, to no avail. The images remained etched in his mind. And there was the stink. Only now did the stench of burnt flesh sting his nostrils and catch in his throat causing him to gag. For want of food, all he could render was bile. The bitterness burnt his throat as his stomach continued to spasm. He slumped to his knees, his hands grasping the sides of the toilet seat, tears streaming down his cheeks.

Washing, shaving and dressing... nothing could erase the nightmare. Not even listening to the radio. Monday. The beginning of most people's working week and he was doomed to a day off. He couldn't bear being stuck in his flat haunted by a dreadful odour of grilled flesh. It was still early but he resolved to get out and reassure himself Mandy was safe. Her flat was not far away. Pulling a cap down over his eyes and the collar of his coat up around his face he tried to hide from the awakening world. Several people recognised him as he hurried along the streets of Avan. He grunted inarticulate replies to their greetings.

In the entrance to Mandy's flats, he glanced at the letterboxes. To his astonishment he found no mention of Mandy Delaney. He climbed the stairs to the first floor. There was no name by her doorbell. He tried the door and found it open. Inside the flat was completely empty. It was as if no one had ever lived there. He went to the window and looked out, hoping for some clue that would make sense of the nightmare. All he saw was a grey day beginning. Violent fury swept like wildfire through his veins. He wanted to beat the hell out of somebody, anybody. He wanted to smash the windows with his fists, causing panes of glass to cascade onto the street below. He wanted to kick and scream and bite and stamp.

Instead he strode out of the flat, his teeth and fists clenched, leaving the door wide open. He vaulted down the stairs three at a time, shoved open the front door causing it to crash noisily against the wall and hurried out into the street, panting. He finally came to a halt at a newspaper stand where he stared unseeingly at the headlines.

"Wanna a paper, guv?" the newsagent asked.

He fished some coins from his pocket without bothering to count them and took the nearest paper. "A good day to yer!" Jock vaguely heard the man say as he strode away.

Not paying any attention to where he was going, he stumbled on a giant crater criss-crossed with coloured ropes. It took him a while to realise he was in Hoyt Park. How the hell had a crater got there? He glanced at the newspaper, hoping it would supply an answer. Terrorists wreak havoc in Hoyt Park the headlines said. Astonished, he was about to read on when a headline further down the page caught his attention: A great man dies. He skimmed the article about the death of a university professor.

What he read made him feel queasy. Was he going nuts? He circled the crater, stepping over the coloured markers, and tried to clear his thoughts. If he wasn't crazy, then something very peculiar was going on. He painstakingly went over what he knew, but it didn't add up. Too many bits were missing. Mandy for a start. He went to pull out his phone only to discover he didn't have one. Another missing part.

He turned and hurried across the footbridge over the River Bree and stopped at a tobacconist's. He asked the guy, whom he knew well, if he could use his phone. He wasn't about to phone his boss. He'd only get a dressing down for not taking a rest as he'd been ordered to. Instead he phoned a colleague and asked if Mandy was there. "What do you mean she's resigned?" he shouted, flabbergasted. His colleague made a rude remark and, with some coaxing, explained they'd received a letter saying she had left for a new job. Things were just getting worse.

In a daze he stepped outside, no idea where to go. He ambled along the high street to the market place trying desperately to shake off the dull ache of incomprehension that made his brain sluggish. Here and there shopkeepers who were laying out their wares greeted him. He barely acknowledged them. Instinctively he turned in the direction of the old railway station and found himself outside the police station.

Drat! He hurried on, lowering his head and pulling up his coat even higher around his neck and face. Standing under one of the trees in the courtyard of the old railway station he pulled the day's newspaper from his pocket and re-read the two articles on the front page. Professor Rafter. The name rang a bell. If he had no memory, he'd have to go on hunches. The telephone directory in a phone booth indicated that the Professor had lived not far away.

At the end of the drive to the Professor's estate sprawled a pile of blackened rubble. He shuddered, recalling his dream. He turned his back on the ruins and was about to leave, when he spotted a neighbour taking an early morning walk through his garden. He hailed the man and explained he was from the police. A detective, he said. The lie would make his questions seem more plausible. The man willingly told him all he knew. Amazing how trusting people were if the tone was right!

Breakfast at the Old Lodge

Brent crossed to the buffet and helped himself to a coffee, wrapping his fingers around the cup to warm them. He had just come from a wind-swept walk along the sea wall.

He joined Tom and Martin who were seated by a window overlooking the lawn that stretched away to the sea some fifty yards beyond. Tom had a bowl of untouched muesli in front of him. Martin, in contrast, was finishing his fourth slice of toast and marmalade.

"I'm not going back to the Reaches," Tom confided. Martin shot him a startled look. "I'm too much of a liability. What's more I have no particular gift to contribute. I'll return to Switzerland and go back to journalism. At least there I know what I'm doing."

"That would be a shame," Brent said, He knew Tom was right about being a liability, but he liked the man and didn't want to see him go. Tom was playing out a story that had no need to be so tragic. All the same, Brent felt guilty, as they all must, knowing that if Tom hadn't been with them in the Reaches he would never have been handicapped like he was. On the other hand, a lot of people would have died if he hadn't been there to save them.

"I've been thinking about it for a while," Tom pursued. "Now that it's time for you to leave, my choice seems obvious."

"What does my sister think?" Martin asked, concern in his voice.

"Jenny's not happy. She wants to return to the Reaches and she wants me to go with her. But she doesn't want to hurt me. And I don't want to stop her going…"

Their conversation was interrupted by the arrival of Dieter and Anju. "I don't care what you say, I don't like it," Anju was saying, oblivious to the others. She looked drawn as if she hadn't slept.

"There's no reason to get annoyed," Dieter argued, nodding cursory greetings to Brent and the others. "It's all your imagination."

The trouble with imagination, Brent thought, was that it was just as real as all the rest. His stories depended on it.

"Yeah, sure!" Anju said, grabbing herself a bowl of muesli. "I saw her in your arms."

Pauline, Brent realised. So that was the problem.

"If I hadn't caught her," Dieter explained, making a show of being patient, "she'd have fallen to the floor."

Their tortured feelings were driving a growing wedge between them. Brent wondered if he should intervene. He couldn't fix every rift between his friends. Yet Anju looked miserable, munching her muesli in brooding silence as she sat opposite Dieter. Brent took a deep breath and launched into a story, knowing that the tone of his voice would captivate those listening and make them experience his story as if it were happening to them.

"Bill and Betty lived in adjacent houses, but a high wall ran between the two marking the border of their respective countries. They met only once, but that brief encounter had bewitched them. Unbeknown to Bill, Betty stood in front of the wall each day picturing what he was doing. He would surely not be interested in her, she had so many failings. And there was that girl who lived near him. No wall separated them and she was attractive and intelligent. Bill must surely be enamoured of her. Not like her neighbour's son. Betty couldn't stand him. And Bill, in turn, stood on the other side of the wall convinced Betty loved the neighbouring boy. The boy was handsome with good prospects, surely Betty would fall for him. She couldn't possibly love someone as insignificant as Bill. He drew up a list of his shortcomings to shore up his judgement. And so they spun their hopeless tales on either side of the wall till both of them were miserable and desperate." Brent plunged his listeners in a bottomless pit of despair, letting them wallow in self-pity and hopelessness.

"Now you might not believe in dwarves, but they do exist and walls are no barrier to them." A damp earthy smell invaded the room as dark energies swirled here and there and indistinct forms shifted amongst them. "So the dwarf knew exactly what was going on. Dwarves can be very patient, but his patience had its limits. He stirred himself from his perch and decided to open a small door in the wall thinking that the two would be delighted to see each other. But instead of rushing into each other's arms as he expected, they stared at each other, silent and unmoving, fearful even. Judging from their faces they seemed to have become even more miserable. The dwarf couldn't stand it. He stomped around the Bill and gave him a hefty kick in the butt sending him flying forward flat on his face on the ground. He did the same with Betty. Both lay wailing at their ill fortune, their fingers now only a short distance apart." Brent allowed the absurdity of the situation to permeate the whole room. "The dwarf wanted to tell them to stop being so stupid and to make a move towards each other, but he could not talk to humans, so he was condemned to watch. Finally. disgusted, he slammed the door and left them to their isolation." At the sound of the door slamming, Brent let the waves of desolation and a feeling of utter wastefulness break over his audience, then he allowed the emotions to slowly recede.

Both Anju and Dieter were in tears when the story ended. Dieter flung his arms around her and she sobbed as she cuddled up close. "I'm so sorry," she repeated.

"I'm sorry too," Dieter assured her.

Brent looked up and noticed that most of the Dream Class were now in the dining room and stood listening, transfixed. "Anyone else got a problem?" Brent asked jokingly.

He saw Jenny make a move to say something, but finally she held back.

"Or is it that you are starving and were just politely waiting for the end to be able to eat?"

"You are unbearable, you handsome man," Sally said running her fingers through his hair. Before he was able to defend himself, she silenced his unspoken words with a kiss.

The will

"I don't get it," Sally complained.

"It's the will," Mae said, as if that explained everything.

"But how can a notebook be a will?"

"Maybe he wanted to do things differently."

"He certainly succeeded." Sally flicked through the pages for the second time. "But at least he could have written something." Irritated, she flung the blank book onto the floor.

"Perhaps he wanted you to write in it," Mae replied remaining exasperatingly calm as she bent down to pick up the notebook.

"But it's his will, not mine," Sally shouted, pacing the room.

"Maybe he wanted to test your reactions," Mae said, a smug smile on her face.

"Yeah sure," Sally snarled and flung herself at her sister, her fingernails foremost like a wild cat's claws. But instead of venting her fury on Mae's scalp, she fell flat on her face. Stunned, she looked round to find Mae watching her calmly from an armchair across the room. Sally scrambled to her feet and grabbing a vase from a low table she flung it at Mae. To her annoyance it bounced off the empty chair and smashed on the floor. Mae was now seated peacefully elsewhere. Sally collapsed in an armchair and burst into tears unable to bear the frustration. As if that wasn't enough, Mae stood behind her and shook her shoulder...

"Wake up," she heard Mae say, as her sister shook her shoulder gently. "The solicitor has just arrived."

Sally shuddered, resisting the impulse to lash out. She took a deep breath and got shakily to her feet. "I need to splash cold water on my face," she muttered and hurried off to the bathroom.

She was in the glass-covered corridor that linked the old and new buildings and the bathroom was close to the Old Lodge. Inside she stumbled on Jenny who was leaning against the washbasin, tears streaming down her face.

"What's the matter?" Sally asked, putting an arm around the young woman's shoulders.

"It's Tom. He's leaving." Jenny burst into sobs.

Sally put her other arm around Jenny and pulled her closer. When Jenny finally calmed, she explained that Tom was very unhappy. He was a liability to the group, he said, and had nothing to offer in the way of a talent or a gift. He didn't want to go back to the Reaches, preferring to return to Switzerland where he would try to get a job as a journalist.

"If we could manage to heal his back, would that make a difference?" Sally asked.

"It might. But we tried everything with Ma'gina."

Sally remembered their desperate efforts. Tom was lucky to have survived at all. "Would he agree to return to the Reaches one more time to try to find a way of healing him?"

"He might." Jenny splashed water on her face and wiped it dry before leaving to look for Tom.

"Good luck," Sally called after her.

"This is John Dafydd, your father's solicitor," Mr Peters told Sally.

The man, who, as his name indicated, came from Wales, was not very tall and had a considerable paunch. His face was round and red and jovial. He made Sally think, somewhat disrespectfully, of Humpty Dumpty. He took a step towards her and held out his hand. He smelt of cigars.

"Pleased to meet you," she said.

Once they were seated, Mr Dafydd pulled out a large buff envelope and ceremoniously removed the seal. "A seal is no longer required. But your father wanted to do everything in style." He pulled out a wad of papers and laid it in his lap. "I will not formally read the will, unless you request it. The document is complex and, as you can see, quite long. Instead I suggest I give you the gist of it and then you can read a letter the Professor wrote you."

"That's fine with me," Mae said.

Sally nodded her approval. She felt more like she was sitting an examination than awaiting the confirmation she was rich. What with her dream and then the encounter with Jenny, her nerves were on edge.

"As you may know, in complex inheritances the will generally names an administrator, someone who makes sure the deceased's wishes are correctly carried out. In this case, Prof Rafter named Mr Peters his administrator and I was named as his replacement, if ever anything happened to him." He paused a moment to see if there were any questions but as there weren't, he continued. "As the Professor transferred most of his property into your joint name a good many years ago no inheritance tax is due on those gifts. Even the house he was living in belonged to you. He paid a minimal rent for its use."

The idea that they should charge him rent to live in his own house struck Sally as shocking and she was about to say so when Mr Dafydd explained. "I say rent, but the sum was symbolical."

"So on the books," Mae said, "our father was poor."

Both Mr Dafydd and Mr Peters smiled.

"It might sound odd, but fiscally speaking, yes. Prof Rafter did everything within his power to provide for you two and leave no obligations behind him. He even set aside a sum to pay my fees."

"But how could we own all his property, including this one," Mae said waving her hand in the air, "without ever knowing?"

"We set up a trust that was initially called the M & S Rafter Trust that was recognised as a registered charity with a view to handling your property," Mr Peters explained. "Technically you own the properties but any income from them is handled by the trust in your name."

Sally realised that they still did not know the extent of their fortune.

Mae must have been thinking the same thing. "Exactly what are the properties held by the Trust?"

"Apart from the Lodge and the Professor's house which is now in ruins, the largest properties you own include a disused factory in Wales, a small castle in Scotland and a large farm in the Lake District. There are other, smaller properties scattered around the country and abroad, a flat in London, for example, a cottage in Northern Ireland and a small holding on one of the islands off the north coast of Scotland. There are also a number of companies including the one that runs events here at the Lodge."

Sally was astounded. She had known Rafter for a number of years, but at no time did he strike her as rich. He was no tycoon. How could he possibly have amassed such a fortune? "I find it difficult to imagine my father was so rich."

Mr Peters smiled knowingly and turned to the solicitor.

"Maybe your father's letter will help you understand." The solicitor pulled a small envelope from the pile of papers and handed it to Sally. "We'll let you read it in peace." Mr Dafydd got to his feet and made for the door followed by Mr Peters. "We'll be outside if you need us."

Sally handed the letter to Mae saying, "You're the eldest. Can you read it out loud?"

Mae took the letter in the tips of her fingers, apprehension written all over her face. Breaking the seal on the back of the envelope she pulled out a single sheet of paper, unfolded it and began to read.

"Mae and Sally, I want you to know how much I love you." Mae's voice broke at that moment. She could read no more. She handed the letter to Sally.

"I wish that circumstances had allowed us to spend more time together. I regret many of the choices I made that kept us apart and if I could live my life over again I would change those but I would never change the fact that I had you."

It was Sally's turn to break down. Tears made further reading impossible. She handed the letter to Mae who cleared her throat and read on.

"I have done everything within my power to make your future life comfortable. I was lucky that my father was a successful man who left me a considerable fortune which people like Mr Peters have helped me make the most of. I have complete confidence in him and strongly advise you to continue working together. Your idea of the Dream Class is excellent. I have always thought the university was not the right place to learn the most important things in life. Maybe the riches that my father left me and that I now bequeath to you can be put to work to make the Dream Class become a reality. Not that I think that a great deal of money will be required. But it will help. May a good wind fill your sails and the sun continue to shine on you. And know that I will always be with you, in spirit at least. Your father, John Llewellyn Rafter."

Mae put down the letter and looked at Sally.

"I really believe he is with us," Sally said, giving voice to a deep feeling that grew stronger and stronger. Being able to feel his presence reassured her and filled a rift between her and the world she hadn't realised existed. She held out her hand to Mae who took it and then pulled her sister closer till they laced their arms around each other and sat in silent embrace.

Flirt

"We've got an appointment at the studio with Collin to look at the material he filmed," Jenny explained to Brent who was lounging in Keira's arms. The three were seated on the terrace of the boathouse. It was high tide and waves broke on the stones of the sea wall.

"Mind if I tag along?" Brent asked. "I have no idea how long Sally is going to be with Mr Peters and the solicitor."

If he were honest, he was growing increasingly impatient. He yearned to be with Lucie. He was worried. When they left the Reaches a couple of days earlier, Lucie and most of the population of Granwich were fleeing hoards of wild men commanded by Horst. The power-crazed villain had followed them to the Reaches and taken over the town. Their stay in Avan had been limited to the weekend, but now with talk of a memorial ceremony, the date of their departure was uncertain.

Keira absent-mindedly played with his ears, rocking his head in tiny movements from side to side against her breasts. Her playfulness reminded him of their torrid encounters in the Dream World on their way to the Reaches. He might have declared his love for Sally, but he still felt a strong physical bond with Keira or Mia as she was called in the Reaches.

"I thought I'd find you two together," Sally announced as she arrived across the lawns from the Old Lodge. "I'm glad you're baby sitting, Jenny. Lord knows what they'd be up to otherwise." She bent forward to give Keira a welcome kiss.

"How about me?" Brent demanded, extracting himself from Keira's arms.

"I'm not sure you deserve a kiss, you naughty boy, running off with another woman at the first occasion." But she gave him a kiss, all the same.

Brent was relieved that they'd found a playful relationship between the three of them. Keira had been jealous at first and he got on much better with the joyous, carefree side of her.

"Does the babysitter get a kiss?" Jenny joked.

"I thought you'd never ask," Sally said, breaking free of Brent's embrace. She cuddled up in Jenny's arms. The girl looked taken aback. They were good friends, that much Brent knew, but he didn't think the two had ever been lovers.

"Well if things are like that, I'm going back to Keira," he said and lay his head back on Keira's breasts.

She pushed him away, pouting. "You only want me when you can't have Sally."

"Ok! I get the message," Brent said as he stood and made a move towards the exit. "I can see when a man is not wanted. I'll leave you girls to your business."

He didn't get far. Sally jumped to her feet and grabbed his hand, pulling him into an embrace.

At which Keira got to her feet and strode over to Jenny. "I seem to have been abandoned." She snuggled up to Jenny.

Over Sally's shoulder, Brent could see the look of surprise on Jenny's face, but the girl did not push Keira away.

"Where's Mae?" Brent asked.

"Aren't three women enough for you?" Sally quipped.

Brent tickled her, causing Sally to wriggle in his arms. What with the embraces of Keira earlier and now Sally, Brent would willingly have returned to bed but there were things to be done if they were to return to the Reaches as soon as possible.

"I'll return to your arms, Jenny," Sally said. "Brent has a bad habit of tickling me whenever I ask him a difficult question." But she made no move to change.

"Who said you could have Jenny back," Keira commented, pouting as only she knew how. "I think I'll adopt her. Her arms are a delight."

Jenny, who had been running her fingers lightly through Keira's hair, stopped and was now blushing. "Stop tormenting Jenny," Brent said. "She's not used to your salacious games."

Keira burst out laughing. "Salacious? Me?" She took hold of one of Jenny's hands and began nibbling the tips of her fingers and running her tongue over them.

"You see what I mean?"

"Jealous?" Keira asked.

"You're impossible," Sally remarked. And both Sally and Brent bound to their feet and began tickling Keira. A game that Jenny joined them in.

Finally collapsing in four separate chairs, laughter still lighting their features, all four gazed out to sea, watching a flock of gulls skimming the waves.

"When do you plan to hold the memorial ceremony?" Brent asked, turning to Sally.

"Are you in such a hurry to return to the Reaches?" Keira asked, grinning.

To Brent's surprise Sally turned pale and sat bolt upright, her mouth fallen open.

"What's the matter," he asked, alarmed. When she didn't answer, he repeated his question.

"Never!" she cried in despair.

All eyes were turned on her.

"What do you mean?" Keira asked.

Sally swallowed hard several times, apparently finding it difficult to talk.

"Are you ill?" Jenny asked.

"It's the ring," Sally told them.

Brent didn't understand. "What ring?"

"To go to the Reaches we need Rafter's ring."

"Have you lost it?" Brent asked, horrified.

Sally nodded.

"But surely there's also Mae's pendant," Keira said.

Sally shook her head. "As we sat watching over our parents in the conservatory, the Professor was holding his ring in his fingers and Mae laid her pendant on Teresa's chest. We were upstairs when the fire broke out. There was no way we could get back downstairs. In the urgency and panic neither of us thought of the ring. It's only now that I realise what happened. They must have been melted in the intense heat of the fire and are lost forever." She broke into tears.

Brent glanced around the faces of the others. All reflected the horror and concern that must surely be seen on his own face.

Distracted

I can't get no …

Tiny fragments of lyrics whirled around Mee's mind as he flitted between the volumes in the immense hall of Akashic records. Unlimited access to knowledge was intoxicating and the list of topics to explore grew by the minute. He might be able to move instantly from one source to another and digest it in a flash, but he could only do one thing at once. So he tried to waste as little time as possible.

A faint fluttering at the limit of his awareness caught his attention. Intrigued, he dropped the records he was reading, metaphorically at least, and rushed to find a closer vantage point. "That's extraordinary…" Jenny was saying as she had Collin roll back the recording and play a segment again.

The startling images of colourful lines scissoring the surface into a wide variety of segments, each radiating an inner light, reminded him of a medieval stained glass long since lost with the destruction of the monastery that had housed it. He checked the reference in the Akashic annals, dashed back to the editing studio, whispered the reference in Jenny's head not waiting to hear her reaction and then returned at lightening speed to his list.

Some times he wondered at the haste. He could go slower, of course. He was free to. But why waste time. He preferred to make the most of every fraction of a second.

He caught a glimpse of a desolate Jock making his way by a local train to the University halt. The man was wondering what he'd find at the Lodge.

Mee hurried to the Lodge where he found Mandy talking to Mr Peters.

"I gather the Dream Class are about to leave on a voyage," Mr Peters was saying. "I'm not sure if you should go with them or make the most of their absence to visit all the properties belonging to the Trust."

Mee whispered a warning in Mandy's mind. Not sure how she would take it, he lingered to judge her reaction.

"It might seem odd," Mandy said, "but a voice just told me that Jock is on his way."

Mr Peters took it all in his stride. "I'd send you to visit the disused factory in Wales right away, but I gather there is to be a key meeting of the Dream Class and I'd like you to attend. So I suggest you ..."

Mee had heard enough. Back in the hall of annals he resumed his breakneck perusal. Each new record sparked new interests. It was like an unending tree shooting forever upward. He ventured up those branches till he felt the onset of vertigo.

To counterbalance his frenetic pursuit, he kept a constant eye on the Dream Class. His brief forays into their adventures were a welcome relief.

"What will happen to the Theosophy Department with the Professor gone?" Fran asked Lyra.

"A new Professor will be named. We hope it will be Chris, but that is not sure at all."

Mee knew things would be otherwise. He'd briefly sat in on a meeting of the administration. He whispered something of the Senate's plans in Fran's ear causing her to gasp.

"Mee says the Senate hope to be able to shut down the Department."

He didn't wait to hear Lyra's reaction, preferring instead to check if the Senate were allowed to do such a thing. Unfortunately, the statutes were on the side of the authorities. Was it ever otherwise, he mused as he flitted back to his research. Amongst the many things he was investigating, he wanted to know why he could not access the annals of the future.

He'd just found an interesting passage by an alchemist when a disturbance at the Lodge caught his attention. Jock was berating Pauline. Unable to calm the irate policeman, she called Mr Peters.

Mee returned to his reading, sure the manager would deal with the situation. The trouble with the writings of alchemists was that they were unendingly ambiguous. From reading alone you could never be sure you'd got it right. He returned to Madame Blavatsky's books in the hope they would clarify things.

In the distance he caught a glimpse of An attending school with her friends for the day. "What subjects do you study at school?" the English teacher was asking. Knowing something of An's situation, Mee drew close to hear her reply.

"We don't have school where I come from."

The teacher looked shocked. "Poor things. So many children are unable to attend school for lack of funds?"

Mee found the teacher's assumption amusing.

An smiled. "We do not have the concept of school, as you call it."

The teacher was so sure An was unschooled and therefore ignorant, she failed to see that An's intellectual competences went far beyond her age. Human interactions fascinated Mee. Behaviour was mostly predictable, but it was those odd bits which didn't fit that he found endearing.

The teacher was floundering in her attempts to understand An, much to the amusement of An's three friends. "So you know nothing of mathematics or grammar?"

"No. If I had had any use for them I would have learnt them."

"So what can you do?" the teacher asked.

"I can defend myself if I am attacked. I can heal all sorts of illnesses. I can talk to birds and animals, … oh yes, and I can also deal with impossible situations like taking part in a group, in an institution, in a system that is completely alien to me."

Mee decided not to wait to hear the teacher's reply, although he did hear the applause of the other girls as he returned to his records.

He hadn't got far with Blavatsky when he heard Sally telling Mae that their key to returning to the Reaches had been destroyed. Mae reacted quite calmly, maybe because she had taken a much smaller part in the adventures there. He remembered Rafter's little box and told them both it might contain a solution.

Anju must have resolved her difficulty with Pauline because Mee found them working out together in the dojo in the sky. He loved to watch the movements of their lithe bodies. Their mock combat was like making love without the sex. He missed having a body. There was so much he couldn't feel.

Below, Mandy had joined Sally and Mae and were talking of the meeting they planned for the end of the afternoon. An was returning to school after the midday break. Brent, Keira and Jenny were ... Tom had just ... The cook was furious at the ... Dieter was making ... Ben was kissing ... Fran hadn't really ... and Mee was exhausted and exasperated. He even told Sally, whom he found alone in the library in the Old Lodge. They had the longest conversation they'd had together since the explosion and he'd lost all anchorage in the material world.

Everything is accelerating, he admitted.

She commiserated. Is there no place you can rest? What do the others do?

Others? He'd noticed no others. Could he be the only one? I think I was afraid of the void, he mused.

Maybe you should seek help, she suggested.

It was good to feel her concern. He'd lost touch with such feelings, always flitting here and there. So he settled down and spent a long while reading the book she was reading, over her shoulder as it were. He hadn't read a novel for ages, especially not one about dwarves and giants and fairies and the like. It had never been his genre.

Their silent communion was interrupted by the return of Brent from town. Mee no longer felt the same jealousy when Sally and Brent interlaced in a passionate embrace, but he didn't have to put up with it either. So he went in search of 'others' as Sally had put it, wondering if he'd simply not noticed what must have been there all the time.

The word of the Gods

Mae turned to Ben and smiled. She couldn't help feeling aglow after their night spent together. She had waited so long for that moment and had been surprised and delighted at the tenderness of their lovemaking.

Returning to the present, she glanced around, waiting for everyone to settle in their seats. The whole Dream Class was gathered in one of the meeting rooms of the New Lodge. Only An was absent. She hadn't yet arrived from her visit to her friends' school. With Pauline's help they had rearranged the seating so everyone sat around a large round table. Like King Arthur, Pauline had commented.

"I have asked Ben to join us as he and I will be spending some time together," she said, getting to her feet. When several people whistled and some stomped their feet, she couldn't help blushing. "I have no idea how we define membership of the Dream Class, but I'd like you to accept him."

Everyone applauded and Ben stood and bowed, grinning. Mae then turned to Mandy who looked apprehensive. "On a suggestion from Mr Peters, I have also invited Mandy." Several people nodded. "She is to work on our security. Mr Peters thinks she should get to know us better and I am inclined to agree."

Everyone approved.

"We have a problem," Mae began, getting down to business. Well at least that got everyone's attention. "We may not be able to return to the Reaches."

Those who didn't already know were shocked, but not as deeply as Brent or Keira or Jenny or Sally had been. Mae went on to explain how the talismans they used to travel to the Reaches had been destroyed. Several people asked questions, some made suggestions, but none were viable.

"There is a possible solution," Mae said, putting an end to their discussion. "The Professor asked me to fetch a small wooden box from his office. I had no time to look inside as we left immediately to fetch Teresa, but we hoped that maybe there was another talisman in it."

Everyone was excited at the news and several people began speaking at once.

"Where is it?" Dieter asked once Mae had called for quiet.

"It was hidden in Sally's flat," she told them.

"Let's go fetch it," Martin said, getting to his feet.

"We already have," Mae informed him.

"So?" Martin asked.

"It contained a small hand-written note book in a language none of us understand."

The disappointment was palpable.

"We want to show it to An. Maybe she can read it," Sally spoke for the first time. "But she has been attending school with her friends all day."

I doubt she'll be able to read it, a voice said in their heads.

"Why do you say that, Mee?" Sally asked.

Because it is written in Amarian.

"Don't you mean Aramaic?" Brent asked.

Mee laughed. No, it is nothing like the Syrian dialect. Amarian is the ancient language of the Gods, the everlasting word.

"Can you read it, Mee?" Mae asked.

No, but I'll see if I can find someone who can.

There was a whooshing sound as he dashed off. Sally burst out laughing. "He's becoming theatrical in his old age."

"Excuse me if my question is naïve, but aren't there other ways to travel between the worlds?" Mandy asked.

Mae was pleased that the former policewoman had spoken up.

"The only other one we know consists of travelling through the Dream World," Keira explained, glancing at Brent. "But that is long and hazardous."

Mae reckoned they could go no further with the discussion. "I suggest we wait and see if Mee can help. We'll leave for the Reaches as soon as we have found a solution. Hopefully soon after the memorial ceremony, which will take place on Friday morning."

The meeting broke up with most people heading for the Old Lodge. Only Mae remained in the room with Brent, Sally, Keira and Jenny. Pauline popped her head around the door, asking, "Would you folks prefer a smaller, more intimate room?"

"We're always in favour of the intimate ..." Brent began, but Sally nudged him in the ribs.

"That would be great," Mae said.

Pauline led them down a corridor away from the reception and out a side door into the grounds in the opposite direction to the Old Lodge. Mandy was waiting for them there. "Mr Peters wants Mandy to see the place I'm taking you to."

They followed a winding path amongst the trees that grew progressively closer together until they broke through into a small clearing in which a hunting lodge was concealed. Paint was peeling off the shutters, a drainpipe hung broken and the gutters were full of birds' nests. But the inside was strikingly different.

"This place is a concealed bunker hidden within the old house," Pauline explained. "It's used only for important strategic meetings. No one will disturb you here."

She led them through into a large room that had comfortable armchairs and a low table. "There is a bar through there." Pauline pointed to a neighbouring room. "There's also a coffee machine and a tea maker, if you need something hot to drink." She handed Mae an iPad saying, "Send me a message when you're finished or if you need anything. You can also use it to take notes if you want. It's wirelessly linked to that projector so you can all look at what is being written."

Mae thanked her and Pauline left.

"Let's have a look at that notebook," Sally suggested.

Mae pulled it out of her bag.

"I can hardly believe the Professor wrote this," Brent mused as he and Sally thumbed through the pages.

"The handwriting is so different," Mae admitted. They took it in turns to look through the notebook, but it brought no new solutions.

I've found the very person we need, Mee's voice said. Let me present Joshua.

What happened then was hard to describe. It was like a train rushing into a tunnel, Mae thought, when the pressure forces the windows outwards and pops your ears. The pressure in the room suddenly went up, pushing the space outwards extending the room to new dimensions. A deep voice, almost like stone, rumbled greetings making Mae and all the others tremble. Mandy gasped in shock.

"Greetings, Joshua," Mae said, awed by the presence.

So this is the book, Joshua voice rang out in the very stones of the building. Turn the pages for me.

Brent began turning the pages cautiously.

Faster, Joshua insisted.

Brent began flicking over the pages as Joshua hummed softly to himself. When Brent reached the end he closed the book. A pregnant silence filled the room.

There are many things in these writings, Joshua boomed in their heads. Are you looking for anything in particular?

Mae explained their dilemma, her voice sounding thin and insignificant.

The person who wrote this text was seeking the very solution you are. Although he did find the answer, he was unable to use it.

Disappointment washed over Mae at the irrevocable nature of Joshua's words. They rang like a God-sent judgement. So the Professor had been searching too. How could they possibly expect to succeed where he had not?

Despair is not appropriate, Joshua commented, his voice soothing. People who have the ability to travel between the worlds can learn to do so without artefacts.

Mae felt hope kindle. "Does it say how?"

Yes. The writer describes how, but, as he didn't have the ability himself, his description is incomplete.

"Could you teach us to read the text?" Mae asked.

No. I am not allowed to reveal the secrets of this language.

Mae thanked him. And Joshua left, leaving them all feeling like they needed something akin to a spiritual decompression chamber to recover from his visit.

In the cathedral

Mae and Sally insisted money be provided so that the members of the Dream Class be suitably dressed for the grand memorial ceremony. They had long discussions in the loft of the Old Lodge, that had quickly become the group rallying point, as to what was appropriate to wear. Most opted for simplicity with dashes of bright colours in more sober clothes, although there was no uniformity in their choices. The tailors had done a good job given the limited time available.

Collin insisted on doing a series of individual and group portraits in their new clothes. It turned out that he was an excellent photographer. In fact he had been documenting the events of the weekend and showed some of his photos to Jenny.

"They are really stunning," she told Sally and Mae. "You should have a look. I believe it would be good to exhibit some of his photos during the ceremony."

So the two sisters selected a couple of photos of Rafter giving his talk in the library and begrudgingly included a photo of themselves. The photos were to be hung in the porch of the west entrance to the cathedral so people could look at them before moving on into the nave.

Mae and Mr Peters had worked hard on preparing a list of guests. They didn't want to hold a crowded public event, but were obliged to invite many people. The Professor was well known and appreciated in town. Sally wanted to use the photo of Rafter and Teresa on the invitation but Mae refused. She did agree that a copy would be made and displayed along with the other photos in the porch.

They had a long discussion about who should speak. Sally categorically refused to let the Rector or anyone from the university administration speak. She held them partly responsible for her father's illness. Instead Chris would speak for the Department.

The surprise had come from An who had convinced the music teacher at her friends' school to have St Mary's girls grammar school choir sing at the ceremony and Keira was preparing them to perform several of her songs. Collin had suggested getting the TV to cover the event, but both Sally and Mae had refused, arguing that it was a private ceremony.

Jenny, Sally and Keira spent a long time exploring every nock and cranny of the cathedral discussing how they would decorate it for the ceremony. Sally was not happy at using a Christian building for such a ceremony. "It goes against all that John Llewellyn stood for."

Luckily Jenny and Keira found a solution. "The energy lines weave the most extraordinary patterns in this building," Jenny told them.

"If we were to find a way to accentuate those lines and make them apparent," Keira suggested, "that might bring forward the more ancient nature of this place."

They experimented various ideas, but finally opted for something Sally had suggested: she slightly changed the colour of the stone floor, the pillars and the walls so they corresponded to the lines of force in the building. She used the colours that Jenny suggested for the different energy sources. The difference was subtle but sufficient to be troubling.

They strengthened the impression by placing plants and flowers using the same colour scheme. Mr Peters had reached an agreement with the ecclesiastical authorities that allowed them relatively free rein providing that everything was back to normal after the ceremony and that nothing sacrilegious was done in the building.

During their time in the cathedral, Keira tested the acoustics and with Sally's help they adjusted the shape of certain surfaces so that the cathedral responded better to her voice, yet kept its deep resonance. They also moved some of the higher windows so they would better catch the rays of the morning sun, sending bright paths of light into different corners of the building.

All was ready when St. Mary's girls' choir filed into the cathedral for their only rehearsal there before the event. Keira had carefully chosen where they should stand so as to make the most startling impact with the new acoustics. She had already worked several times with them in the school and was pleased to find the girls delighted at such a chance to sing.

Talking to Tricia and the others, she realised that part of their enthusiasm was the promise of singing with someone who was a fast rising star. Although they had refused to let the event be filmed, the two sisters had accepted to have the singing recorded. Collin had organised that with people from the BBC.

When the time came for the memorial ceremony to start, Sally and Mae stood just inside the west entrance and greeted people as they arrived. There were so many present that a lot had to stand along the side aisles and at the back of the building. There was much surprise at the appearance of the building and the place was abuzz with quiet conversations as people struggled to figure out what, if anything, had changed.

Once the last people had entered, Mae and Sally made their way down the central aisle at a stately pace till they reached the pew reserved for them at the front. It was then that Keira began to sing a slow, haunting lullaby that made good use of the modified acoustics of the cathedral. The girls' choir joined her on the following verses as both the strength and the warmth of the young female voices rang in the air.

When the song came to an end, Mae rose, climbed the steps before the altar and turned to face the congregation. Brent had taught her how to project her voice so even those perched against the farthest walls could hear her.

"We would like to welcome you all this morning and to thank you heartily for taking the time to join us in this memorial celebration for Professor John Llewellyn Rafter and his wife, Teresa who both passed away last weekend. Although it is a sad occasion for many of us, neither our father nor our mother would have liked this celebration to be steeped in sadness. To honour their wishes, we have prepared a ceremony that includes songs as well as a few tales of the Professor and his life. We ask you not to applaud at the end of the performances. Once the ceremony is over, we invite you to join us in the Community building across the square for an aperitif."

As Mae returned to her seat, Keira sang a sea song in which she made her voice echo back off the walls like the distant calls of sailors at sea. The choir added a soft whooshing sound that rose and fell in time with her song. For all Mae's promise about avoiding sadness, the effect was heart-rending.

Professor Chris Dryman took his place at the top of the steps before the altar and unfolded a piece of paper he pulled from his jacket pocket. Gone was his usual joviality and relaxed manner. He seemed tense and tired, his shoulders unusually slumped. His week had been a nightmare involving bitter discussions with the university authorities about the future of the Theosophy Department.

"Professor Rafter," he began, his voice catching on the name causing him to pause a moment, "was many things in his life, but for those who worked with him he was a friend and a mentor. He encouraged each and every one of us in both small and larger ways. The Department as it stands today was his brainchild, but he involved all of us actively in its development. He had confidence in his staff and was open to new ideas and innovative suggestions. The Department thrived and grew during his time at its head. His task was far from easy. Our Department is the only existing theosophy department in the country. As he so rightly put it, our work was often at odds with the logic of the rest of the university.

"It is not for nothing that the Department is built on a island in the River Bree, joined to the remainder of the university by a narrow bridge. Rafter once half jokingly told us that we would wake one morning and find the whole department, us included, cut adrift and out at sea en route for untold adventures. The recent audit carried out by the university administration is typical of the miss-match. It would be an exaggeration to say that the increasing hostility of the authorities towards him and the department broke his heart, but it certainly didn't help to keep him in good health.

"Now that he has left us, the university is doing its utmost to undo all that he did with an alacrity that can only be called tasteless and lacking in dignity. They will probably succeed in doing away with the Department, but they will never be able to get rid of the heritage he left us. It will live on in all the people who worked and learnt with him. It will live on, above all, in the work of his two daughters, Mae and Sally Rafter, and their talented friends.

"I would personally like to thank him for all he gave us. I will always remember him for his playfulness and his generosity. I am proud to count him amongst my best friends and I pledge myself to pursue his work and support his daughters in doing so."

The atmosphere in the cathedral was electric as he came down the steps where he was welcomed by Mae and Sally, who both stood to embrace him.

As Chris accompanied the two sisters to the front pew, the choir began singing softly. It was a love song that Keira had written specially for the occasion. Rare were the people in the cathedral that did not have goose pimples as the melody rose and twined its way upwards carrying Keira's solo voice above it into the heights of the cathedral and beyond. The sun appeared from behind a cloud at that moment sending bright rays through the small windows perched high in the walls causing the crisscross of coloured lines that traversed the building to glow and dance.

Naniu and Alo came to stand at the top of the steps, waiting for the music to end. Both were well-known figures in town. Naniu, who was dressed in one of her typical oriental costumes, was world renown as a singer and had taught both Keira and Sally singing. Alo was a shaman who lived on a hill above the town. He had helped the Dream Class in their adventures in other worlds.

Alo told the story of Rafter's early adventures while Naniu improvised a musical accompaniment. The effect was almost eerie, giving the listeners the impression they were transported to another world. Alo spoke of a group of friends, of quests, of secret passages, of strange encounters and joyous meetings. When the two finally ceased and made their way to join Sally and Mae, many were those who wondered what exactly it was they had heard.

Their place at the top of the steps was taken by a young girl who couldn't have been more than ten years old. She was all dressed in white. Those who attended the concert at the Arena would have recognised Sarah, the girl who had accompanied Keira and told the most marvellous tales. Hardly had Sarah begun to speak than the entire congregation was enthralled. She led they by the hand through the meanders of a tale of love between two young people, John Llewellyn and Teresa, making every heart in the place beat faster. As the story of their separation was briefly evoked, the girls' choir sang softly, underscoring Sarah's words as wave after wave of sadness filled the air. The young girl touched briefly on how the couple were finally reunited with their long lost daughters as the Professor lay dying. When Sarah brought the story to a close there was not a dry eye in the place.

Sally stood up and climbed the steps to join Sarah who stood motionless but watchful, suspended, as it were, at the end of her story, waiting. Sally embraced the young girl and then, holding her by the hand, spoke.

"Mae and I thought it would be most appropriate to end this ceremony with the words of our father, John Llewellyn Rafter," she said. "Much of what we have chosen to share with you comes from things he said to us in private. He spoke to us, the group of young people he'd gathered to accompany him in his final hours, in a last effort to share with us as much as he could before he left."

Sally wiped the tears from her eyes, blew her nose and, pulling a paper from her pocket, began to read.

"Always remember that you can learn something from everyone you meet and every situation you find yourself in. Professors and experts have no monopoly on knowledge, neither do schools nor universities nor churches. Your own experience is like a beautiful garden that you should seek to nourish and enrich at every moment throughout your life. Material goods and facts and figures are not enough to nourish that garden. Pursuit of them alone has left us stranded, confused and unable to understand the wider world we live in.

"What is needed is transcendence: that which is beyond and above the normal range of human experience. Transcendence is the essence of life, its specialness, its joy, its magnificence, … the search for transcendence gives our lives a much deeper meaning. With such practices as music and dance and art and story-telling and dreams you can go further, stretching out beyond the limits of the material universe, rediscovering forces that the ancients were aware of, forces that are the motors of our world and many others too.

"But in that quest, be cautious of those ideas that spring to mind spontaneously from your upbringing or your education. They might mislead you. Be careful of words too. They can betray. And beware of those people who adopt extreme positions, they will try to force you to the extreme. Each of us has special gifts or aptitudes. Don't let anyone tell you otherwise, however intelligent he or she claims to be.

"Should you make use of your gifts with moderation and restraint? Maybe not always! Sometimes excesses can be the most joyful expression of being. When Sally dances or Keira sings, they do so with their whole heart. Just like Mae who organises things with all her heart and soul. Should you refuse to use your gifts? Surely not! It would be a dreadful waste. So what should you do? Cultivate your gifts in your beautiful garden, seek out the transcendent and share what you have learnt with others, that is the deeper purpose of life."

A profound silence filled the cathedral as if the whole edifice was holding its breath. Mae rose to join Sally and Sarah as they descended the steps and, holding hands, all three began to walk down the central aisle. Ben and An followed as did Anju and Dieter, along with Martin and Fran and Jenny. Keira left the choir and joined them. Only Tom was absent, they had been unable to convince him not to return to Switzerland. He had left the day before.

The group, followed at a distance by St. Mary's girls choir still singing, made their way slowly towards the west exit, the doors of which now stood open letting bright sunlight flood into the cathedral. The congregation remained in their seats a moment not knowing what to do, then, when the music ceased they rose, stunned, and made their way to the door.

The Dream Class crossed the threshold and as they stepped out into the waiting sun Mae relinquished her hold on Sally's hand and turned to beckon Ben forward. Behind, a throng was exiting the cathedral and flowing out across the steps just as a cloud passed over the sun. Grasping Ben's good hand, Mae turned back to follow Sally and Sarah, only to see the two girls vanish in a shower of fiery stars that sank to the stones of the Starless Square and blinked out.

The author
Alan McCluskey

One of his pupils once confessed, with typical candour and ambiguity, that Alan McCluskey had taught her the creative value of madness. His work, whether as a teacher or a video artist or a company director or a scientist or a novel writer, has always been marked by a need to question the obvious, adopting what he calls the Martian perspective in which the self-evident is not taken for granted. He has brought that questioning perspective, along with a passion for images and what they can reveal, to novel writing, together with a long-standing fascination for the dream world and the magic of fantasy.

For information about Alan McCluskey, his books and artwork, see:
Secret Paths: http://author.secret-paths.com
Facebook: http://www.facebook.com/Secret.Paths
Pinterest: http://pinterest.com/almacme/

The Reaches

The Storyteller's Quest Book One
by Alan McCluskey

The quiet town of Avan with its port, its provincial university and its conservative seafaring folk would hardly be the place you'd expect to run into an adventure and frankly neither Brent nor Sally nor Keira were going out of their way to have one. At least nothing more than the occasional torrid love affair and the awkward self-questioning typical of many young adults like themselves. Sally was finishing her studies in the Theosophy Department of the University hoping to become Professor Rafter's assistant, Keira, Sally's best friend and lover, was a young librarian who occasionally sang in a popular folk group and Brent was a would-be writer who couldn't quite get his act together and who spent hours wandering the streets and lanes of the town in search of inspiration. Yet unbeknown to them forces had long been at work that would throw them together in a series of adventures that were going to tax them to the extreme forcing them to develop abilities that went way beyond what would seem possible during a voyage from the real world to the realm of dreams and on into another world called the Reaches that at first sight looked deceptively like their own.

The Keeper's Daughter

The Storyteller's Quest Book Two
by Alan McCluskey

It wasn't Brent's fault if he was stuck in the form of Jake the Owl, at least he didn't think it was as he sat on a branch preening despondently. The threads of all his stories had become inextricably muddled in his owlish head. To think that he'd once prided himself on being a storyteller. His stories had become adventures and some of those adventures had become nightmares, and now he was stuck with them. He'd flown in search of his friend and lover, Mia. She'd been dragged off by a band of thugs just when it was time for them all to return to their world. Only Sally, their mutual friend and lover, had made it back from the world of the Reaches to their hometown of Avan. Hearing her story, despite the dangers she'd had to face, her friends suggested Sally teach them to travel to the Dream Realm and beyond to the Reaches. The idea appealed to everybody. Not that Sally knew how to get back to the Reaches, but the idea of a 'dream class' as they called it pleased her and, above all, she wanted to return to the world where her newly-found half-sister lived and where her two friends had so abruptly disappeared.

Boy & Girl
by Alan McCluskey

When Peter awakes in the head of a girl, he is both delighted and alarmed that his secret yearnings have become reality. Very quickly, however, his error is apparent; this girl is not him. Kaitling –that's her name– is twelve years old, like Peter. She's the daughter of a magician, a prominent figure in another world. Boy and girl travel back and forth from each other's minds, but have little time to get acquainted before Kaitling's island is overrun by warrior priests and she has to flee. At home, a conflict erupts in Peter's family forcing him to take refuge at a friend's place. Meanwhile at school, a haughty new girl goads him about his girlishness and, spitting in his face, vows to rid the earth of people like him. The stage seems set for a desperate struggle to survive, but will ingenuity and youthful fervour be enough against folly and fanaticism?

In Search of Lost Girls

by Alan McCluskey

If you listen carefully you can just hear the mournful tolling of a convent bell over the shuffle of girls' feet as they traipse to Mass, nursing bruises and a numbing despair. No one cares. No one is there to stem the torrent of injustice and abuse. They are lost and forgotten. In another world, the walls of the cathedral still reverberate to the sound of angelic singing as the mourners make their way to the exit, heads bowed, voices hushed. If only they knew that those girls who delighted them with their music were really boys in disguise, sanctity would would flee in the face of raging indignation. The scene is set. The author picks up his pen with trembling fingers and begins to write. Time to tear Kate and Peter apart. The thought of making her life hell has him dribbling in anticipation. He ought to know better. Things rarely turn out as an author expects.

www.ingramcontent.com/pod-product-compliance
Lightning Source LLC
Chambersburg PA
CBHW051438260626
47162CB00001B/152